King—
of Kearsarge

By
ARTHUR O. FRIEL

Frontispiece by
JOSEPH M. CLEMENT

THE PENN PUBLISHING
COMPANY PHILADELPHIA
1921

ISBN 13: 978-1-4344-8512-0

To

My Mother

LUCY LOCKE THOMPSON FRIEL

Contents

6   *CONTENTS*

Ye who love the haunts of Nature,
Love the sunshine of the meadow,
Love the shadow of the forest,
Love the wind among the branches,
And the rain-shower and the snow-storm,
And the thunder in the mountains,
Whose innumerable echoes
Flap like eagles in their eyries ;—
   Ye whose hearts are fresh and simple,
Who believe that, in all ages,
Every human heart is human . . .
   Listen to this simple story.
               —The Song of Hiawatha.

King of Kearsarge

CHAPTER I

A CALL FOR HELP

THE big man standing on the steps of the village post-office glared down at the open letter in his hand and growled.

The sound was inarticulate, but eloquent of supreme disgust. His face, too, was heavy with angry disappointment, and his hands gripped the close-typed page as if itching to rip it apart. As he hastily reread it he growled again. Then he crunched it in one fist.

Scowling, he stared down at a bulging packsack leaning against a piazza-post; looked into the grinning face of his partner—and suddenly grinned himself.

"That's right, laugh, you high-geared giraffe!" he grumbled. "It's all your fault anyway. If you hadn't suggested that we stick around until this mail was shuffled I wouldn't have gotten this letter for another week, and we'd be humping ourselves back to camp without a care in the world. Now I've got to hike out of here for Manhattan, and our happy home is busted up."

His tall companion, lounging on the steps, suddenly straightened up. The smile vanished, and concern showed in his eyes.

"What's up?" he asked.

" Pendexter's sick. Caved in all at once, Wightman writes, and will be laid up indefinitely. Overwork, I guess; the old boy's a glutton for detail. That leaves Wightman with more than he can swing, and this is his wild wail for hellup, hellup—S O S—C Q D— P D Q!" He glowered once more at the crushed note. " So little Harry Miller has to shuck off his wilderness garb and go back to town. Don, you sphinx, why did I ever become a lawyer?"

If Don knew, he did not say. He stared down at Miller's packsack, and hitched his broad shoulders under the weight of a similar pack which hung on his own back. His rotund mate resumed:

"Yep. Just what I was thinking. Here we've just gone and bought oodles of grub because we'd decided to stay a while longer—and now what'll we do with it? It's twelve long miles from here to the top of old Kearsarge, and all up-hill; and I'm not pining to tote all this stuff up there when I won't get a chance to eat it. These New Hampshire mountain roads of yours are no dream of bliss for a splay-foot fat man like me. You nearly walked my legs off coming down here."

Don smiled again, and gazed thoughtfully up the street, where the prim houses nestling under the big elms drowsed in the warmth of late afternoon and the shadows slowly lengthened as the summer sun drew ever westward. Several overalled men, loitering around the post-office with ears wide open to the conversation, stared unwinkingly at the two. Flannel-shirted, knee-booted, wide of hat and broad of shoulder they were; but there the resemblance ended.

Miller, the shorter by half a head, was broad all the way down: a solid, square-faced and square-jawed chap whose mountain garb could not for an instant conceal the fact that he was city born and bred. His mate, though his bearing was that of one who belonged to the great world outside this quiet town, fitted into his wilderness clothing as if he belonged in it: his long legs and lithe body were those of the trail-follower, and his deep gray eyes those of the hillman, accustomed to looking out across wide vistas. To the loungers who watched, somehow the pair suggested a mastiff and a greyhound.

" Cache it," decided Don.

" Huh? Cache it? Where? "

The attentive audience looked at the well-filled packs and opened its ears a little wider. Don glanced lazily at his partner, hitched his near shoulder, and began to drift across the road. Miller jammed the letter into a shirt pocket, slid into the packstraps, and plodded after him. When they were well out of earshot Don elucidated:

" Camp."

" Whaddye mean, cache it in camp? " expostulated Harry. " What's the good —— Oh, I get you. Thinking about that hunting trip next fall, eh? "

The other nodded.

" Good hunch, that. This is mostly canned stuff anyhow, and it'll keep up there forever and a day," Miller approved. " But nix on the long hike back, I tell you. Not as long as I've the price of a horse and wagon to tote me and my chattels to the foot of the mountain. After that we've got to hoof it, allee same jackass."

They turned a corner and swung into another road which ran sharply down-hill to the railroad station. Up the steep grade two girls were coming, and they looked in frank curiosity at the big men bearing down on them. Across Miller's face broke a friendly smile, and he hunched his right shoulder as if to loosen the packstrap preparatory to lifting his hat. Then he changed his mind.

The girls passed him without speaking; and their gaze, slipping off him as if he were a post, rested on his companion. When they had passed he turned and looked after them—to find that they, too, had turned their heads and were looking back at the silent Don.

"Uh-huh. Thought so," he remarked, sotto voce. After a couple of steps he added: "Don, I nearly stubbed my toe that time,—started to lift my hat to your friends. Thought you knew everybody in this town."

"Men, yes."

"Men, yes!" mimicked Harry. "Oh, sure. But you never, never speak to the ladies. Being an old married man, you look right over their heads without a quiver. And me, now—*me*, a merry bachelor, heart-whole and fancy-free—they never even see me when you're around. 'Tain't right, I tell you! When I get elected to Congress the first thing I'm going to do is to jam through a bill to protect fat bachelors. Make the married men grow spade-shaped beards or wear rings through their noses or something. Then maybe we chaps who are still foot-loose will get a kindly look once in a while—even if we are built like toads."

As before, Don smiled but said nothing.

They crossed another sandy road, tramped along the echoing platform of the station, and dropped their packs against the wall. Harry entered the building and busied himself with the writing of a telegram.

Don filled a pipe, lit it, and sat down on his pack. Reflectively he watched the smoke curl away from his lips and drift down along the track on the wings of a tiny breeze. As it vanished his gaze roved on down the shining twin rails to the point where they converged and were lost in the hills. A frown darkened his face, as if he were visioning the roar and heat and strife of the cities toward which those rails led. After a time his eyes came back up the creek which flowed sluggishly beside the railroad embankment, and rested on the thick growth of alders, overtopped by tall elms and drooping willows, basking in the sunshine on the farther shore.

Through the open window beside him clacked the stutter of the Morse as Harry's message started southward. When it ceased, the smoker tapped an ash from his pipe, sighed, arose, and turned toward the door; then halted and smiled at a sudden thought. When Harry emerged he was stooping to lift his pack.

"Well, it's done," grumbled Harry. "I, as party of the first part, have informed Wightman, party of the second part, that I start for New York to-morrow. Now to charter a horse and get a-going for camp. But say, aren't you going to wire your wife?"

"Guess not."

"Oh! Then you're going to stay up here?"

Don shook his head.

"Going back with me?"

The other nodded.

"But she doesn't expect you back for at least a week yet, does she?"

Again his partner shook his head.

"Slip in and surprise her," he explained.

Harry smiled boyishly back at his chum. Then suddenly he scowled and began to fuss with a packstrap. It took him some time. He stared at it thoughtfully, then flashed another glance at Don. They had been roommates at college, these two, in the days when "Silent" King had been known as one of the foremost athletes of his time; and Harry knew him as only a man's roommate can know him. Yet now he hesitated and covertly studied his mate. He noted anew the strong, earnest face, with its firm nose, long jaw, and kindly mouth; the steady gray eyes, now looking dreamily at something far away; the broad brow, the broad shoulders, and the broad fighting-man's hands. His glance traveled down the tall body and dropped again to the packstrap in his fingers. He opened his mouth, then closed it; contemplated the platform without seeing it; opened his mouth once more—then shut it and swung the pack to his back.

"I haven't the heart to say anything," he thought. "Besides, it's none of my business anyway."

CHAPTER II

THE house was dark. Don set the dunnage bag on the top step and pulled out his watch. It was nine o'clock. He stepped softly back down the walk and looked up again at the bedroom windows, seeking the faint glow of the little night-lamp which often burned beside her bed. But the room was black. The windows were raised just five inches, and he knew the burglar-locks were on.

Back to the piazza he strode, picked up the bag, fitted his key to the lock, stepped inside, and with the surety of long practice pressed his thumb on the wall where the little black-and-pearl button jutted out. The hall leaped into light. He listened a moment. No sound came to him.

" Hello, Ruth ! " he called.

Despite the darkness and silence, he half expected a cry of " Why, Donald ! " and a rush of slippered feet to the head of the stairs. When they failed to come he felt disappointed.

"Anybody home ? " he asked loudly.

No answer. The maid was out too. Hanging his hat on the rack, he set foot on the first stair. Then he halted.

Softly, so softly that he would not have heard them

if the house had not been so still, little footsteps were padding down the hallway. He peered over the rail to meet a pair of great round eyes.

"Greetings, Rajah," he saluted, and stepped back. The big tiger-cat, tail in air, marched decorously up to him, mewed plaintively, and rubbed against his leg. He set down the bag and lifted the animal by the erect tail until his claws dug into the rug, then let him gently down again. This was their regular form of salutation: the hoisting by the tail, followed by a vigorous rumpling of fur—a proceeding which Don himself called a "Fiji massage," which Ruth termed "barbarous," and which delighted the cat beyond measure. Rajah rolled on his side now and wormed himself expectantly along the floor, as he always did when the tail-stretching was over and the rumpling was due. It came speedily—a tousling and tickling which ended when the big fellow bounded up with a little excited yowl and scampered to the end of the hall, where he waited with shining eyes for his master to pursue him. But Don smilingly shook his head and yawned.

"Tired, Rajah. Rough-house you again to-morrow." Grasping the bag again, he marched up-stairs.

At the door of Ruth's bedroom he paused and peered within. The faint light from the street lamp showed him that the bed was tenantless. He rubbed his chin a moment and considered. Perhaps she had gone over to her aunt's to stay during his absence. But no, Rajah was here, sleek and well fed, and she would not have left Rajah to the perfunctory care of the servants. She would soon come home. So he went on into his den, where he threw up a window, pulled down the curtains, and snapped on the light.

For a moment his eyes wandered over the familiar walls, where his own face looked back at him from framed groups of athletes. It smiled boyishly among husky lads who, in his prep-school days, had plunged and slid on gridiron and diamond and sped around the cinder-path. Stronger and more mature, it gazed out from teams which had fought the battles of sport during his years at college. Here and there, mute veterans of bygone struggles, hung a battered nose-guard, a splintered hockey-stick, a disreputable baseball mitt. In sonorous Latin phrases a parchment proclaimed that a great university had honored Donald Warren King with the degree of "Artium Liberalium Baccalaurei." Smaller frames there were, too, holding snapshots of a girl—always the same girl; and from these his gaze traveled to the oval silver frame on the bookcase, whence smiled the same girlish face—the face of Ruth, mistress of the house.

Deep, dark eyes beneath curving black brows, with more than a touch of mischief in the tiny droop of one long-lashed lid; a little nose " tip-tilted like the petal of a flower"; a tiny rosebud mouth with lips deliciously curved, and a rounded chin that hinted at wilfulness— the face of a girl who would turn to pleasure as a flower to the sun. Perhaps a disinterested observer, studying that portrait, might have said that the little mouth spelt selfishness, and the chin stubbornness: that this beautiful woman had known only ease and plenty, and would have her own sweet way regardless

of others.   But to the quiet, indulgent Donald such an
intimation would have been blasphemy.   Straight to
his hungering heart that picture spoke, and drew him
across the room to take it in his hands and lose himself
in memories and dreams.

Back along the golden lane of retrospect drifted the
vision of this wife of his as she had first come into his
life.   Three years ago he had left the grinding city behind him for a time and fared north to New Hampshire, his native state, there to camp alone on Black
Mountain, one of the three humps of old Kearsarge;
and on a day when all the mountain lay silent in siesta
he had climbed up to the bare summit, which turned up
to the sky like the blank face of a giant petrified in
sleep.

Dreaming in languorous sunlight, splashed darkly
hither and yon by the drifting shadows of lazy clouds,
Mount Kearsarge drowsed in the golden haze of that
midsummer day.   In all its loose-lying length nothing
moved, save the moccasined man who drifted across its
Titanic face as silently as a wind-blown ghost, and who
finally sank from sight into a little triangular niche at
the northern edge.   And there, alone amid the infinite
peace and the majestic solemnity which is the heritage
of the mountains, he sat wrapt in contemplation of
the far-flung panorama, where for hundreds of square
miles the living green rolled away over the hills to the
hazy horizon; the sombre carpet of the pines checkered
with vivid patches of farm-land, splashed with silver
lakes, yellow-threaded with sandy roads; a smiling
land of thrift and homely virtues, where great cities

were not, and small cities lay buried out of sight in the river-valleys. Provincial, pastoral, peaceful it was, yet stern and strong beneath its velvet mantle, and from the dawn of western civilization a breeder of men: men with souls unbending, unwavering, unflinching: men who were the backbone of the nation, as the granite whence they sprang was the backbone of their eternal hills. But now, in that vast expanse of man-tilled and man-bearing territory, no man was visible from this lofty eyrie. Under the summer sun the country lay dreaming like a fairyland, so beautiful that it enthralled the senses with the sheer loveliness of it, and so tremendous that it whelmed the soul with awe.

And while the deep-eyed disciple of the Red Gods sat thus hidden in his niche, a little breeze sprang up and frolicked around the summit. Across his reverie it smote with a rustle and swirl of darting draperies which flared out from the stone above him and drew his gaze sharply up to his left. He stared astounded; for where he had thought himself far from human-kind, he was not alone. Above him stood a wondrous girl.

Perched on the brink as if about to take wing, and utterly unconscious of his presence, she cared nothing for the pranks of the breeze. Her soul was far from the austere mountain-top, and the unseen man gazed his fill: gazed at the wayward tendrils of dark hair blown about her cheek, and at the rich color in that cheek; at the long-lashed, enraptured eyes, and the rosebud lips half parted as if they too would drink in the beauty of that scene; at the patrician lines of her figure outlined by the pressure of the wind against her filmy gown—a gown never made for mountain-climbing, for it was soft and fluffy as the feathery edges of a cloud which floated in the sky above her. In truth, she seemed a princess who had floated hither upon that cloud from the far land of dreams, and had dropped from it as lightly as a snowflake; and he watched her with bated breath, as if fearing that any sound would dissolve the vision and leave him staring at the empty sky.

A leg-muscle, grown cramped by his unchanging posture, gave him away. It twitched involuntarily, and as his foot moved it hit a small fragment of granite lying loose on the ledge. At the tiny rattle she turned swiftly, stepped back in startled amazement, stared down at him as he had stared at her. For a long moment her dark eyes and his deep gray ones held each other. Then both laughed.

In this high realm of the Red Gods the petty conventions of Town, demanding formal introduction and social small-talk, had no place. In two minutes they were acquainted; in three, they were marveling that they should meet up here—for she was cousin to a classmate of his, Bob Delancey, from whom she had heard much of " Silent " King's athletic prowess. So, too, she had heard of the reason for his sobriquet— the taciturnity of a man who was silent to empty babblers and revealed himself to but a few kindred souls. And presently he, who had habitually fought shy of women because he considered them gushy and silly, found himself talking to her without restraint; for she did not chatter inanities, but showed an eager interest in the country about them which quickly put him at his ease and led him naturally to tell her of himself and his early life in this northern State. Such confidences inevitably become reciprocal. Thus, sitting side by side in the little niche up there amid the vastness, they quickly formed a better acquaintance than months of conventional meetings in town would have given them.

All too soon, of course, they were discovered by her companions—a party of youths and girls, chaperoned by her aunt, who had motored over to the foot of the mountain from Lake Sunapee. Before them Donald became his usual laconic self, holding himself somewhat aloof from their babble and badinage. Yet, when they started downward, he walked with them to the timber; or, rather, walked with Ruth, some distance behind the rest. When she was gone and he stood alone among the stubby spruces he found in his heart a vague unrest, a strange yearning coupled with a sense of loneliness, as if the Red Gods with whom he had communed now had forsaken him. And they had; for, though their tall disciple did not yet realize it, he had fallen under the spell of another god—a little god, a blind god, but a mightier god than they.

That mischievous little god of the arrows had not left him long in ignorance. Alone in his woods, hearing in the sighing mountain winds a voice of music, seeing in his campfires a face demure but bewitching, feeling in his soul a mysterious call from the shores of blue Sunapee—he had answered the call. Down to his

Lady of the Lake he had gone, heedless of his wilderness clothing, contemptuous of the stares and sniffs of the silked and flanneled fashion-slaves who thronged the hotel piazzas, and paid his court in the straightforward way that was his nature. And, as swiftly as a forest fire springs up in that land of hills and sweeps all before it, he had won. A wondrous night of stars —a canoe on the lake—a ride to the home of a kindly old country pastor—it was done. In less than a fortnight from their first meeting she was his own.

That was three years agone. And now, freshly returned from the mountain where they had first met, looking once more into the loved face which seemed turning to him for a kiss, he felt anew that his gods had been good to him. Ay, far better than he deserved, he told himself; far better than any ordinary fellow like him deserved. The modest heart of him never told him that the very strength of his untainted manhood had drawn her to him as the upstanding oak attracts the vine.

A soft body bumping against his leg recalled him from his land of dreams. It was lonesome Rajah, who had stalked into the room and now rubbed his sleek side against his master, blinking up at him the while.

"I'm lonesome too, Rajah," smiled Don. "But we'll surprise pretty mistress soon, boy."

Suddenly he started. His hat, hanging in the hall, would be a dead give-away. Better make the surprise complete: wait until she started up-stairs, and then meet her half-way. He ran down, retrieved the hat, put out the light, and returned to the den, where he began to unpack.

The cylindrical bag held only his personal camp-kit, the bulkier articles having been sent by express for delivery on the morrow. Curled luxuriously in the big armchair, Rajah watched with one sleepy eye as his master unrolled corduroys and flannel shirt, smoothed out a rumpled hat, and laid aside the belt axe, knife, lamp, and various small camp tools. Both eyes flew open, however, when a long army six-shooter tumbled suddenly from the leg of a hunting-boot and whacked solidly on the floor. Don caught the startled look and chuckled.

"Old Meat-in-the-Pot, Rajah," he said, patting the gun. "Handier than a rifle. Like this."

Out darted his arm, and the empty weapon menaced a huge white owl which, cunningly mounted, brooded on an imitation limb high between the windows. Though he knew nothing of guns, the cat instantly sensed the threat of the attitude; and his eyes began to glow, for with all the strength of his feline heart he hated the pompous owl which stared so glassily at him from its secure perch. Many a time he had sneaked into the den and, with tail twitching and claws hooking the rug, had glowered at that bird which he could not reach. Now something was going to happen! And when the owl came tumbling down he would pounce on it and rip the stuffing out of it!

But nothing happened. The weapon sank. Don snapped out the cylinder, peered through its six deadly chambers, and slid the ejector up and down.

"A little dusty," he thought. " Oil her up to-mor-row." He laid it on the table. Rajah slowly subsided.

The camp equipment was stowed away in a closet until only the revolver, the belt of cartridges, the felt hat, and a pair of light moccasins remained. The hat needed cleaning, the cartridges must be boxed, and the moccasins would be a comfortable change for his tired feet. Kicking off his shoes, he pulled on the soft Indian footgear, then ousted Rajah from the chair and lay back with a long sigh.

For the past two days he had been traveling: first a slow, tedious journey by wagon to the village, where they had missed a train and had to wait until afternoon; then by rail to Boston, where they had stayed overnight so that Harry could see to some business this morning. To-day they had sped through Massachusetts and Connecticut to the great city on the Hudson, dined leisurely at a Broadway hotel, and endured the dead air of the subway to lower Manhattan. There they had swung across the bridge and out on the Brighton line, left the train at Beverly Road, walked westward a couple of blocks and separated with a mutual " See you to-morrow." And now he was tired.

Reaching out, he snapped off the light and raised the curtain. A breath of air swept in, and he swung his chair to meet it. Then he jumped erect as a piercing shriek rose from beneath his feet. His heel had come down on Rajah's long tail.

" Why, Rajah, old boy! Come here! " he coaxed. But the outraged cat, thus rudely roused from dreams of white owls which he was rending limb from limb, would have none of him. He heard the little feet dash through the doorway and down the hall. Laughingly he pursued them to the head of the stairs. When he heard the bump announcing Rajah's arrival on the lower floor he turned aside into Ruth's bedroom.

The soft glow of the shaded boudoir lamp revealed a symphony of pink and gold. The spread on the shining brass bed was pink beneath its lace. Across the back of a chair hung a pink silk kimono. The long side curtains at each window were pink. On the pink walls hung a few small water-colors framed in dull gold. The one note of masculinity in the room was his own picture in a square silver frame on the dressing-table. One could easily guess that he had selected that frame as a gift to her, for it was such as a man would choose.

A little pile of snapshots lying just beneath his picture caught his eye, and he lifted them nearer the light. Two of Ruth's girl friends standing beside the fountain in Prospect Park; Rajah snoozing in the sun; and ——

His pulse stopped an instant and he grew tense.

Elliott Duncan!

Elliott Duncan, insolently handsome, at the wheel of his fast gray car; his cap tilted at a jaunty angle, his powerful figure lolling back against the cushions, his heavy mouth twisted in a half-cynical smile. A big, fresh-skinned man at whom both men and women looked twice: the men searchingly and the women wistfully. To the women, who glanced elsewhere when he returned their regard, his face bespoke easy goodfellowship; but to men, who met his gaze squarely, his cold eyes told of unscrupulous determination to take whatsoever he desired. Don laid his thumb over the lower half of the pictured face, and instantly the good humor was gone from it. Above his nail the eyes stared as cruelly as those of a shark. His fist closed as he recalled sinister rumors regarding this man.

There was Virginia Davies, a dark-eyed little beauty, who for a few short weeks motored and danced with Duncan. Then they were seen together no more. A tall blonde, said to be a divorcée, took Virginia's place in the gray car. From Virginia's laughing eyes the light fled, and beneath them grew dark hollows. Then she disappeared. And four days later, lashed by a northeast gale, the snarling green waves of the Atlantic flung her body out on the Brighton sands.

"It's the same old thing, Don," a cynical newspaper man had said at the time. "One more unfortunate—and so on. And you can't hang it onto him so that it will stick. He's clever, he's rotten with money, and he's got a pull with the big boys in politics."

And this was the man whose picture, taken with Ruth's own camera, lay on the dressing-table beneath his own! Decidedly, he must speak to her. She could not know what Duncan was. Man-like, he hated the retailing of sordid gossip, and he had never told her of the ugly rumors, for it had never occurred to him that she might meet this man. Hastily he ran through the other pictures, but found only landscape studies taken in the park. Turning out the light, he went back to his chair in the den.

Shaken despite himself, he stared out at the stars and recalled other things of Duncan. Ever at his brain hammered the questions: Where, and when, and how had Ruth met him? Their acquaintance must have begun during his absence in camp, and it could be no more than a casual friendship. Friendship? He laughed at himself. It could hardly be even that; and it would assuredly be anything but that, when he had told Ruth a few things for her own protection.

Why worry? Duncan was dangerous to girls who were unprotected or easily deceived, but not to the wives of men who would strike swift and hard to defend them. He stretched his arms over his head and relaxed, his mind at ease. It would all be cleared up as soon as she arrived.

Dreamily he smiled up at the far worlds twinkling in the deep blue. It was good to be home once more. His heavy eyelids drooped, opened sleepily, closed again. Slowly he slipped down in his chair.

CHAPTER III

DON AWAKES

RAJAH loved music. Not weird minors, or plaintive melodies with an undertone of tears—these filled his heart with woe. But the gay, lilting things which his mistress usually played exhilarated him until his regal dignity slipped from him and he became the veriest buffoon.

The music was strangely muted to-night, but it affected the tiger-cat as it always did. First he prowled uneasily about the room, peering into corners in search of some mouse, or even a big white owl, upon which he might pounce. Then, as his tingling nerves became more and more surcharged with the exciting rhythm, he broke into a spasmodic trot, broken by sudden whirling jumps which brought his nose where his tail had been a moment before. This in turn was succeeded by foolish little tumbles on the rug before the man who lounged indolently in Donald's big leather chair and stared down at him with cold contempt.

Rajah rolled on his back, rooted his nose along the floor, yanked himself sidewise and whirled over into a crouch, his snapping eyes fixed on the white buckskin shoe which stretched lazily from the big chair. Unconsciously that foot was beating time. Perhaps the cat's intoxicated imagination translated it into his deadly enemy, the owl. His haunches grew tense, his fur bristled, his tail twitched as he poised for the fatal spring. Of course, he did not really mean to attack that foot, but it was vastly exciting to "make believe."

Into the cold eyes above him stole a crafty gleam. They glanced swiftly at the girlish figure at the piano, and saw that her thoughts were floating far away on the tide of the music. The foot began to jerk at unexpected instants, tantalizing the quivering cat until he could stand the strain no longer. Into the air he launched himself. And into the air shot the white foot to meet him. The hard toe caught him square on his sensitive nose, and with a little startled yowl of pain he whirled over backward, striking hard on his head.

For an instant he sprawled helpless where he had fallen. Then he lurched to his feet, pawed at his nose, and sidled dizzily out into the hall. As the pitiful little figure disappeared in the shadows the man chuckled.

The soft music stopped. Ruth swung about and smiled into the smiling face of the visitor. Then her gaze roved about the room.

"Did I hear Rajah cry?" she asked.

He laughed, and lied with smooth skill.

"Hardly that. I think he was trying to burst into song. As a contortionist he's a wonder, but as a vocalist—well, when he heard his first note he ran away from it."

Ruth's merry laugh rang down the hall, where Rajah had begun a halting ascent of the stairs. Still dazed, he turned his head toward his mistress' beloved voice—

and bumped his aching nose against the next stair. It stung so sharply that he recoiled, slipped, and rolled down three steps before his claws caught and held. Both people heard the noise.

"And now, having convinced himself that he's no soloist, he's trying a one-step out in the hall," laughed the man. Ruth giggled and jumped from the bench.

"Isn't he the silliest thing? He's so funny when music stirs him up. Let's go and see what he's doing, Elliott."

Duncan rose swiftly and caught her arm. It was not his desire to let her see the cat's hurt face. Besides, he had other things in view.

Again Rajah stumbled whimpering up the stairs. His head and nose ached so cruelly that tears blinded him; but the worst hurt of all was not physical. In all his proud life he had never met treachery or inhumanity. Now he had been deliberately goaded into an excess of playfulness and made the victim of stark brutality. And as he slunk into the friendly darkness the man had laughed—and his mistress had laughed! Heart-broken, he sought the one comfort left in all his bitter world—the caress of his master's hand.

In the dark upper hall he paused to lap his nose and paw his singing ears. Then, at a shambling trot, he entered the den and plumped himself into the sleeping man's lap. Donald stirred, blinked, and ran his hand slowly down the cat's back. At the kindly touch Rajah snuggled closer; and as Donald drowsily stroked him again and again, the pain grew dull and the load of grief was lifted. He was safe, and was being petted as of old.

A little laugh came from below. The stroking hand stopped suddenly. A sheepish grin stole across the man's face as he rose and gently laid Rajah in the chair. So he'd been asleep! Fine watchdog, wasn't he? Must be company down-stairs. The Mackenzies, perhaps, from next door.

Shod in silence, his moccasined feet made no sound as he passed along the hall and down the stairs. The narcotic of sleep had not quite passed from his brain, and near the bottom he hesitated, peering downward and feeling unsteadily for the floor with one foot. His palm, grasping the rail, squeaked sharply.

"Wonder what that was?" queried a masculine voice. It was not Mackenzie's voice. Donald halted in some surprise. Then came Ruth's reply—a chant intoned in mock-solemn cadences:

"His—Royal—Majesty, Rajah,—has caught—a big —fat—squeaky—squirmy—mouse!"

Donald laughed silently. The other man chuckled— a short, rather hard chuckle. Ruth's soft voice came again:

"Now, you must let me go. I'm very much interested in Rajah, you know."

A chill crept over the man on the stair. This unknown man must let her go! Was he holding her? Who was he?

The answer came quickly—a little gasp, and a cry: "Elliott! You big bear, you're crushing me!"

The chill in Donald's blood suddenly became an icy

tide which whelmed his heart. He swayed as if struck
from behind. The gloom of the hall deepened to a
black, whirling void. Dazedly he told himself that this
thing was impossible. His little wife, his goddess who
had come to him on a cloud-chariot from dreamland—
she could not be a traitress. No. No. She could not
be! He had not heard aright. This was some terrible
trick of imagination, some waking nightmare which
would pass—which *must* pass!

Little by little his vision cleared. Vaguely he felt
that minutes had elapsed while he stood there, that
words had been spoken which his stunned brain had
not received. He must look into that room. His eyes
could be trusted, if his ears could not. With uncertain
step he went down the few remaining stairs, and
passed to the open door beyond which glowed the soft
light of the big rose-globed lamp.

Beside that lamp he saw two figures blended into
one. Clasped close in Duncan's arms, Donald's wife
was not even making a pretense of trying to evade him.
Passive she stood, smiling up at the man whose photograph lay on her dressing-table up-stairs. And even
as Donald looked stupefied on his princess of the mountain-top unresisting in the embrace of a known *in-
trigant*, Duncan's lips met hers and clung there through
a long moment. The last hope of the man in the hallway snapped under him and fell away.

In most men lie latent traits of the wild things of the
woods: traits which, through the countless ages of evolution, have remained ever the same. Wound a fighting animal slightly, or even seriously, and you but

madden him; and then beware, for he will leap and
rend you with tooth and claw. But wound him mor-
tally—then, sick with shock, he turns to the darkness
and the solitude where he may suffer alone. His madness comes not then, but later. When the awful after-
agony seizes him, however, his devastating wrath is
more to be dreaded than the swift fury evoked by a
lighter hurt; for then, if the thing that struck him
down be still within his reach, he is likely to destroy it
utterly, or, failing that, to rend himself.

On Donald the clean-hearted, Donald the unsuspi-
cious, this revelation of faithlessness fell like a bomb.
It struck his soul into the dust, smashed thought from
his mind and sense from his brain. Far down within
him stirred the blind instinct of the stricken animal;
and, knowing not what he did, he turned slowly away
into the dark.

From the lamplit room behind him, where stood
those two so intent on each other that they were totally
unaware of the silent spectre which had taken shape in
the doorway and faded out again, floated another
laughing protest.

" You're a dear boy, but must I remind you again
that a girl isn't made of rubber and rawhide? I truly
believe your earliest ancestors were grizzly bears."

" Pardon, lady mine," came Duncan's apology. " I
don't want to let you go for a single minute. However
—is that better? "

" Much better." Came the sound of a long breath.
" Why, Elliott! Do you know how late it is? Just
look at that clock! You must run along home now—

the maid may come in at any minute, and maids have very loose tongues sometimes."

"Ye-es, I suppose so." The tone showed he was loath to go. "You should have a Jap, like mine. He sees nothing, hears nothing, says nothing—like the three little monkeys of his native isle. No matter how often you come to see me, my Lady Ruth, you need never fear *his* tongue."

"I believe you. He's an Oriental sphinx. Really, I don't think I ever knew the exact meaning of the word 'inscrutable' until I saw him. He's silent with his face and eyes as well as his tongue. But these maids —and the neighbors! How do you manage your neighbors, Elliott? Have you trained them as well as the Jap?"

"Oh, they've learned that it's wise to keep out of my affairs," was the significant reply. "There's more than one way of convincing neighbors that it's best to be deaf and dumb. Are yours too nosey? If so, perhaps I can find means of ——"

"Oh, no, no!" she interrupted. "The best way to keep these people quiet is not to let them know anything. And your car is standing outside, and if anybody's watching——"

"Meaning that I must cast myself into outer darkness. But first, where shall we meet to-morrow? Shall I call here again?"

"No." She considered. "I'll meet you in Manhattan. I don't suppose those garage men will have our car back here to-morrow—they keep saying they have found something else wrong with it, so that they can run up a bigger bill, I suppose. So perhaps I'd better take the subway to the Grand Central ——"

"Too far!" he decreed. "You don't want to ride all that distance in the stuffy old tube. I'll be in Wall Street in the afternoon anyway, and we can meet at the subway station—say about three o'clock. Then we'll motor up to one of those live places on Broadway where we've been before—or try a new one, if you like. And after we've lunched and danced to our hearts' content,—well, we'll see."

Numb, dumb, moved only by that ancient instinct of the animal with a deadly wound, Donald was creeping up the stairs toward his dark den. The words which came to him seemed to break against his mind and drop away like arrows splintered against a dead wall. Yet even on a dead wall arrows leave their marks.

"Three o'clock, then, at the Wall Street station," Duncan repeated. "You'll be there?"

"Of course. Haven't I always met you when I said I would? Now run along, run along, or I'll call my trusty cat and have him chase you out."

Laughingly they came out into the hall. Up above, Donald looked dully down at them with a curious feeling of detachment. A sort of mental anæsthesia seemed to envelop him. He saw Duncan hold her close; heard her promise again to be on time; saw her watch as the car started away, then turn back into the music-room. Somehow all this didn't hurt. Vaguely he felt that it ought to. But it didn't.

Like a man walking in sleep he passed to his den. Into the darkest corner he turned. There, bolt upright, as if dead and frozen on his feet, he stood blank-eyed, staring at the unseen wall. Formless thoughts flitted bat-like through his darkened mind and were gone. Time was nothing. Space was nothing. The man who had gone, the woman down-stairs, and he himself—all were nothing.

By and by the woman came up-stairs and went into another room. After a while she passed along the hall. At the open door of the den she stopped and stood very quiet. Presently she spoke.

" Rajah! Rajah, are you in there? "

The cat's paws bumped on the floor as he left the big chair.

" Rajah, you're a naughty, bad cat. Haven't I told you not to push doors open? You gave me quite a fright, sir, and I've a mind to spank you." Then her half-chiding tone melted. " Still you were a lonesome boy, Rajah dear. Now run along into my room. Scamper, you rascal, scamper!" The door shut firmly.

In the black corner the tall, silent shadow turned it-self about. It did not advance. It did not speak. As before, it only stared at the darkness. But where the gloom had been mere emptiness, now it was shot athwart with blood-red specks. Far down in Donald's blood the chill began to thaw and a black broth began to form: the poison distilled of wrath and hate and an-guish, which drives men to kill. The formless thoughts flitted back again, not so formless now. There were certain things to be done.

A snake had crept into his Eden. When one found

a snake one killed it. Of course. Still, this snake had crept in because the woman opened the gate. Perhaps the woman had even met it half-way and invited it in. Probably that was true. Then it might not be exactly fair to kill the snake. Of course, it must be beaten, broken, driven hence forevermore. But what about the woman, who had ——

Something snapped in his brain. The merciful numbness of the first shock, the feeling that nothing could hurt, dropped away as if struck aside by a mighty hand. Poignant as a spear-thrust came full realization; and the things he had seen, the things he had heard, became whips in the hands of vindictive Furies, lashing, lashing, lashing him until he writhed.

"God!" he spat through clinched teeth. "God!"

His hands groped out before him, caught the edge of the heavy table, and clinched on the hard wood until his nails bled; and clutching it as a man in a maelstrom clings to anything within reach, he fought off wave after wave of the anguished frenzy which beat upon him and almost engulfed him in the wild abyss of madness.

How long he fought that bitter battle only the Recording Angel knows. At last he drew a long, tortured breath and passed a shaking hand across his brow. He felt sick. The dazed feeling came over him again. He got into his chair, but could not rest there. Mechanically he bent over and laced his moccasins. Mechanically he returned to the table. His hand felt along it for his hat. It encountered, not the Panama, but the felt hat he had worn in camp. He put it on. The hand went back and sought something else—just what, he hardly realized. It met steel; cool steel; the steel of his gun. Down that steel it slid to the butt. It lifted the weapon, and the thumb pressed back the spring, letting the cylinder drop out sidewise. The other hand groped; found the belt of cartridges; loaded the revolver; closed it noiselessly. Then the left hand lifted his light silk vest. The right hand shoved the weapon down inside his trousers, under the belt. The left hand dropped the vest. The whole thing was done without conscious purpose, almost without volition. His body simply went ahead and armed itself without consulting his mind.

The black broth was beginning to simmer. Before long it would boil.

He passed into the hall, where total blackness reigned. From the pink-and-gold bedroom came no light, no sound. Groping, he found the door of his own room; entered, and snapped on the light. Then he stood frowning, trying to think what he had come in here for. Disjointed sentences tore at his mind like the talons of vultures: "*Three o'clock at—maids have loose tongues—ought to have a Jap—live places on Broadway where we've been before ——*" His teeth clenched hard and his brow knotted. *What* did he want here? A knob on the wall caught his eye—oh, yes: money. He was going away. He needed more money. There was money in the wall-safe; money left there in a past life, before he went camping. About three hundred. Yes. Three hundred.

"*—Always met you when I said I would—you're a*

dear boy ——" taunted the whirling ghosts of dead words. What was that combination, anyhow? He tried, and tried, and tried to open that little safe. With sudden fury he yanked at it, tried to pull it bodily out of the wall; but he only hurt his fingers. Click, click, click-click—the combination came back to him now. Presently the little door swung outward. The money was there. Jamming it into a pocket, he strode back to the light.

In the act of turning it out he hesitated, his eyes on the drawn curtains in the doorway connecting his room with hers. His hand dropped; went to his inner coat pocket; emerged with a folded sheet bearing sundry rough notes.. Smoothing it out, he held it against the wall. On the back he wrote his farewell.

> Came home to-night. Am now going away again. This time I won't come back.
> You may as well spare yourself the trip to Wall Street. Duncan will not be there.

The pencil dropped on the floor. Through the portières he passed, found the boudoir lamp, and twitched the little chain.

She lay asleep. Tranquil, peaceful, her soul wafted far away into the mysterious realm of slumberland, she seemed hardly to belong to the world of human error and frailty. Lightly on her rose-petal cheeks rested her long lashes. Half-parted, her curving lips seemed to smile. Framed in her dark hair and softly tinted by the pink-shaded light, her dreaming face seemed a picture of purity from which all evil things must slink away abashed.

Out of the black poison seething in his veins there arose a black demon, which shouted that she had no right to that fair face, that upon it should be stamped the scarlet brand of shame. His fists knotted hard. Then the frozen look came back into his face. Slowly he turned from her and laid his note beside the light.

A picture looked him in the face—his own photograph in its silver frame. It had no business here now. He pulled it from the frame, crumpled it into a broken paper ball, dropped it, and jerked the chain again. The room was dark.

Curled up in a furry ball at his mistress' feet, the big tiger-cat watched his master's tall figure loom suddenly black between the curtains; saw the light in that room, too, wink out; heard the front door open and close. Then, in all that house, he heard no sound but the soft, regular breathing up among the pillows. He yawned, stretched, turned about, lay down again, and let his sleepy eyes close once more. He was at peace with all the world. The kick he had received, the bitterness of being laughed at, were forgotten. Little did Rajah know, or care, that his dumb appeal for comfort had launched against the man who kicked him a living thunderbolt of wrath. But so it was. And even now the bolt was on its way.

CHAPTER IV

MAN TO MAN

In all the twelve massive stories of the Alden Arms apartment house only one space was lighted. That was the wide entrance, where twin clusters of white globes flanked the stone steps and the spacious vestibule glowed bright with its all-night welcome to late-returning revelers. Above, the stone front towered up into the night, every window dark.

Wide open stood the big glass-and-iron doors—wide open to admit any wandering breath of coolness that might steal up from Riverside Drive and the Hudson, some three blocks away. They were supposed to be closed, of course, as were also the inner doors of plate-glass. But the liveried, liver-hued elevator pilot had his own ideas on that subject, and at this time of night he put them into practice. From his brilliantly lighted cage he blinked somnolently out through the marble hall at a dark motor-car across the street: a town car with a sedan top, from which four people had gone into the opposite house not long ago—two men and two women. Idly he wished he owned it, wished he could be a sport. Then he wished the hall-man would come back, so that he could talk to him. 'Deedy, it was pow'ful slow round yere in de long hours befo' mawnin'. With a wide yawn he turned to one of the

41

mirrors in his cage and became absorbed in contemplation of a lump on his dusky nose.

Two motor-cars swept past, and he did not turn—even though from one of them rang the reckless laughter of a girl who had been drinking too much. That was " old stuff " in his blasé life. Of a sudden, though, he stood very still. His head began to turn stealthily, as if he were afraid he might see something, and equally afraid he wouldn't. *Something* had been near him: something silent as the dead, swift as a vanishing ghost: something dread and uncanny. Not a living thing was in sight. The ornate hall was vacant. No noise came to him save the familiar night-sound of the great city. Yet he felt in the marrow of him that *something* had flitted past. Superstitious as all his race is, he goggled fearfully about the empty vestibule, and finally, almost shivering, crept to the door and peered up and down the street. Nobody lay dead on the sidewalk. Nothing unusual was in sight. Nervous, uneasy, he crept back into his elevator and wished daylight would come.

Meanwhile, on the second floor, a moccasined man stole from door to door, peering at the name beside the entrance to each apartment. Not finding what he sought, he turned to the stairs and resumed his search on the floor above. His movements were silent, but not stealthy. He cast no look behind to see whether he was watched. No burglar or bum was he, but a man driven by a fixed, implacable purpose. Beneath his felt hat-brim steely eyes glittered through narrowed lids; his face was flint, his mouth a steel trap; his hands opened and shut as if throttling something. Had the scared negro caught one good glimpse of that grim figure, he would have fled into the street and bawled for a policeman.

From door to door, from floor to floor, Donald passed with never a sound. From one card he straightened up abruptly. His finger jammed hard against a button. Somewhere inside an electric bell rang.

Minutes dragged away. Nobody came to the door. He set his thumb on the button and held it there. The bell pealed in one continuous, imperious summons.

A bolt snapped back. The door was yanked inward. In the opening stood Duncan himself, attired in pajamas and ugly at being roused from sleep.

"What d'you want?" he demanded savagely. "Who the ——"

The sentence stopped unfinished. Warned by the baleful glimmer in those half-shut eyes, he tried to slam the door. But he was too late. The door jumped back at him. The intruder leaped at him. A pile-driver fist smashed into his face. He reeled back into the dark.

The door swung shut of its own accord. Instant blackness filled the corridor. Donald swung again at the place where Duncan should be. His fist met nothing, and he nearly fell. His quarry had staggered back out of reach. He sprang forward a pace, then stopped suddenly. Unfamiliar with the place, he might run headlong into a wall. So he stood still and felt for a match.

Several feet away, Duncan spoke. He completed the question which he had started to ask.

"Who are you?"

"Light up, and see!"

The other did not comply.

"Ashamed of your name?" came a sneer through the dark. "Or did your mother forget who your father was?"

At that insult Donald forgot matches, walls, everything. Forward he strode, hands clutching for that obscene throat.

"I'm King!" he grated. "King, you sneak!"

A startled "Hm!" came to his ears. A barely audible movement followed—a retreating movement. Still his lunging hands met nothing. Duncan was giving way before him, keeping out of reach. Swiftly he pursued. The sound stopped. An instant later he struck a blank wall.

Light leaped into the corridor: light shining from a doorway beside him, and flooding a luxurious bedroom. Of the sybaritic splendor of that room Donald saw nothing; for his flaming gaze was fixed on the heavy figure which, in its white silk pajamas, stood beside the massive bed and scowled at him. Into the room he strode. As he did so, Duncan coolly sat down on the bed and waved a hand toward a chair.

"Perhaps I ought to apologize for that remark," he said easily. "It was rather nasty. Still you'll admit that when a chap rouses you from your virtuous couch and greets you with his fist, it's apt to upset the usual social amenities. Besides, I'd hardly say your own manners are impeccable, if this is a sample. Before we carry the matter any further, perhaps you'll be so good as to explain."

Amazed at the effrontery of the man, Donald stood glowering at him. He seemed not in the least alarmed, nor even perturbed. On the contrary, he emanated an arrogant assurance, as if he had but to lift his hand and precipitate this troublesome fellow into annihilation. His insouciance stirred Donald's memory to recall sinister rumors as to this man's power, and the things which had happened to men who opposed him. One of those men had disappeared bodily, and had never come back. Don whirled and looked behind him. Nothing was there.

The sudden movement seemed to amuse Duncan. He laughed—a mirthless laugh.

"Don't be afraid, King. I'm all alone. I let my Jap go out for the whole night, and there's nobody here to listen. Sit down and tell me what's on your mind."

"You know well enough. You've sneaked into my home."

The other's brows lifted slightly.

"Oh, no. 'Sneaked' is hardly the word. I never 'sneak' anywhere. Please clarify your statement."

"Clarify?" exploded Don. "Stand up on your legs and I'll clarify! I'm not here to bandy words."

Duncan smiled insolently and remained seated.

"No? Perhaps I'll stand up when you've told me just why I should. Meanwhile it's much more com-

fortable to sit. Now just why did you think I'd
' sneaked into your home,' as you express it? "

Donald took an iron grip on himself. His answer
came crisp, incisive.

" I was at home to-night. I watched you. I listened
to you. You will not meet my wife to-morrow."

" Why not? " Duncan leaned forward. " Have
you hurt her? "

" *Why not!* Because you won't be able to. *She's*
safe. I don't fight women."

" I see. Very commendable, I'm sure."

With another irritating smile Duncan lolled back
on one elbow. His right hand slipped under a pillow.

" So you've learned that she doesn't care for you
any longer," he went on. " Rather a blow to your
vanity, eh? But there's no need of kicking up such a
rumpus about it. More than one man has had the same
experience, you know." Cold, calculating, his shark
eyes stared unwinking at the menacing figure before
him. " Besides, I'm amenable to reason in a case of
this sort. Be sensible, now, and state your terms."

Not understanding, Donald scowled down at him.
Slowly the unspeakable meaning of the suggestion
dawned on him.

" You—you rotten slaver! " he choked. " Think you
can *buy* her? "

" Oh, no indeed," deprecated the other. " Of course
not. You shouldn't be so brutally direct—it's quite
bad form. There's no thought of ' slavery '—pah! a
most disgusting word! It's merely a matter of every-

body being satisfied. These triangular arrangements are not new in the world, by any means. Be reasonable, my dear fellow, and I'm sure we can—er—arrive at a settlement advantageous to all of us. One good turn deserves another. I'll overlook the impetuosity you've displayed thus far, and I can get you almost anything you want. I have a habit of getting things." He paused. Then, as if it were a mere afterthought, he added: " Of course, if you persist in being disagreeable, I can also get you some things you don't want."

Though uttered so casually, the threat was unmistakable. Again Donald thought of the man who had disappeared; of others who had met sudden and complete ruin; and—of little Virginia Davies.

" One evening last week, when I was in camp," he stated with slow significance, " a very filthy skunk crossed my path."

The cold eyes watching him narrowed a bit.

" I killed the skunk." .

For an instant the eyes became venomous. Then across Duncan's face, like a mask, dropped a slightly bored expression.

" Very interesting," he yawned. " But if you've any lurid ideas, forget 'em. The sort of thing you're thinking about isn't being done nowadays. I've suggested a reasonable proposition to you, King, and you'd better consider it carefully before doing anything rash. How about it?"

Never yet had Donald hit a man who was not on his feet. Seething with wrath though he was, yet his

fighting code held him back. Through rigid lips he
spat his answer.

"Stand up on your hind legs, skunk!"

Unperturbed, Duncan shrugged a shoulder, and replied in the same silky tone: "Still determined to be
nasty? You're only running headlong into all kinds
of calamity. May I ask just what you propose to do?"

"Hammer you into a pulp."

"Ah, yes. A most laudable intention, to be sure.
But I think you've overlooked a bet." The insolent,
mirthless smile flitted again across Duncan's face.
Very casually, as if to ease his shoulder muscles of his
weight, he rose from his elbow to a sitting posture;
but his right hand remained hidden under the pillow,
and his eyes were watchful.

"In the first place, you've forced your way in here
in the small hours, with burglarious or other felonious
intent. You are wearing—er—some sort of footgear
never worn in this city, with the evident purpose of
muffling your footfalls. I am alone and unprotected."
Again the derisive grin. "In the second place, I have
some influence among the Powers that Be. Therefore,
if you should meet with—er—an untimely death up
here, I should have no difficulty in hushing it up and
in avoiding any unpleasant consequences. People frequently are mistaken for burglars in the night, and re-
grettable accidents happen."

He paused, and glanced at the knotted fists hanging
at his antagonist's sides. He was very sure of himself—so sure that he was contemptuous.

"Again, even if it should become known that you

came up here because of—ah—your jealousy, I could prevent the yellow press from digging too deep. I have a way of fixing things. I might even become quite a hero; and you would be far too dead to dispute any claim I might make. My advice to you is to slip out of here as quickly as you came in. Otherwise ——"

He paused again. His hand began to creep out from under the pillow. Suddenly his voice lost its specious suavity and became harsh.

"Get out!" he snarled. "I'm sick of looking at you! Get out quick, or you'll go feet first!"

The black broth in Don's veins boiled over. With the deadly silence of a jaguar leaping on his prey he sprang for his enemy's throat. But even as his feet left the floor Duncan's right hand licked out, gripping a wicked automatic. A thin pencil of flame stabbed at him. A sharp report filled the room. Something stung the tip of his left ear. As his heels struck the rug he whirled sidewise and backward, and his hand streaked to his waistband where the big revolver hung.

Crack! spat the automatic again.

CRASH! roared the army gun.

His coat, hanging loosely unbuttoned, whipped violently back against his left arm as Duncan's bullet smote it waist-high. The concussion of his own weapon seemed to burst the walls asunder and split his ear-drums. Acrid powder-gas stung his nostrils. The hammer of his gun rose half-way, then slid smoothly down again. There was no need of another shot.

Duncan's automatic dropped. His left hand fluttered to his throat. Into his eyes crept an awful fear. Suddenly he seemed to cave in at the middle, and with a short, bubbling sigh he fell forward to the floor.

Between his shoulders a red stain spread rapidly on the back of his white jacket. For a moment the grim-jawed man standing over him stared at it. Then he understood. The heavy bullet had driven clear through Duncan's body.

CHAPTER V

A FRIEND IN NEED

A HEAVY, muffled thump suddenly jarred the ceiling. In the apartment above, a man had leaped from bed. *Thump, thump, thump* went bare heels across the room. They stopped, and the listening man pictured the unknown fumbling in his clothing. *Thump, thump, thump* they came back to the window. An instant later the resonant, far-reaching call of a police whistle sang out into the night.

Across the court a window squeaked violently, and a man yelled: " Hello, Marbury! Where's the shooting? "

" Down-stairs in Duncan's apartment," came the reply overhead. " Three shots. The last one sounded like a cannon. See anything? "

" There's a light in his bedroom, but the curtain's down. I'll be over as soon as I can get into some clothes."

The whistle blew again—three long blasts, followed by short urgent ones close together. Somewhere down the street another whistle answered. Then a nightstick began to beat the pavement in the rallying signal of the police fraternity. The blue cordon was beginning to close in.

Donald looked again at the figure on the floor. Into his mind flashed Duncan's remark about the yellow press; and close on the heels of this thought came a vision of his own face, Duncan's—and Ruth's—spread across a printed page for the delectation of the morbid public. He recalled the big headlines and the sordid details of certain murder cases. Anything but that! For his own future he cared nothing—it held only misery; but for the preservation of his shamed home from the eyes of the curious he cared much. He might yet escape. Shoving the weapon back into his waistband, he bolted down the corridor.

As he ran, he heard the clang of the elevator gate down below. Opening the door a narrow crack, he peered out to see a light stealing up the elevator shaft. In a moment the car rose, hesitated while the scared negro glanced about him, then went on upward. As the floor of the cage passed the ceiling Donald pulled his hat low over his face, darted out, and closed the door without a bang. But just as his hand left the knob the door across the hall opened and a man in night-gear and trousers leaped at him.

Without a pause in his stride Donald swung a frightful blow flush on his assailant's jaw. The man crumpled backward through the doorway. From within the apartment shrilled the shriek of a terrified woman. Down the stairs flew the fugitive, while above him rose an uproar as men popped into the hall and yelled at the still ascending elevator-man.

At the entrance he stopped and peered out, while through his brain flashed a dozen plans of action. He could not run far before meeting a patrolman. He could not hide in this hornets' nest. He might walk away in leisurely fashion, trusting to his nerve to carry him through if stopped. But no! his moccasins would make him an object of instant suspicion, and the police net would seize and hold anyone who didn't look just right.

That automobile across the street! Why not? If he could only get a mile away—he darted from the vestibule and leaped across the pavement. But as he ran he saw that the machine was no longer empty, for a man occupied the driver's seat. The car began to move, and the man yelled: " Keep off! "

But Don jumped to the step. It was his one chance, and he would not let it slip. The big gun leaped to his hand again, and he jammed it into the other's face.

" Drive! " he commanded hoarsely. The car jumped, and he swung himself into the rear of the tonneau.

" Keep going, and keep your mouth shut! " he rumbled into the driver's ear. " Squawk once and you're dead! "

The other suddenly turned and squinted into his face.

" Good Lord! Don! " he ejaculated.

" Harry! " gasped the hunted man.

The car almost stopped.

" For the love of Mike, what's up? " blurted Harry. " Have you gone nutty? Where——"

" Police are after me. Never mind why. Get me away from here."

Blank astonishment overwhelmed Harry, but he turned to the wheel and the machine shot ahead. "Down in the back!" he grunted. Don dropped to the floor.

Around the next corner dashed a patrolman. At sight of the car he leaped to the roadway and barked: "Hey, there! Halt!"

The machine stopped with a jerk. Black rage swept over the man crouching against the cushions. So the game was up! Well, he would fight it out! Better to go down fighting, if need be, than be dragged to the Tombs and perhaps to a shameful death in the grim chair up at Sing Sing. His hand closed over the butt of his gun.

"All right, officer," came Harry's voice in well simulated surprise. "What's your quarrel with me?"

Harry was trying to bluff it out. It was a desperate chance, but—the fugitive flattened himself as far as he could, turned up his coat-collar, put his hands under him, and pressed his face to the floor, so that no telltale gleam of white should show if the officer glanced in at him. The darkness of the tonneau and Harry's nerve might save him yet.

"Who are you, and where you goin' so fast?" snapped the policeman. Alert, suspicious, ready for anything, he stood poised just out of Harry's reach, while with eyes hard as chilled steel he bored into Harry's face.

"Why," laughed Harry easily, "my name is Miller, and I'm going home. Here's my card. What's the row, anyway?"

The man-hunter glanced at the card, and his voice changed. "Oh, attorney-at-law, eh? Of Pendexter, Wightman and Miller. Sure, I know about ye, Mister Miller. What's this shootin' down beyant?"

"Hanged if I know. I heard some shots over this way when I was about a dozen blocks up on the Drive, but I haven't seen anything. It sounded to me as if it was back where you just came from, though."

"Did it so? That's the trouble wit' these tall build-in's—they take holt of a noise and break it up and t'row it around amongst 'em till ye can't tell where it starts. And ye saw nothin'?"

"Nothing unusual."

Another patrolman suddenly ran up, panting, and fixed his baleful glare on Harry's face. The other turned to him.

"Nothin' here," he began. "This is Mister——"

He broke off short and grabbed his mate's arm.

"'Tis there it is! Down the block—there goes one of the boys into the buildin'!"

He leaped away. The other flashed one more look over the car, gazed fixedly at the number, probed Harry's honest face an instant, and followed. He had not said a word.

Slowly Harry started up the car. For blocks he moved at the fair speed of a man going home, but in no hurry about it. Then the machine began to pick up, and steadily but swiftly ran northward. All the time Donald crouched on the floor, bumping and sway-ing, but ever holding his head below the level of the door. At last the car slowed and stopped, and he peered out across a gloomy, unfamiliar country. The city, with its lights and its whistles and its ten thousand policemen, lay behind them.

"Whe-e-e-ew!" whistled Harry. "That was a narrow squeak! If I hadn't had my card, or if the cops had looked into the back—Gee! it would have been all off! Now explain yourself. Were you in that shooting I heard?"

Don straightened up stiffly and laid a hand on Harry's shoulder. For a long moment the two looked into each other's eyes. Through the mind of the man who had just left his broken life behind him trooped memories of the years of comradeship which he and this chum of his had lived as roommates at college and as clubmates in after years. Always Harry had been ready to fight for a friend; and now, when a friend had come leaping desperately out of the night and demanded his aid, he had given it loyally, unhesitatingly, though that friend bore in his hand a freshly fired weapon and on his face the look of a hunted criminal. He deserved nothing less than the stark truth.

"I have shot Elliott Duncan," said Don.

Harry's jaw dropped.

"You—have—shot ——" he whispered. He stared at the haggard face above him, and his own ruddy color fled. "So!" he went on in a hushed voice. "I was afraid there would be trouble—but not that bad!"

The hand on his shoulder closed like a vise.

"You were afraid? Then—you knew! And you —didn't—warn me!"

Harry's head went back defiantly. For an instant he glared. Then, as he read the misery in the other's gaze, his expression softened, and he spoke with quiet dignity.

"Donald man, I knew your wife was motoring with Duncan. I knew they met at *thés dansants* uptown in the afternoon when you were at your office. But I didn't believe she really would double-cross you. She seemed above that sort of thing. And I didn't say anything, Don, because I'm not the man to tell a man things about his wife, or a woman things about her husband, unless I'm absolutely sure—and even then I'd hesitate a long time. I believe more domestic unhappiness is caused by tale-bearers than by any other one thing. But now—I wish I *had* told you!"

The merciless grip on his shoulder relaxed before he was half through. Now it tightened again in a brief, affectionate clasp. Donald understood, and honored his friend the more.

For a moment they stared out into the dark. Two questions were hammering at Harry's throat, and finally he broached the first.

"Don, are you dead sure you had reason to shoot up Duncan?"

"Positive." The tone was hard and flat.

"And—you laid him cold? Killed him?"

"Yes. Through the body."

Harry shivered. His lips went dry, and he moistened them twice with his tongue before he spoke again.

"Well, you've got to flit from this state," he an-

nounced briskly. "The nearest state is Connecticut.
If you could get north of Massachusetts you could
work straight up into Canada and lose yourself. Let's
get out of New York state right away."

"No. You turn back. I'll shift for myself."

"Huh? Sit down, you long-legged centipede, or I'll
yank the car out from under you. We're going into
Connecticut, I said." The car shot ahead, and Donald
sprawled violently back on the cushions. He made no
effort to get up, for a reaction had set in and he felt
sick. The machine hummed swiftly on through the
night, and they had covered miles before the driver
spoke again. He was thinking hard, and as they passed
a marshy spot he slowed down.

"It might be a good idea to heave your gun over
into the swamp there," he suggested. "You don't need
it any more, and it's mighty bad evidence."

Without a word Donald drew out the weapon and
hurled it from him. It plunged sullenly into a black
pool and was gone.

"Good head, Harry boy!" thought Harry. "It
won't be long before he'll be alone and the black despair
will get him, and if he had that gun then he'd spill his
brains sure. Now get him over here and talk to him."
Aloud he said: "Climb over here beside me. When
we hit a town you can climb back and squat while we
pass through. There, that's more like regular folks.

"Say, wasn't it lucky I was on the job when you
came hot-footing it out of that place? You know I
left this car to be overhauled while we were in camp.
Well, when I got home there she was, clean as a

whistle; so after I got bathed and fed up and so on, I went out for the first spin in three weeks. Had some spin, too! Finally I got hungry again and dropped in at a cabaret for a bite and a peep at the dancing, and found Ed Halliday there with his wife and a Miss Lawrence—Mrs. Halliday's sister; so we made a foursome, and finally I took 'em all home and went inside a little while. I'd just got settled in the car again when the shooting broke loose, and while I was trying to figure out just where it was you popped out and came for me.

" I didn't know you at once, and I was just getting ready to hand you a stiff jolt on the chin when you poked the steel under my nose. Of course, that altered circumstances immediately, and I turned on the juice. Gee, I was scared green! "

Don smiled faintly. He knew Harry was afraid of nothing.

" I was doping out some way to dump you when you spoke again. Then I recognized your voice, though I couldn't believe it until I saw your face."

He fell silent again. By and by he resumed his monologue.

" The odd thing about those shots, though, was that although they were right across the street they seemed to come from the next block. I can't figure that out yet."

" The room was down the corridor, on the court," explained Don.

" Oh! Gee, that's it! The sound rolled out the back way. Say, that's what gave you a chance to get under

cover—the cops probably ran over into the other street
first."

They neared a town, and Donald crawled back out
of sight until the electric lights lay behind them. For
a long time thereafter he sat gazing at the road rushing toward them in the glare of the twin lamps. At
length Harry asked: " Say, Don. Did you—were the
—did all three bullets hit him ? "

When no answer came he looked up to find a bewildered expression on his companion's face.

" I counted three shots," he added.

Then the light broke on Don's mind.

" I shot him *once!* " he replied. " He fired at me
twice."

" What ! " cried Harry. The car wobbled violently.
He spun the wheel back again. " Why, I thought ——"

" Great guns ! " exploded Don. " Did you think I
shot him to pieces? In cold blood ? "

" No—not in cold blood—but maybe in hot blood.
Who fired first ? "

" He did. Also second. I shot last."

The machine stopped with a squeal of brakes.
Harry whirled on him.

" What the blazes are you running away for, then?
You shot in self-defense—his gun would show two
shots gone, and he couldn't fire after he was dead.
You wouldn't be convicted—perhaps you wouldn't
even be indicted! I never handle criminal cases—cor-
poration's my line, you know—but I can get you a
first-class criminal lawyer. Come on back ! "

" No ! " An iron hand seized his arm. " What have

I to go back to? The yellow press—and a ruined home."

"Oh!" said Harry. After a moment the car moved forward.

The full measure of Harry's fealty swept over Donald in a warm flood. Ever since he had admitted the shooting Harry had believed that, infuriated by the discovery of his wife's faithlessness, he had shot down an unarmed man. Although the very roots of his being were fastened on the bedrock of the Law, although his whole legal and social career were imperiled by making himself an accomplice, he had throttled every instinct save that of whole-hearted comradeship to aid the escape of a man whom he looked on as a murderer. Truly, friendship could go no deeper than that! The love of woman had proved a treacherous spark which at the last had blasted the whole structure of Don's life; but among the blackened ruins the clear, clean flame of man's love for man still burned steady and true. Something blurred his sight, and he gulped and drove his nails deep into his palms, thankful that Harry was watching the road.

"Here's Bridgeport ahead," warned the driver. "Crawl back into your hole."

They swung through the city without a hail. When he emerged from the obscurity again he saw that the sky ahead was beginning to pale. They would reach New Haven at dawn; and there the ride must end, for the pitiless daylight would reveal his presence in the car sooner or later, and he would not further jeopardize Harry. So he sat staring at the brightening

sky as he had stared at the lighted road; and back into
his mind came the memory of other risings of the sun
which he and Harry had seen from the bald summit
of Kearsarge only a few days ago. A few days! It
seemed years. And as he remembered those care-free
days he decided where he should go. Not into Canada,
as Harry had suggested; but back to old Kearsarge,
in whose tangled forests he could hide himself as
effectively as the wild things which prowled by
night.

Mile after mile fled behind them, and moment by
moment the protecting shadows stole away into the
west. A pucker between the driver's eyes grew into
a worried frown. Finally he slowed, stopped, peered
at a dial, and muttered to himself.

"Gas is running low," he said, meeting his passenger's questioning gaze. "I drove quite some distance early to-night, and I've got to fill her up again in
New Haven. That means a garage—and daylight."

He rubbed his chin and stared at the sky. Donald
climbed out and extended his hand; but Harry's mind
was elsewhere.

"If you can hide out somewhere along here until I
get back," he went on, "I can get the juice and buy
some grub. Then we'll streak straight up the Connecticut Valley——"

His eyes dropped to Donald's face, and then to the
outstretched hand. In both he read a final farewell.

"Oh, nix, Don!" he protested. "I'm going to tote
you to Canada before I quit. I'm just getting warmed
up to this ride."

"No. You've risked too much already. Get your gas and go back home."

Harry opened his mouth—and closed it. The quiet finality in the other's attitude was unmistakable. He opened the door and stepped out into the road.

"Have you any money?" he asked, reaching into a pocket.

"Plenty, thanks. Won't need much. I'm going to travel by freight. Safest way."

For a long minute they stood under the swift-coming dawn, each gripping the other's hand.

"Old man ——" Don began brokenly.

"Say, you green-headed gorilla, if you try to thank me I'll bust you wide open!" raved Harry. Then, in a more normal tone, he added: "Let me hear from you when you can, Don. I know your writing — you needn't sign it."

Don nodded, and turned on his heel.

"So long!"

"So long!"

Harry stood watching until his mate had disappeared toward the railroad. Minutes later, faint and sweet, came the whistle of a whippoorwill. Harry tried to answer, but somehow his lips quivered and refused to frame the call. He bounced into the car and violently jabbed the horn three times. Then, slowly, he started toward the rising sun.

CHAPTER VI

THE SPY

BEYOND the tumbled New Hampshire hills the sun had gone down. The long, skinny clouds near the horizon had lost their rosy glow, and now stretched blue-black against a pallid sky. High in the upper air the night-hawks veered and swooped after luckless insects; but the birds of the woodlands, busy during the sunlit hours, now had sung their tributes to the departing day and tucked their sleepy little heads beneath their wings. Dusk was creeping from the east, filling the hollows with transparent but ever deepening shadows. It was not quite time for nocturnal beasts and birds to issue forth and prowl the earth and air; not quite time for the lighting of lamps in the homes of men; but the hour when an infinite, solemn peace broods over the land, soon to be veiled in night.

Slow-flowing, shallow, choked with sunken shavings and sawdust from Ela's mill, the creek which the Warner villagers dignify by the name of " river " became in the half-light a thing of beauty, gleaming like polished steel, and reflecting darkly the tangled brush and bending trees which grew along the farther shore. Behind that fringe of bush lay the village baseball field, flanked and backed by wooded steeps and barren pastures.

64

Along the hither bank stretched the railroad; and up on the crest of a steep slope, parallel with the right-of-way, ran the elm-shaded main street of the town.

On the platform of the railroad station, where an idle group awaited the coming of the last up train, a small boy yelled: " Here she be!" All eyes turned to the southeast, where something black had darted out of a sandy cut. The rails began to sing. Swiftly the oncoming locomotive grew larger, and the hum of the steel changed to a rapid *clackitclackitclackit* which in turn was drowned in a rising roar. A jet of steam shot upward, and the shriek of the whistle tore across the silent hills. Bell clanging, steam hissing, the train thundered in and stopped.

The weird, thin whistle of the air punctuated the scuffle of feet on the platform, died, and was succeeded by the panting of the engine. Trainmen swung outward from the coaches and stood by the gates. Dusky porters descended from the Pullmans. The baggage car ejected a few trunks and bags. A handful of passengers picked their way down the steps. The conductor waved his hand, the engine coughed, the trainmen swung aboard, and the cars began to move. The wheels rácketed across a siding, and the train diminished until it whisked around a bend. Two minutes later the station was deserted, except down at the far end, where the agent juggled an unclaimed trunk into the tiny baggage-room. Silence and solitude and deepening dusk brooded over the creek.

Behind a big tree, which drooped over the darkening waters and whispered mysterious things to them as the passing breeze touched its leafy branches, a head stole warily out and reconnoitered. As the agent slammed the door and started toward the office it dodged back out of sight. Minutes later it emerged again. Then a tall figure detached itself from the tree and glided across the flimsy foot-bridge leading to the baseball field. Along the narrow path through the brush it strode, wheeled abruptly to the right, and was screened from the sight of anyone on the railroad side by the wall of trees and underbrush.

The train had brought one passenger who had not paid his fare; who, while all minds were centered on the platform, had ducked from under the cars and taken refuge behind the friendly tree. In fact, for three days and nights (especially nights) this passenger had journeyed northward by slow stages, unseen by train crews. Stowed away in box-cars, crouching on coal flats, or walking long, weary miles over the ties, he had crawled up across two states, traveling all night and sleeping fitfully by day in coverts such as a genuine hobo would have despised. Ever in his mind had been the necessity of evading the human eye; and in consequence he had eaten scarcely at all, invading tough dens near the railroad yards only when he grew giddy from hunger, and then wolfing his food, with wary glances at the rough men about him. Then, as he neared New Hampshire, the strain, the sleeplessness, the partial starvation, the blistering heat, and the sombre thoughts that ever hammered at his brain engendered in him a reckless fever to reach the cool, sweet forests and disappear; and, caring little whether he fell beneath the deadly wheels, he had ridden the "rods" and the "blind baggage" of express trains. Had Harry stood beside him now in the big, dim field, he would scarcely have recognized his old-time chum. Gaunt, hollow-cheeked, blackened by cinders and smoke, eyes bloodshot, face bristling with a four-days' beard, hands swollen by cuts and blisters, clothing wrinkled, he bore little resemblance to the well-groomed Donald of other days.

The long flight was nearly done. Between him and the wild upper reaches of his protecting mountain lay four toilsome leagues of dusty roads—and the village. He could not go through that village, for he was known there, and the electric lights would unfailingly reveal his identity to some sharp-eyed observer. He must follow the meandering creek, dodging the sight of man, until he could reach a little branch road which would lead him to the Kearsarge road. Even then he might be seen and recognized. But his overmastering desire to reach his refuge goaded him on, refusing to let him rest here until sleep should fall on the town and permit him to pass through undetected. He must run the risk.

Wearily the fugitive turned and pushed through the dew-laden grass. His step was lifeless, and his shoulders drooped. Hunger gnawed fiercely at his vitals; but he could not eat for many hours to come. The one compelling fact was that he must go on until he reached safety or dropped. Doggedly he drove his lagging legs along beside the stream until it swerved toward the railroad. Through an old covered bridge he picked his way, and up along the creek again he trudged to a point where it turned a sharp angle and started on a long sweep toward the main highway.

There, at the bend, the low-lying river bank suddenly rose steep and bushy, with a narrow, sandy path scaling its side. There also lay a deep, dark pool hollowed out by the steady current from above. A ledge, dropping straight into the depths, made a first-class diving platform; and, as he stopped a moment to rest, the impulse to take a cool plunge and a refreshing swim overpowered him. The quiet waters smiled up at him, the willows along the shore nodded in friendly fashion, and the only sound was the far-off barking of a dog. He stripped, balanced an instant on the brink, and dived.

Just as he plunged, a footfall crunched on the steep path and some small stones rattled down. At the sound of the splash, the man above stopped instantly. When the swimmer broke water again and blew spray from his nostrils there was no sound from the brush-screened path. Whoever was there apparently did not care to reveal his presence.

A big night-flying moth veered across the bend, flying aimlessly about and showing against the sky like a drifting, crazily flopping leaf. Donald floated luxuriously on his back and watched it. By and by it jerked sidewise as if a string had pulled it, and was gone in the trees. He paddled to the ledge and crawled out, pushed his streaming hair back from his forehead, and listened. Utter silence lay over the creek. He stepped to the edge and dived again.

As he struck the water the unseen listener leaped
down the path, darted into the underbrush fringing the
stream, and was lost in the shadows. When he heard
the swimmer come to the surface he stood motionless a
minute, then worked stealthily forward. His movements were like those of a weasel—slinking, furtive,
yet sinister. In appearance, too, he was more than
suggestive of that deadly prowler: beady eyes, pointed
nose, cruel mouth, bat ears, sandy hair; body wiry,
sinuous, capable of lightning movement. Besides these
physical characteristics he possessed a restless wander-
lust, an uncanny faculty for making his getaway, and
a habit of sniffing the air, which long since had decided
his "moniker." To the underworld and the police of
a dozen cities, and to the wardens of three peniten-
tiaries, he was known as "Sniffy the Weasel," robber
of small post-offices and occasional stick-up man.

With slow overhand strokes Donald drifted back to
the rock, rested his hands lightly on the margin, and
scanned the shore. After a moment he emerged,
walked up the stone, and listened intently. The ferret
eyes of the spy narrowed, and he became thoroughly
interested. Hitherto he had been merely inquisitive;
but this unknown swimmer was entirely too cautious to
be a mere countryman taking a bath. "Stop, look, and
listen seems to be this guy's motto," he thought. His
keen brain began to speculate, and he watched every
motion.

Don stepped to the path, scooped up a handful of
fine sand, returned to the water, wet the sand, and
began to scrub his face and neck. Sand is not the

most soothing substitute for soap; but, well mixed with water and elbow-grease, it makes a most efficient scouring substance. Don needed to be scoured, and he went at it thoroughly. Handful after handful of sand traveled from path to river until the bather's whole body glowed. Then he dived again, but came up before the Weasel could move. Piece by piece he picked up his clothing, surveyed it, and dropped shirt, socks, and underwear into a separate pile. When he looked at his blackened collar his nose wrinkled in disgust, and he whirled to throw it into the stream; but a quick thought stayed his arm. The collar would float, and it had a laundry mark. He fumbled in his vest, found matches, and burned the inside of the collar until the ink marks were obliterated. Then he knotted his tie around it, fastened a good-sized pebble to it, and threw it well up-stream, where it sank at once.

The Weasel's growing suspicions crystallized into an avid desire to get into this man's pockets. As Donald dipped his union-suit into the stream and began to scrub it between his fists, Sniffy slipped forward a bit, planning attack. A rush, a blow with a blackjack, a shove into the creek—then the Weasel reconsidered. Don was wringing the garment dry; and the sight of the rolling, writhing muscles of his arms and shoulders was enough to give pause to a bigger man than Sniffy.

This guy, he reflected, was too leery anyhow, and he didn't look to be either muscle-bound or slow. He probably would leap like a wildcat and hit like a sledge-hammer. The Weasel had a gun, but he also had excellent reasons for not wishing to use it in this town at this early hour. As silently as his animal prototype he began to retreat.

" Got to get my bonehead and let him be the chopping-block," he grinned to himself. " That gink's fist would muss up my fatal beauty for fair."

At the edge of the brush he dropped to all fours and crawled down the field. He had to get across that field and up the slope, beyond which lay long piles of boards stretching down to the railroad track. He had not much time, and he was used to taking chances, so he took one now. Instead of working down along the brush to the railroad and then scooting through the dim light to the hill, he became a snake and cut across the field on his belly. He was expert at crawling, and he reached the slope and wriggled up it unobserved. But at the top he slipped, and a stick cracked.

He cursed horribly under his breath, and lay quiet for several minutes before he crept over the edge.

Back at the bend Donald sprang erect. Only the near-by chirp of a cricket and the distant chanty of a whippoorwill came to his ears. The field was empty. But he had caught the snap of that branch, and after a tense moment he pulled on his clothing.

CHAPTER VII

THE WEASEL BITES

THE Weasel crawled on hands and knees until he was well away from the declivity. Then he darted among the board piles to a solid stone wall, running away at right angles from the river. Beyond that wall lay the village cemetery, guarded on the creek side by tall pines which stood in serried ranks along the precipitous bank. The Weasel scuttled across the barrier and hurried to a dreary corner where the gloom lay thick. A surly, burly, bullet-headed creature slouched forward to meet him.

"Where yuh been?" growled the latter. "Where's yer water? Yuh didn't even bring back th' can."

"Sssst! Shut up, simp!" hissed the spy. "There's a job handy. Found a classy lad takin' a swim. I think he's got coin."

"Hmph! Did yuh see th' coin?"

"No, but ——"

"Aw, piff! These hicks ain't got nothin' in their jeans. Y' could roll a dozen of 'em an' not git six bits. Lay offen that stuff."

"Lay off it yourself. Listen here, while I spell it out for you. This lad is no hick. He's just lit, he's travelin' light, and he's on the dodge—looks like he'd been ridin' the rods. He threw away his collar because it was dirty, and he burned the laundry mark off first. His clothes were built in Manhattan—I spotted the cut when he lifted 'em. I tell you, Bull, this lad's a fly cashier or somethin' like that, and he's ducked out about two jumps ahead of the examiner. I'll bet he's got a wad pinned in his inside pocket that'll make this post-office job look like small change. We've got him right where we want him. Get me?"

"Yeh, I gotcha. Where'd yuh leave this pretty bird?"

"Down at the bend, washin' his shirt."

"Washin' his—hmpff! One uh these Li'l' Lord Fawntuhroys, huh? I bet he's rotten wit' per-fume. Lead me to 'im."

The Weasel made no reply. Though he was utterly vicious himself, Bull's crudities sometimes grated on him—for the Weasel had once had education, social standing, and sensibilities. Bull, though endowed with a low animal cunning and brute courage, had never been anything but a roughneck. He was the brawn of this combination, as Sniffy was the brains. The brawn had lately become rather domineering, largely because the last two "jobs" which the pair had tackled had been defeated by circumstances beyond the Weasel's ken. Now, as Sniffy led the way among the ghostly gravestones, he grinned wickedly at the thought of what Bull was about to go up against. He had no misgivings as to the outcome—he had seen Bull beat up too many men; but he suspected that "Li'l' Lord Fawntuhroy" would land a few smashes that might make Bull sing small for a while, and the prospect filled him with malicious glee.

As he placed his hands on the wall preparatory to vaulting over, Sniffy ducked, and Bull followed suit. Up at the corner, just at the edge of the bank, a tall figure loomed and began to crawl over into the cemetery. Donald had dressed, and now he was continuing along that upper curve in the creek.

"Walkin' right into our hands!" whispered Sniffy. "I thought he'd go along the rails. All we have to do is dodge up on him. Don't stub your foot on the gravestones." Stooping, they started to cut across and get their man on the flank.

Under the shaggy pines it was now very dim, and Donald, invigorated by his cold bath, was walking swiftly. The two thugs, ducking among the burial plots, moved more slowly and lost sight of him, so that when they neared the brink he had passed the spot where they planned to intercept him. Bull arose, saw his prey escaping, and, with a muttered oath, darted after him. Sniffy trailed at his heels.

At the thud of feet on the needle-carpeted ground Donald whirled like a cat. Bull suddenly checked his rush. He had looked for a soft, dandified chap whom he could beat down in two blows. This fellow was lean as a wolf, his shoulders were formidable, and his fists hung poised as if he knew how to use them. Bull did not know that his opponent's leanness was due to a ravenous hunger which had sapped much of his strength. He was disconcerted. So, for a tense instant, the antagonists stood sizing one another up.

Through Don's mind flashed the thought that this heavy-jowled man and his ferret-faced partner were detectives. Through Sniffy's brain darted the first suspicion that Bull might have more than he could handle, and he felt for his blackjack. Through Bull's thick head soaked the feeling that it would do no harm to temporize. Temporizing, to Bull, meant threatening his man instead of beating his head off.

"Come t'rough wit' th' coin!" he snarled. "We seen it on yuh. Come acrost, an' we'll leave yuh go."

Sharp relief swept over Donald. This was not arrest, but a plain hold-up. He knew Bull lied, for ever since leaving Harry he had carried his money in his moccasins, thus obviating the chance of having it jolted from his pocket in jumping trains. It was there now, all except a small bill or two in his trousers. He smiled, and waited. The smile stung Bull. He lowered his head and started forward.

It occurred to Don that he was standing on the edge of the bank, and that he was one against two. He stepped away from the brink. Seeing his man give ground, Bull grunted and rushed. Don ducked his swing and shot a terrific jolt to Bull's bloated midriff.

"Oomphuh!" gasped Bull. So uncouth and unexpected was the noise that Sniffy snickered—but pulled his blackjack.

Bull's rush was stopped and the wind was knocked out of him, but he was game. He chopped a blow at the jaw and sank the other hand for an uppercut. Don blocked the first and side-stepped the second. Then he stepped in and threw his whole weight into a right hook. Bull saw it coming. As his up-shooting fist plowed past Don's shoulder he tried to duck. The hook missed his chin, but smashed home under his ear. Bull wavered, reeled, and pitched backward down the steep bank.

Like a shadow the Weasel glided behind Donald. With lightning speed he struck. The blackjack thudded square on Don's head. He dropped as if smitten by a thunderbolt.

A resounding splash came up from below. The Weasel's lips formed a soundless whistle.

"Whew! All the way to the bottom! Bull must be out cold."

He dropped on his knees beside the unconscious man. Bull could sink or swim. Rapidly unbuttoning the light vest, he dived a hand into the inner pocket. It came out empty. Then it slid into the inside coat pocket and seized a flat packet of paper. A triumphant grin cracked Sniffy's face. But it soon faded, as his fingers told him that this was not money. Still holding it, he pulled out his electric flashlight and spread its rays over his find—and hurled it from him with a biting oath. It was only a dirty time-table of the Boston and Maine Railroad, evidently picked up beside the track, and open at the map. With a vicious yank he tore open Don's shirt and felt next the skin for a money-belt. When he found none his brows knit in perplexity, for his instinct insisted that this man had money on him, and that he was hardly likely to carry it loose in his outer pockets. Nevertheless he began a methodical search, commencing with the vest.

The upper pockets yielded only a fountain pen and fragments of a cigar. Lower down, however, his fingers encountered a smooth metal disk, and he drew out a watch, with a slender chain and gold cigar-clipper. Sniffy loved a good watch, and as he examined this one under his flashlight his eyes sparkled. "Cost a century if it cost a cent," he muttered, and he squatted for minutes absorbed in inspection of the works. Then he spent other minutes trying to decipher the small, conservative monogram on the case; but the letters were so cunningly looped that finally he gave it up, wrapped the timepiece in a handkerchief, and slipped it gently into his coat.

"I knew you had class, sport," he informed the prostrate man. "This ticker was worth sluggin' you for, even if you had nothin' else. Now turn over here and lemme get into your pants pockets."

With some difficulty he rolled Don on his side, and was about to continue his search when he started up in half a panic. Something was crawling up toward him.

Sniffy was not given to superstitious terrors, but while he knelt beside his victim the eerie whisper of the breeze in the pines and the depressing influence of the silent dead around him had been working on his subconsciousness. Of all weird places after nightfall, a dark country cemetery is the most uncanny; for it is the abode of silence and mystery, and when, among its awesome shadows, something begins an invisible, creeping, stealthy movement, imagination dethrones reason in a flash and conjures up unnameable horrors.

It was because a graveyard usually is shunned after sundown, and thus they could best escape observation here, that the two yeggs had chosen to hide here until the time came for what they had to do that night. But now Sniffy quaked and squinted fearfully into the gloom. The sound itself was unnerving: a cautious, slithery advance, stopping at times, then coming on with the utmost care, and so slight that he could not tell whether it came from the air, the ground, or—beneath the ground! At that appalling thought his blood turned cold. His trembling hand went back to his hip, but he did not draw his gun: his scared brain told him he could not shoot a dead thing crawling up through the earth, for bullets would not harm it. He strove to regain a grip on himself, to tell himself that it was Bull crawling back up from the river; but that thought brought a fresh access of terror. He had left Bull to drown, and perhaps Bull had drowned, and perhaps he was coming back after drowning! Of Bull alive he had not the slightest fear; but of Bull's avenging ghost —if Sniffy's throat had not been paralyzed he would have squeaked out loud. If only he could see something move! But his starting eyes saw only the glimmering tombstones, the sombre pines, and the man who lay as if dead at his feet.

By a supreme effort he nerved himself to advance toward the creek. His quivering nerves rebelled, and his leaden heels dragged. The dread sound died out of the air.

In the dense shadow of a towering pine he leaned and listened, trying to stab through the void below with swift yet shrinking glances. So profound was the silence that it seemed to press inward upon his eardrums. The tenuous susurrus of a tiny breath of air in the needles far above him became audible. His cautious breathing seemed harsh and irregular—or was it his breathing? Slowly he drew a full breath and held it; and the respiration continued! In a moment he located it, a little below him, a little to the right. Whatever this thing was, it was alive. The worst of Sniffy's fear was lifted by this assurance, and as he turned his torch toward the spot his hand was almost steady. When he raised his arm he could hear his sleeve swish, and perhaps the unknown heard it too, for the breathing stopped, then came again as if held under restraint. Sniffy pressed the spring, and the light shot straight to the place where the creeper lay—straight into the red, wet face of Bull.

Blinded, Bull whimpered and dodged. The Weasel became himself again.

"Come out of that, you bum white hope!" he sarcastically advised. "There's nothin' to be afraid of. Lord Fauntleroy is takin' a snooze."

"Douse th' glim!" rumbled Bull. As Sniffy complied he scrambled up over the edge and pawed off some dead pine needles which had stuck to his face during the ascent. "Did he beat it?" he asked.

"Beat it? No, bonehead. I told you he was takin' a snooze. I knocked him out."

"Huh? Youse? Ho, yas yuh did! He c'd smash yer conk wit' one wallop."

Sniffy laughed jeeringly. "So? Come take a slant

at him." He led the way to where Donald lay, and
turned on the light. Bull's visage contorted with rage.
He pulled back one foot and kicked the unconscious
man savagely in the face. Don's head jerked back,
and blood oozed from a gash in his forehead.

The Weasel whirled in white fury. As stated before, he had once had sensibilities, and they were not
quite dead. Had Don recovered consciousness and
started to rise, Sniffy himself might have kicked him
down again. But the utter brutality of this reprisal
got under his skin. Moreover, he had to get the whip
hand of Bull once more.

"You dirty, stinkin' gutter-pup! You sneakin',
snivelin' son of a dog!" he hissed. "Do that again
and I'll lay you stiff!"

Before this outburst Bull gave back. But the initial
attack was nothing to what followed. When the
Weasel was aroused his tongue was keen and venomous
as a serpent's fang; and he was more than likely to become a true weasel—to be overwhelmed by blood-lust,
and to kill. He had smarted for days under Bull's
growing insolence; he was nettled by his failure to
find a large sum on Donald; he was enraged at himself for his recent yielding to the ghostly terrors about
him; and he was infuriated by Bull's kick. All these
causes rushed together like storm-clouds and burst in
cyclonic wrath. Sniffy knew Bull's every weakness,
and with vitriolic phrases he flayed him alive. In
thirty seconds Bull was positively foaming with helpless rage—helpless, because he knew that in his present
mood his slighter mate was deadly, and he dared not

attempt physical retaliation. In another minute the impact of Sniffy's words had knocked the wind out of him more thoroughly than Don's fist had done. And when Sniffy was through, Bull cringed like a whipped cur.

The Weasel had regained his grip with a vengeance. Seeing Bull utterly cowed, and having vented his spleen, he now remembered that he needed this brute in his business, and moderated his tone. However, he did not at once resume the rough-and-ready comradeship between them. Instead, he put Bull on the defensive and gave him a chance to save his face.

"What were you sneakin' up on me for?" he demanded.

"I wasn't," defended Bull. "I t'ought he'd laid yuh out, an' I was crawlin' back easy so's tuh nail 'im when he wasn't lookin' fer me." Sniffy said nothing, but waited for the other to establish his alibi. "Me foot caught on a root or sumpin'," added Bull after a pause. "I'd uh had this mutt down in 'nother minute if I hadn't fell over th' edge. I might uh got drownded, though, fer all youse did tuh help me out."

"No danger. I knew you could take care of yourself. Besides, you were never born to be drowned."

"Meanin' I'm booked to git hung?" asked Bull with a sickly grin.

"You said it."

The Weasel was half right. Bull never would be drowned; but neither would he be hanged. Could the plug-ugly have had a prevision of the doom awaiting him, however, he might have been tempted to roll down the bank again and stay down. But the future was still unborn, and his thoughts were all with the present and the recent past.

" How'd yuh do 'im? " he wanted to know.

" Beaned him. He came right after me when you went shootin' the chutes, and we went duckin' and dodgin' all over the place. He's the swiftest hitter I ever saw." Bull nodded, and Sniffy grinned mentally as he saw his yarn was being swallowed whole. " But I ain't so awful slow myself, and I let him fan the air until he saw he couldn't hit my jaw and swung for my wind. When his fist went by I dropped the shot on his nut. Come on, now, let's frisk his wad."

" Ain't yuh got it yet? "

" No. I was just gettin' at his inside pocket when I heard you crawlin' up. Come, get busy! "

Together they searched Donald's pockets, each keeping a watchful eye on the other. When they straightened up Bull looked hard at the Weasel.

" T'ought yuh said this guy had coin," he grumbled. " Eight dollars an' twenty cents. Chicken-feed! "

Sniffy was nonplused. Suddenly he had an inspiration. He knelt again and explored the victim's armpits and the backs of his legs. Then he felt the whole body over, seeking any unnatural lump. He found none.

" He's either lost it or eaten it," he conceded at last. " I'll bet my shirt he had it."

Sourly Bull surveyed the dim, motionless figure on the ground. After a minute he bent and stripped off Donald's coat and tried it on. It fitted fairly well.

" What's the idea? " puzzled Sniffy

" Eight-twenty split fifty-fifty makes four-ten," figured Bull. " I git four bones an' a dime fer fightin'
this guy, fallin' a couple uh miles, an' takin' a bath. I
kin wear his clo'es, an' they're a long shot better'n
mine, so I'm coppin' 'em."

He pulled off the rest of the suit. As he did so,
he noticed that the shirt was torn out at the waist-line.
He did not raise his head, but his piggy eyes lit with
suspicion.

" So yuh got it! " he thought. " Snitched his money-
belt, yuh did, an' yuh been stallin' ever since. I'll git
yuh yet, Sniffy." Aloud he said: " Will we shove th'
gink down th' bank, or leave him lay here? "

" Aw, let him alone. We'll be miles away before he
can do anything."

The Weasel turned away. Bull picked up his own
coat, and with it and the stolen vest and trousers
across his arm he followed. In a few seconds the two
were swallowed up in the gloom.

CHAPTER VIII

THE VOICE

FAR up above the pines the stars marched, in straggling array, steadily across the velvety sky. By and by a lopsided moon poked itself above the horizon and sailed upward, dropping a faint light which the shadows seemed to swallow as it fell. Among the branches of the mournful pines a fitful wind murmured and died, came again and crooned in doleful monotone, passed and was gone. Up over the river bank stole a thin mist, dank and chill as death itself, which drifted in among the cold white headstones and further blurred their outlines, already dimmed by the dark.

At last a quiver ran through the half-clad body lying sprawled as Bull had left it. A twisted arm straightened out, and a sigh broke from the pale lips. A moment later the eyes opened in a vacant stare.

Slowly Donald realized that the tiny point of light on which his gaze rested was a star, peeping down through an opening among the tree-tops. Flat on his back he was, and chilled by the breath of the river. He rolled his head sidewise and peered at the graves, then lay inert and tried to remember.

The shock of his fist on the big fellow's ear—the

ugly face falling back into the shadows—and then chaos. Something had smashed him senseless—but what? Not the man whom he had fought. Now he recalled the other man, the smaller chap with the wizened face; and he understood.

His whole forehead felt top-heavy and his eyes curiously swollen, and he tried to brush away the feeling by rubbing his hand over them. It came away smeared with something, hesitated, went back and fingered the cut on his brow, then passed slowly over his head, finding the tender lump on his crown. Suddenly it fell away, as he stared at his shirt-sleeve. He lifted his head again quickly and looked down at his body; and as he saw that his clothing was gone he started up.

As he reached his feet a violent dizziness seized him, and while he and the graves and the pines whirled together he almost fell again. But presently the attack passed, leaving behind it nausea and a grinding headache. When he surveyed the bare knees between his short union-suit and his socks he felt an odd sensation of being lost; for civilized man, when his clothing is taken from him, is for a time as helpless as a little child. The facts that he had been starved, beaten, and robbed, that he was a homeless fugitive, that he was exhausted to the point of illness, were as nothing compared to the circumstance that he had no trousers. For an instant he felt a mad impulse to tear off his shirt and underwear and make a complete job of it. Then the pendulum swung the other way and he laughed—and his laugh was not good to hear, for it was the unhealthy cachinnation of a man who has been strained too far and is about to break.

Still grinning, he looked down at his feet, and cackled afresh when he saw that the moccasins were laced. So the thugs had missed the money after all! That was a most ludicrous joke. And his feet were dressed, anyway. Now if he could only find his hat he would be covered up at both ends, even though the six feet of him in between were not up to Fifth Avenue standards. He poked around with his foot until he found the hat, and pulled it down as well as he could on his puffy forehead.

Ouch! it hurt. And it would get all bloody, too. Oh, well, never mind the blood. Blood? Who said blood? That square white tombstone over there looked something like the back of a pajama-jacket with blood on it. Was that Duncan's face leering at him just over the stone?

He straightened up with a jerk, and over him crept a chill that was not the clammy touch of the mist. These unwholesome fancies must be shaken off. Jaw set, chin in air, hands clenched, he fixed his eyes up the creek and marched ahead as resolutely as a soldier going into battle. He had yet to round the upper loop of the river, to cut across the fields, to brave the main highway, and to enter the branch which would lead him to the Kearsarge road.

Fickle Fortune, having led him into a trap, now smiled again. His progress to the highway was uninterrupted by sight or sound of human life, and ere long he stood beside it. Across the way opened the branch road, revealed by an electric light and flanked by a house on each corner. One house was dark. The other was lighted, but its occupants were not in sight. After a glance up and down the highway he dashed across the lighted area and into the welcoming gloom beyond. The sprint cost too much, as his heavily pounding heart and splitting head told him when he slowed again into his weary stride; but it was the only way. Fighting off an impending attack of vertigo, he trudged the short distance to the point where the sandy track turned sharp to the right.

As his breathing became regular the pain in his temples grew easier, but he felt unnaturally hot. A little way ahead a tiny brooklet babbled to him of cool refreshment. When he reached it he knelt and plunged his arms into it up to the elbows. For a moment the sensation was delightful; then he was seized with a shiver so violent that his teeth rattled. The grim hand of fever lay heavy upon him, but he would not admit it. Instead, he told himself that he must get some clothing.

Before him were two houses, both dark, facing each other across the narrow way. The doors and windows of country places, he knew, were as a rule insecurely fastened; but he did not care to burglarize a house. In the barn there should be some old clothing. He stole up to one of the barns and investigated it. The doors were fastened, but a high window at the rear stood half-way open, and he might pull himself up and wriggle in. But then a horse stamped inside, and he decided against that attempt.

When he passed the other house he observed that it was trim and well kept. The barn, however, was dingy and weather-beaten—apparently much older than the dwelling. Its big front door sagged, and no sound came from within. Evidently these people kept no animals. A circuit of the structure disclosed one window, which was immovable. There was, however, a small rear door which looked promising, for the faint moonlight showed that it had shrunk away from the casing, leaving a wide crack.

Behind the building was a small garden, in which he hunted for a stick. At the edge of the plot he found plenty of them—short, firm stakes which evidently had been used around young plants. Armed with one of these, he went back to the door and felt up along the crack until the stick encountered a strong hook. Holding his improvised jimmy against the iron, he hammered it upward with the heel of his hand, making hardly a sound. The hook clung stubbornly to its staple until the repeated shocks against his arm had set his head to throbbing fiercely. Then suddenly it gave, snapping upward with a noise that seemed like a pistol-shot. But it failed to reach the sleeping ears in the house, for he could detect no movement anywhere. The door swung open, disclosing only cavernous blackness. With every sense alert he entered.

At the fourth cautious step a plank groaned beneath his weight. Something scurried across the floor, and he stopped, nerves tense. But it was only a rat, and after a moment he went on, hands groping ahead, toes feeling for an obstruction or an open trap-door. He would never find anything in this blackness, he told himself, and he began to consider the advisability of opening the big door and letting in the faint moon-shine. As he advanced, however, his bare knee bumped against wood. His exploring hands felt the rounded side-board and smooth handle of a wheel-barrow. Then they touched cloth—a thin, tough fab-ric hanging over the handle. It felt like the material of which overalls are made. He pulled it out of the barrow and retreated to the door.

Outside he held his find aloft, and a dangling leg confirmed his surmise: he had a pair of overalls. He shook out the other leg and pulled them on. They were a miserable misfit, for the owner evidently was rotund of body and short of leg, and Don's shins were uncovered from a point midway below the knee. How-ever, they were trousers of a sort.

A moment's thought convinced him that his chance of finding a coat in the blackness of the barn was virtually nil. So he shut the door and wedged it with the stick. Then, instead of returning to the road, he went straight to the woodland a short distance behind the barn; for at the corner where the branch de-bouched into Kearsarge street there were houses and another electric light. Moreover, the brook ran out of the woods, and his mouth was parched. When he was well inside the shadows he lay flat and drank. Then he started slowly for Kearsarge.

The going was hard. Dry, dead branches stuck out like bayonets and stabbed rents in his new-found

breeches. Others, live ones, switched him across the
face. His toes collided with sudden stumps. His
heels dropped into unexpected hollows with a jar that
shook his head into savage protest. The trees he could
dodge, but the treacherous undergrowth seemed to take
spiteful delight in snaring him, and the forest floor
laid swampy traps. Now and then he had to stop, lean
against a tree, and get his bearings.

Not only did his feet try to mislead him in the gloom
and the helter-skelter openings, but his mind was wandering again. A thudding like far-away artillery filled
his ears. Strange figures took shape and gibbered at
him; and when he stopped to look at them they were
gone. Some small animal, which was a cat and was
not a cat, rubbed against his leg, only to vanish when
he swerved. Cold eyes bored into his back, or glimmered fishily out of a dim bush ahead of him. And
then a voice, clear and sweet, called from nowhere:

"Don! Donnie boy!"

A horror seized him, and he turned short and fought
blindly, fiercely, like a man in a whirlpool, toward the
Kearsarge road.

The forest seemed to hurl itself at him, to clutch
his arms and legs, to combat his rush and try to thrust
him back. When he reached the stone wall where the
trees ended his clothes and his skin were torn in many
places, his breath whistled in his throat, and his eyes
were red with a fighting glare. The thudding in his
ears had swelled to a roar, and the pounding of his
heart seemed to shake him from head to heel. He
threw himself over the wall and strode past a house

which lay buried in silence and slumber, out to the open
road.

At last his tortuous dodging was at an end, and out
ahead of him, fair and free, ran the way to his mountain. In the sickly light of the moon it gleamed like
a stream of dull silver, undulating over the rolling
hills. Houses there were, he knew, scattered at far
intervals along it; but the hour was late, and the eyes
and ears in them would be closed. Looking neither left
nor right, he pushed on, trying to hold his head erect
and banish the phantasms which had just driven him
from the wood.

Both efforts failed. His head was too heavy and
too full of pain, and despite himself it drooped; and,
though he fixed his gaze unswervingly on the sand, he
knew that grotesque things were flitting along among
the roadside bushes and pointing derisive hands at him.
They were making fun of his ragged, scant overalls;
they were laughing diabolically at his staggering gait;
they were jeering at him for a blind fool, who had
allowed another man to come into his home and steal
his one great treasure. When the bushes gave way
to broad fields his tormentors ran along the walls, and
others waited for him behind the trunks of the black
trees which drooped over the road ahead. He could
hear the rustle of their shadowy feet, the whisper of
the wordless jests which they passed, the soundless
laughter with which they received one another's gibes.
And by and by, from a bare field, rang again the silvery voice:

"Donald! Donald!"

He swerved as if lashed across the face by a whip.
Out over the empty field darted his gaze, and then
back along the road. Nothing moved—nothing was
there. Cold sweat bedewed his forehead, and he
trembled as he started on.

Now the bushes lined the stone walls again, and just
ahead, at his right, drooped silvery birches which he
remembered, for behind them lay a small graveyard.
As he passed it the tremulous leaves of the birch-trees
shivered suddenly, and a wind smote his hot cheeks.
In normal moments he would have said that a breeze
had sprung up; but now he knew that the wood-
demons had been clinging in the branches like bats
while he halted, and that the rustle and the breath of
air were caused by their jumping down again to march
beside him. As before, he would not delight them by
noticing them, but doggedly kept his eyes ahead. But
soon one of them perched on his shoulder, where Rajah had balanced himself when he was a kitten. He
struck at it, and it was gone.

Yard by yard he strode on into the hills, the invisible
goblins trooping beside him. A gap opened in the
walls, and two houses fronted him, their windows staring like lidless eyes at barns across the road. The
ground rose in a slow, long pitch, and then began to
crawl rapidly up, up, growing steeper with each step.
He realized that he had reached Tory Hill, a grinding,
back-breaking climb. Its high crown was bare of
trees, he recalled, and houses were fairly close together
on the long level reach beyond. There, perhaps, the
ghostly entourage would leave him. But now, among

the big trees flanking the lower part of the hill, they took grisly shapes.

One of them flashed out an arm in a loose white sleeve and pointed an automatic at him. He dodged and grabbed at his waistband for a gun; but there was no waistband—only the high front of his overalls. And then cold eyes were everywhere, glowering at him with malevolent hate.

Something was pushing against him, weighing him down, choking off his breath; and he was so hot that it seemed his head must burst. Somehow he was not making much progress. First he was on the left side of the road, and then almost falling into the right-hand ditch. A red mist was settling over things. He could make the climb—he *would* make it, despite death and the devil! But he must not hear that voice again, or it would drive him mad. It was the voice of a woman who now was dead—the woman who had destroyed his home and driven him out as a wanderer on the face of the earth.

Then it came again—from the vacant road behind him.

"Donald! Where are you?"

He clutched at his throat. His dim eyes rolled up to the sky. The stars and the moon wavered, danced madly, rushed together in crashing collision. He reeled in a desperate effort to keep his feet. Then, with a gasp, he fell across the road and lay still.

CHAPTER IX

PANSY GIRL

THROUGH endless æons Donald fought in a red inferno against hordes of fiends which issued from caves and charged on him with a clattering roar like that of a railroad train. They stabbed at him with dry, dead branches, they climbed upon his back and choked him, they stripped his clothing from him and rushed back to their lairs. And then female demons came out and pointed at him and shrieked in malicious glee as he turned and fled.

When he reached the protection of a shadowy forest the trees sprang to life and flailed him with their branches and hurled him back to the caves, where an army of huge spiders, covered with cold eyes, dashed out and swarmed up his bare legs. He beat and kicked them off, and out from the caves boiled a vicious crew with faces all alike—the face of Duncan—and attacked him with police clubs, amid a screaming chorus of police whistles. He tried to shoot them with a revolver which would not explode, and they in turn drew pistols and riddled him with bullets; and when he was down they sneered and flaunted newspapers from which flared the word " MURDER " and his own name, and a picture of himself strapped to the electric chair.

94

He bounded up, and they changed to heavy-jowled thugs who demanded that he "come t'rough wit' th' coin," and he knocked them out one by one. They be-came weasel-faced, and got behind him and slugged out his brains. Then he was alone, and from some-where far off came a voice calling: "Donald! Don-ald!"

Out from the shadows came a girl with rosebud mouth, who clung to him. He knew only too well that she was false, and he would have thrown her off, but his arms were paralyzed. She lifted her lips to his— and suddenly she stabbed him through and through. And then he was in a place of tombs, where the wind soughed through the pines, and from the branches dropped weird things which gibbered and pointed and laughed soundlessly. From the graves rose the de-mons, and again the battle raged.

Sometimes the red mist thinned and the clangor in his ears sank to silence. Then he looked up and saw a pair of deep blue eyes watching him from a sweetly anxious face—a face he had never seen before. Some-thing cool rested on his brow, and he was at peace. But then the mist swirled back and he plunged into a whirling abyss where his torments recommenced.

Came a time when the haze vanished as if blown aside by a mighty wind, and he found himself staring up at a flat white space. Across it ran zigzag cracks, and his gaze followed one of these until it met a pa-pered wall. Then a rectangular lighted space drew his eyes, and he saw that it was a window, covered by a thin roll-curtain on which the sun was beating. Like the wall-paper, the curtain was old and faded. It moved slowly in and out as if pushed and pulled by wandering breaths of air. At the bottom it did not quite meet the sill, and there such a powerful light poured in that his eyes hurt, and he turned them away.

Something moved on the other side of him. He rolled his head and met the gaze of a pair of deep blue eyes—the eyes which had come through the mists at times and brought a temporary truce to his fight. They were wide, frank eyes, set in a girlish face tanned by the summer sun and aglow with health; but below them were dark hollows which bespoke lack of sleep. Squarely, unfalteringly, they met his questioning stare. After a moment they began to smile, and she spoke.

" Howdy! Feelin' better now? "

He nodded. The simple movement tired him. He closed his eyes and sighed.

Somewhere in the room a fly buzzed. Somewhere outside a grasshopper chirred.

" You been pretty sick," added the girl. Donald exhibited no interest in the information. There was a long pause. Then he heard her rise from the chair.

" Hungry? " she asked.

" Uh-huh," he grunted.

" Oh, you can talk, then. I was beginnin' to think you was deef an' dumb."

And with that she went out.

By and by his eyes opened again and strayed over the room. It had one window and two doors. Its furnishings were few and plain—a huge bureau, topped by a narrow mirror, across one corner by the window;

a small, marble-topped stand in another corner, holding a big earthen pitcher full of black-eyed susans and buttercups; two chairs—one a small rocker, the other a stiff-looking thing; and the bed on which he lay. All the furniture was that of a bygone day— heavy, quaint, built to last a hundred years; the sort of furniture almost invariably found in a New Hamp- shire farmhouse.

The door at the foot of the bed opened, and the girl reappeared, holding a bowl that gleamed white against her dark blue dress, and from which the handle of a big spoon projected. For an instant she hesitated on the threshold. Then, seeing that he had not fallen asleep, she came forward, carefully balancing the bowl, and sank into the chair beside him. From the earthen vessel rose an appetizing odor that made him feel hollow to his feet.

" It's pretty hot," she warned. " You better use the spoon. Can you set up?"

Don struggled up—and fell back. His arms would not support him.

The girl set the bowl on the floor and passed her strong young hands under his shoulders. He put forth every ounce of power left in his body, and after a clawing, kicking scramble, aided by her upward pull, he leaned dizzily against the headboard. With one hand she pushed him forward and balanced him, while with the other she arranged the pillows behind his back.

It was the first time in his life that he had known real weakness; and, as is usual in such case, he was filled with fierce rage at the insubordination of his muscles. To be lifted and pushed around by a woman, like a puling infant, accentuated his wrath.

"You ain't very stout yet, be you?" said the girl, as she reached for the bowl. Knowing the New England idioms, he knew she did not refer to his woeful thinness, but meant that he had no strength; and although the innocent remark was prompted by sympathy, to his raw nerves it seemed like a taunt. He bent a withering glare upon her. For an instant amazement stamped her face. Then a red wave swept over it. Without another word she fed him spoonful after spoonful of chicken broth until the bowl was empty.

When he had finished she made no effort to assist him to lie down, but when he had slipped into a prone position she shook the pillows and placed them beneath his head. As he looked up he saw in her face the hurt expression of a child who has been slapped and does not know why, and he was stricken with remorse. It was not her fault that he wasn't "very stout yet." On the contrary, she was doing her best to restore his strength.

"The broth was fine," he whispered. Her face brightened a bit, but she looked at him coldly.

"Mebbe next time I'll give you hearty vittles," she said. "Now go to sleep."

Without question or argument he obeyed. She hovered over him until his breathing became regular and he lay quiet. Then she smiled, as if he were a naughty youngster whom she had forgiven, and tiptoed out of the room.

The dull *tonkatonk* of a cow-bell passing near the window roused him from his nap. On the upper part of the curtain the sun still lingered, but the lower half was in shadow. Outside he heard the girl's clear voice.

"Go on, Molly girl. Blackie, you've had all day to eat—git along, git along!"

Followed the clatter of bovine hoofs on a barn floor, a rattle of chains, and sundry bumps of horns against the poles of the tie-ups. Soon he heard the clank of a pail, the squeak of a windlass, and the rattling, bumping descent of a bucket into a well. The squeaking redoubled in volume as the bucket was reeled up, succeeded by a rush of water into the pail. The voice came again, receding toward the barn. This time it was uplifted in song.

"Abide with me; fast falls the eventide,
The darkness deepens. Lord, with me abide——"

The old hymn stirred Donald strangely. Not for years had he heard it, for he was not a church-goer. Coming now from the quiet fields where the dusk would soon be gathering, it brought home to him the blackness into which his life had been plunged and the dismal future stretching ahead, in which he must live a lonely, furtive existence like that of the wild things. For days he had wanted nothing so much as to reach the mountain fastness and vanish; but now, somehow, he envied the simple, honest life of these country-dwellers, who looked all men in the face and went about their humble tasks with a song in their hearts.

For a long time he lay staring upward, and his face was sombre.

By and by he heard the girl moving about in a room near by, and the rattle of a stove-lid came to his ears. She came once to the door and looked in. He closed his eyes and lay as if asleep, and she went away, leaving the door ajar. Soon thereafter he heard the clump of heavy shoes entering the other room.

"Evenin', Pop," saluted the girl.

"Evenin', Pansy gal," replied a masculine voice. "How's thet tramp o' yourn doin'?" The voice had the nasal twang of the true Down-Easter, and the first word of the question was pronounced "haow."

"He ain't *my* tramp," flashed the girl. "I didn't find him."

"Heh, heh, heh!" chuckled the other. "Wal, I brung him home, tubby sure, but ye ain't let me see him sence. Guess them black eyes o' his'n has bewitched ye, ain't they?"

"Pop, you git more foolish every day. Mister Tramp is pickin' up."

"Wal, that's good news. Now mebbe ye'll be willin' to go to bed agin. Ye're beginnin' to look kinder pickid, settin' up so much. What's he got to say for himself?"

"Nothin'. He's got over his fever, but he's awful feeble. He et a big bowl of broth an' went to sleep. Supper's all ready, Pop. Set up."

A chair moved up to the table, and the small noises of a meal began, mingled with scraps of conversation concerning the cows, the hens, and kindred topics.

In the deepening shadows Donald lay feeling very small, very cheap, very mean. Those dark circles under the blue eyes came back to accuse him. She had been losing sleep to watch over him, a " tramp "—for he certainly must look like a tramp, and a tough one at that—and he had repaid her by an exhibition of nasty temper. He vowed to make amends at the first opportunity. But then came a cynical thought which never would have entered his head until the last few days.

They had removed his clothing, of course, before putting him to bed; and no doubt they had examined it carefully in an effort to ascertain his identity. Thus they probably had found the money in his moccasins. In New York that amount would seem almost trivial; but up here among the hill farms it was a large sum. The cause of her solicitude was very evident. Her vigils, of course, were prompted not by sympathy, not by kindness, but by the hope for reward.

Well, she could have it all if she wanted it—he was willing to pay for the care he received. He smiled grimly up at the ceiling and fell to wondering what " Pop " meant by calling his gray eyes black. Finally he turned over and went to sleep again.

CHAPTER X

THE FACE IN THE DARK

NIGHT lay over the land when Donald awoke, tortured by a burning thirst.

The door at the foot of the bed was wide open, and on a table in the room beyond shone a light. It did not penetrate beyond the threshold, for between him and the lamp stood a pasteboard box, the sides of which had been bent outward so that they threw the light toward the farther wall. On the other side of the table, in the full glow of the flame, sat " Pansy gal " with her eyes on a book.

Her figure had a tired droop, and her lids hung heavy. Against the wall beyond her stood a tall clock, whose solemn ticking was the only sound to break the utter stillness of the night. The hands pointed to half after ten. Beside the clock a window stood open.

An artist might have found inspiration in the scene, Donald thought—the young girl lost in the shadowy imagery of romance, and the ancient clock measuring off the flying minutes of her own golden youth. It was the first time he had had opportunity or inclination to study her face, and he choked down his thirst to look at her critically.

Even with her gaze bent downward her eyes seemed

unusually large, and now he noticed that her brows and long lashes were much darker than the masses of golden hair which curved about her temples and hung low on her forehead. It was the contrast, he decided, that made the eyes so noticeable. Her nose was straight, her mouth a cupid's-bow, and her chin—his gaze lingered there. It was a firm little chin: rather resolute, in fact, and yet not aggressive. The face was not at all defiant, not at all selfish. On the other hand, it was not in the least insipid or weak. The dominant note was that of sweetness, of sunny temper.

He followed the line of her neck to the rounded curve of her breast, half revealed, half concealed as it rose and fell beneath the plain little dress. As if she felt his gaze, she lifted her head and looked straight at him; and as he, unseen, continued to study her winsome face, irresistibly there came to him the thought: " She'll make a fine wife and mother."

Whereupon an ugly little demon, born of bitterness, sat up in his brain and sneered: " Bah! They're all alike!"

Hearing no sound from the bedroom, she glanced at the clock, yawned, and once more became absorbed in her book. For a time he continued to watch her. Suddenly, unaccountably, his gaze shifted to the open window beyond her. It was nothing but a square black patch on the wall, like any other window gaping at the night. Yet, somehow, he began to wonder what lay on the other side of it—an empty field? a pasture? a woodland? Well, what difference did that make? He moved his head impatiently, remembered his thirst, looked at the girl, and opened his lips to call for a drink; but closed them as his eyes swerved again to the window.

It was black and empty as before; yet he sensed the presence of something beyond it—an evil thing lurking in the gloom and looking in. Only the measured tick tock, tick tock, tick tock of the big clock came to his straining ears. A creepy feeling began to crawl up his spine.

Slowly, as he concentrated all his senses into that of vision, a vague blur began to grow in the outer dark —a formless, oval shade not quite so black as the rest of the square. It did not move. By and by he told himself that it was a mere illusion, an after-image left on his brain by his long stare at the golden-crowned face beside the lamp. He shut his eyes, and kept them shut. When several minutes had passed he opened them and looked again—and his muscles stiffened.

The thing had advanced and taken form, and now it was a face, hanging disembodied in the window-frame and strongly delineated by the rays of the oil lamp. It was a swarthy, black-bearded visage, with black hair growing down almost to little black eyes set so close together that they seemed to grow out of the coarse, flaring nose dividing them. The eyes were fixed on the girl. They swept over her from head to foot, and slowly back again; and in them grew a greenish glow, and the black-haired lips opened until the teeth showed behind them. Lust, primal lust was stamped in every wicked line of the face, in the red mouth, the twitching nostrils, the gloating gaze which

followed the soft lines of her slender figure. Perhaps
she felt it, for she stirred uneasily and lifted one hand
to her breast in an involuntary, protecting gesture.

The sick man's presentiment had been correct: this
was an evil thing, hovering like a hawk over the innocent girl. Red rage gripped him, and he leaped out
of bed.

Gaunt, spectral in the ill-fitting nightshirt which had
been put on him, he stalked out into the light. With a
gasp of terror the girl sprang up, the book thudding
on the floor. The leering face at the window vanished
like a wind-blown mist.

" Why—why ——" stammered Pansy. " Oh, you
scairt me most to death! What are you gittin' up for?
You're sick! "

He wavered and grasped the table. Wrath had carried him this far, but with the disappearance of the
face his false strength left him. Had it not been for
the fact that the broth and the dreamless sleep had
already begun to restore his vigor, even his anger could
not have brought him across the threshold. Now he
leaned heavily on the table and thought swiftly. Why
alarm her further? The foul thing outside would do
no harm to-night. It was scared away.

" I want a drink," he mumbled.

" A drink? Then why on earth didn't you say so,
'stead of traipsin' out here like a gallopin' spook? You
git back to your room! "

Meekly he turned and forced his wobbly legs to take
him back to bed, where he collapsed. When the room
ceased to whirl she was beside him with a big pitcher

and a tin dipper, and he drank and drank until she refused to give him more.

"No more now, or you'll founder yourself," she smiled. "You can have another drink by an' by. Now why didn't you holler?"

"I'd been asleep. Woke up thirsty. Forgot," he replied.

"Don't forgit next time," she commanded. "Now go to sleep."

But this time he disobeyed orders. She needed sleep too, and he cast about for a way to send her to bed without letting her know he had overheard the conversation at sundown. Finally he asked: "Aren't you reading rather late?"

Her eyes dropped, and she flushed a bit.

"Ye-es. But I got pretty int'rested."

Even as she spoke she set her teeth, and he saw that she was fighting to stifle a yawn.

"What's the book?" he queried.

"I've a hoe."

Don blinked.

"Mebbe you never read it," she went on. "It was writ by a feller named Scott, an' it's about things in England hundreds of years ago."

"Oh! Ivanhoe!" said Don. "Like it?"

"Middlin' well. Some parts seem so furrin I don't rightly understand 'em—the Templars, an' sech things. An' that Rona girl don't seem human, some way; more like a doll."

"Rona? You mean Rowena. I'll tell you about the Templars to-morrow."

"Ro-we-na," she pronounced "An' you said *I*-vanhoe?"

The sick man nodded. She flushed again, but looked straight at him.

"I guess you think I'm awful ignorant," she said. "But I ain't had as much schoolin' as I might, an'— well, I read about everything I can git, but that ain't much, an' Pop don't keer for readin', so—so there ain't anybody to explain it to me."

It was bravely said. There was not the slightest note of self-pity in her voice, not the least trace of shame in her face, though the tired eyes were a little wistful as she said that she got little to read. It was a straightforward explanation of a deficiency which she felt keenly, but for which nobody was to blame. Don felt very uncomfortable, and wished he had not corrected her. But as if she read his thought she went on: "Thank you for tellin' me those names. I'll git 'em right the next time."

After a silent moment he suggested:

"Don't you think it's time for little girls to be in bed?"

"Why ——" she hesitated, then continued: "I'm goin' soon. Soon as you git to sleep."

He dropped his circumlocution and made a direct attack.

"Look here! Are you sitting up on my account?"

Yankee-like, she replied with another question.

"Well, somebody has to set up an' look out for you, don't they? An' Pop's too tired."

"No. I'm all right now. Go on to bed."

She stood looking at him for a moment.

" Promise not to git up agin ? "

" I promise. Just leave some water on the chair."

" Promise not to drink so much you'll swell up an' bust ? "

" Yes. I'm pretty well busted already." He eyed her keenly as he spoke. Her face became sober, and again the cynical thought of money slipped into his mind.

" Poor feller," she said softly. A question trembled on her tongue, but she thought better of it. Instead, she asked another.

" Sure you'll be all right ? "

" Dead sure. I'm going to sleep as soon as you've retired."

" Then I'll go," she decided.

Taking lamp and pitcher, she went out, and he heard her pouring water from a pail. Presently she returned, set the pitcher on the chair by the bed, laid the dipper beside it, and exacted one more promise from him.

" If you want anything before mornin' will you holler ? "

" I'll holler. Good-night."

" Good-night. I'll leave the door open, an' turn the light down low."

" No. Take it along. Good-night."

" I think you better have it."

" Don't want it. Good ——"

The tall clock gave an odd click, as if clearing its throat, and began to strike. Eleven times its hammer

came down on the bell. The last stroke seemed to
quiver and linger in the air, as if Father Time, too,
had decided that Pansy girl should be in bed, and was
emphasizing the lateness of the hour.

"—night," finished Donald.

" My, I *am* sleepy! Good-night."

She passed out, went to the window beside the clock,
and shut it. Then she picked the book from the floor,
and, with it under her arm, crossed the room. Softly
she stole up creaking stairs, and the light faded out.
For a little while he heard her moving about overhead. Then all was still, save for the measured swing
of the pendulum opposite his door.

CHAPTER XI

SUSPICION

PANSY kept her promise, for the next day she gave her tramp hearty victuals. He awoke late, to find his door closed; but before long he heard her come softly to it, and it swung open to admit her golden head. Finding his eyes open, she nodded brightly.

"Mornin', Mister Spook," she smiled. "Can you eat a reg'lar meal?"

He nodded, and she went away. Soon she was back with a bowl of hot oatmeal and a generous pitcher of cream. He sat up without assistance this time, and adjusted his own pillows. She watched him demurely, but with a twinkle in her eye; and then, observing the vigor with which he attacked the cereal, she disappeared, to return presently with lightly browned toast, crisply curling bacon, and big gold-and-white eggs. Now, a man can sit up in bed and eat quite comfortably with a spoon and a bowl; but when it comes to plates and knife and fork, he is up against a different proposition. So, after studying the problem a minute, Donald began to look about the room.

"Salt an' pepper?" asked Pansy. "I'll git 'em."

"I want my trousers," he explained.

An odd look flitted across her face, for hitherto she had met the word only in books. Up here the men spoke of "pants" or "britches."

"Why?" she demanded. "You can't wear 'em in bed."

"I'm getting up. If I don't get 'em I'll get up without 'em."

Whereupon she fled. Donald juggled the plates over to the chair, and hitched himself to the edge of the bed. It seemed that she was gone a long time, and he began to eat some toast. Finally she returned and laid something over the footboard.

"You can have those for the time bein'," she announced. "The things you was wearin' when you come here ain't decent."

Suddenly remembering the nature of the "things," he grinned at the idea of dignifying them by the name of trousers. She giggled, went out, and shut the door.

"Hurry up," she called, "or your breakfast'll git cold."

Thus admonished, he scrambled out and grabbed the garment, noting that the fabric was coarse, but tough and serviceable, and that this really was a pair of trousers. He had some difficulty in getting into them, for his equilibrium was uncertain and his knees weak, and his attempt to stand on one leg nearly resulted in an unpremeditated backflip. So he sat down and pulled them on, then stood up, surprised to find how well they fitted him. They belonged to a man nearly as tall as he, and clung so snugly to his waist that no support was necessary. This was fortunate, for his hostess had forgotten to provide belt or suspenders.

" Got 'em on? " rang her voice outside.

" Got 'em on," he echoed, sitting down and starting on the bacon and eggs. The door swung wide, and she reappeared bearing a big cup of coffee.

" Your father," commented Don between mouthfuls, " must be about my size."

Her glance went to his legs, and a shadow crossed her face.

" Those pan—*trousers*—ain't his," she said. " They're brother Tom's."

He raised his brows. He had heard nothing of a brother.

"He went away three years ago," she went on. " He used to go huntin' and fishin' when Pop thought he ought to be workin', and they had an awful row and he went away mad. He never come back—he never even wrote. We don't know where he is, or whether he's even alive or not. I'm kind of afraid he—he won't never need those pants again."

She bit her lip and turned her head aside. Then abruptly she went out.

He finished his meal in silence and sat looking dubiously at the dishes, debating whether he could carry them out. His vitality was rapidly reasserting itself, and the strong coffee had filled him with a pleasant exhilaration. Still, he remembered how his knees had wobbled last night, and again to-day when he had donned the trousers; and he had no mind to emulate the comedy waiter who sprawls on his face amid crashing tableware. So he decided to take a preliminary turn about the room to test his underpinning. Thus he had to approach the bureau; and as the reflection of his shirt in the narrow mirror caught his eye he turned and faced himself.

"Great guns!" he ejaculated. As he realized that the countenance staring back at him was his own he felt as if someone had smitten him in the stomach; for it was almost the face of a stranger.

He understood now why Pansy's father had called him "tramp" and referred to his black eyes. They were black—the black eyes of the prize-ring. Blue-black patches surrounded his bloodshot eyeballs, and above the right eye opened a red, partly scabbed gash —the wound left by Bull's kick. Added to this, the unkempt stubble which covered his chin and cheeks, and the frowsy hair which stuck out at every angle, gave him so disreputable an appearance that he resembled not only a hobo but a bum. But it was not these externals alone that startled him. He had been bruised and battered many a time in his football days and in swift bouts with the gloves; and a razor and a comb would quickly alter his wild appearance. There was something else, which was not due even to the ravages of hunger and illness: a grim, sombre expression which no physical suffering could have produced. About his mouth and eyes were lines which never had been there before,—scars burned into the flesh by the agony which had seared his soul. And the eyes themselves, which before had been only earnest, now held in their depths a brooding shadow. And these were marks which no brushing or scrubbing could ever take away.

He laughed harshly and turned his back on the glass. "A man's a man for a' that," he muttered, and took a deep breath, stretched his arms wide, and swung them smartly together before him. The sharp rip of rent cloth startled him.

"Oh, dear! There goes Pop's best nightshirt!" came Pansy's dismayed voice at the door.

Twisting his neck and hunching one shoulder forward, he ruefully surveyed his back in the mirror. From midway of the shoulders nearly to the waist-line the cloth was split and the skin exposed.

"Turn round here," she ordered, getting behind him. "Yes, I'll have to run a seam right down here," and with one finger-tip she traced a line down his back. It tickled, and he jumped.

"Be you ticklish? That's a bad sign," she reproved.

"Sign of what?"

"Sign you like the girls. Do you?"

"No!" barked Don so sharply that she started and jabbed her finger into his ribs. Whereat he jumped again. She stifled a giggle and dropped her dancing eyes to something which she carried over her arm; and when he faced her, her expression was demure— almost solemn.

"If you're goin' to tear things up mebbe you better put on your own clothes," she suggested. "I was jest bringin' 'em in when you got rambunctious. Be you goin' to stay up?"

"Yes. I'm sorry I tore ——"

"Never mind," she interrupted. "Pop'll never notice it after I sew it up. But if you git another tearin'
tantrum I shan't mend your clothes agin." And with
that she flitted out, leaving him staring rather foolishly
at the little bundle which she had passed him.

Shirt, union-suit, and socks, freshly washed and
ironed, and fragrant with the sweet odor of garments
dried in pure air and sunlight; all the clothing he
possessed, except his hat and moccasins; a mere handful of cloth, which would not ward off wind or rain
nor keep him warm in the chill mountain nights. However, a man would not freeze in midsummer. He
shook them out, and then he caught the significance
of her threat not to mend them again: for his silk socks
had worn through in his long flight, and both shirt
and underwear had been torn in jagged rents by his
mad dash to escape from the ghostly woodland; and all
had been mended. There were hundreds of neat, firm
little stitches in the upper garments. The socks had
been carefully darned. She must have worked for
hours on this job, he thought.

Then up sat the ugly little devil Suspicion, which
once already had whispered to him.

"Oh, well," it sneered, "she expects to be paid for
it."

He shut the door, dressed himself in his own clothing and brother Tom's, and sought his moccasins. Under the bed he found them, powdered thickly with the
dust of the country road, in which showed the impress
of big fingers—obviously those of "Pop." Jammed
far up in the toe of each, where he had tucked it days

before, was his money, undisturbed. He shoved it into
a pocket, pulled on the moccasins, picked up the dishes,
and went out.

The room into which he passed was empty of life,
for its sunny-haired mistress had gone up-stairs, where
he heard her moving about and singing soft and
low. Depositing the dishes on the table, he looked
around.

It was the kitchen—or, rather, a combination of
kitchen and " settin'-room "—and it was full of doors.
Beside the doorway through which he had entered, another opened, disclosing the stairs. Beyond that stood
a closed door, apparently that of the " front room."
Then came the corner, and in the middle of the next
wall rose a huge fireplace topped by a high shelf; but
the opening had been bricked up, and before it stood
a modern range, glistening with a blackness that be-
tokened faithful polishing. Two more doors flanked
the bricks,—one, he was to learn, shutting in a big
dish-closet; the other opening into a generous pantry,
where he could see a big water-pail enthroned on a
small platform over the sink. Then came the wall
with which he was partly acquainted—where the clock
stood and the window had framed the evil face.

Obeying a sudden impulse, he stepped to that window and looked out.

Apple-trees, gnarled, contorted, but full-bosomed
with foliage and immature fruit, stood in orchard-
array near the house. Beyond lay a close-cropped
field, where the haying recently had been done; a lopsided field, for one side dipped and the other swelled

to a big knoll. And past the stone wall marking its farthest boundary stood the forest, a veritable sea of trees which rose and fell along the hills like huge rounded waves sweeping on to engulf the puny toil of man. High over all blazed a glorious July sun, bathing the dark-green pines in a glossy shimmer, outlining every stone in the gray-white wall, beating fiercely on the bald knoll, ripening the little sour apples and throwing beneath the twisted trees patches of deep shadow and glaring light.

The black-bearded beast of prey evidently had come from the forest; had stolen down stealthily among the apple-trees, slipped up closer and closer ——

"My! You're real spry!" said Pansy's voice behind him. As he turned she advanced from the foot of the stairs, smiling.

What a little thing she was! The top of her head was hardly up to his shoulder. Yet she was no child; fully nineteen, he decided, and ripening into womanhood, for all her girlish ways. With more interest than hitherto, he noted the great mass of shining hair, so heavy that it was always tumbled and unruly, yet finespun as the gossamer webs which the morning sun finds gemmed with dew among the grass-stalks. And then his gaze dropped to the eyes looking up at him from beneath the long dark lashes: eyes like forest pools plashed with sunlight—clear, cool, yet with mysterious depths—the eyes of a maid, whose mind no man may clearly read.

"Will you know me the next time you see me?" she inquired mischievously. A little touch of deviltry twinkled beneath the silky lashes, and she gave him back stare for stare.

"I hope to," he replied coolly. With which he turned his back on her and passed to a small mirror in a wall-cabinet hanging beside the window, where he inspected the cut in his brow.

"That's an awful bad cut you've got," said she, ignoring his aloofness. "It was all full of dirt, too. You must have got a bad fall."

"I did. But I got this after I fell. Guess one of those bums kicked me."

"What bums?"

"Couple of toughs. We had a scrap."

"A—a scrap? A fight? Where? What was you fightin' about?"

"Down Warner way. They thought I had money."

Sudden silence followed. Turning, he found her watching him with eyes wide.

"I—wonder!" she said slowly. "Oh, I bet it was the robbers!"

"Robbers?"

"Yes. There was two fellers tried to rob the post-office late Sat'day night—the same night Pop brought you here. One of 'em was a big man an' t'other a little one. Some of the Warner men drove 'em away—there was some shootin', an' they think one of the robbers got hit, because they found some blood in the road afterward. Do you s'pose it was the same men?"

"Probably. Did they get anything?"

"Nothin'—one of 'em was workin' on the safe when ——"

Suddenly a startling thought assailed her, and she stepped away from him.

"Did you know 'em?" she asked in a frightened little voice.

Instantly he saw his peril. She suspected him of being an accomplice of the two yeggs, who had quarreled with his mates and been beaten and left for dead. If she suspected him, others would. He might be put under arrest and forced to give an account of himself —with the inevitable result that his identity would become known and he would be haled back to New York.

"No. Never saw them before," he denied, meeting her eye steadily. "They sneaked up in the dark. While I was fighting one, the other hit me with something. When I came to myself they were gone."

The methodical tick of the clock became painfully audible in the tense silence that followed. In the depths of the big blue eyes he saw a little fear, a little doubt, a little defiance, and a great question. His own honest gaze never wavered. Soon the fear vanished from the upturned face.

"Will you know me the next time you see me?" he mimicked.

A merry peal of laughter answered him. The tension was broken. With her next question she banished all thought of robbers.

"Can you shell peas?" she demanded.

"Why—yes. Sure."

"We're goin' to have 'em for dinner, so you can help if you want to." With that she slipped into the pantry, emerging with a milk-pail, full of plump green pods, and two deep pans.

Drawing up chairs facing each other, with the pail between them, they fell to work—or rather to watching each other's hands. He started slowly, noticing how deftly she broke the pods; and thereafter she, beneath the mask of her long lashes, spied on his efforts to make his big hands crack and empty them with creditable speed—and laughed in her heart, though her face gave no hint that she knew him to be a " city feller."

CHAPTER XII

FOR some time no word was spoken. The tiny snapping of the pods, the drum of the peas in the pans, and the pulse of Time were the only sounds.

But as they worked, it seemed that now and then there came to his ears a murmur—a vague, elusive something which was a sound and was not a sound: something felt rather than heard, suggesting the rumble of an artillery duel far off, beyond the rim of the world. It came and went, and its elusiveness bothered him. By and by it became more distinct, and still it seemed like the faint growl of heavy guns.

He glanced up to see if Pansy heard it; but she was absorbed in the shelling of the peas. At that he scowled and tried to shut his ears, deeming it a recurrence of the thudding which had troubled him before he fell in the road; but it came back oftener and deeper, as if the tide of distant battle were sweeping up over the horizon. It died, and for breathless minutes the air was still. Of a sudden it broke forth in a tumult that seemed to quiver along the ground, and at once a shadow fell on the room. The golden head flashed up, and her startled gaze encountered his.

" Oh, Lordy! " she breathed. " We're goin' to have a storm! "

To her it seemed strange that his face showed relief; she did not know that he was glad to find it real, not a trick of returning illness. "You ain't scared of storms?" she asked.

"No. Are you?"

"Yes, I am," she confessed. "It's the only thing in the world I'm scared of. We have awful ones sometimes—they swing round the mountain all of a sudden——"

"What mountain?" demanded Don quickly.

"Kiasarge, of course. We're almost under Black Mountain, you know—oh, I forgot! you didn't know, but——"

Boom! Rrrroomboommm! rumbled a hoarse salvo of the onsweeping thunder. The shadows about them deepened swiftly until the corners were choked with gloom. Through the open windows, in the hush following the detonation, came a soughing sound which grew and grew—the rush of the wind in the forest.

"We've got to shut the doors an' winders, or we'll git blown inside out!" cried Pansy. "It'll be comin' full pelt in a minute!"

She sped into the pantry, and a window dropped, followed by the sharp click of a hastily raised latch, the sound of her flying feet, and the snap of another latch. He strode to the orchard window, tugged at it, found it immovable; tried to raise it higher with no better success; gave it up and retreated to the bedroom, where he engaged in a similar struggle with his own window. Somewhere outside resounded the heavy bump of a closing barn-door. Then the quick patter of feet came back into the kitchen, and the window which he had been unable to move slammed shut.

" How do you close it? " he called.

" Pull the pin! The pin at the side! "

Then he saw a small iron pin projecting from the frame, lifted a little, pulled the pin inward—and the erstwhile immovable window jumped from his fingers and fell so hard that he dodged, expecting the glass to splinter. But the panes were small, and though they rattled they did not even crack.

" Did you shut it? " laughed Pansy outside.

" No," he grumbled. " It shut itself."

" Then come coax this one to shut—I can't budge the pin. It's the most aggravatin' thing ——"

He found her on the side of the room which he had not yet inspected, and which, he now observed, contained two windows and a door. Strange, he thought, that he had neglected this side; then he recalled that she had interrupted his investigations and kept his mind busy ever since. The door and one window she had closed. At the other frame she was pulling in vain. As he strode to it she sprang away and darted up-stairs, where more windows began to drop. Forcing the stubborn pin from its socket, he lowered this window without mishap, then stood looking through it at a sandy road, where great clouds of dust were whirling past as if fleeing the wrath to come. Across the road lay a small field, beyond which rose a steep wooded slope. Before the furious wind the trees were bending against a menacing gray-black sky, across which flickered sudden sheets of lightning. Not a drop of rain had fallen, but from everywhere came the howl of the wind, hurling gusts of sand against the walls, shrieking in the chimneys, rattling the windows and wringing groans of protest from the tortured joints of the old house.

A sharper flash leaped across the sky.

Rrrrrrip! Whoooooommmm! roared the Storm King.

From up-stairs came a frightened little cry, so muffled by the thunder that it sounded like a squeak. Rushing feet tumbled down the stairs, and Pansy burst into the room and slammed the door behind her. She was flushed from her haste, but the rosy glow quickly vanished and left on her face a strange pallor.

"Oh, Lordy!" she gasped. "It's awful!"

Flash! Rrrriprrrriprrr! rattled the tossing clouds, as if machine-guns mounted on swift-flying battle-planes had loosed a tearing volley; and immediately, like bullets thudding against walls and roof, came a downpour of hailstones. So sharply did they crack against the window-sills and the frames enclosing the small panes that Donald drew back, not being minded to have the glass splinter into his face, and crossed the room, pausing to smile down on the pale-cheeked girl and endeavor to reassure her.

"Cheer up!" he said. "It won't last long."

"Mebbe not," she replied through set teeth. "But it's lasted too long already."

Inasmuch as the storm had hardly commenced, he made no further comment, but passed on to the rear window where he could get a broader view of sky and forest. The vicious outburst of hail thinned, then stopped. For a moment the air was clear, and as he looked out across the low-lying forest to the left its resemblance to an onrushing sea became truly terrifying; for now the erstwhile quiet trees writhed and tossed under the mighty wind, giving the rolling hills a plunging motion like the lurch of huge, oily billows. Upon the leaden sky crinkled jagged streaks of lightning, mostly plunging downward, but some crackling horizontally across the racing clouds. The boom of the heavy artillery had ceased for a moment, and it seemed that the wind was passing. Those zigzag lightning streaks, Don told himself, were wireless orders flashing from the Storm King's headquarters to the fighting line, and this lull preceded a fierce drive.

Scarcely had the thought crossed his mind when a blinding flash seared his eyes and a rending crash split the heavens. Stunned, groping, he staggered back. A shriek echoed in his deafened ears, something collided with him, and a pair of arms went up over his shoulders. He grasped it instinctively, and felt—his aching optic nerves refusing to work until they recovered from the shock—felt the quivering form of Pansy in his clasp, and her hair pressing against his breast.

When his eyes became normal again he peered about the gloomy room, sure that it had been struck, and marveling that they were still alive. But everything looked the same, so he turned to the window and saw the work of the bolt on an apple-tree close by, along whose dark-gray side gleamed a ghastly gash, and from which one heavy-fruited limb drooped to the ground.

"Only a tree," he murmured to the golden hair. "Look!"

"I won't!" came her muffled voice from somewhere in his ribs. "Oh, d'you s'pose—we'll ever live to ——"

"Why, of course," laughed Don, himself again, and patting her shoulders soothingly. He would have said more, but suddenly heavy drops slammed against the window, and in an instant a roaring deluge of rain smashed like a solid wave upon the roof. The forest, the hill, the field itself vanished in a smother of water, through which only the nearest apple-trees showed faint and blurred. The tumult of it filled the house and drowned his words; and so, falling silent again, he stood watching the fury of the storm, utterly unconscious of the fact that one arm held her close and the other hand caressed her hair, as a big brother might shelter a little sister from her fears. And she, overwhelmed by terror, clung closer and kept her face hidden in his broad chest, just as she would have snuggled in the embrace of that lost brother Tom and drawn comfort from his calm strength.

Thus, while the cloudburst raved and rioted and crashed around them, they stood locked in each other's arms without thought save of the elemental violence which terrified the one and awed the other. And neither knew that the door had opened and shut, and that a dripping figure stood in the room,—a black-bearded figure in whose close-set eyes, as he viewed the lover-like embrace outlined against the lightning's glare, there flamed a malevolent hatred that menaced death, and worse than death.

Abruptly, as it had come, the rain slowed to a drizzle and ceased. The dazzling flashes faded, the smashing concussions swept away eastward, the earth-shaking tumult of the heavy guns followed more slowly. Once more the hill and the forest sprang into sight. Far in the west grew a brassy yellow glare, spreading rapidly as the last wild wrack of clouds fled after the thundering battle-line. Soon a wave of light came speeding eastward, and suddenly the sun flashed out more brilliant than ever on a countryside left battered and torn by the receding hosts, where crops and uncut hay lay trampled flat as by the hoofs of mighty chargers; where trees sprawled uprooted, or stood splintered and gashed as by the rending explosion of shells; where hillsides were gullied and slashed as by the plunge of solid shot. And as suddenly as the reappearance of the sun there came to the man and the maid a consciousness of the closeness of their embrace, and their arms dropped and they stepped apart, flushing and avoiding each other's eyes.

More to relieve his embarrassment than for any other reason, Donald opened the window, while she pushed her disordered hair up from her forehead and peeped out at the damaged apple-tree. From trees and eaves came a rapid, steady drip; and, now that the thunder had diminished to a far-away grumble, it seemed that a slower drip sounded in the room itself. Pansy's ear caught the sound, and with a little pucker on her brow she turned and scanned the ceiling for a leak. At that the figure by the door moved. Instantly her gaze dropped. With a smothered gasp she seized Don's arm, and at the imperative grasp he whirled.

So unexpected was the apparition confronting him that Don was truly startled. It was as if the black womb of the storm had spewed forth in its mighty travail the ugly demon which had tortured it—an ungovernable Spirit of Violence, in whose blue-black beard and smouldering eyes still lingered the deadly glint of the lightning. His squat, broad body, sloping shoulders, and long gorilla-arms furthered the resemblance to a primitive creature hurled down astride a thunderbolt—misshapen, clumsy, but withal fierce and powerful. So, for a space, Don stood staring at this thing which had sprung from nowhere. Then, as he recognized the face and remembered the leer which he had last seen on it, the muscles which Pansy's fingers clasped grew hard and his hands curled into fists, while into his own eyes came a glare before which the intruder's gaze wavered and shifted to the girl.

"*B'jou*, Mees' Lucee," he spoke in a hoarse, alien voice. "De rain, she's drive me een."

"Why, howdy, Jules," she replied (not very cordially, Don noticed; but her hand dropped from his arm). "You scairt me at first. I didn't hear you come in."

"*Mais non*—de storm she's mak' too beeg smash, an' you was too eenterest'." Pansy blushed from throat to hair, but her chin rose defiantly and her cool gaze never dropped. Don took a slow step forward.

"Ho! How de ween' blow, an' de tonnerre roll, an' de ligthtn' flash! An' de trees go *crrrack!* an' de branches bus' an' fall, an' de trees fall too, *comme—lak* dey wan' to keell me. An' de rain—by gar! she's come so fas' I mos' git drown. She's wan bad storm, *sacre!* So I drop down de heell an' ron for de house." He waved a hand upward at the forest slope across the road.

Pansy made no reply. Straight and cold she stood, with her chin in the air. After a moment Jules moved toward the door.

"*Mais* now de storm ees gone, an' I go too." His eyes reverted to Donald and measured him in a long, slow stare, as if he were sizing up an enemy—as, in truth, he was. Don took another step forward, silent and menacing as a bulldog. For an instant they fronted each other, and then Don spoke.

"Keep away from the windows!"

Instant malignity swept the other's face.

"Ho! W'at you mean?"

"You know what I mean. Keep away!"

"So? An' who are you, *m'sieu,* to tell Jules LeNoir w'at he do?"

"None of your business. *Keep away!*"

Jules' glowering eyes swerved to the girl's frankly astonished face; and, seeing that she did not understand, he burst into a loud laugh and significantly tapped his head. With a smothered growl Don started for him. But Pansy stepped in front of him, and as he tried to pass her she seized him.

"No!" she commanded. He could not get by without trampling her, so perforce he stopped.

Jules opened the door with exasperating delibera-

tion. On the threshold he paused and laughed again,
—a harsh, mirthless laugh. Through narrowed lids
his eyes glittered venomously at the tall, scarred fellow
chafing in the girl's grasp.

"Mebbe we meet again, *m'sieu!*" he said softly.

Turning, with catlike tread he crossed the road.
Through the window they watched him stalk athwart
the little field to the edge of the woods, where he
turned and stood, a menacing blot on the peaceful landscape, scowling back at the house. Then he plunged
in among the trees and was gone.

CHAPTER XIII

THE CRIPPLE

"I FIBBED to you a while ago, but I didn't mean to," confessed Pansy, without looking at him. "I said I wasn't scared of anything but storms. I'm scared of Black Jules."

"What did you stop me for?" demanded Don.

"Why,—I don't like fightin'," she faltered. "An' besides, you ain't strong enough to fight Black Jules—yet."

At that last word he swallowed his annoyance. She was right; and by her interference she had saved him from a merciless beating, at the very least.

"Why are you afraid of him?" he quizzed.

"I don't know. He never done anything to scare me, except look at me; but every time he comes here he looks an' looks—oh, I hate him!" she flared. "He ain't been round here sence spring, an' we thought he'd gone for good. He lives all by himself somewhere in the woods—I guess he's part Injun, anyway; an' most everybody's scared of him,—men an' all, even dogs. What did you mean about winders?"

He made no reply.

"Did you ever see him before?" she persisted. "D'you know anything about him?"

Don considered. He had determined not to tell her

of the face at the window; but if he denied having
seen the fellow before, his recent action would seem so
unreasonable as to justify Jules' aspersion on his san-
ity.   It would do no harm merely to admit that he had
seen Jules; and he knew something about him—
namely, what she had just told him.   So he nodded
guardedly.

"Where?   What's he got to do with winders, an'
why did you fellers act like two dogs gittin' ready to
bite?"

"Little girls shouldn't ask too many questions."

She pouted.   After a pause she returned to the attack.

"Will you tell me sometime, if you won't now?"

He nodded again.

"Ain't you afraid you'll hurt yourself, talkin' so
much?" she teased.   "I never see a man that wasted
as many words as you do."

Whereat he smiled, but remained dumb as an oyster.

Glancing at the clock, she picked up the pans of peas,
gauged their contents, and decided that enough had
been done.   Quickly she made preparations for a fire.
When he offered to help she ordered him away,
and so, after opening the other windows, he went back
to his chair.   As she worked he sat staring out at the
sunlit field and forest, thinking of many things. Pansy,
too, was silent, but she also was thinking.   It was high
time, she told herself, that she knew who this fighting
man was; and now she abandoned her pointblank questioning and went after what she wanted with feminine
indirectness.

"I s'pose you've been round here before," she said, with her back to him. "This is Joe Dale's place, an' I'm Lucy Dale."

He looked up, surprised. Lucy? Her father had said "Pansy." He opened his lips, but in the nick of time remembered that he was not supposed to have heard the supper-table conversation of the previous night, and choked back the words on his tongue. Then he started, as he saw her object. She had told him her name, and it was his move. He had not thought of an alias, and he had to have one immediately. So he grabbed the first name that came to mind—his own, with a variation.

"My name is—Macdonald."

"Oh! You're a Scotchman. We're English, I guess. My first name is—oh, I told you."

"Yes. Mine is—Walter."

His hostess stood very quiet, looking down at the range. He could not see her puzzled expression, but somehow he felt that the name he had given did not fit; and he was vastly relieved when she said: "Walter? I don't like that name very well. I s'pose most everybody calls you Mac?"

"Yes. Either Mac or—or Don."

"Don? That's better. Reminds me of the Spanishers—I mean Spaniards—that come over here after Columbus an' stayed in the West Injies. I read a book once about the dons. They used to fight a lot, didn't they?"

Before he could answer, a step slithered in the grass just outside—a halting, painful step. As the screen-door opened Don looked up at an elderly man in overalls and hickory shirt; a square-built, muscular man, stooping slightly at the shoulders, whose close-cropped iron-gray beard and mustache fringed an open, weather-beaten face, and beneath whose shapeless felt hat twinkled a pair of blue eyes keen as the November frost. His solid frame bespoke a slow, ox-like strength; and yet, somehow, in the carriage of his arms there was an indefinable suggestion of something missing—the touch of oddness which so quickly focuses our attention on a man who is maimed. At the second glance Don saw what it was. The left hand was gone at the wrist.

"Why, Pop!" cried Pansy, fluttering over to him. "What are you home so soon for? Why, you're lame!"

"Rob's hosses run away an' throwed me off the load, an' I wrenched my laig," answered her father, his eyes on Don. "'Tain't nawthin' serious, though it hurts some. But the red hoss tore hisself all up on a rail fence, an' Rob had to shoot him, an' then he tol' me to go hum for the day, an' I come. Howdy, mister! Ye're lookin' pretty peart agin."

"I'm much better, Mr. Dale, thanks to you and Miss P—Dale." Their hands met, and Don's jaw set as the farmer gave him a mighty grip. Dale's keen eyes bored into his battered face as if taking the measure of the man beneath it; and as the handshake ended, a satisfied, kindly smile crinkled the crow's-feet beneath his gray brows.

"I see ye know my name. But don't call me Mister

Dale. Folks allus calls me Joe, an' this little gal is Lucy. We're jest plain folks, an' if ye git to misterin' an' missin' us we might swell up an' git too toney to talk to the neighbors. Heh, heh, heh! An' don't thank *me* for nawthin'. Ye can thank Lucy all ye want to,—she's the one that brung ye round."

"Pop, you set down this minute an' let me git at that leg! Mac—I mean Don—will you git the liniment in that cabinet? Now pull up your overhauls, Pop—is it your knee? I should think Rob would have brought you home instead of makin' you walk."

"Wal, Pansy, I'd ruther walk. The white hoss was bunged up some too, an' scairt to death besides, an' most likely he'd of run away agin if Rob'd harnessed him into the buggy. One runaway a day's enough for me—I ain't a hawg on speed. Heh, heh, heh—ouch! That's a laig, Pansy gal, not a post. Rub easier right thar."

"Pardon me," Don broke in, "but did you say 'Pansy'?" He meant to get this name settled once and for all.

"Yas. Oh, I see: I told ye 'Lucy.' Wal ——" he hesitated, and grew suddenly grave.

"Her name is Lucy," he went on after a pause. "But when she was little her mother was livin', an' Mother was awful fond o' pansies,—allus had a big bed of 'em out front here under the winders. 'They're sech human little things,' she useter say, 'with their sweet little faces turnin' up to the sun, an' they seem jest like young 'uns—young 'uns that never cry, but are allus smilin' an' cheery.' She was delikit, Mother was, an' she kep' failin' all the time. An' one day a little while before the end she laid lookin' at a big bowl o' pansies beside the bed, an' she says, ' Lucy dear, ye're jest like one o' my pansies—a little yeller pansy with big purple eyes, allus sweet an' smilin'. Ye're my Pansy gal ——' "

He stopped, swallowed, and winked rapidly at the wall. And now that the reason for the name was revealed, the listener marveled that the similarity had not occurred to him before; for, with her slender, graceful figure, her great blue eyes, and the aureole of fair hair surrounding her sunny face, the girl was in truth a living pansy: a dainty floweret without the majesty of the rose or the stately beauty of the lily, but with a quaint freshness and charm all its own.

" Ever sence then Lucy's allus been ' Pansy gal ' to me," finished Dale. " Thankye, Pansy, that feels a sight better. Don't rub it no more now. Gimme my pipe."

Fumbling in a pocket, he produced a plug of tobacco, which he gripped against his body with his maimed wrist. From somewhere she brought out a short clay pipe and an open knife, and he whittled slivers from the plug and filled the bowl. She held the match, and after a few puffs he sat back contentedly.

" What made the hosses run away, Pop?"

" The thunder scairt 'em. We had the rack pretty nigh full o' hay, an' cal'lated we could make it a full load an' drive right into the barn before the rain hit us. But we waited a little too long. The lightnin' bruk out so sharp the hosses jumped an' throwed Rob off, an' then they run wild ontil they hit the fence. I was on behind, an' when the rack smashed into the fence I got throwed into a big bloob'ry bush. That eased up my fall, so all I got was a jolt an' a twisted laig. Lessee, mister, did Pansy call ye 'Don'?"

"Er—yes. My name's Macdonald. Walter Macdonald."

Dale fell silent. He took out his pipe, looked at it, tamped down the ash with a hard thumb, put it back between his teeth and resumed his puffing. His frosty eyes rested a moment on Don, then strayed to his daughter, who had passed behind their guest to restore the liniment to the cabinet. As she met her father's look she raised her brows and gave him a perplexed little smile. Don, of course, did not see this; but again there crept over him the curious feeling that his name did not fit.

"Wal, thar's reasons for everything, tubby sure," was the farmer's cryptic remark. Carefully he rose, favoring the game leg, and moved toward the door. "I cal'late the rain must of give the peas an' beans an awful peltin'. D'ye wanter come out an' look at the garden while Pansy sets the table, Mac?"

But Don was overtired already, and mumbled something to that effect.

"Then ye better lay down a while," suggested Dale. "We'll call ye when dinner's ready."

When the meal was on the table, however, Donald was buried in slumber; and Pansy tiptoed away from the door without waking him.

"Yas, let him sleep," said her father. "He's recooperatin', an' folks needs lots o' rest while they re-cooperates. He kin eat any time."

The wise old man was right. But even he was surprised by the length of his guest's nap. The sun was far down the sky, and the level shadows of late afternoon were stretching across the land when Don awoke. As he stepped into the kitchen he found the girl setting the table for the last meal of the day.

"Howdy, Mister Sleepyhead! Are you hungry yit?"

"I could eat a raw dog with the hair on!" he growled.

"Heh, heh!" sounded Joe's chuckle in the screen door. "Sorry we ain't got no raw dawgs, but mebbe ye kin make out a meal." Entering, he cast his hat at a chair and went to wash his face. "Set right up, Mac. I'll be with ye in a minute."

But Donald remained standing until his host and hostess were seated and his own place was designated. The table, he noticed, was set for four. Only three of the places, however, were graced with side-dishes of "sass." The fourth plate, at the farmer's right, was turned down.

"Thar's only us three, Mac," explained the farmer, catching his guest's glance at the empty chair. "That place is Tom's—my boy's. He was too high-sperrited to stay to hum with the ol' man, an' he went away. But he'll come back sometime—sudden, like he went. So we allus keep his place ready. Help yerself to the vittles—it's kind of onhandy for me to pass plates. Sail into them hot biscuits."

Don sailed in, with a relish that brought a grin to
Joe's face. The one-handed farmer was no mean
trencherman himself, but he had to cry quits long before his guest called it a meal. Then, asking if Don
smoked and receiving a nod in reply, he told Pansy to
bring another pipe. With a fresh, clean clay between
his teeth, Donald sat back in well-fed content and
asked how he had reached the shelter of this home.

"Wal, Pansy's got to milk the cows, so I kin tell ye
about it while our vittles settle in our stummicks."

The old man hitched his chair around and gazed reflectively at the smoke drifting across a golden shaft of
sunlight. Presently, when his daughter had gone to
the barn with a couple of clinking milk-pails, he told
his tale.

CHAPTER XIV

A TALE AT SUNSET

On Saturday night Joe had borrowed a horse from his neighbor, Rob Clarke, and driven down to Warner village to buy some needed supplies. There he had spent some time in talk and jest with old friends, so that it was late when he started his return trip. Tired by his week's work, he sank into a doze, from which he was suddenly aroused by the abrupt stopping and backing of the horse. When the animal was quieted he found that he was half-way up Tory Hill, and that across the road lay the body of a man.

Instantly the thought of his missing son Tom sprang to his mind. Hoping that this was his boy, fearing he might be dead, he quickly turned the prostrate form over and wiped the dust and blood from its face. The fever-heat of the gashed brow told him that this man was not dead; but the light of a match showed him that this was no kin of his, nor even an acquaintance.

"I didn't know what to do with ye," he admitted. "O' course I thought o' the doctor, but then I rickollected somebody sayin' he'd gone over to Punkin Hill to take keer of a woman that was expectin' a young 'un, an' so thar was no knowin' how long he'd be away. I couldn't leave ye layin' thar like that, so finally I put ye in the wagon an' brung ye here an' put ye to bed."

Then he had waked Pansy. She saw at once that
the stranger was " real sick " and must have medical attention. As it happened, such attention was within
reach; for a medical student named Martin, a
nephew of Rob Clarke, was spending a few days at the
Clarke farm. Forthwith Joe summoned him—a summons which the student answered with whole-hearted
enthusiasm, for this was his first " case." For two
days and nights he and Pansy coöperated in caring for
the sick stranger. Then an unexpected telegram came,
telling Martin of serious illness in his own family, and
he had to go.

" He said ye'd got by the wust of it, though, an'
Pansy said she could see ye was easier," added Dale.
" So he told her what to do for ye, an' sence then she's
been yer doctor."

" How long have I been here? "

" Wal, lessee. I found ye Sat'day, an' to-day is
Thursday. Most a week."

Don did some figuring. For at least two weary
nights Pansy had gone sleepless, and on the other three
her rest had been considerably curtailed; and she must
have kept a watchful eye on him through the days as
well, in addition to performing the many small duties
of the country housewife in her father's absence. No
wonder she had looked tired! And she had given him
no hint of her vigils, save the reluctant admission that
" somebody has to watch out for you, an' Pop's too
tired." Another moment's thought convinced him that
her lost sleep had been a vicarious sacrifice to her missing brother Tom, whom she would have nursed with

the same unflagging care had he been brought home desperately ill.

"Takin' it all round," drawled Joe, "I cal'late 'twas jest as well for ye that I found ye when I did. Ef ye'd laid thar till mornin' ——"

He blinked thoughtfully.

"Well?"

"Wal! The last time Martin was here he'd heard some news. He wanted to know jest what time I found ye, an' what kind o' clo'es ye was wearin'. Arter I told him he figgered a minute, an' then he says ye couldn't of had no hand in the ruckus at the pust-office. That was the fust I'd heard about the robbery."

"Robbery? Oh, yes. Pansy said two men tried to rob the post-office."

"Uh-huh. An' she told me two fellers fit ye that night becuz they thought ye had money. Must of been the same fellers—one big man an' one little 'un."

"Right. One looked like a rat and the other like a big bum. City crooks, probably. Tell me all about it."

So Joe, nothing loath, told of the biggest event this quiet town had seen in many years.

The failure of the attempt to burglarize the post-office had been due to a dog. He was not much of a dog—just a flea-bitten terrier which had drifted into the town sometime before, made himself at home there, and been named "Tramp" by the villagers. Since nobody owned him, nobody tied him up; consequently he had the run of the town at all hours. And thus it came

about that he nosed into the affairs of Sniffy and Bull
and barked his way into fame.

The whole town was sound asleep when the shrill
yapping of the terrier aroused several families living
near the post-office. Finally, growling, some of the
men arose to " make that pesky critter shet up." Their
wrath dissolved into astonishment and conjecture,
however, when they found that Tramp was barking at
a big stranger on the post-office steps who seemed to
be trying to coax him within reach. The wary animal
refused to be coaxed. He kept away and continued
his clamor until one of the spectators raised a window
and shouted. After that there was no doubt as to the
stranger's character. He threw up a revolver and
fired at the man who had called out.

" Right thar was when Tramp skedaddled," narrated
Joe. " When that ree-volver went off he done a back
somersault so quick he 'most snapped his tail off, an'
he went somewhars else. I cal'late all the folks that
was watchin' done the same thing. Heh, heh, heh!
That is, all but Joel Morgan. Joel, he fit in the Fillypeens durin' the Spanish War, an' he ain't afraid o'
nawthin'. He jumped an' got his pants on, jumped
agin an' got his repeatin' rifle, an' then run down into
his yard an' got behind a big elm-tree.

" The big feller see his shirt in the dark an' fired at
it—come darn nigh hittin' Joel, too. Joel fired back
but missed. A little feller come runnin' out o' the
pust-office, an' both of 'em fired into Joel's tree. Then
they turned an' run full pelt down the street toward
Lower Warner."

Morgan, who had brains, did not fire again at once; for the fleeing yeggs were passing houses set close together, and he realized that a hurried shot might easily kill or wound one of his neighbors. Also, he guessed that the men would leave the poor sidewalk and run in the road, where the going was better. If they did, he could fire on them without endangering his fellow-townsmen. Wherefore he ran to the middle of the road and peered down its length.

His surmise was correct. Stumbling on the narrow and broken walk, the bandits soon turned out into the soft dirt. Morgan glimpsed them against the dim shine of an electric light beyond and sent two bullets after them. As he expected, they returned the fire. Heedless of the leaden death whining around him, the veteran coolly marked down one of the revolver flashes and shot low.

Only one bullet came back. It struck in the sandy road before him, bounced, tore one leg as it passed, and spattered dirt into his eyes. The flesh wound did not bother the ex-soldier, but the blinding sand did. Stumbling over to a tree, he worked on his eyes until tears had washed most of the grit from them. Then, his fighting blood thoroughly aroused, he went after the robbers.

From tree to tree he rapidly worked his way in true bush-campaigning style, making sure that his enemies were not waiting in ambush behind any of the big trunks. Thus he came to the electric light whose sheen had revealed their indistinct figures during the fight. He looked, listened, saw only an empty road. So he

stepped out into the sand under the light and scruti-
nized it. He found tracks—marks made by a man
falling and struggling up—and a splotch of blood.

That sinister blot in the sand was the beginning of
a red trail. His bullet had struck so shrewdly that the
track of the yegg's staggering feet was lined by a
streak of his life-blood, so plain that it was visible even
in the gloom. Down this line went Morgan, swift and
vengeful, rifle ready and nerves tense. But the red
mark was short, and it ended as suddenly as it began.

Under another electric light, on the boards of a
bridge across a little brook, were several wet red
smears. Beyond these there was nothing—not even a
footprint. Morgan knew his quarry had dropped over
into the water and waded. This move left him nonplused, for the bandits might have gone in any one of
four different directions. They could wade up-stream
and then cut across into the Pumpkin Hill road; or
they could go down to the near-by river, which at that
point was so shallow as to make easy wading, and there
they could double back up the river or go on downward. He had no light, he could hear no suspicious
sound, and his torn leg began to hurt. So he reluctantly gave up the hunt and turned back.

" The danger bein' all over," concluded Dale, " Joel
found the men all out in front o' the pust-office tellin'
each other how they went lookin' for guns an' couldn't
find 'em right off. He laffed at 'em, washed his face,
tied up his laig, an' went back to bed. An' that's all."

" And they've found no trace of the robbers? "

" Nary a trace. They clean dis'peared—hide, horns

an' all. They come from nowhar an' I guess they went nowhar."

The latch clicked, and Pansy reëntered the pantry with her pails.

" Pop! " she called. " The wood-box needs fillin'."

Dale glanced out of the nearest window, and perceived with surprise that the sun had vanished and the gloaming lay over the fields. At once he arose and started out. Don laid down his pipe and followed.

CHAPTER XV

EVEN-TIDE

THE barn was small, snug, well kept. At their tie-ups stood one black cow and two Jerseys, contentedly chewing their cuds, and in the cavernous blackness of a horse-stall showed the diminutive hindquarters of a calf. At one end a huge doorway stood wide open, framing a broad dooryard, a strip of road, the field and forest beyond. At the other, two open windows showed the evening sky; and beneath them low tiers of firewood stretched from wall to wall. Thither went the farmer and his silent shadow, and in the crook of his maimed arm Dale began to pile sticks of "soft" wood which would make the swift fire needed for the cooking of the morrow's breakfast. Donald, too, reached for a handful, but his host forbade him.

"Ye can't kerry nawthin' heavy till ye git yer strength back," he decreed. "Ye'll help me more by jest openin' the door."

So Donald, realizing anew that his legs were shaky, contented himself with the office of door-tender until the wood-box was crammed. Then, still trailed by the convalescent, Dale went out and latched the door of a chicken-house.

"Got to be keerful," he explained. "Weasels an' skunks like chicken jest as well as we do."

The mention of these night prowlers suddenly recalled to Don the leering face at the window. Abruptly he asked: " Did Lucy tell you Black Jules was here today?"

"Yas, blast him!" roared Dale. The violence of his reply astounded Donald and apparently surprised the old man himself; for after opening and shutting his mouth two or three times, he added in his normal tone: "Ye caught me onexpected, Mac, or I wouldn't of bellered like that. But jest 'twixt ourselves, I'd ruther have a rattlesnake livin' under my doorstun than know that feller was loose round here. I c'd kill the snake."

"What have you against him?"

"Nawthin' — yit. But I mistrust him. Thar's lots o' things I don't know, Mac, but thar's two things I do—I know hosses an' I know men. An' I tell ye Jules is bad, pizen bad. He come here for no good cause an' he'll come to no good end. An' when I tell ye that I tell ye all I know about him, an' I know it jest becuz I feel it, sartin sure. Whar he come from, an' why, I dunno—nobody knows, onless mebbe *ye* do." The glance accompanying his last words was significant.

Don caught the look, but did not understand it. Therefore he determined not to commit himself and to let matters shape themselves.

"Why should I know?"

Beneath the gray brows grew a quizzical gleam which said as plainly as words: "Mebbe ye think ye're foolin' me, young feller. But I warn't born yestidday an' I'm a wise old owl." Deliberately he produced from his overalls pocket his ever-present pipe, and deliberately he touched a match to the charred tobacco remaining in its bowl.

"Oncet when I was a young feller," he said, with apparent irrelevance, "I lost three good friends. Three on 'em, all to one whack. An' I lost 'em by not mindin' my own business. That larned me a lesson. Sence then I've tended pretty strickly to my own affairs." Puff, puff, puff.

"Ye needn't tell me nawthin', an' I don't ask ye nawthin'. But Pansy tol' me how ye give Jules a warnin', an' that ye'd met up with him afore, an' that ye nigh tackled him; an' ye wouldn't ack that way onless ye had suthin' agin him. I kin see jest as far through a stun wall as the nex' feller; an' I don't mind tellin' ye I know ye're arter Jules—an' I hope ye git him."

And then Don saw, in one illuminating flash: saw not only the significance of that glance, but also what a beautiful explanation of his presence lay ready to his hand. Dale had put two and two together—and made five. His own reticence, instead of exciting suspicion that he was a malefactor, had by his fortuitous antagonism of Jules created the impression that he was trailing a malefactor. He knew the unreasonable tenacity with which countrymen cling to an idea once formed. In fact, he doubted his ability to convince his host of his error, even had he been minded to do so—which, of course, he was not. All he had to do was to play the hand which had been dealt him; and this he proceeded to do by making the old man defend his deduction.

"Supposing you were right," he said, with feigned

reluctance, " Jules would have recognized me, wouldn't
he? But he didn't."

" Humph! With that face? With yer eyes bunged
out an' yer forrid split? An' would ye be apt to go
arter him lookin' jest like he see ye last?" Dale
waved his pipe contemptuously. "Mac, I'll bet a
dollar to a doughnut ye had a heavy beard, or anyways
a mustache, not so long ago."

The farmer was dead wrong, but Don made no effort
to win the dollar. He merely smiled, a smile which
might mean anything or nothing. Then, tersely, he
told his host of what he had seen last night.

When he finished, Dale stood like a statue, his gaze
fixed on the far distance. He swallowed once noisily,
and wet his lips twice with his tongue before he spoke.

" Fust I los' my hand in a sawmill," he said in an
odd, strained voice. "Then I los' my fust baby—
killed by a hoss. Next I los' my wife. Then I los'
my boy Tom—though he'll come back. An' if I should
lose Pansy ——" His voice died away, and he swallowed again.

" Blast his rotten soul!" he suddenly flared. " He's
snoopin' round here nights, is he? I ain't seen him
sence spring, an' las' time I did see him I told him
right out I didn't want him round here no more. I
was afeared, Mac,—I allus s'picioned he was arter
Pansy. But he wunt never git her! I'll kill him fust!"

" Have you a gun?"

" Nope. I never liked a gun, though Tom was allus
a great hunter. But I don't need no gun for that
stinkin' blacksnake! I'll take an axe to him, or a

pitchfork! An' thankye, Mac, for tellin' me—ye say ye didn't tell the gal?'"

Don shook his head.

" Right, boy, right! Don't say nawthin' to her. I'm awful glad ye was here to-day when he come in, an' glad ye was awake las' night. An', Mac, I've got this to say to ye: I know ye're arter Jules, whether ye admit it or not, an' I don't care why; but in yer own good time ye'll git to him, an' when ye do, remember Pansy's been good to ye, an' don't show him no mercy!'"

" I won't!" promised Don, and his eyes glittered. The older man laid a hand on his shoulder.

"An' one thing more: ye'll wanter be goin' on soon, I s'pose, an' doin' what ye've got in mind—though I don't need to tell ye ye're welcome to stay here as long's ye like. But what I'm gittin' at is this: I'm workin' for Rob till his hayin's done, an' Rob's place is quite some ways from here, an' I'm gone all day. So I'd take it kindly, Mac, if ye'd promise to stay round here till my job's done, an' keep an eye out for Jules. I wouldn't feel right to leave the gal alone now, ye onderstand, an' I need Rob's money. Will ye stay?"

Don was staggered. Each day he lingered within the reach of man would increase the chances of discovery. Yet—he squared his shoulders and nodded.

" I'll stay."

" Good! An' now le's be gittin' in."

" Just a minute. I don't admit I'm after Jules. I don't admit anything. But if I stay here, I don't want it known. If Jules comes here, well and good. But if he doesn't ——"

"I onderstand. My mouth is shet." He turned and led the way to the barn, where he shut the sliding-door with a resounding thump that startled the calf into a scared whimper and brought a protesting grunt from sleepy hogs somewhere down below.

When they entered the kitchen Pansy was wiping the last of the dishes, and the milk had disappeared, presumably into the cellar. The room now was aglow with lamplight, and on the table Don observed the worn copy of "Ivanhoe." Evidently she meant to hold him to his promise concerning the Templars. As he ruffled its dog-eared pages she came swiftly to him.

"Please tell me what this means," she requested, opening the volume to a place marked by a hairpin. "Let's set down an' be comf'table."

Dale, wordless, seated himself beyond the stove and refilled his pipe. Donald drew two chairs up beside the lamp. In a moment his head and Pansy's were bent over the printed pages, and, throwing aside his usual taciturnity, he was clarifying the references to feudal times and customs and weaving in many touches of mediæval history of which she never had heard. And as he talked, the "furrin" characters which she had striven so hard to visualize became living entities, agleam with clashing mail, rustling in gorgeous apparel, and actuated by the emotions common to all mankind as well as by the exalted ideals which made the days of chivalry fit material for the glowing pen of the lame Scotsman.

These romantic figures of the olden time held little interest for the hard-headed farmer sitting back in the shadowy corner, except that Donald's evident familiarity with them confirmed an unexpressed opinion that "this feller's got a darn good eddication." But his kindly, wise old eyes saw something else which did interest him mightily—the rapt attention with which Pansy hung on the words of their mysterious guest, and her steadfast gaze at the strong profile beside her. He studied that profile anew, did Dale, and the stalwart figure beneath it. He had spoken truly when he said he knew men. Just as he had sensed the evil in Black Jules, so he felt that here was a clean, brave heart. And now, watching the two young people sitting so close together and bound by a tie of mutual interest, he grew very thoughtful and sat very quiet.

It was the meddling old clock that brought them all back to realization of the fact that bedtime approached. With firm emphasis it announced that nine hours had passed since noon. Dale yawned loudly.

"Hi, ho, hum! Wal, boy an' gal, I'm goin' to Bedlam, as the feller says. Gittin' sleepy, Mac?"

"Dead tired," Don admitted.

"Then git to bed, boy, git to bed. Pansy, ye'd oughter be ashamed of yerself, keepin' the poor feller up so. Travel up them stairs, young lady! 'Night, Mac. Sleep tight."

Haltingly he clumped up the stairs. Pansy, with a smiling nod, followed. Donald trudged into his room, leaving the tall clock to rule its kitchen domain.

But he did not sleep at once. For some time after the floor overhead had ceased to creak he lay staring at the dark, thinking of many things: the fury of the storm, and the second appearance of Jules; Dale's account of his rescue; Pansy's eager interest in the history and romance of a bygone day; Joe's request that he stay and guard his home—this touched him deeply; and finally, the tramp dog and the battle of the post-office.

So Joel Morgan, who fit in the Fillypeens, had winged one of those thugs who had assailed him in the cemetery. Good for Joel Morgan!

Not knowing who had kicked him when he was down, nor who had saved him from another kick, Don held a grudge not against Bull, who had stood up and fought him face to face, but against "that little rat" who had struck him down from behind. And as his drowsy eyes closed he hoped that Joel's bullet had struck down Sniffy the Weasel.

And his wish had come true.

Black, uncanny, sullen and slow, the Warner River wound among the rolling hills below the village and skirted a stretch of desolate pasture. A few feet from the water, up a little gully cut through the barren land by some spring freshet, lay all that was left of Sniffy the Weasel. Unwinking, unseeing, his blank eyes stared straight up at the far-flung stars, as if seeking the malign planet which had guided his devious destiny through many an evil deed and then had set for all time. His lips had fallen away from his teeth, leaving his weazened face fixed in a horrid grin. Below his ribs, far back close to the spinal column, rested the bullet of Joel Morgan.

A week ago, before a tramp dog nosed him out, he

had been a fierce, forceful creature able to overmaster his brute satellite by sheer dominance of will. Now he was nothing—an empty shell, stripped of life by the rifle of a " hick "; stripped of everything valuable by the despoiling hand of Bull, who had waited for him to die writhing in the gray dawn of Sunday morn, then plundered the body and fled.

And somewhere out in the dark, while Don slept peacefully at the foot of the mountain and Sniffy lay stark and stiff on the lonely river bank, Bull was wandering aimlessly like a hulking, rudderless boat blown along by the winds of Chance. And as sleep is much like death, and as death sees things beyond the normal human ken, perhaps it was not mere coincidence that Bull's scarred victim laughed suddenly in his sleep, and that the pal whose body he had rifled now grinned that ghastly grin. Perhaps both the living and the dead caught a fleeting fore-vision of what was to happen to Bull.

CHAPTER XVI

THE OPEN ROAD

CAME an unbroken succession of perfect hay-days—clear, clean, golden-hot days when the sun jumped pink-faced out of bed, swept the heavy dewdrops from the nodding grasses, and broiled the juices from the stalks which the mowing-machines and hand-scythes laid low before him; when lusty breezes frolicked along the fields and aided the forks of the farmers in tossing the half-dried hay which had lain in bunches and windrows over night; when huge racks wended their sedate way to the barns, where the brawny arms of the haymakers hurled the winter feed of their beasts upward by great forkfuls into the yawning mows. From sunup until sundown the fields sang with the shrill chirr of grasshoppers rejoicing in the heat; from dusk till dawn they resounded with the monotonous chorus of the crickets. By day and by night the skies were clear save for an occasional fleecy cloud which drifted lazily along as if out for an airing, without the slightest evil intent toward anyone.

Through these long, quiet days the Dale farm lay in peace. If any sinister black-bearded shadow lurked in the edge of the woodland it took good care to remain masked by the undergrowth, and the alert eye of Joe Dale's tall watchdog spied no marauder except one

mountain hawk, which swooped down from the clouds
and beheaded a pompous young cockerel. The fowl
was a little too heavy to be carried away before the
long-legged Donald arrived with a pitchfork; and so
his tender body garnished the table of his owner instead of forming a bloody repast for his slayer, which
escaped only by dropping its prey.

Through these days, too, the convalescent "recoop-
erated" rapidly. His hollow cheeks filled out and,
under the fierce sun, took on a coppery glow. The
ugly bruises above his cheek-bones faded until his eyes
once more were clear and gray. No longer did his ribs
project like the hoops of a barrel; no more did he have
to refrain from turning quickly, or sit down at fre-
quent intervals to rest. Had it not been for the scar
on his forehead, the lines eaten into his face by the acid
of mental torment, and the fuzzy brown beard which
he allowed to grow, his exterior would have been that
of the Donald of old.

That beard bothered Dale, for it tended to upset his
theory that Don had worn one when Jules last saw
him; but the farmer maintained his policy of minding
his own business, contenting himself with the hypothe-
sis that his guest had at least possessed a flowing mustache. Joe was little in evidence these days, for when
Don arose in the morning the old man had gone to
work, not to return until the sun hung low, when he
trudged into the house, washed his face amid much
puffing and splashing, combed his gray hair up into a
stiff pompadour, and demanded his "vittles."
Through the evenings he seemed content to sit in his

corner and smoke, watching teacher and pupil at their lamplight sessions with that same gentle look in his eyes, until his head began to nod and he climbed aloft.

Somewhat to his surprise, Donald found himself looking forward pleasurably to the evening quiz. The reason for this was twofold: a kindly interest in sating Pansy's thirst for knowledge of past and current events, and a feeling that thereby he was discharging some of his obligation to her. There was no doubt of the effect of these talks on the girl. Not only was her face alight with interest throughout the explanations, but her quaint mode of speech, already far superior to the out-and-out colloquialism of her father, began to improve as she absorbed the urban diction of her preceptor: she now used " run " and " see " and " come " and kindred verbs in the past tense, and painstakingly avoided the solecism " you was." These things Donald noted without comment, but with the secret satisfaction of one who sees that his efforts have not been spent in vain.

However, few activities of man are purely altruistic; and Donald, though totally unconscious of any selfish interest in these sessions, nevertheless was actuated in part by their soothing reflex upon himself. First, they busied his mind with wholesome activity which, for the time, shut out the sombre wraiths of the past. Again, they gave him the comfortable feeling that he was not altogether useless; for he was not fitted by training or inclination for the monotonous tasks of farm life, and, though he pottered around the place all day doing little chores which came his way, he often thought himself

hopelessly inefficient. This sense of futility was en-
hanced by the circumstance that the vigilant watch he
kept on forest and road met with no result. But when
the day was done and he clad himself in the mantle of
the oracle all his distrust of himself fell away, and he
felt like a man who, after traveling over a stretch of
dubious bog, suddenly steps again on the firm soil of a
field which he knows.

Besides all this, the subtle charm of the dainty maid
herself went far to weave about these hours a golden
spell: the appeal of her flower-like beauty, her winsome smile, her unconscious grace, and her great eyes
—eager, wistful, merry, demure, transparent, and baffling, all at once. And no normal man, even though
embittered by past betrayal and cynical toward all
womankind, can remain totally insensible of the glam-
our of such a comradeship. Had anyone suggested
to Donald that this charm even existed he would have
repudiated the suggestion with fierce scorn. Yet—
would he have found equal enjoyment in imparting the
same heterogeneous information to old Joe?

But these lamplit hours were few and short, while
the useless days and the shadowy nights were long
and filled with rankling rebellion against the malice of
fate. The past would not down. Black moods often
drove him to avoid the girl by day and goaded him
by night to leave this home and vanish into the forest.
At times he cursed himself for passing his word to
remain here, and at other times he answered Pansy's
cheery talk with morose silence or replies so curt that
she flushed and wondered how she had offended him.

Joe too noticed his recurrent sombreness and pondered as to its cause; and, though he asked no questions, he reached a conclusion near the truth.

"It ain't that he's mad at us, or nawthin' like that," he told Pansy. "Suthin's a-plaguin' him. Mebbe we'll know what it is sometime, but it ain't none of our business onless he wants to tell us."

Since Donald did not tell them, they gave no sign that they observed his moods. They treated him always with a simple courtesy and an unexpressed sympathy to which, in his better moments, he responded in kind. And as the days drifted past, the evenings knit about these three a fabric of whole-souled affection, light as gossamer and strong as steel.

Then came the day when Rob Clarke's haying was finished. And into the peaceful fields of the Dale homestead sprang a beast of the forest.

That morning the lure of the open road overpowered Donald. Lounging in brilliant sunlight at the barn door, he surveyed the farm for the thousandth time since his appointment as watchman; and for the thousandth time nothing new met his scrutiny. Then his gaze roved on down the sandy highway, and over him suddenly swept an irresistible desire to stretch his legs and look at new things just around the bend.

Well, why not? Nothing had happened in all this time. Black Jules never appeared in daylight, it seemed. Once he had crept in from the night, and once he had sprung from the storm. But in the full glare of the forenoon sun—one might as well expect to see an owl or a bat abroad at that time of day. So, for the first time since his arrival, Donald stepped outside his sanctuary—and thereby forsook his trust.

It was to be only a little stroll, of course. But by physique and by instinct Donald was unfitted for strolling; his legs were too long, and his muscles worked too smoothly, and he found too great a pleasure in a swinging stride to idle along the way. So it was but a moment before he was marching away at better than a four-mile gait, head up, shoulders back, lungs swelling with deep draughts of air; and the farm fell away behind and disappeared around the curve.

To right and left rose steep banks, heavily grown with brush and trees. Soon the right-hand slope dropped abruptly, and he looked out across a maze of tumbled hills and woods which were utterly unfamiliar. As he topped a little rise the incline to his left began to recede, and not far ahead he glimpsed open ground. His stride lengthened an inch or two, and soon he reached the point where the forest ended and a rolling, rocky stretch of pasture lay open to the sky, saved from utter nudity only by clumps of unkempt trees.

Far up along the rambling ridge the pines swung in a broad belt, dividing the yellowish fallow land from the baby-blue sky; and against the dark green tree-line glimmered a little grayish blotch. It had a regularity and rigidity of outline which could belong only to a house. There was but one house on these mountains that Donald recalled. It was the Half-way or White House, an abandoned shack beside the trail, where chance campers sometimes stayed and porcupines gnawed the boards at night. At sight of it the mantle

of unfamiliarity fled from the countryside, and for the
first time Donald got his bearings.

He knew this great bleak pasture—had cut across it
more than once to save miles of the rambling trail.
Only a little way down the road, around a sweeping
bend, lay the little branch road which broke away from
this one at right angles and ended at what once had
been a toll-gate, where the long trail began. But he
need not use the lower part of that trail; he had only
to climb up across this barren land to that little gray
blotch, and he would be among the protecting pines
which had held out their shaggy arms to him ever
since he and Harry had fled toward the dawn.

The call of the high, silent places suddenly assailed
him as had the lure of the open road. All he had
to do was to crawl over that stone wall—and yet he
could not; for he was bound by his promise to the Dale
farm.

The thought fell like a wet blanket on his impatience.
With it came a realization that he had been derelict in
his duty, and that he must return at once.

Resolutely he turned his shoulder to the distant
Half-way House and started back.

CHAPTER XVII

FIST AND KNIFE

THE way was longer than he had thought, as it ever is with those who go adventuring and wheel at the call of duty. As he strode along there awoke far down within him a subtle sense of alarm, of impending evil, almost of fear, which he could not analyze, but which drove his marching feet until his steady tramp became a double-quick. It was preposterous, he told himself; nothing untoward could be happening at the Dale farm this glorious morning; he had been tied to the place so long that his constant vigilance had become a habit, and now he was merely feeling the guilt of truancy. But the feeling would not down; rather, it increased as he neared the house. When at length he passed the final turn in the road and saw the little homestead dreaming as peacefully as ever, without a hostile figure anywhere in its homely fields, the wave of relief which swept over him was so intense that he snorted in disgust and called himself a fool.

Still something urged him on. Everything was peaceful outside the house, it whispered; but how about matters *in* the house? His pace, which had slowed, quickened again. But once more he derided the silent monitor, and compelled his eager feet to adopt and hold a more leisurely gait. So it happened that when he left

163

the road and turned into the yard his tread was well-nigh soundless.

"No! You can't come in, I tell you!"

He stopped in his tracks. The voice was Pansy's, and it held a note of fear. It came from the kitchen door, which he could not see; for between him and the "el" jutted a corner of the main body of the house. Scarcely breathing, he poised himself for advance and listened.

The screen door around the corner rattled violently under an angry hand. Evidently it was fastened.

"*Ouvrez!* Open, Mees' Lucee, or I'll bus' it open!"

"You go away right now, or I'll call somebody that'll make you!"

"Ho! By gar, you t'eenk I scare, *moi? Tres bien,* Mees' Lucee, hollair all you want. Your fathair ees wit' Rob Clarke. Your lovair ees a mile down de road. Now weel you open dat door?"

"No! I won't!" Beneath the defiant tone the undernote of terror was more noticeable.

A harsh laugh answered her. *Rrrip!* came the sound of a tearing screen. Pansy screamed. The kitchen door slammed shut. The bolt snapped home.

"*Sacre!* So I mus' come een t'rough de weendow, ma pretty wil'cat?"

His moccasined toes falling light as thistledown on the turf, Donald flitted around the corner like an avenging fury. Framed in the open window stood the girl, white-faced, struggling to pull the clumsy side-pin and drop the sash. Outside, his eager arms stretching in to seize her, was Black Jules.

Don's big right hand shot out. Jules, leaning forward, presented no mark for a blow. The hand darted over his shoulder, gripped his face, and hurled him backward and down.

The shock of his impact against the solid ground would have stunned an ordinary man; but the Frenchman whirled like a cat, rolled over feet foremost, and leaped erect so quickly that he seemed to rebound like a rubber ball. At sight of his assailant the rage in his swarthy face flamed to fury. He grinned a deadly grin.

" So we meet again, *m'sieu!* "

With that he rushed.

More than half-way Don met him, with two lightning smashes that stopped him in his tracks. Another blow, starting below the hip, straightened him out of his crouch. Instantly Don launched a knockout for the bearded jaw. But one smooth-soled moccasin slipped on the grass, and he had to pull the blow or fall.

Jules dropped back into his crouch—head in, body hunched, arms low, hands curved like talons. He had not struck a blow. He was not a fist-fighter. His style of combat was that of the gorilla he resembled—to seize, crush, break and mutilate.

Warily the half-breed circled his steel-fisted antagonist, seeking the slightest opening for a lunge and a clinch. His fingers worked slowly, as if they itched to claw into the other's vitals, and his eye was that of a basilisk. But those fists always fronted him, and his feints opened no unguarded point.

Suddenly Don's left hand licked out. Jules in-

stinctively threw up a protecting forearm. Too late
he saw it was a feint, and tried to duck. That low-
hanging right fist crashed into his mouth, and the
swift-following left thudded against the side of his
jaw. He staggered, fell, rolled on his side, and lay still.

"Get up, you scum!" grated Donald. He had
missed the corner of the jaw, and knew it. But Jules
lay utterly nerveless, his face hidden by his beard and
by one arm thrown across his eyes. After watching
him curiously for a moment, Donald stepped up to
him, put a foot against his chest, and gave a shove to
roll him over.

In a flash the fallen man threw aside his feigned
insensibility and struck—low and foul. But he moved
a shade too soon. The foot against his ribs shot him
and his intended victim backward simultaneously, and
he missed by inches. For an instant, however, Donald
was off his balance; and in that instant the Frenchman
seized his ankle and yanked him off his feet.

Hardly had he struck the earth when Jules was upon
him, clutching for his throat. And now the two-fisted
fighter found himself at a deadly disadvantage, and the
ape-like Jules came into his own. Hitherto superior
science had been thrashing brute strength. But with
arms obstructed by the ground and by his antagonist's
body, Donald could only deliver short, uncertain jolts
and grapple with those talons which were striving to
choke out his life. If once they wound around his
windpipe, he knew, they would clamp home in an iron
grip which he could not break.

Over and over they rolled, arms and legs thrashing

the turf and each other like the tentacles of fighting devil-fish. Again and again Donald blocked those hands; but always they darted back. Once a hard thumb raked across his forehead. Once a long nail bit into his nose. Jules was trying to gouge his eyes. And again, as the two heads came together, he heard a snap of teeth at his ear. He dodged away and shot another short blow into the wicked face, forgetting the menace of those clutching hands. And then the hands got him.

Gasping already from his fierce struggles, Donald felt the universe begin to whirl as his breath was shut off. Desperately he strove to break away, to batter those iron arms aside, to whip a knockout blow to the jaw above him; but all in vain. The fingers sank into his neck until it seemed that they would squeeze his head from his body. A confused roaring grew in his ears. Floating spots of flame came between him and the leering face which gloated down on him. The world began to slip away.

In his extremity his legs saved him. Intent on his enemy's throat, Jules had neglected to pinion either his legs or his body. Now, in a convulsive contortion, that tortured body shot those legs upward. One knee smote the half-breed in the abdomen. He grunted and relaxed his grip. One gasp of air got into Don's bursting lungs. His knees struck again with terrific force, and a grimace of pain twisted the black-bearded visage. The hold on his windpipe broke. He threw himself backward, rolled out of reach, and staggered to his feet.

Through the haze dancing before him he made out
Jules rising, poising an instant, then lunging at him
with head lowered. Instinctively he again used the
knee. It smashed into the other's face so hard that
he snapped erect, tripped over his own feet, and
sprawled sidewise. He did not get up at once; nor
did he again feign unconsciousness. One hand gripped
the ground, while the other fumbled in a dazed way
at his head. Donald seized the opportunity to rub his
aching throat and draw deep, invigorating breaths.
The haze disappeared, and when Jules again started up
Don stood alert.

This time the half-breed did not leap to his feet.
His rising was springless and uncertain, and his hand
still rubbed his puffy eyes. The second he stood clear
of the ground Donald tore into him with a hurricane
of blows that sent him staggering. For the first time
he began to use his fists, sending back swings that were
clumsy but powerful, and doing his desperate best to
duck or block the sledge-hammer smashes shooting
into his face and body. He was fighting on the defensive now; and in this his physique, his posture, and his
primitive strength aided him far more than his hands.
For Jules was no bloated Bull, but an iron-hard creature of the wild, who could take a terrific beating and
still fight on. Moreover, his squat neck and hunching
shoulders gave him a natural crouch, bringing his
jaw near his chest and making it hard to hit. And
so, despite the merciless battering, he kept his feet.

Back, ever back he reeled, trying at times to side-
step, but instantly overwhelmed by a fresh assault.

Back, gasping, striking, dodging, until once more he came to the window where Pansy stood, a terrified but fascinated witness of the first real man-fight she had ever seen. There a swift side-glance showed him that he was being driven into a corner. Another glance at his relentless antagonist told him that he would meet no mercy now, that he would soon be beaten utterly senseless. Down he dropped on his hands, gathered his legs under him like a wildcat, and launched himself head foremost at his punisher's body.

So unexpected and so quick was the manœuvre that Don barely sensed it before the human projectile was hurtling at him. But he had not played football for nothing. He swerved and threw out a stiff arm to ward off the tackle. He deflected it, and evaded the clutching arms; but the Canuck's shoulder struck him a frightful blow under the ribs. A sickening pain darted through him, and his strength seemed to vanish like the air from a broken balloon.

Pansy caught the involuntary grimace that passed across his face, and as he clapped a hand to his side and turned with halting step toward his enemy her cheeks went white again. Jules, scrambling up from the ground where he had sprawled, caught the anxiety on her face—anxiety which held no thought of peril to herself if her defender should fail, but which spoke sympathy and yearning tenderness. For a second he stood poised, then took several steps backward out of Donald's reach, keeping his eyes riveted on her until her own gaze swerved to him. The look of absolute loathing she gave him stung worse than Don's blows.

Of a sudden he laughed—a venomous laugh. His hand dropped to his waist. From some place of concealment inside his trousers a knife leaped into his fist.

Hand low by his side, blade turned forward for the deadly up-thrust, bloodshot eyes glittering with hate, he advanced toward the man who had thrashed him before the girl he desired. At sight of the naked steel Donald stopped abruptly. He poised himself to side-step, strike, and seize that murderous right hand. To wrest the knife away was his only hope. So he stood tense, waiting, while with cruel deliberation Jules crept nearer, a wolfish grin playing across his lips.

A startled cry rang from the window. The door sprang open. Little feet rushed across the grass, and Pansy threw herself between the two men, facing Jules with eyes flaming. His arm, rigid for the up-drive, relaxed, and he halted. A sneer twisted his mouth, and he growled deep in his throat. The growl was echoed by Donald, who put a hand on the girl's shoulder and tried to swing her back out of the way. But she turned and flung both arms around him, clinging so close that he could not put her aside without brutal force. Over her shoulder she cried to Jules: "Would you stab my brother?"

Astonishment, incredulity, and perplexity flitted across his swarthy face. Motionless as a statue of Murder he stood, eyeing them.

"Please, Pansy!" urged Donald, trying to disengage her arms, and warily watching his antagonist.

"No, no!" She resisted determinedly. "I ain't goin' to have my brother killed!" His fingers tightened on her arms, and his mouth set in a straight line. He must fling her aside, he decided. But, divining his intention, she whispered, " Oh, Don, please don't! Let him go, or he'll kill you sure—and then what'll become of me?" At that he hesitated, for he knew well that an unarmed man had small chance against a knife-fighter; and with him out of the way ——

Jules stepped back a pace. His knife hand rose to his waistband, and his thumb hooked over his breeches.

" Your brothair? Ees he your brothair? "

" Yes, he is my brother! " fibbed the girl defiantly. " An' jest because you can't lick him you want to murder him! " At that ugly word the half-breed started, and his gaze wavered. "You ain't even a man! You're a sneakin' coward! " Jules winced under her scorn; then his face grew menacing again. " D'you know what they do with murderers over to Concord? They tie their hands an' put a rope 'round their neck an' hang 'em! Hang 'em till they're choked to death! "

Fear dawned anew on the knife-fighter's swollen features. He glanced swiftly to left and right, licked his lips, and stepped backward another pace. By some feminine intuition she had struck the yellow streak in his make-up.

" I was meestake," he excused hoarsely. " I know you got a brothair w'at's been gone a long tam, *mais je* nevair seen heem. I deedn't know he's come back." He paused, and seemed to struggle with himself. As if ashamed of the knife, he slipped it hurriedly back into its hidden sheath. Then he spoke to Donald.

" Eef I knowed you was her brothair I would not

have fight. Mees' Lucee was meestake, too,—all I want was a dreenk of watair. She lock de door an' tell me no, I mus' go, an' she mak' me a leetle mad, so I wan' to—w'at you call—plague her. I wouldn' do no harm. *Sacre!*" A sudden grin split his beard. "We have wan beeg scrap, *n'est-ce-pas?* An' all because we don' onderstand. Now for why can't we be friends?"

Hot disgust against posing as Pansy's brother and thus saving himself rose up in Donald. Hiding behind a woman's skirts was not in his creed; and, despite her warning pressure on his arm, he was about to disclaim all relationship and renew hostilities, when he realized that by doing so he would again imperil her. The Canuck's feeling against him had been the hatred of jealousy. Now that he believed this jealousy to be baseless, he would be more circumspect; he was already trying to make amends. And there would come another time, Donald vowed, when he would see to it that Jules neither choked him nor drew a knife. Now he must think of Pansy first. So, for her sake, he played the hand she had dealt.

"I told you once to keep away from these windows," he growled. "You've no business here. You're no friend to any of us. If you come around here again you'll find me waiting for you with an axe. Now get out!"

The other's black eyes narrowed evilly. His hand twitched slightly toward his belt, but dropped again. He shrugged his shoulders; opened his mouth, shut it without a word; wiped his bloody nose on the back of his hand; stared first at the man, then at the girl; drifted slowly backward, turned, and slouched away toward the forest. Several times he looked back, and at the edge of the woods he stopped, as on his previous appearance. Then the trees swallowed him.

The man and the maid looked at each other. Her hand still rested on his arm, and she was very close to him. Unconsciously he put both hands upon her shoulders and drew her nearer, unresisting. Into her cheeks crept a deeper color, like the soft flush of the dawning day. Upon her sunny face a virginal soul stood forth, pure, trusting, unafraid. And deep in her eyes shone a wistful tenderness which a man far more dense than he could not fail to read. For a long minute he looked down into those eyes, and his own gaze grew troubled. Then, with a sigh, he dropped his hands and stepped back.

"Guess I'd better wash up," he said in a very matter-of-fact tone. Turning, he strode away toward the well.

CHAPTER XVIII

THAT evening Joe Dale rode home in state, driving the white horse which had once run away with him and launched him on his flight into the "bloob'ry bush." Beside him sat an erect, alert little man whose ancestors, back in the early stages of evolution, must have been chipmunks; for he still retained the inquisitive nose, the bold eyes, the reddish hair and the snippy ways of his squirrel progenitors. All he lacked was a fuzzy tail, a black stripe down his back, and a pile of stones to frisk upon. As he rode he talked incessantly, his gaze meanwhile roving over everything, near and far, within his range of vision. This was Rob Clarke.

In the barn, where he had chained the cows and given them their evening feed, Don stood still as he heard the squeak of an ungreased axle up the road. Then, as he always did when vehicles approached, he sought cover. Up-stairs into the hayloft he climbed, closed the trap-door behind him, and took his stand well up on the mow, where he could see and hear through the big open hay-door without revealing himself.

The intermittent squeak grew louder, and Clarke's

incisive voice became audible, punctuated at intervals by Dale's brief replies. The dull plunk of hoofs swerved into the yard and stopped to a resounding "Whoa, boy!" Donald shifted his position a bit and stood narrowly scanning Dale's companion, who took the reins as Joe clambered out.

"Thar ye be, Joe, home agin all right side up with care. Whoa, gol darn ye! Stan' still, or I'll skin ye alive! Now don't it beat all, Joe, how hosses will act! Here ye been drivin' all the way, an' the ole plug went along easy as a yeller dawg, an' now when I take the reins the darn fool gits jumpy the minute I tech 'em. What ails him, I wanter know?"

"I've told ye before, Rob. Ye want to gentle 'em, not yank their mouth off an' yell their ears out. Hosses are like humans,—it all depends on how ye handle 'em."

"Wal, mebbe so, mebbe so. I ain't got much patience with hosses or humans either. Got yer tools all out yet? All right, take yer time, take yer time. Mebbe ye kin drive a hoss better'n I kin, but when it comes to pickin' things out of a wagon that ol' stump o' yourn ain't much good, is it? Ha, ha! Wal, if thar ain't Lucy! Howdy-do, Lucy! Whar ye been keepin' yerself all this time? Mom was sayin' only yestidday, she says, 'I guess Lucy Dale must of died or got married or had some other bad luck,' she says. 'She ain't been nigh us for weeks,' she says, 'an' I can't git over to see her with a passel o' hungry men allus hollerin' for vittles,' she says. Ha, ha! Why don't ye come over an' see Annie? Ain't mad at none of us, be ye?"

Into the picture framed by the barn window moved Pansy, cool and self-possessed.

"There's lots of things to do, an' I've been busy all the time. You don't know how much work there is around a house."

"Yas, that's what Mom's allus sayin', but I dunno, I never could figger whar a woman puts in so much time. Whoa, thar! O' course, thar's a lot o' cookin' to do over to our place jest now with the hayin' an' all. But it ain't so here—ye've got all day an' nothin' much to do, seems to me, an' ye might come over an' be sociable. Annie'd be tickled to death to see ye."

"I'd like to see her, I'm sure. Why don't she come over here?"

"Wal, she's busy helpin' Mom—ye know Mom's kind of porely this summer—but she's been dyin' to see ye an' find out all about this feller ye got stayin' here. Ha, ha! That puts me in mind o' what she says when Mom was talkin' about ye—Whoa, I tell ye!— Annie says 'I guess mebbe Lucy's fell in love with that tramp feller that Martin went over to see,' she says. 'She's got a mighty good chance to, with her father away all day!' Ha, ha! Ye ain't done nothin' like that, have ye now? Wal, by cracky! Look how red she's gittin', Joe! By gorry, mebbe Annie hit the nail on the head!"

He turned his grinning face toward Dale, who had removed his belongings from the rear of the "democrat" wagon and stood leaning on a pitchfork. Joe made no reply, no motion; but all at once Clarke's grin became vacant, then sickly; then it faded and disappeared. After an awkward pause, during which the hidden listener longed to get hold of that chipmunk nose and twist it till its owner howled, Clarke turned again to the girl.

"Now, Lucy, I was jest jollyin' ye. I'm allus jollyin' somebody. I know ye wouldn't fall in love with no tramp. Annie was jest jokin', too." His glance darted back and forth between father and daughter, both of whom stood mute. Another strained silence followed. Then, in a clumsy effort to cover up his *faux pas,* he rattled on.

"Annie's been crazy to see this feller, though, ever sence Martin come back from over here. Martin says the feller was kind of a myst'ry, an' mighty well-built, an' he jedged he'd be real good-lookin' when he got well agin. Whoa, ye bag o' bones! Annie'd of been over here before now, only thar was so much to do. Ha, ha! Gals are funny, ain't they? But say, whar is this feller, anyway? Trot him out an' lemme look at him. Yer pop wunt tell me nothin' about him, an' I'm most as cur'ous as Annie. Whar is he?"

"I don't know," the girl replied coldly. "Gone for a walk, perhaps."

"Wal, I swan! Ain't he got nothin' to do but go walkin'? Ef he was over to my house he'd be workin' for his keep, an' don't ye forgit it. Look at that screen door, now! Hole in it big enough to drive a hawg through! I'd make that feller patch it up quick. I'm s'prised at ye, Joe—ye allus did try to fix things right away, 'stid o' leavin' 'em hangin' like that. How'd ye bust that door, anyway?"

Joe stared blankly at the sagging section of screen, and then at Pansy. Something in her answering look warned him.

"I done it this mornin', Rob," he lied. "Thinks I, 'That screen looks kind o' rawtten. I wonder if it'll give.' So I put my foot agin it. It give."

"Ha, ha, ha! I sh'd say it did! Whoa, consarn ye! Wal, it's sundown already, an' ef I'm goin' anywhar to-night I got to be movin'. Got all yer stuff, Joe? Wal, now come over an' see us, Lucy. Giddap! Go on, darn ye, or I'll skin ye alive!"

The horse bolted, as if to forestall execution of the threat by jumping out of his hide. The ungreased axle recommenced its lament, which came back in rapid diminuendo from down the road and soon ceased. Donald raised the trap-door and descended.

"Who done that?" demanded Joe, looking at the torn screen.

"Black Jules. He was here to-day an' he kicked his foot through it."

Joe started. Consternation overspread his face as he looked again at his daughter. But her calmness reassured him. Then, hearing Donald advancing, he whirled on him.

"Gorry mighty, boy! Ye fit Jules, didn't ye? Yer face is swole an' scratched! Did ye lick him?"

Pansy's clear laugh forestalled any reply Don might have made.

"Lick him? Oh, Pop, you'd ought to have seen Jules when he went away! He couldn't hardly see out of his eyes, an' his whiskers weren't black any more

—they were red! An' he wouldn't have got away at all, only he had a knife an' Don didn't."

"A knife! He didn't cut ye, Mac, did he? Ye're all right, ain't ye?"

"All right, thanks. I saved myself by a very brave act—hiding behind Pansy."

"Why, Don! You didn't! Don't you believe it, Pop,—it ain't so!"

"I don't b'lieve it, Pansy. I know Mac better'n that. But come on, le's go inside, boy an' gal, an' tell the ol' man all about it. By gorry, ef that mis'rable Canuck's comin' round here with a knife I'll have the law on him!"

The cows had to wait for the draining of their distended udders that night, for it was long past the usual milking hour when Joe consented to let his daughter relieve them. Somewhat to Donald's surprise, his host warmly commended him for "keepin' his head" and permitting Jules to think he was Pansy's brother.

"It's the bes' thing ye could of done for all of us," he declared. "This Jules was crazy jealous, an' now he'll quiet down. Ef ye'd killed him it would of made a mess with the law. Ef he'd killed ye—that would of been a darn sight worse mess. Pansy, I'm proud of ye! Ye're a brave little gal, an' ye showed quickwittedness—an' sometimes that's a hull lot better'n bein' jest brave."

He smoked thoughtfully, and Pansy arose to light a lamp.

"By gorry, I'd of give a y'ar o' my life to see that fight!" Joe burst out. "Mac, ye ain't the fust feller

that's tried to lick Black Jules, but ye're the fust man
I know on that's done it. He jest about kilt the other
fellers. He bruk Nate Gorman's laig so bad Nate
warn't no good for nigh onto three months, an' mashed
his face flat besides. He hurt Silas Pettengill so he
couldn't work for a fortni't. He darn nigh bruk Walt
Hanscom's back, an' twisted his arm most out o' the
sockit, an' caved in his ribs. Walt's got two brothers,
Seth an' Roy, an' they went arter Jules with rifles, but
they couldn't find his shack—nobody never knew whar
he lived, 'cept it was on Black Mountin somewhar.
But while they was scoutin' round a bullit come from
nowhar an' hit a tree right ahead of 'em, an' when they
stopped an' looked round another bullit knocked the
rifle clean out o' Roy's hand. An' they couldn't see
nawthin', so they got out. But they said arterward
that thar warn't no explosion to them shots—jest a
kind of a whine, an' the rattle o' the bullit through the
leaves, though Jules must of been clus by, becuz they
was in the woods an' a bullit couldn't travel fur. An'
thar's another funny thing about that Canuck—no
dawg'll go nigh him. An' when dawgs allus bristle
up or run away from a sartin man, that man's bad!

"Gee whillikers, though, I'd like to of seen ye beat
the stuffin' out o' Jules! But ye bruk away jest in
time when he was chokin' ye, boy. He'd of started to
bust yer bones an' cripple ye as soon's ye couldn't fight
no more. That's the way he does."

A resounding bawl from the barn echoed out across
the fields. Pansy looked at the clock and fled to the
shed, where she lit a lantern and picked up the milk-

pails. Her father suddenly remembered something.

" By gorry, I've lef' my tools layin' all round the yard. Rob's hayin' is all done now an' I'm through, so I fetched my stuff back to-night. Ever see my workin' harness? Made it myself—leather sleeve an' a hook. I kin pitch on a load o' hay as well's the next feller when I've got it on. Come look at it."

When the harness, with a pitchfork and a rake, had been gathered up and carried into the barn Donald inspected it with interest. As he was about to comment on it Joe knocked the words from his mouth.

" Oh, by gosh, I lef' my papers in the wagon!" he exclaimed blankly. " Pansy gal, I got a lot o' noospapers for ye to read. Rob give 'em to me—they kep' comin' for Martin arter he went, an' the Clarkes don't read much—an' now I've let 'em git away. What an ol' fool I be! But thar, I'll waylay Rob when he comes back. He'd oughter be comin' along soon—he jest went over to Si Pettengill's. Thar's a big bundle of 'em under the seat—Bawston an' Noo Yawk papers mostly, Rob said."

The breath caught in Donald's throat as if a hand had clutched it. Boston and New York papers! Out of the dark leaped two spectres to confront him—twin demons which, while he lingered here, had prowled just outside his sanctuary: the argus-eyed, clarion-voiced Press, and the hydra-headed, club-fisted Law. And now the first of these twain was hard upon him.

He caught himself glancing toward the big open

door, beyond which lay the all-concealing night. Then he called himself coward and fool; told himself that the Dales knew him only as a stranger from nowhere; assured himself that even though the New York papers called Donald King a murderer, he still was safe. So he forced his thoughts to concentrate again on Joe's harness, which he praised highly, much to the farmer's delight.

Yet, when the milking was done and all three had returned to the kitchen, Pansy and her father noticed that their guest had become taciturn, and that now and again he looked toward the front windows as if expecting something. He was. He was waiting, with mingled defiance and dread, for the Press to come back.

At last, from the brooding silence of the velvety night, there came a tiny sound like the squeak of a baby mouse. Again and again it came, growing louder with each repetition, until it was unmistakable—the protest of the unoiled axle. Joe arose and lumbered to the door. Pansy, who had been knitting a woolen sock, dropped it. Don glided into the semi-obscurity of the buttery.

" Jest a minute, Rob," came Joe's voice outside.

" Whoa, consarn ye! " bellowed Clarke. The squeaking stopped.

" I forgut my papers."

" Wal, by cracky, did ye now? So ye did, so ye did! Here they be under the seat. Wal, now, if I'd took 'em back hum that'd been a good 'un, wouldn't it? Ha, ha! Got 'em all right this time? Say, ye wasn't

goin' to look for nothin' perticler, was ye? 'Cuz Mom
used some o' them papers to wrap up things in, an' the
ones I give ye was jest what we had layin' round.
Wal, that's all right then. I kin see Lucy in thar by
the light waitin'—s'pose she'll read her eyes out now.
Ain't she the beatinest gal to read? Gorry, I don't see
what fun folks git out o' readin' noospapers, but then
it takes all kinds o' folks to make up a world, as the
feller says. I don't see that tramp o' yourn in thar—
ain't he back yit? Ain't lost him, have ye? Ye wanter
work him, Joe, work him hard while ye got him.
Annie says—er—ah—ump—wal, I gotter be movin',
Joe. Come over an' see us now, both of ye. Sure ye
got everything? Wal, g'night. Giddap, darn ye!"

Pansy pounced upon the big bundle of papers,
roughly corded, which her father deposited on the
table. When he was sure that Clarke was well along
the road, Don drew a chair up on the other side of the
lamp and straightened out a journal from the top of
the pile. At a glance he saw that it would not contain
any account of the Duncan killing, for it was from
Boston, and but a few days old. But, feeling Dale's
watchful eye on him, he forced himself to assume an
interest in the current news, to turn the pages leisurely,
and even to read an item or two aloud to Joe. Then
Pansy read from the sheet she held, and in the interval
the fugitive's eye leaped from headline to headline,
stole a surreptitious glance at the girl's paper, and saw
that it was the New York *Bulletin*.

A wild impulse to seize it from her taunted his
muscles. But he crushed it down.

"You fool, there's plenty of time," he told himself. "These papers won't get away. Hold hard!" Nevertheless the smouldering fire of impatience mounted again as the moments passed, and when she discarded the newspaper he barely restrained his desire to grab it. For a minute longer he stared at his own publication, seeing nothing; and when he laid it down he picked up the *Bulletin* with far less show of interest than the girl had displayed.

This time the date was dangerously close to the one he sought. He had shot Duncan on Thursday night. This paper had been issued on the following Monday. With quickened pulse he skimmed its news columns. The thing which he dreaded was not there.

Perplexity gave way to irritation. There *must* be a story on Duncan here somewhere, for his killing formed a piece of news that would not die in a scant three days. The paper felt strangely thin. He looked at the page numbers: page 2—page 5! Turning to the back, he discovered that pages 9 and 10 also were gone. Somewhere, somehow, a whole sheet had dropped bodily out of the paper. The malicious Press was playing a scurvy trick on him: arousing all his fears, tantalizing him, then baffling him by hiding away the one story he must see.

When he laid the *Bulletin* down he found that Pansy had gone through three more papers, skimming the cream of the news and leaving the residue for another day. He gathered them all up at once, looked at the dates, found them widely divergent, picked the most likely issue, and resumed his circumspect perusal, uncomfortably conscious of Dale's continued stare, which to his supersensitive nerves seemed laden with suspicion. As a matter of fact, the old man was not paying the slightest attention to the younger man's actions; his unwinking gaze was absent, and his mind was filled with a visualization of the fight this foster-son of his had waged that day. Ignorant of this, however, Donald kept control of his every movement. And so the game went on, and the kitchen was silent save for the rustle of the turning pages and the solemn tick of the old clock.

All at once Pansy's golden head became very still. Slowly the paper in her hand rose until its extended sheets hid her from the men. It stayed there, suspended in the lamplight glow, for an interminable time. The little hands holding it began to tremble. It sank again, and her wide blue eyes studied Don's face; dropped to the paper, lingered there; rose again, and searched his countenance with an intensity that drew his own gaze swiftly to her.

" What is it? " he demanded, dropping his paper.

" I—you ——" she stammered, and stopped.

Dale's rambling thoughts abruptly returned to the present. He took the pipe from his mouth and stared at his daughter.

" Are you ——" she recommenced in a very small voice—and stopped again. In the silence a vagrant breeze stirred the apple-leaves outside. She had an inspiration. " Did you—hear anything? "

A keen look flashed between the men. They came out of their chairs as if propelled upward by springs.

Both turned to the door. The younger man grasped the other's arm and stopped him.

" Go out through the barn," he ordered. " Get your axe. Then sneak around the barn. I'll go the other way."

Comprehension and appreciation of this bit of strategy lit up the old man's face. Without a word he turned and tiptoed out through the shed. Closing the screen door softly behind him, Donald stole around the corner of the house and began a stealthy reconnaissance.

Pansy stood in the middle of the floor, casting rapid glances around her like a cornered field-mouse seeking a hiding-place. She stepped toward the buttery, and halted: turned toward the stairs, whirled back again: hesitated, then fled to the tall clock. Opening its narrow door, she threw the paper into the black lair of the pendulum. When the door was shut she stood unconsciously intertwining her fingers and staring at the lamp. In her face was the hurt, dazed look of one who has been dealt an unexpected blow.

At the second corner Donald halted and reconnoitered the orchard, where the twisted trees loomed vague, formless, against the gloom of the moonless night. One by one he picked out the tree-trunks, narrowly watched two or three protuberant boles which resembled peering heads, and decided that no enemy stood upright among those shadows. A stealthy slither in the dew-damp grass caught his ear. Squinting around the corner, he saw a figure advancing close to the house.

"Halt!" he commanded, leaping out. The figure stopped.

"All right, Mac," drawled Joe's voice. "By gorry, ye've got a bark like a rifle. See anything?"

"No. I forgot you were coming that way."

"Heh, heh! Wal, I'm glad ye stepped out jes' then. Ef I'd run onto ye sudden around the corner I'd of split ye to the neck, mos' likely. S'posin' we take a walk through them trees." They traversed the orchard, finding nothing. Joe rubbed his ear with the axe.

"Now I was sartin I heard suthin' when Pansy spoke. But thar ain't nawthin' ——"

The leaves tossed again, smitten by another errant wind. Both started, then looked at each other rather sheepishly.

"I cal'late 'twas the wind, arter all," judged Joe, in a tone of mingled relief and disappointment. "We're gittin' skeery as a couple of ol' maids, Mac." He sniffed the breeze and scanned the murky sky. "Thar's rain behind that wind. We'll git it before mornin', mos' likely. Wal, le's go in."

They returned through the barn, where Joe hung up his axe and rolled the big door shut for the night. The thump startled Pansy out of her daze. Darting back to the table, she opened another paper. When the men reëntered the room she sat apparently absorbed in its columns.

"By gorry, she's gone back to her paper already!" laughed Joe. "I bet she don't know we been fightin' a hull army o' desperaydoes out in the orchard. Wake up, gal! We kilt forty-seven on 'em, an' the rest flew away in their airyoplanes."

His raillery brought a wan smile to her lips.

" I heard you talkin' outside, Pop, so I knew there wasn't anything around. I'm gettin' nervous, I guess."

" Wal, it's been a tryin' day, honey. Mebbe ye'd better go to bed an' leave yer readin' till to-morrer night. It's arter nine o'clock, an' I'm goin' to lay down till mornin' myself." He fetched a long yawn.

She folded her paper and laid it aside, glad of the opportunity. " I guess I will." Her eyes rested on Donald's, and she seemed about to speak further; but then she turned, hurriedly bade them good-night, and ran up the stairs.

" Ye forgut yer lamp," called her father.

" Never mind," she replied, and was gone.

" Pore little gal!" sympathized Dale. " She's like her mother was,—brave when thar's danger, narvous when it's over. She didn't even remember to light my lamp. Thankye, Mac,—I'm allus scairt o' bustin' that glass chimbley. Wal, good-night, boy. See ye in the mornin'."

CHAPTER XIX

RAIN ON THE ROOF

GENIAL old Joe was doomed to disappointment. He was not to see his fighting guest the next morning, nor for many mornings thereafter.

Left alone, Donald attacked the remaining papers, casting most of them aside after one glance at their dates. A few, which looked promising, he examined thoroughly, running a finger down each column to make sure he did not miss a head. But his search proved fruitless. There was no New York paper of the date he most desired to see; the editions issued nearest to that day were those of Boston publications; and there were wide gaps between dates. Evidently Clarke had spoken true: he had given Joe " jest what we had layin' round."

Methodically he gathered them up and arranged them in a neat pile. Then he closed the windows and made sure that the door was locked. Absent-mindedly he blew out the light, and started for his room; but before he reached it he stopped again, wondering if he had not skipped a paper or two, and whether he should go through them again. Undecided, he stood staring toward the old clock, now invisible in the gloom.

Slowly, regularly, with dignified finality, the ancient

timepiece beat out the measure of the passing minutes. It faced him squarely as he stood by the table;
and into the mechanical swing of the pendulum crept
a hidden significance, an insistent message constantly
repeated. It was saying something which he could not
interpret. Little by little, as he concentrated his attention on it, his brain-cells began to stir, to quicken in
a vague effort to receive and analyze the communication
which lay behind those inarticulate ticks and tocks.
And by and by, as he drifted into a half-hypnotic state,
the solemn cadence became verbal.

"*Tick—tock. Tick—tock. Time—flies. Time—
flies. Your—time—has—come. 'Tis—time—to—go.
Go—now. Go—now. Tick—tock. Go—now.*"

And as he still stood motionless, the clock developed
an impatient little click between ticks, adding another
syllable to its warning.

"*Tick-click—tock. An-nie—says. An-nie—says.
Tick-click—tock. An-nie—says.*"

The listening man threw up his head. He had the
message now. Spiteful tongues were at work behind
the back of this pure little girl-chum of his. The
tactless Clarke had already revealed one innuendo
which the females of his tribe had loosed against her.
Was it at all likely that inquisitive, envious Annie had
not said other things—and worse? And there was another and even weightier reason for his speedy departure—the thing which had troubled him that afternoon when he searched Pansy's eyes and read their
open secret.

The all-seeing old servant of Time which had ruled

this room so long was wise with the wisdom of age. Through the years it had watched Pansy girl grow from cooing infancy to alluring young womanhood, her body and mind aglow with life and youth, and her heart as responsive to the whispers of the little blind god as the dainty pansy of the garden to the caress of the summer breeze. Through the weeks just past it had watched her and the tall newcomer in their intimate rôle of preceptor and pupil, and old Joe sitting in his corner, looking through the tobacco-haze at things gone by and things unborn. And now it had spoken forth right manfully, hammering home its wordless warning until this dull mortal caught it at last. His work here was done. He must go—now.

A stair squeaked. Turning toward the closed door at the foot of the staircase, he listened. Soft little feet were stealing down from above. Pansy had changed her mind, he decided, and was coming down to get her lamp.

In the darkness he moved toward the high shelf, intending to light that lamp and hand it to her. But as he reached for it a quick thought stayed his arm and whirled him about. She probably was in her nightgown, and would be overwhelmed with mortification if she found herself in a lighted room. Silently he stepped across to his own door. He was just a little too late. As the knob turned under his hand the next door opened, and Pansy stepped out and collided with him.

With a startled little cry she recoiled. Her head bumped hard against the door-edge. The impact **and** the sharp intake of breath showed that the blow hurt. Don forgot her dishabille. His right arm swept around her.

" I'm sorry, Pansy girl," he apologized. " I tried to get out of your way and blundered right into it. You got a nasty blow."

" I hit the—edge of the door," she answered in a dazed way. " I wonder if—it cut."

His free hand, rising to feel the back of her head, became entangled in a great braid of hair. He pushed it aside, and it slipped caressingly down over his bare forearm. His nerves tingled and his pulse quickened. High on her crown his exploring fingers found a swelling lump.

" It isn't cut," he announced. " It's a bad bump, though."

Somehow his voice sounded hoarse. The hand in her hair trembled a little. A hot tide flooded his face and neck.

" It's—it's all right now, thanks," she said in an oddly repressed tone. But his arm, instead of loosing her, clung tighter. Gently, but firmly, she pushed with both hands against him.

" You must let me go, Don."

Slowly his arm fell, and he stepped away.

" I'll get your lamp," he offered confusedly.

" No. Please don't." He felt that she was blushing. " I'll find it all right. Good-night."

Unwillingly his feet turned again toward his own door.

" Good-bye," he whispered.

She stood very still. Into the silence between them came a sound—a gentle drumming which merged into a mellow murmur, soft and low: the beat of summer rain on the roof.

" Did you say—good-bye? "

" I—I meant—good-night, of course."

Slowly his door swung open. Though the face up-turned to his was indistinct in the darkness, he sensed in her attitude deep trouble.

" What is it? " he demanded.

" Nothing—now," she replied at length. " Good-night."

He passed into his room and closed the door behind him. Without touching the lamp that stood ready on the little stand, he sat on the edge of the bed and waited.

A narrow slit of light appeared under the door. Presently it grew dim and faded out. The stairs squeaked again, and soft footfalls sounded above his head. For a time he sat quiet, listening to the steady drizzle of the rain in the orchard outside and drinking in the cool dampness wafted in at his open window. Then, hearing no further sound from above, he arose, lit his lamp, and returned to the kitchen.

The door at the foot of the staircase was closed. In the familiar lamplight the room looked homely and prosaic as ever. Father Time, who had given him cryptic counsel, now was merely a battered old clock staring vacantly past him. Nevertheless he nodded to the timepiece, and murmured: " You were right, old scout. I'm going."

He failed to notice that the door of the pendulum-closet, tightly closed as a rule, now stood slightly ajar.

Out into the barn he passed, his light throwing fantastic shadows among the tie-ups, chests, and barrels. The cows lifted their heads and stared with great melting eyes. The calf kicked his hoofs against the side of the stall, and for an instant Donald feared the little fellow would scramble up and bawl; but after his first start he lay quiet. From a rack holding three axes Don took down the longest. Heavy-headed, razor-keen, it would be a prime necessity in the wilderness, forming a tool of many uses and a deadly weapon. From a box he took a double handful of nails, which he dropped into a pocket. Stepping softly, he returned to the kitchen.

He would need food, of course. But there was canned food enough for a week or two hidden away at the top of the mountain, where he and Harry had cached it when they broke camp. The cooking utensils had been left there, too. So the only thing he took from the house itself was a plentiful supply of matches, which he wrapped up carefully and stowed away inside his shirt. Then, with paper and pencil, he sat down to write.

At first the words would not come. Over in the corner he saw gentle-hearted old Joe, his maimed wrist resting in his lap, his one hand holding his pipe, his blue eyes beaming on his " boy an' gal." Beside the table he saw the girl whom he had just held in his arms, her face aglow and her eyes alight with pathetic eagerness to learn. The sobbing beat of the rain on the roof and its plash on the windows crept into his heart. His eyes grew misty, and a big lump formed in his throat.

By and by he wrote haltingly, with long pauses between sentences:

DEAR JOE AND PANSY:
  After you went to bed to-night, old Father Time stepped out of the clock-case and said: "Move on!" I am obeying orders.

  I do not want to go. If I could do so, I should like to stay on here forever. But it cannot be. The darkness and the rain are calling, and I must go to them now. What lies ahead I do not know. Perhaps we shall meet again. Perhaps not. But in any event, the memory of your kindness, your generosity, and your staunch belief in me, will go with me to the end of the Long Trail.

  You do not know how much your trust has meant to me. It is not altogether on my own account that I go now like a thief in the night. If I were to stay longer we all might regret it.

  And so, my very dear friends, I now say
Good-bye.
DON.

From the closet he brought a big plate, which he placed conspicuously in the middle of the table. Digging up his roll of bills, he counted out a hundred dollars. This he laid in the plate. On it he put the unfolded note. Then he picked up axe and lamp and returned to his room, where he pulled on an old coat which Joe had given him, and took his hat from the bureau. He was ready to go.

Yet he lingered, looking about the room where he, a dirty tatterdemalion picked up out of the road, had found sympathetic care and the beginning of loyal friendship. Into his mind crowded bitter-sweet memories of the weeks just gone. Now that he stood facing night and storm and loneliness, the silent forest awaiting him seemed bleak and cheerless. The words he had just written down ran through his head like a mournful litany.

" I do not want to go. I do not want to go."

While he thought, he revolved his hat absently in his hands; and at each revolution his finger-tips rubbed against something on the leather band inside. Its recurrence aroused a subconscious curiosity which prompted his fingers to cease moving the hat and follow the outlines of the oddity. They found it to be a series of perforations.

Vaguely aware that something demanded his attention, he lifted the hat and glanced at the band. Suddenly every nerve sprang awake as if the innocent felt had leaped up and hit him.

The little round holes stamped through the leather formed his initials—D. W. K.

Furthermore, the band bore the imprint of a Broadway hatter.

No wonder that Pansy, and Joe too, had been silent when he gave his alias! Beyond a doubt they had examined this headgear when first he came among them. They could hardly know that D. W. K. stood for Donald Warren King; but they could not fail to know that it did not stand for Walter Macdonald. Decidedly, he was a rank amateur at criminality. As he recalled the extreme pains he had taken to sink his collar, and then stared at this telltale hatband, he snorted in disgust.

Clapping the hat on his head, he turned up his coat-collar, picked up the axe, blew out the light, and turned to the door. In the doorway he halted. There was no particular use in unlocking the outer door, and he wished to leave the house safe from intrusion. So he turned back, threw a leg over the window-sill, and pulled out the locking-pin until the sash began to descend, when he wedged it with the axe and swung his body through.

A moment later the window was down. Blank, black, forbidding, it barred him out from the room where Pansy girl had brought him up from the red abyss; from the home where he had been protected, restored to health, treated with homely courtesy and good-fellowship; from the hearts which had opened wide to him, had adopted him as son and brother, had perhaps held him closer even than a relative. He felt a childish impulse to smash it, crawl back in, and go to bed. But he squared his shoulders and closed his fist on the axe. Without a backward look, he trudged away through the soggy grass to the road.

Straight away he marched, along the sandy track where he had wandered away from his duty that morning. So indistinct was it now, in the watery gloom, that he had to peer intently downward to make it out. Ere long he found himself slipping off into a ditch, and knew he had reached the first turn. And there he turned his head, hardly hoping to see anything but blank darkness.

A rectangle of light, its edges blurred by a nebulous aura of mist, stared after him. The lamp in Pansy's room still burned.

Irresolute, he leaned on the axe and gazed at that light, wondering whether he had made a noise and roused her, whether she were ill, whether anything had happened wherein his assistance was needed. Twice he picked up the axe and took a step toward the house; and twice he halted short. No shadow passed across the rectangle. No sound came to him but the beat of the rain. The light did not grow bright or dim. At last he concluded that she had gone to sleep without extinguishing it. So, with an involuntary sigh, he turned away and plodded on. When he looked back again he saw nothing. The trees had swung in behind him, and the house was blotted out.

Steadily, relentlessly fell the rain on field and forest, on hill and hollow, on ridge and road. It dripped drearily from the sombre pines. It oozed along little ruts and depressions, collecting in dirty little pools which lay in wait for fugitive feet. It chilled the hands and seeped through the worn clothing of the heavy-hearted man who fared onward through the murk. Behind him it pelted the heelless, shapeless imprints of his moccasins, sliding the tiny grains of sand over them until it obliterated all semblance of a human track. And back where the trail began it kept up its soft, persistent weeping on the roof.

Though old, that roof was tight; and the raindrops,

unable to creep through it, had to roll down to the eaves and drop off. Yet, in the little room beneath it where the light still burned, and where Pansy girl still lay awake, the pillow beneath her head was wet. Face down she lay, silent, motionless save for an occasional convulsive quiver of the shoulders.

On the bed beside her lay the New York newspaper which she had hidden in the clock.

CHAPTER XX

THE TRAIL OF THE RABBIT

MID-SEPTEMBER dawned on Kearsarge. The myriad brilliant stars low-hanging in the east grew pale, then dim, then faded out in the brightening sky. Far down on the sky-line the feathery edges of a tenuous cloud became suffused with dull pink, which deepened to a ruddy glow, then flamed into a fiery flare. At once the shadows beleaguering the mountain-top began to sneak down into the timber, leaving behind them a half-light which was no longer night and was not yet day. Then, in his wave-tossed bed in the Atlantic, seventy miles to the east, the sun sat up and squinted over the horizon at the bald-headed old mountain, sprawling lazily among the hills and lakes. Finding the shaggy giant still buried in his million-year slumber, he flung across the lesser mountains a shaft of light; and instantly the shadows still lurking below the summit dodged behind trees and rocks, there to cower and slink throughout the day.

Swiftly the light spread down through the wilderness, where the horrent heads of the pines broke it into irregular patches on the needle-carpeted ground. Into one small gap among them it poured in a flood—a gap not made by Nature, which abhors emptiness and ever strives to fill blank spaces with growing green. Only a little time ago this patch on the mountainside had been filled with trees which swayed and rubbed shoulders with their brothers and sheltered the furred and feathered ramblers of the wild. Now the spots where they had stood were marked only by stumps, whose peaked yellowish tops bore mute witness to the deadly swing of man's axe; and the severed trunks, stripped of branches, lay piled upon one another in four log walls, notched at the corners and roughly thatched with spruce boughs.

The cabin was very unobtrusive. Instead of standing aggressively out in the open it snuggled back among the trees, flanked by squat scrub pines whose low branches masked it at the sides, and partly concealed at the rear by a jutting boulder. Its bark walls and its bough thatch harmonized with the needle-carpeted forest floor and the evergreen conifers, and only in front, where the narrow doorway opened black, was there anything to draw even the keen eyes of the forest-dwellers. But there was scant chance of any prowler approaching from the forest; for the house stood on a natural terrace, and a stone's throw from the door the mountainside dropped away at a steep grade which the slippery pine needles made doubly difficult of ascent. Behind it, a similar sharp slope fell from the summit, and from it oozed a tiny spring, cold and crystal clear. Though a true woodsman might have grinned at the crude construction of the cabin, he would have instantly acknowledged its cunning concealment and its strategic location. Here a man might live for years undisturbed, unknown, his very existence unsuspected save by the dumb kindred of the wild.

Somewhere up in a hairy pine a bird piped his tribute to the sun—a lonely, sweetly sad little song of two notes which spoke the spirit of the solitude. Other sound there was none; and when the bird wearied of his efforts the silence hung so heavy that the tiny impact of dead pine needles dropping against the branches became audible. By and by the sound of a soft tread crept into the air—slow, deliberate, with intervals between footfalls. Through the shadows came a belated porcupine, wending his sluggish way back home. At the edge of the clearing he paused, goggling his beady eyes at the stumps; resumed his progress, stopping again to stare at the rough rock fireplace before the cabin; nosed around the stones, grunted once in the depths of his belly, and shambled onward into the woods. Utter stillness settled again.

By and by a man stepped through the doorway. He glanced to right and left, listened, and strode to the spring, where he threw himself face down and drank. Then he moved down along the tiny channel worn by the overflow, and at a little pool well below the drinking-place he performed his morning toilet.

He was thin, was Donald: thin with the leanness of one who had worked hard from dawn to dusk day after day, whose sleep had been restless, and whose food had been scant. The contents of the cache might have sufficed thus far for a mere camper, who had nothing to do but ramble and loaf; but he who swings an axe all day three thousand feet above the sea must not try to

cheat his body of the fuel it craves. That way lies
physical discomfort, mental gloom, and fitful sleep
wherein the past rises up and torments the ragged
nerves. Yet, though he was lighter by far than when
he had put Pansy and Joe behind him and trudged
away through the storm, he was not emaciated. The
dry air of the mountains, the clean fragrance of the
pines, and the pure water flowing from the living granite formed three of Nature's most potent tonics; and
though he was lean as a wolf, he had also the wolf's
endurance.

On him the wilderness had set its seal. His hair
was shaggy and his beard was thick. His face and
hands were weather-beaten, his nails were long, and his
palms were calloused. His old coat and trousers were
ripped. The torn remnant of his silk shirt (the wilderness does not like silk shirts) was stained and
smeared with the pitch of the pine. His moccasins
were worn thin; and he had not a sock in the world.

Having washed up, he got breakfast. This was a
simple task. From the cabin he brought a stew-pot
containing remnants of a rabbit which he had snared
the day before. Among the rocks he built a small fire;
and when the meat was warmed through he squatted
and ate it. Then, stowing the pot away in the hut, he
picked up his axe and swung away toward the trail.
He needed boards for his roof, and the nearest boards
were at the old Half-way House, two miles distant.

The axe he carried in his left hand. His right fist
curled about a rounded stone, approximately the
weight of a baseball. As he passed down the trail,

silent and stealthy as a hunting panther, his eyes plumbed every shadow, spied around every bend of the path for an unwary bird or beast which he might be lucky enough to kill with his stone. For a ball-player this is not an impossible feat, especially if he possesses the hunting instinct. In bygone days Donald's deadly throw had sent many a base-runner to the dugout in chagrin. More recently, it had brought occasional meat to his stew-pot. So now he held himself ready for instant action. But he saw no living thing; heard nothing but an infrequent bird-cry off in the wilderness.

Well down the mountain, a huge uprooted tree loomed athwart the trail, flanked by several great boulders to the right. He crawled over the obstruction, leaving it unmarred by the axe; for it was not his policy to do any work along the path which would show that a man was using it often enough to justify the task of keeping it clear. Soon he passed from Kearsarge proper to Black Mountain, around which the trail swung on its way to Mission Ridge. The grade ceased to drop and began to ascend. Then it ran fairly level, twisting short around projecting boulders. And just around the next sharp turn he saw what he sought.

A rabbit stood at the side of the path, nibbling at something in the shadow of a young hemlock. He stood broadside on, and his long ears stuck up to catch the slightest sound; but so absorbed in his breakfast was he, and so stealthy had been the hermit's approach, that he knew nothing of the doom impending. Sud-

denly a frightful shock smote him. The earth jerked
out from under him. He struck against a tree,
bounced back, rolled over. Dazedly he sensed a huge
man-animal leaping at him. He got his big hind legs
under him and jumped. The man missed him and fell
sprawling.

He was crippled, was the rabbit, but far from dead.
Though a broken shoulder made one foreleg useless, he
still could hop. Now he hopped headlong away
through the thick brush, which entangled and obstructed and tripped his pursuer. Terror lent wings to
his three remaining legs; and although now and then
the dread thing crashing along behind nearly got him,
always he kept ahead.

Down through the wilderness they plunged. Under
old tree-trunks, rotten these many years, dodged the
quarry, and over them leaped the man. Across little
bogs the rabbit gained while the other floundered in
mud. Now they sped through spaces where the forest
floor was firm and clear of brush, and here the distance
between them rapidly lessened. Again they veered
into undergrowth, and the fleeing coney drew away.
Here and there an uprooted tree loomed, its branches
towering in air and forming a veritable chevaux-de-
frise against Donald while opening free avenue of escape to his prey; and these let the rabbit lengthen his
lead by yards while the man was struggling through.

And so the chase kept on along Black Mountain's
rugged side, neither man nor beast recking where it led.

Great boulders and a frowning ledge started out
from the trees. Between them showed a big black

hole. To the tiring rabbit that dark opening meant concealment and safety, and he headed for it. One last scrambling plunge carried him into the gloom.

Behind him Donald checked himself in mid-stride. The black opening was a doorway. Cabin walls flanked and topped it. He hesitated only an instant. Then he dashed in and yanked the door shut. A minute later the rabbit's mundane troubles all were over.

Holding the warm, limp body over his arm, he stared about the place. It had a small window at a rear corner. The light entering there was dim, as if obstructed by something outside. He stepped over and peered through the dirty pane. The sheer face of the ledge, he found, swung outward behind the house, leaving only a short outlook along the base of the cliff and cutting off much of the light from above. Turning back, he saw another little window—hardly more than a slit —in the door. He threw the door open and examined the interior.

The cabin was small and dirty. Along the side nearest the ledge ran a bunk, whence floated a musty smell suggesting that its blankets were seldom aired. At the foot of the bunk stood a crude table, on which were several coarse, dirty dishes; a glass lamp with a sooty chimney; a jumble of odds and ends shoved against the wall, and—he looked closer—two quart bottles of vile whiskey. Along the walls hung clothing and cooking utensils. Glancing upward, he found that the roof had no ridge, but sloped all one way—away from the cliff. Poles ran from the eaves to the opposite wall, forming an unfloored loft; and on them he saw something resembling a sledge or toboggan. Beside it lay a pair of snowshoes. They were not of the usual pattern, but longer and more narrow; about five feet in length, he judged, and a scant foot wide. In the triangular fore-frame of one shoe the gut had been broken and patched with leather strips. The thought came to him that in damp snow that patch would leave a telltale mark.

Turning toward the door, he observed in the corner behind it a small sheet-iron stove, on which stood a blackened pot or two, and above which were several shelves bearing supplies. Hungrily he glanced over the bags and cans. For a minute he considered taking a few things and leaving some money on the table. But the plan died stillborn. This cabin, so far from the trail, hidden among boulders and under a ledge, had been built primarily for concealment. To take anything, and especially to leave money, would be to notify the owner that his covert had been discovered—and he would not rest until he had hunted down the discoverer. This place could belong to only one man. And Donald, weaponless, was not yet ready to settle accounts with Black Jules.

He peered out, saw nobody, and strode swiftly away until the sheer cliff turned into a timbered hill. Here he halted, at a loss. Jules must have a path somewhere, for man always follows a path; if there be none, he will make one. But at first no sign of a track was discernible; so he got his bearings by the sun, and started toward the far-away point where the chase had begun. And then, having ceased to look for a path, he found it—an elusive track which the feet would follow, though the eye could scarcely see it: a cunning, evasive trail which skirted thick brush instead of cutting straight through, as an honest man's would have done; ever following the line of least resistance, but always working toward the six-foot trail which formed the mountain highway.

Eyes and ears alert, he followed it until he became convinced that it led whither he would go. Then he turned back, determined to take ambush and see what befell. Behind a tree where he could squat and watch both approaches to the cabin he settled down to wait.

For a long time nothing happened. The sun rolled ever higher, filling the cool depths of the forest with a mellow warmth. A wandering bee bumbled aimlessly around the tree, droned away, swirled back again, rested a while on the watcher's hat, made up his mind to go somewhere, and departed like a bullet. An ant crawled up until it reached Don's collar, hesitated, ran back and forth, began to promenade his neck, and was snapped into the air by a hard finger. Otherwise nothing moved. Everywhere brooded the eternal silence, intensified rather than relieved by the occasional timid chirp of an unseen bird.

His squatting position became intolerable, and he rose to his knees. By and by this posture also grew strained, and he sat down. As he did so, somewhere off in the woods rose a dull sound—the muffled roar of rising grouse.

Long minutes dragged away. He turned about and lay flat on his stomach, watching with a somnolent squint. Presently he caught himself drooping forward, half asleep. He jerked his head up; but ere long it began to sink. After all, why wait longer? Jules might be gone all day. He decided to inspect the inside of the cabin a little more closely, to see if any weapons ——

He froze to the ground. With Indian silence, Black Jules had stepped out into the open. He came from the heavy timber down behind his cabin. One fist held a brace of ruffed grouse; the other clutched a rifle. His gaze swung around the limited circumference encompassed by the trees; but it was the perfunctory look which does not expect to see anything new, but which has become habitual. Straight on to the dark doorway he came. There he dropped the birds, leaned the rifle against the wall, and went in.

Don cast a quick look behind him. He had all the information he needed, and it was high time to retreat. Bushes flanked his covert, and would mask his exit if he got beyond them; but he could not go through them from his present position, for the inevitable snap of twigs would betray him. Directly behind, however, stood scrub pines beneath which no bushes grew. He started to turn about. But abruptly he abandoned the effort. Black Jules had reappeared in the doorway, wiping his bearded lips on the back of his hand. The gesture recalled to Don's memory the bottles of whiskey.

The Frenchman stood so long at the door that the motionless watcher hugging the ground began to think he had been seen. He waited for the rifle to leap up

and spit death toward his tree. At length, however,
Jules sat down on the sill and began to clean the
grouse. The prone figure at the rim of the bush did
not move until he was thoroughly absorbed in his task.
Then it began to worm its way backward, dragging the
dead rabbit.

Inch by inch, ever narrowly watching the cabin, feeling for obstructions with outstretched toes, pausing for
minutes at a time, Donald worked back until he pushed
himself through the low-hanging pine boughs. Then,
on hands and knees, he crawled on into the timber until
it was safe to stand and walk. On a long arc he picked
his way back to that elusive path; and once on it, he
made mental notes of rocks, trees, logs, patches of bush
as he went, for he felt that he would come this way
again.

At length there arose before him a conical boulder,
shadowed by two big pines. He stepped around it and
found himself unexpectedly in the trail. Up and down
it he looked, and saw no life. Turning back, he found
that the odd-shaped stone made an ideal lookout post;
for here the trail was visible for some distance on both
sides, and the deep shade of the trees would go far
toward concealing a motionless figure. With a shiver
he thought of the gay little parties of vacationists who
came up this trail in the summer—oftentimes young,
pretty girls; of those sinister bottles in the cabin; of
the lecherous leer he had once seen on the breed's face.
But those girls, reflection told him, always were amply
escorted; and not even Black Jules would dare attempt
an abduction in the face of several men. So he dis-

missed the thought, marked the spot in his memory, and strode away up the trail to retrieve his axe, which he had dropped when he sprang at the rabbit.

As he repassed the conical boulder on his way to the Half-way House, a sudden thought halted him. He had heard the grouse rise down there by the cabin: Jules had killed two of them,—with a rifle: and he had heard no shots! The roar of a grouse's wings, he knew, would be audible for only a short distance, while the bark of a rifle would reverberate far along the silent mountainside.

Old Joe Dale's voice came drifting across the gulf of many silent days: "*Thar warn't no explosion to them shots—jest a kind of a whine, an' the rattle o' the bullit through the leaves.*"

Decidedly, there was something queer about that gun. All the way to the old shack he puzzled over the problem of this noiseless shooting. Now he regretted that he had not looked more closely at the weapon when it leaned against the wall, and wished he could see it again.

He was soon to get his wish.

CHAPTER XXI

PANSY SAYS SOMETHING

Don lost his pipe. A new, clean, sweet-smoking briar it was, just broken in, and a wondrous solace to the hermit in the long, lonely hours which nightly grew longer and more lonely. Discovering its loss late in a day devoted to work on his new roof, he forthwith abandoned his job and hiked out to a small open space on the trail where he had rested and smoked after toting a load of short boards up the mountain. He knew just where he had sat—down beside a cold little spring—and fervently he hoped to find his incense-burner there.

All the way from Andover that pipe had come, over fourteen miles of tortuous country road; for, driven by desperate necessity, the fugitive had emerged at last from his mountain fastness and, on a day of heavy fog, gone out among men to buy food, clothing, blankets, and tobacco. Disguised by his heavy beard and long hair, favored by the blurring fog and by the fact that he had never before been in Andover, he had made the trip without arousing suspicion that he was anything more than a stray wood-chopper,—an impression which he had deliberately encouraged by imitating Joe Dale's down-East dialect while buying his supplies. Now he had plenty of food, new clothing and heavy boots, and snug blankets to keep out the bite of the fall nights. But he would rather have lost all his new outfit than that little, crooked, black-bitted pipe, which had cost a quarter and was worth its weight in gold.

Luck was with him; for down beside the spring he found the missing briar, unharmed. Clutching it in one fist as if afraid it would try to escape him again, he turned and retraced his steps. Just as he emerged from the underbrush two figures stepped out from the trees at the upper end of the open space. He stopped, half-whirled to slip back into the bushes, then halted. They had seen him. Also, at second glance he had seen them more clearly. They were the Dales.

"Wal, by mighty, ef 'tain't Mac!" blurted Joe, as he drew near. Pansy said nothing, but stared as if a ghost had risen from the ground. "Wal, I be tee-totally darned! It's Mac, sartin sure! How be ye, boy? Gorry, but I'm tickled to see ye! Fine crop o' whiskers ye've raised—I cal'late it'd cut about ten ton to the acre. Heh, heh, heh!" He put down his axe, and their hands met.

"Howdy, Joe. Cheer up, Pansy! Did you take me for a gallopin' spook again?"

"H-h-howdy, Don! Yes, I—I did for a minute," she laughed, her eyes still wide and startled. "Whatever are you doin' up here?"

"Living here. And you?"

"Oh, we—we've been up on top for a little picnic." She put out her hand and touched his, as if to assure herself that he was real flesh and blood. " Why, Don, have you been livin' up here all this time? An' you never came near us once, or let us know! "

" Yes," he admitted, somewhat ashamed. " I've been busy—building a house."

" Whar is yer house? " asked Joe bluntly.

" Over yonder." He hesitated. " Want to see it? "

" Gorry, yas, ef 'tain't too fur. We'd oughter be hum now, with the cows waitin'."

" Then come on." He forged ahead, and the Dales followed him along the terrace. As they went, each watched the woods: the girl darting glances here and there, looking for birds or squirrels, and paying not the slightest heed to direction; her father shrewdly " gittin' the lay of the land " by close attention to such objects as would guide him if he wished to come this way again. But even Joe's keen eye failed to detect the little house masked by the pines until the guide stopped with a wave of the hand. " Welcome to our lodge in the wilderness," said he.

" Wal, I be darned! " ejaculated Joe, staring at the doorway beside him. " Ef that'd been a cat 'stead of a cabin, he could of clumb up my laig an' bit my nose off before I'd of knowed he was thar." With that he fell silent again, looking over the stump-studded clearing, the crude fireplace, and the cabin itself.

" Oh, Don! Is *this* where you live! " Pansy's tone was shocked. " Why—why, you ain't even got a whole roof! An' no stove! An' not even a real bed! " She looked aghast at the bare interior.

" Rome wasn't built in a day," quoth he. The allusion was new to her, but she quickly caught its import. Joe, too, nodded.

"Buildin' a cabin all alone ain't no cinch, 'specially when ye have to knock the trees down fust. Considerin' everything, I think ye've done pretty well." He turned away. "We'd like to stop an' visit with ye, boy, but it's gittin' late. I bet that Molly cow is bawlin' her head off right now. Want to walk down a piece with us?"

"Gladly."

So they went back through the timber and swung down the trail. They walked in unusual silence for a time; for somehow Joe's customary flow of conversation seemed to have dried up, and he tramped as if buried in thought. The girl too was oddly quiet, and flitted along ahead with hardly a backward glance at the men marching side by side. Upon Donald crept an uneasy feeling that something was amiss.

"We never mistrusted ye was livin' up here," said Dale at length, awaking from his abstraction. "I figgered ye hadn't gone very fur, though Pansy was afeared ye'd lef' this part o' the country for good. 'He's gone,' she says, 'an' we wunt never see him no more.' But I says, 'Oh, we'll see him agin sometime, when he gits ready.' Still, somehow I didn't think o' ye bein' so clus by us. Yer shoe-lace is ontied, Mac."

His taciturn companion looked down, stooped, and retied the trailing string. Pansy, heedless of the halt, passed on.

"Boy, why did ye leave us so sudden-like?" asked the old man under his breath.

Involuntarily Don's glance went to the girlish figure down ahead. Joe followed the look.

"M-hm. Never mind, lad. I onderstand—mebbe better'n ye think. I knowed ye was squar when I fust looked ye over. Ef I hadn't I never would of left ye alone with my little gal as much as I done."

The keen old eyes that met Don's embarrassed gaze were very kindly. They rounded two turns of the trail before he spoke again.

"Ye hadn't ought to of left us jest the way ye done," he reproved. "Pansy felt awful bad when she read yer note. So did I. An' ye hadn't ought to of lef' that money. We ain't runnin' no hotel or no hosspittle, an' we didn't want none o' yer money—didn't even know ye had any. Howsomever, it's too late to argy about it now, becuz some of it is spent. Pansy sent some to that feller Martin that doctored ye, an' ast him to git her some good books. He sent back a hull box—I cal'late he must of put in a lot of his own, becuz Pansy only sent ten dollars. But anyway, she's got 'em."

"I'm glad she has."

"Yas, so am I. She gits a lot o' comfort out o' readin' 'em. Arter ye went so sudden she was kind o' low an' fidgety, 'specially when night come on an' thar warn't nobody but me to talk to. An' I couldn't tell her a lot o' things she wanted to know—I ain't got the eddication. Besides, she's been lonesome. I wisht ye ——" He bit the sentence off short. After several steps he concluded: "I wisht her mother was alive."

By tacit consent they lengthened their stride and soon caught up with the girl.

At length they came to the bend below which stood
the conical boulder. Here, of all places, Donald
should have become cautious. But it is a trick of
human nature to grow careless when one has passed
a danger-point many times with impunity; and already
he had acquired the habit of casting merely a perfunctory glance at the spot where his enemy's path
ended. So now, with his friends beside him, he
thought of Jules only in a hazy sort of way, and asked:
" Jules hasn't bothered you, has he? "

" No," said the girl. " I guess he thinks he'll get
another lickin' if he comes nigh us."

Joe trudged on, saying nothing; but after a minute
he began to chuckle, a contagious sort of chuckle
which brought smiles to the younger faces. They
were abreast of the stone when Donald jestingly
urged:

" Cheer up, Joe. What's on your mind? "

" Heh, heh, heh! I was jes' thinkin' how mad
Jules'd be ef he knowed ye warn't Pansy's brother
at all. Gorry, I bet he'd spit fire! "

" The last time we saw him he was spittin' blood,"
recalled Pansy; and, for the first time that day, shè
laughed up at Donald as winsomely as the Pansy of
old.

As they passed out of earshot something moved
stealthily in the dense shadow under the pines. A
squat shape sidled around the rock. A venomous face,
distorted with fury, peered down the trail, and its
black-bearded mouth hissed an oath out into the still
air.

"So you lie to me, leetle *diable!* He ees your lovair! An' you laugh at me, at Jules LeNoir! I speet blood, hey? I speet fire, hey? *Oui, ma'mselle*—an' now I speet lead!"

A rifle leaped to his shoulder. Its muzzle covered the defenseless head of the man who had thrashed him. The trigger crept back.

But in the last fraction of a second, when a hair's weight more of pressure would have struck Donald dead in his tracks, cunning caution stayed the half-breed's trigger finger. There were three of them, the monitor whispered; it would not do to kill and leave witnesses alive; if he did, every farmer in the valley would join a posse to hunt him down. Then his murderous hate flared out again. *"Kill 'em both!"* it counseled. *"Kill the old man too—and take the girl!"*

While he hesitated, the trio swung around the next turn.

The gun sank. His thumb uncocked it. Crouching low, he stole down the trail. As he went he cursed in a fierce whisper,—cursed the men and the girl, too, with the vilest oaths his misbegotten brain could conceive. At the bend he sank to hands and knees, spying ahead. Then, satisfied, he slipped into the undergrowth and was gone—gone through the trackless woods, by a route which he alone knew, to wait and watch at the Half-way House clearing.

All unconscious of the dread wood-demon stalking them, the three passed on down the mountain, halting only when Donald stopped in the clearing and extended a farewell hand to each.

" Wunt ye come along with us, boy? " urged Dale. " We'll give ye a darn good supper."

" Yes, do come down an' stay to-night," seconded Pansy. " You can come back here in the mornin', if you want to."

But Don shook his head.

" Not now, folks. Some other time."

" Remember, that's a promise! " said the girl.

" Yas, Mac, that's a promise. Good luck to ye, boy! " Their hands gripped.

" Good-bye, Don. Take care of yourself. If there's —anything we can do for you any time—be sure an' let us know." The girl's parting handclasp, though far less powerful than her father's, was none the less cordial.

" I will. I'm not going to say good-bye, but *au revoir.*"

" What's that? I saw it in a book."

" It's French, and means ' Till we see each other again.' "

" Oh! That is better. *Au—re-voir!* " She pronounced it with difficulty, and ran after her father. But after a few steps she slowed, turned, and saw the lonely man still standing and watching her. She reached a sudden decision.

" Don," she said, low and sweet, " it ain't any of my business, I s'pose, but—but it seems to me you—ought to let your wife know where you are! "

With that she fled.

CHAPTER XXII

THE SILENT GUN

For minutes after Pansy had disappeared over the stone wall Donald stood rooted in his tracks. Let his wife know where he was! How did Pansy know he had a wife? How much more did she know? He took one swift stride forward to pursue her; then turned back, with a hollow laugh. Let his wife—humph! Hardly! Slowly he started back up the trail.

Up under the trees Jules slid away again into the woods, a wicked grin on his face. His wits had cleared, and he was content to let the Dales go for a time. Nor was he minded to kill this man here. He knew where he could get him, up the trail where no-body could know. So he darted away toward his look-out post, and he gloated as he went.

The sun had gone. In the eerie stillness of twilight a subtle sense of impending danger crept into Donald's consciousness. He tried to shake it off, telling himself that he was getting old-womanish, afraid of the dark; but the feeling persisted. Twice he was sure he heard a rustle of leaves off to his right; and though he reasoned that it was the hour for nocturnal animals to come forth, and that there was nothing alarming in the mere movement of a few leaves, the

sound seemed sinister. He wished he had his axe,
which he had left at the cabin. But he wasted no time
in vain regrets, nor did he slow his stride. Only, as he
passed over pebbly patches, he scanned the stones.
Presently he found one which suited him, and picked
it up. Farther on he spied another. With a missile in
each fist he marched on through the gathering dusk.

Off to the right sounded a dull crack—the snap of
a rotten stick. He stopped short. Prowling porcupines would not break sticks like that. Not far ahead
was that danger-point where Jules' path ended. He
looked ahead, behind, and at the tangled forest growth
on both sides. Then he faded away into the brush on
the left.

By a cautious détour he swung around the point
which he had reason to avoid. It was slow, confusing
work, and he did not wish to spend all night at it; so,
though his passage through the bush was soundless,
he cut his arc a bit too short, and returned to the trail
at a point visible from the conical boulder. For a
time he stood behind a tree at the edge, watching.
Beneath the twin pines down the trail nothing moved.
No sound came to him. He stepped boldly out into
the open and started on.

His moccasined foot came down on a mossy, slanting
stone. He slipped, fell to hands and knees. As he
went down a little puff of wind flitted past. A stone
up ahead jumped from the ground.

Powwww! The scream of a glancing bullet split
the stillness.

Instantly he knew the meaning of those rustling

leaves and the broken stick; knew Jules and his silent gun were on murder bent; knew another bullet would follow. Leaping up, he plunged headlong into the bushes.

Swift flight was his only hope. He tore away toward the next bend, where he could emerge unseen and run without hindrance. Another bullet slammed through the thick undergrowth to his left. A third ripped past his right ear, so close that he felt its deadly breath. A fourth rattled among saplings farther to his right. Jules was spraying the bush with lead.

Scratched and bruised from collisions with branches, Don popped out into the trail again. He was beyond the turn. No more bullets searched the woods. But he knew well that Jules had not given up, that he would follow like a bloodhound; and with all speed he dashed for the next bend. As he fled he scanned the sides of the trail, seeking a covert where he might in turn ambush his pursuer—for he had no intention of running any farther than he had to, and he still clutched his two stones.

But the woods offered no place where he could safely lie and wait. So he sprinted on, rounding one turn after another, now and then catching the rattle of stones dislodged by following feet. At every stride hot rage flamed fiercer within him. He was not accustomed to running away from any man.

Athwart his path suddenly loomed the fallen tree. His face lit up. Here he could hide and strike down the assassin as he struggled across. But second thought whispered that Jules, a crafty prowler of the

wilderness, would not rush blindly at an obstruction
so obviously adapted for the last stand of a desperate
man. Halting, he glanced around, and spied the boulders near the roots of the prostrate giant. There the
shadow lay thick. Snatching off his hat, he threw it
down beside the tree, where it lay as if knocked off by
a branch. Then he leaped across the trail, sprang
behind a boulder, and crouched.

He had time to control his rapid breathing before
the enemy arrived; for Jules was shorter of leg and
perhaps of wind, and was burdened with a rifle. Ere
long, however, the rattle of another stone came to the
waiting man's ears. Flying feet thudded faintly on
the earth. Panting, Jules dashed up—and halted short.

The rifle rose half-way, and stopped. The hammer
clicked back. The hoarse breathing ceased while
Jules held it to listen. Then it came again explosively,
as his straining lungs mastered him. Up the trail
ranged his keen gaze, and back to the darksome tree,
and down to the hat. To Donald it seemed that the
half-breed stood an interminable time, watching that
tree with narrowed gaze. Not until his harsh breathing became slow, inaudible respiration did he move.
Then, with the smooth silence of a snake, he crept
forward.

Tense as a dog held in leash, the hidden man watched
that deadly figure advance. His nerves rebelled
against longer inaction, demanded that he rise and
hurl his stone. But he held himself down, steady, motionless, while the assassin worked up closer.

Once Black Jules stopped and flashed a glance at

the boulders. He seemed to hesitate, and Donald barely restrained himself from leaping up and at him. But it was only for an instant. Then, concentrating his attention once more on the tree, the Frenchman resumed his noiseless progress.

With gun almost at his shoulder and finger ready on the trigger, Jules stopped just beyond the tip of an outflung limb.

"Stan' up an' fight, you beeg pansy-picker!" he jeered.

Donald promptly obeyed.

His stone flew low. It missed the black head by more than a foot. But it struck Jules' left arm with paralyzing force. Smitten from an unexpected quarter, he staggered. His gun jumped. Flame spat from its muzzle. The recoil kicked it out of his be-numbed left hand.

A hoarse cry of pain, rage, and shock burst from him. He whirled, trying to pump another cartridge into the barrel. But his stricken arm only fumbled clumsily, and it takes two hands to work a repeating rifle. Before he could even swing up the gun his quarry threw the second stone. It smacked into his face. He went down as if shot.

From his covert Donald leaped forth and snatched the gun from the breed's nerveless hands. Down and back he yanked the lever. The spent shell tinkled on the rocks, and the cold muzzle which had sought his life now menaced the man on the ground. But after a moment it sank, as one good look told Don that his enemy knew nothing of his predicament. Square between the eyes the stone had got him. He was out cold.

The victor laughed grimly. Jules might be dead, and Donald rather hoped he was; but he doubted it, for that beetle-browed skull looked too hard to be broken by anything less than an axe. He watched the sprawling figure for a time, but could perceive no sign of life. So, with a grimace of distaste, he picked up one thick wrist and found the pulse. It still beat. Dropping the arm, he involuntarily wiped his hand on his trousers. Then he stood frowning in perplexity.

Now that he had Jules, he didn't know what to do with him. He knew well enough what Jules would do if their positions were reversed. He remembered Joe Dale's exhortation, delivered weeks ago under darkening skies: " Remember Pansy's been good to ye, an' don't show him no mercy! " And his grim promise: " I won't! " But it is one thing to kill a man in fight; it is another thing to slay him when he lies disarmed and helpless. Disgusted, Donald turned away and sat down on a stone.

If the would-be murderer recovered consciousness, he thought, he might throw the fear of death into him and drive him off the mountain. He would not lift a finger, however, to bring that venomous creature back to life. While he waited he examined the rifle. The secret of its noiseless shooting, he found, was like all other secrets—very simple when explained. In this case the explanation was at the muzzle of the weapon, and was nothing more nor less than a little cylinder, which he recognized as a modern silencing device.

He had thought of that possibility, but had discarded it as unlikely; for it had seemed improbable that this ignorant Canuck would know of up-to-date refinements in gunnery. As he looked at the rifle itself his surprise increased. It was a beautiful gun: far too good for any backwoodsman to own, far too modern and well-equipped for any small-town store to handle. With its walnut shotgun butt, its engraved pistol-grip and fore-end, its three-quarter magazine and graceful half-octagon barrel, its multiple sights and its silencer, this weapon must have been bought in a metropolitan gunshop by a man who knew guns. There was only one way whereby this uncouth brute would ever get such an arm,—to steal it.

Though this was merely a surmise, and though Donald never knew where the rifle came from, his deduction was correct. Prowling through the woods a year before, Jules spied on a couple of city sportsmen, and coveted this weapon. Trailing them to their camp at the end of the day, he lay in the bush for hours, waiting with stoical patience for his chance; and when at length sound slumber had overwhelmed them, he crept into their tent unseen, unheard, and crept out again; and with his booty he slipped away into the trackless forest, leaving no trace behind. For a year his stolen prize had done his bidding. Now it had passed into the hands of a better man, who meant to keep it.

Levering a cartridge from the barrel, Donald examined it and found it to be of a calibre commonly used. He nodded approvingly, for it would be easy to obtain a supply of ammunition. As he closed the breech-bolt he observed that the magazine was well filled. Evidently Jules had reloaded before starting his pursuit. Glowering at the senseless figure by the tree, he wondered anew just what to do with him.

Darker and colder it grew. He was becoming abominably hungry. To kill this beast, he argued, was the only logical solution of his problem: thereby he would protect the Dales, as well as himself. But he could not do it. Killer he might be, but he was no butcher. And Jules showed not the slightest indication of recovering his senses and renewing hostilities.

Hunger finally forced a decision. He would leave the vanquished foe where he was. In the morning he would come back. If Jules died, well and good; if he lived, they would undoubtedly settle accounts later. Rising, he shook himself to drive the chill of the fall night out of his bones; stepped over and picked up his hat; prodded the motionless form with the rifle-butt. Then, hugging his new gun lovingly under one arm, he crawled across the big tree and picked his way up the trail, where dense darkness now reigned.

The next morning Jules was not there.

CHAPTER XXIII

DEAD AND BURIED

VENISON, like gold, is where you find it. You may snoop for days—yes, for weeks—around the places where deer should be, and get nothing. And then again, in the most unlikely spot, a big buck may stalk out within easy pistol-shot—usually astounding you so thoroughly that you forget you have a gun until he is gone again.

So it was with Donald. Taking a vacation from his carpentry, he and his silent gun had prowled the woods all day without spying anything larger than a red squirrel, which he scorned to shoot. Now, his back against a boulder, his rifle across his lap, and his arms folded behind his head, he was lolling back in the semi-obscurity of a scrub pine and puzzling as to the extent of the Dales' knowledge of his affairs, when out into a small opening sauntered a proud young buck.

Scarcely believing his eyes, the hermit sat breathless, nerveless, motionless while the noble animal passed athwart the little glade, his antlered head high and his dainty hoofs stepping silently as those of a phantom. Just at the edge of the bush the deer halted abruptly, turned his head away from the hidden man, and nervously sniffed the air. In that moment Donald came out of his trance. Swiftly he swung up his rifle, sighted behind the shoulder, and fired.

Even as the silent rifle kicked his shoulder in recoil, out rang the sharp crack of another rifle. One convulsive leap—a crash in the bush—the deer was down. Already on his feet and about to dash forward, Don checked himself. Near at hand, off to the left, sounded the clatter of a breech-bolt ejecting an exploded shell and the tinkle of the shell itself as it dropped on a stone.

Very quietly the hermit levered a fresh.cartridge into his own barrel. Came then the noise of a man running through the forest; and out dashed—not Black Jules, as Donald half expected—but a stranger in the hunting garb of a town dweller.

Over the deer he bent. Donald caught a fleeting glimpse of a smooth-shaven face, partly concealed by a soft hat pulled well down. He moved forward, jaw belligerent and rifle ready. This stranger was not going to walk off with his deer—not by a jugful! Straight to the buck he strode before the other heard him and straightened up.

"Huh!" gasped the stranger, startled. Don did not gasp—he stood dumb. The newcomer was Harry Miller.

Hard on the heels of the first shock of surprise came another. The blank stare of astonishment in Harry's eyes gave way to narrow-lidded speculation, but no gleam of recognition dawned. His old chum didn't know him!

He moved to grab Harry's hand, to chaff him on his

loss of memory; but the motion died almost before it started—throttled by the primitive instinct of the hunted man to trust nobody. An instant later the memory of Harry's loyalty shamed him, and he opened his lips to speak. But in that second of indecision Harry became unfriendly. The slight movement of Don's hand, holding his rifle, had not escaped him and had been misunderstood.

"Well?" he drawled aggressively. "What can I do for you?"

A little imp of mischief prompted Donald's answer. When he spoke it was in the gruff vernacular of the backwoodsman he seemed to be.

"What ye doin' with my deer?" he demanded.

"*Your* deer! Say, Mister Man, *I* shot this deer!"

"Nope. Thar's my bullit-hole jes' behind the shoulder."

"Nothing doing! I plugged him in the ——"

He stopped, his mouth open; bent over the buck; looked up again with a frown.

"Guess you're right, at that," he conceded. "He's shot behind the shoulder. My hole ought to be at the base of the neck—he was almost head on to me."

He lifted the antlered head, and both examined the neck. Sure enough, there was another wound, made from the front. They grinned at each other.

"Guess he's *our* deer," said Harry.

"Yep."

"Want to toss up for him?" Harry drew a quarter from a pocket and balanced it on his thumb.

"Nope. I need meat."

" So do I."

Don stroked his beard, eyeing him quizzically.

" Whar ye stayin'? "

" Camping up on top."

" Alone? "

" Right."

" Been here long? "

" Oh, no. I blew in yesterday."

" An' ye need meat already? "

" I sure do. You see, it's like this: I was up here last summer and had to leave quick; so my partner and I cached a lot of grub, and naturally I expected to find it there yesterday. It's all gone. Some sneaking whelp has gobbled it—and I brought only two days' rations. See? "

Don saw, and repressed a grin. He himself was the " sneaking whelp " who had gobbled all that grub.

" Tell ye what," he suggested. " We're pardners on this deer. I'm livin' up nigh the top. D'ye want to move yer camp an' bunk in with me a while? I've got plenty o' grub—canned stuff and sech-like. What say? "

Harry looked him over. The hermit almost laughed outright, perceiving that he was being inspected from the standpoint of cleanliness.

" I'm game," decided Harry. " But I give you fair warning, partner, I have a whale of an appetite."

" Guess I can fill ye up. Come on."

Stooping, he heaved the buck up on his shoulders. Harry fell in behind, and through the gathering dusk they marched to the cabin.

" This here is my hangout," twanged the hermit. " 'Tain't much to look at, but it's new and clean." Then he grinned and threw off his hat. " And you're mighty welcome, Harry," he added in his normal tone.

Harry's jaw sagged and his eyes bulged. Recognition, amazement, incredulity chased across his face. Wordless, he stared for minutes. Then a frown grew on his brow, and his mouth tightened.

" Thanks. How, do you happen to know my name? " It was Don's turn to stare, and he did.

" Evidently I've changed considerably," he answered, at length. " Mean to say you don't know Don King? "

" I *knew* Don King," said Harry. " Yes, I knew him well—poor devil! And I'll admit that you bear a striking resemblance to him, in spite of your beard. But you can't tell me you're Don and get away with it. What's your game, Mister Man? "

Don blinked helplessly at him.

" You might put that stuff over on me if it weren't for one little thing," added Harry. " That is that Don King is dead."

At this astounding news the hermit gaped.

" Who says—how did—I'm not! " he stuttered.

" Oh, cut it out! Don King is dead, I tell you! I went to his funeral! Now just what do *you* know about poor old Don, anyway? "

" The principal thing I know about Don is that I'm Don," asserted the other. " Would you mind telling me what I died of? "

The shadow of a smile twitched Harry's mouth.

" Oh, all right, go on kidding yourself, if you get

any fun out of it. Don was killed three months ago
by a train at Worcester, Massachusetts—and ground
all to pieces on the track."

"Ground to pieces," repeated Don, dully. "Three
months ago. Hm!" Then, after a pause: "See here,
Harry. This is a ghastly joke. It seems I have to
convince you. Listen:

"We went home because Wightman was sick. I
killed Duncan." Harry started. "You got me out of
town. I chucked my gun into a swamp. Gas gave out
near New Haven, and I left you. I gave you the whippoorwill call ——"

Harry's rifle slipped from his fist and thumped on
the ground.

"Holy—jumping—Judas—Priest!" he gasped.
"It's true! Nobody else could know ——"

Abruptly he sat down on a stump; tugged at his
collar as if it choked him; jumped up again, seized
Don's right hand, and wrung it.

"Well, dog-gone your old hide!" he blurted.
"You're alive! No, confound it, you can't be alive! I
saw your mangled remains—I shipped 'em to Brooklyn
—I saw you buried! And now here you are, hard as
nails and covered with whiskers!"

"There's a huge mistake somewhere, Harry. You
say I was cut to pieces. I came through Worcester
on my way up here, but I didn't leave any chunks of
myself on the track."

"That's just exactly what you did, though. That's
all there was left of you—chunks! You were the
worst mangled-up corpse I ever saw, and I've seen a

few tough ones. You had absolutely no face, and
hardly any head; and half a dozen trains must have
passed over you between dark and daylight. The
trackmen had to pick you up in a basket."

" Then how did you identify me? "

" By your clothes and your watch. That's all that
saved you from Potter's Field. After the authorities
noticed who your tailor was and what a corking good
watch you carried they figured you must be somebody
worth looking up. So it wasn't long before I got onto
it, and I dropped everything and went and had a look
at you—and I don't mind telling you that the sight
gave me a fierce jolt. Now who the deuce was wearing your clothes and toting your watch? And say,
where did you get that scar over your eye? You
never had that when I knew you."

" Great guns! " muttered Don. In a flash he saw
the whole thing. The fight with the two yeggs in the
cemetery—the foul knockout—the awakening, stripped
and bleeding from Bull's vindictive boot—all these
came back. The larger thug, he remembered, was
big enough to wear his clothing comfortably. Evidently Joel Morgan's bullet had hit the " little rat,"
and the big fellow had gone his way to meet a far more
horrid death under crushing wheels. And all the time
he had been leading his furtive existence up here in
the wilds he had been free to walk unsuspected among
men! He laughed mirthlessly. Then, briefly, he explained.

" I see," nodded Harry when he had finished. " And
I certainly have balled things up for fair. And yet,"

defensively, "what was I to think? You told me you were going to ride freights. You were a rank amateur as a hobo, and stood a mighty good chance of falling under the wheels. You probably wouldn't travel as fast as an experienced tramp, and might easily be around Worcester about that time. And it wasn't to be expected that somebody else would be wearing your clothes—and your watch. Confound you, it's largely your own fault! Why under heaven didn't you drop me a line just to let me know you were safe? I asked you to."

"I know it, old man. Sorry I couldn't. Things didn't break right, that's all. I've had no chance."

Again, slowly, Harry nodded. Donald did not explain just why "things didn't break right," and his old chum did not ask. For some time they stared silently at nothing, each thinking of past and future. Then Harry awoke to the fact that darkness was almost on them. He bounced up.

"Say, I'm going up to the tent and wrastle my blankets down here," he announced. "I need a walk, anyhow. I'm dizzy!" Forthwith he turned and tramped away toward the trail, leaving his forgotten rifle on the ground. Donald turned mechanically toward his cabin, brought out food, built a fire among the stones which served as stove and fireplace, and cooked the evening meal. When Harry returned with blanket-roll and a glaring gas lamp he found his supper smoking hot.

Two questions were hammering at Don's mind. He waited, hoping Harry would answer them unasked; but the latter devoted himself whole-heartedly to the work of eating, making no remarks whatever. So finally Donald inquired:

" How about my—er—widow? "

" Can't tell you much about her. Haven't seen her since your funeral. She was—well, very cool and self-possessed then."

Don nodded.

"All right. Now tell me this: Why wasn't there an uproar in the papers about Duncan's death? "

Harry hesitated and looked at him pityingly.

" Well, I suppose I have to spring it," he said. " I wanted to give you time to assimilate the first shock before handing you another. Now I'm going to slip you a swift jolt. Are you all set? Then here it comes:

" You didn't kill Duncan! "

Donald sat stunned. From his lean, tanned face the color receded. Then it flowed again in angry red.

" Harry, you lie! " he charged hoarsely.

" Thanks. I expected something like that. But the fact remains: you didn't kill him. Oh yes, I know you shot him—slammed a big slug clear through him. But you shot a little high, Don—about half an inch too high. What position was he in when you fired? "

" Sitting on the edge of his bed. Leaning forward."

" Uh-huh. And he fell forward, I suppose, and you saw the hole in his back and thought you'd got him in the heart; and you had to beat it right fast, and didn't stop to turn him over. Now here's what happened. Your bullet got him low in the throat and went through

him on a downward slant. Looking at his back, anybody would say he was another little job for the un-
dertaker. He wasn't far from it, at that, for the lead
messed up his cosmos quite considerable. But right
after you flitted from the festive scene some of the
neighbors came bustling in and rushed him to the hospital, along with a chap from across the hall. Say,
how did the other fellow fit into the plot of this piece?
He was knocked cold."

"The man across the hall? He jumped me just as
I was getting away. I smashed him in the jaw."

"Well, he hit the floor or the wall or something so
hard that he got concussion of the brain. You sure did
clean up everybody in sight while you were there. He
came around all right in time, but he was so hazy in
his recollection of what you looked like that he was no
aid to the police.

"As for Duncan—well, you didn't kill him, Don, but
you might as well. You did a lot more to him than
blow a hole through him. You broke him. You
smashed him like a little boy's balloon. You knocked
the legs out from under him and threw him into a pit
he'd dug himself. He's done, through, down and out.
And to a man who loves power as he does, that's worse
than death.

"Here's how it worked out: Duncan's had barrels
of money, and he used a lot of it in politics. Not that
he wanted to hold office—that was too slow for him.
What he wanted was power to do whatever he pleased,
without regard to anybody's laws. This is a decidedly
unprofessional remark for me to make, but it's true: if

you slip plenty of money to the right people you can get away with almost anything in New York—for a while. And he made it his business to keep in with the Powers.

" But it was costing him a huge amount to keep up with the game he was playing, and besides, he was the kind that always wants more money; so he was bucking Wall Street hard.   He was a clever stock gambler, and I happen to know he's made some scandalous hauls in the Street.   But just when you went to see him he had a whale of a big pot on the fire, and it needed some mighty careful watching to keep it from boiling over. And then you and your six-gun tear loose and spill the beans.

" He goes to the hospital and stays there for weeks with Old Man Death roosting on his footboard and making faces at him.   In the meantime the aforesaid pot boils over with a loud, steamy hiss.   Immediately several other hunks of fat which he's had up in the air come tumbling into the fire.   And when he's able to sit up and take notice again, about all he's got left is a burned smell.

" The Powers have no use for a dead one.   And with most of his money gone—pop! goes his pull; and he becomes a very ordinary chap with a fine bunch of enemies who haven't been able to bite back so far, but have been keeping their teeth sharp and waiting. What's more, it wasn't alone the sudden cramp in the middle of his bank-roll that put him on the toboggan. He'd been rolling too high and wide to suit some of the big chiefs—though they're not squeamish.   But just at

this auspicious moment one of his chickens came home
to roost. It was a girl whom he'd thrown aside, as
he's done to others. She happened to be a rather distant relative of somebody very high up; and now she
raised a squawk which stirred up the political gun
aforementioned, and he greased the skids for Duncan's
slide into the ditch, while his genial confrères planted
the boot under Duncan's ear while he was going down.

"He's dropped out of sight lately—cleaned up what
he could from his financial mess and ducked. He
hasn't left town, though. New York is the best town
in the world to hide in, and he's simply submerged himself somewhere. With his ugly disposition, and the
enemies he's got, I wouldn't be a bit surprised to hear
of his being found dead some morning with some East
Side gunman's bullets in him.

"I forgot to say he never squealed on you. He's
vindictive enough, but it probably went against his
swollen pride to admit that he got what was coming to
him for chasing another man's wife. He only said he
surprised a burglar in his rooms. Nobody cared much,
anyhow, as long as he was busted and discredited. So,
old-timer, you can go back to town any time."

Don's face was working. Fists clenched, he leaped
up.

"He's alive!" he choked. "The reptile I killed is
alive! And I'm dead and buried!"

CHAPTER XXIV

PANSIES ARE THOUGHTS

DAWN found Donald sleepless and haggard. All night long he had tossed and turned, wincing under the sharp prods of memory and wrestling with the problem of his future action. Now, as the light of another day stole through the formless shadows of night, he came back to the solid reality of the present. He would take things as they came, and the first thing to come was the work of getting breakfast. Wherefore he arose and started the morning fire.

Harry awoke, yawned, blinked at his comrade's lined face, told him he looked rotten, and urged him to go soak his head. The advice was good, and Don followed it. He returned from the bathing pool considerably freshened but uncommunicative, and while the food cooked he said never a word.

"Why so pensive, little one?" chaffed Harry.

"Thinking."

"Bad business. Thinking at meal-time is contrary to Hoyle and Holy Writ. It draws all the blood away from your tummy into your feet, where your brains are, and your grub doesn't assimilate worth a whoop. Cut it out."

The hermit smiled, but remained silent throughout

the meal. Harry, too, became thoughtful, and nothing more was said until they had finished and lit their pipes. Then they stared at each other.

" Don, you husky ghost, you're in the middle of a tangled web," opined Harry. " What are you going to do? "

" Stay dead."

" Uh-huh. I thought maybe you'd decide that way. But still, there's more than one way of looking at it. You've got to think of others besides yourself, even if the others have slipped you a raw deal. Otherwise the tangle may get worse than ever. For instance, suppose your—er—widow should marry again."

" Marry whom? "

" Duncan."

" Humph! No chance of that."

" Don't be too sure. They were very good friends a few years back, you know; he was crazy about her."

Blank astonishment showed in the other's face.

" That's news to me."

" Yes? I wondered whether you knew it. Sometimes a fellow doesn't know as much about his own wife as other folks do. There's no good reason why she shouldn't have told you about him, as far as I can see; for it seems to have been a sort of boy-and-girl affair, and Duncan wasn't the merciless rotter then that he is now. In fact, they say he was a pretty decent chap until she threw him over. Then he let go all holds and hit up a dizzy pace with the cabaret bunch that made even the old rounders sit up and watch his smoke. He got onto himself after a while and steadied down—some. But he's been a bear-cat with the women ever since."

Slowly Don puffed at his pipe.

"Wonder why I never heard of this," he muttered.

"Well, you couldn't hear it from me, because I just recently learned it myself. And why she never said anything about it I can't say. Maybe she thought you'd be jealous, or —— Oh, well, who knows the workings of a woman's mind? I'm sure I don't. The question remains—what are you going to do?"

For some time Donald did not answer. At length he arose, knocked the dead ash from his pipe, and twitched his shoulders as if to dislodge a burden.

"I'll cross no bridges until I come to them. The first thing before me is to go down into the valley and square myself."

Harry looked puzzled.

"There are an old man and a girl down under the mountain, Harry, who were my friends when I most needed friends. They found me a wreck, and they gave me a new strength and a new faith. Now I'm going down there and tell them who I am. Come on."

Side by side they swung down the mountain, Donald bearing a huge chunk of venison slung on his back, and both carrying their rifles.

"Don't these folks even know your name, Don?"

"No. Only an alias." A moment later he added: "Perhaps I'm wrong about that. Pansy seems to know a good deal about me, though I don't know where she got it."

"Pansy, eh? Pretty name. Let's see, pansies are for thoughts—and heart's-ease. Does it fit?"

"Perfectly. She has grown up among the fields like a flower, and she's sweet and unspoiled and true blue."

Whereat Harry covertly studied him from the corner of his eye and slightly raised his brows. But he said no more, and they tramped on wordless, each busy with his thoughts.

Rounding the turn in the sandy road beyond which lay the Dale homestead, they spied Joe toiling away at the woodpile. As they advanced he straightened up to rest a moment; then, raising his hand to shield his eyes from the bright morning sun, peered fixedly at them. Don flourished an arm, and the old man's maimed wrist rose in recognition. As he moved to meet them Donald noted that he moved but slowly and limped a little.

"Howdy, Mac!" he welcomed them as they strode into the yard. "Whar's the army goin'?"

"The Kearsarge Reserves have been called out to shoot a chipmunk, named Rob Clarke," jested Donald, reaching for his hand.

"Heh, heh, heh! By gorry, ye hit the nail squar on the head. Rob does look like a chipmunk—darned ef he don't act like a chipm—ouch! Go easy, boy! Squeeze my hand all ye like, but don't shake it too hard. My j'ints are full of roomytiz. I'm a-gittin' old, Mac."

"Old? Nonsense! I'll bet you could put me on my back right now."

"Mebbe so. That is, ef I could sneak up behind ye

with a sledge-hammer when ye warn't lookin'. I wouldn't want to tackle the job no other way." His gaze strayed curiously to Harry.

"Joe, this is my friend Harry Miller. Harry—Joe Dale."

He emphasized the word "friend," and Joe grinned and nodded.

"Whar ye from, Mister Miller?"

Before Harry could answer there came an interruption. The door flew open and Pansy came running out.

"Don! Where ever did you drop from so early in the mornin'? I'd begun to think we never would see you down here again!"

The men turned as one: her father with an indulgent grin, Donald with hand outstretched, Harry with eyes full of interest. Straight to Donald she sped, disregarding his hand; drew his face down—and kissed him!

Joe was mildly surprised. Donald was utterly astonished. Harry, seeing that his chum was taken aback by the unexpected caress, snickered quite audibly. The sound drew Pansy's eyes to him, and she blushed but gave him a defiant look as if to say, "Well, it's nothing to *you!*" At this he pulled a mock-solemn face that made her giggle.

"Ye're lookin' fine, Mac," remarked Joe, coming to the rescue of his embarrassed foster-son. "When we see ye last ye looked sort of pickid, but ye've filled out some sence then. Tryin' to fat up for the winter like a b'ar?"

"If I'm putting on weight it's because I get enough meat now," said Don, shaking his rifle. "I've brought some down to you." He unslung his burden. "Pansy, this is my friend Harry Miller."

"Say!" protested Harry. "Just because I'm beefy you needn't introduce me as a piece of meat."

"I didn't!"

"You sure did. 'I've brought some meat down to you—meet my friend Miller.' Why didn't you go the whole distance and say 'Miller, the animated pork-chop,' or something like that? You might as well."

"Oh, go drown yourself!" growled the badgered Don. "Never mind him, folks—he's not responsible. I don't know how he manages to get along in New York, now that I'm not there to protect him."

"Oh! So you knew each other in New York?" asked Pansy.

"He was my best chum before I came up here and changed my name," Donald told her.

"Changed your name! Oh, Don, you've quit pretendin'! I'm so glad! We knew you must be all right, but ——"

"But I acted like a bank-robber?"

"Yes, you did! Always keepin' out of sight, an' givin' us a name that we knew wasn't so."

"I had reason to. I shot a man, and I thought he was dead. But he isn't."

Joe gave a startled grunt. Pansy shrank away, appalled.

"You—you shot a man?"

Grim-faced, he nodded.

" Didn't you know it? "

" Mercy, no! We—we knew you were playin' dead, but ——" Wide-eyed, she stood meeting his steady gaze. Her color came back; and loyally she declared: " Well, if you shot him he needed to be shot! "

Joe gave another grunt, signifying approval. Harry nodded decisively, and the Dales did not miss this confirmation of their own conviction. Both gave him a friendly mile.

" Le's git in whar we can set down an' rest our laigs," suggested Joe. " Pansy, git some doughnuts an' coffee for the boys."

Inside the warm kitchen Dale glanced curiously at the rifle which Donald stood in a corner.

" Whar'd ye git the gun, Mac? "

" Black Jules."

The farmer blinked, stared, frowned in puzzlement. Then his face lit up.

" Gorry, boy, have ye found his hole? Is that the gun that shoots without no noise? Wal, by mighty! Whar's his house? "

" On Black Mountain."

" Shucks, I knowed that. Whar'bouts on Black Mountain? "

" Can't tell you exactly. I can find it, but I can't describe the way so that anybody else could follow it. The cabin's away off in the woods, under a ledge."

" An' ye've got his gun! " Dale stared long at the odd muzzle. Then, shrewdly watching Don, he opined: " Wal, we ain't seen Jules in a long time. I cal'late he must of died."

"Not yet, Joe," laughed Donald, reading his thought. " His head's too hard."

Whereupon he told of his fight with Jules, omitting no detail. Harry listened as eagerly as the others, but he did not keep his gaze fastened on the narrator's face as the Dales did. Instead, he shrewdly watched the varying expressions of the girl, and in them he read much. He saw her loathing for the half-breed; her terror when his comrade's life was menaced; her joy when Jules was struck down, and a tiny touch of apparent regret that the black-bearded prowler still lived. From these he drew a very accurate conclusion as to the reason for the enmity between the two hermits of the mountain; but he took care not to reveal his thoughts. As for Joe, he forgot to eat or drink, and sat with a hunk of doughnut bulging his cheek. When the tale was done he bolted the chunk whole and washed it down with a noisy gulp of coffee.

"Gosh-amighty, that was a narrer squeak!" he cried. "I wisht ye'd busted his head for good with that stun! But say, Mac, that puts me in mind o' suthin'. Ye remember them two pust-office robbers ye fit with? Wal, the feller that Joel Morgan shot has been found."

" The little rat-face? " asked Don eagerly.

" Wal, yas, he was the little feller—I dunno about his face, becuz he didn't have much face left when they found him. He was layin' nigh the water in a big ole pasture down below the village, on t'other side o' the river, whar nobody goes much. A couple o' Warner fellers was comin' up through thar with some pat-

tridges they'd shot, an' their dawg found this desper-
aydo under some bushes, whar he'd laid an' died. The
coroner found Joel's bullit in the ree-mains. So that
settles one o' them robbers. T'other one must of got
away."

Donald and Harry glanced at each other, but neither
of them enlightened their host as to what had become
of " t'other one." Then Pansy spoke.

" Don, you said you'd changed your name. What's
your really-truly name? "

" Donald Warren King, at your service." He
placed a hand on his heart and made a grandiloquent
bow. She dimpled.

" I knew it anyway, but I wanted to see if you'd fib
again. You ain't trusted us as much as you might."
The deep blue eyes reproached him. " But now—I'll
show you somethin'."

With that she rose and climbed the stairs to her
room. Soon she was back with a newspaper page,
folded so that one column alone showed—a column
with a cut well toward the top.

" There you are, Mister Donald Warren King
Walter Macdonald! It's an awful good picture of you
before you covered your face with whiskers."

It was. He instantly recognized the photograph as
one which had been taken only a couple of months before he fled New York. His eye darted to the top of
the column, where the top-head announced:

" SILENT " KING,
FAMOUS ATHLETE,
KILLED BY TRAIN.

With mingled feelings he read his own " obit." It was the usual type of New York news story, printed on an inside page, and telling of the finding of his body at Worcester. It touched on his camping trip to New Hampshire; said he had undoubtedly fallen from a moving train; sketched his life, with especial reference to his athletic prowess, his entrance into business in New York, and his marriage to " Miss Ruth Delancey, niece of Mrs. Gordon Delancey, and one of the most beautiful and popular members of the younger set." The concluding sentence made his lip curl.

> " Mrs. King is prostrated by the news of her husband's death, and could not be seen by newspaper men to-day."

An effective way of dodging the reporters and their questions, he thought. And this was how Pansy had learned he was married. This was why, stirred by sympathy for that unknown woman, she had told him he ought to let his wife know where he was. Again he glanced over the column of cold black printers' ink, and sighed as he recalled how perturbed he had been by Pansy's parting advice on the mountain; how he had dodged and hidden when the world never knew he had shot a man—and all because he lacked the knowledge which this newspaper article would have given him. The thing was grotesque. The goddess Clotho, spinning his thread of life, had tangled it into a wondrous snarl.

" Ye'll eat dinner with us, o' course, Mister Miller," said Joe, breaking the silence.

"I certainly will, thank you," was Harry's instant assent. "Miss Dale's doughnuts and coffee have put a razor edge on my appetite. Besides, for the past few hours I've been forced to subsist on the cooking furnished by our whiskered friend yonder, and if you knew what an atrocious cook he is ——" Leaving the sentence unfinished, he rolled up his eyes and assumed an expression of unutterable woe.

Joe chuckled. Pansy shot an amused glance at Donald. He smiled faintly and rose.

"Hoboes seeking hand-outs must work for them," he declared. Forthwith he stalked out to the woodpile and swiftly began splitting wood. Harry followed, got another axe from the barn, and attempted to make a creditable showing at work with which he was unfamiliar. Joe limped slowly out, found his tools in use, and stood puffing reflectively at his pipe and watching with amusement the "city feller's" awkwardness with an axe.

None of the three spoke. Each was thinking. Donald's thoughts were a complex of past events and future possibilities. Joe ruminated on Black Jules and speculated on Miller. And Harry, slugging manfully away at hardwood knots, said to himself:

"Pansies are thoughts—and heart's-ease. If that little lady would kiss me as she did Don, I'd forget I ever had a worry. He's a fool for luck, and he doesn't know it. Ho-hum. Well, we shall see."

CHAPTER XXV

THE SNOW LADY

OVER the mountain hovered the sullen gray skies of mid-November. Among the pines, whose furry coat changed not with the seasons, the hardwood trees stood gaunt and bare, stretching their naked arms upward to the forbidding heavens as if begging for warmth from the south-swinging sun. Gone was the crisp, racy atmosphere of October, when snappy days had been interspersed with others when it seemed that Summer had hesitated and turned back toward her northern hills. Now the air held the brutish cold of the coming winter, and the leaden clouds were heavy with the menace of snow.

Harry was going home. For a month now he had stayed on, toiling with zest toward the completion of the cabin. When Donald suggested that he was neglecting the hunting for which he had come, he replied:

"Oh, forget it! I didn't come up here for hunting so much as to play around in the air and fill my system plumb full of ozone. Besides, when I was a kid I never had a chance to build a house out in the woods. I always wanted to, but I was a city kid and there were no woods handy, and my folks wouldn't have let me **do** it anyhow. So now I'm getting my revenge. Out of my way, Whiskers, before I bounce a log off your bean!"

So Donald, recognizing the healthy craving to create which exists in every live man's soul, and amused by the thought of what some of Harry's snobbish acquaintances in town would say if they could see him laboring as a wilderness carpenter, had accepted his aid; and now the cabin was complete. In the evenings they sat by the fireplace, smoking, thinking, watching the flames, in that silent communion which only old chums know. Sometimes they talked in serious vein of Donald's future—or, rather, Harry talked and Donald listened. But no urging or argument by Harry could induce him to return to New York. He was immovable as the granite mountain on which he lived. His city life lay behind him, and behind him it should stay.

And now Harry was going. Silently he rolled his pack, and silently Donald watched him. When he saw that Harry was leaving his blankets and gas lantern he protested.

"Oh, I might come back again," suggested Harry. "Keep 'em for me. I've no use for them in town, and I'm not going to tote them to the railroad. Besides, if you should have visitors they'd come in handy."

Something in his tone made his host look oddly at him; but before he could ask a question Harry swung the pack to his shoulders, picked up his rifle, and extended his hand.

"So long," he said simply.

" Not yet," replied Donald. With his own rifle in
one fist he accompanied his partner out to the trail, and
thence on down the mountain. And all the way they
said never a word.

At the end of the trail, where the sandy hill road to
the village began, they halted.

" Don," said Harry, looking him square in the eye,
" there's one thing that has to be done, in simple jus-
tice. If you won't do it I will—whether you like it or
not."

" What is it? "

" Let your wife know you're alive."

Donald frowned; but after a moment he nodded.

" You're right," he conceded.

Their right hands met, wrung, and parted. Harry
tramped away toward the far-off rush and roar and
swirling life of Town. Donald, once more a hermit,
turned and slowly plodded up the silent trail toward his
lonely cabin.

The snow held off. Driven by restlessness, loneliness, and consciousness that his supply of firewood was
none too generous, the hermit became once more a
wood-chopper. For two days he swung the axe from
cold gray dawn to cold gray twilight. On the third
day the blank grayness of the skies thinned and a sickly
sun showed its blurred face at intervals; and Don laid
aside his axe, trudged down to the Warner " deepo,"
and claimed a pair of snowshoes, new moccasins, and
several boxes of cartridges which Harry had promised
to send him from Manchester. Not only that, but he

walked coolly into the village barber shop and had his hair and beard trimmed. Feeling curiously chilly about neck and ears after the shearing of his shaggy mane, he tramped back to the mountain.

The next day he chopped more wood—and tired of it. That night, standing at the door and feeling the threat of the snow which still had not come, he reached a grim decision. It was time to go hunting again; time to rout a certain black-bearded beast out of his dingy lair on Black Mountain.

By firelight he examined the silent gun which once had sought his life; oiled the working parts sparingly to insure smoothness and speed of action; tested the feed again and again to see if a cartridge would jam; made sure that the rifling was spotless and the sights at pointblank range. Satisfied, he loaded it and went to bed.

Contrary to his custom, he slept very late in the morning. Twice he awoke, and twice a dull, sodden slumber overpowered him. When at last he arose he found himself burdened with a heavy cold, due to that untimely hair-cut. Breakfast tasted like chips, and he left it half eaten. Disgusted, dispirited, he felt little like faring forth on a quest where the margin between life and death might be thin as an eyelash. But the sky told him that the coming of the snow was hard at hand, and that when it did come it would stop his hunting for days. So at last, shod in his silent moccasins and armed with his silent rifle, he slipped away toward the trail.

Over the mountain hung a breathless hush. Accustomed though he was to the everlasting silence of the high places, Donald felt this sinister stillness. The stark trees, the naked bushes, the sullen pines, all seemed to await with dread the onslaught of winter. The birds were gone or silent. The beasts had sought their dens. He alone moved in a frozen world. As he passed down the trail his nerves reacted to the threat in the air. He became alert, and at every bend in the path he paused to reconnoiter.

Half-way down to the conical boulder, peering around a turn, he stopped dead. Down ahead the trail ran almost straight for fifty yards or more, dropping at a gentle grade, flanked by the inscrutable pines. And some twenty yards before him, alone in the silent solitudes, walked a woman!

She was no woman of the countryside—her dress proclaimed that. All in white she was, a soft whiteness like that of new-fallen snow. Drifting down that lonely forest trail amid the eerie stillness foreboding the storm, she seemed the daughter of the Snow King, who had preceded her blustering father from the far Northland and now awaited the coming of his whirling host of snowflakes.

Amazed, his grim mission forgotten, Donald stood watching her as she passed on toward the next turn. He never thought of calling to her, or of stepping out into the open and following; and it was well for him that he did not.

She seemed to be scanning both sides of the path, but not once did she glance behind her. At length she reached the bend. A moment more, and she would have faded away among the trees. But just then, from the apparently empty pines beside the trail ——

Out stepped Black Jules.

He blocked her path. She stopped. The breed's teeth flashed across his black beard in a wide grin, and he spoke. After a moment she answered, and a short conversation ensued which the hidden watcher could not hear. Then Jules grinned again, nodded violently, and pointed down the trail. He stepped aside to let her pass. Don observed that his enemy had obtained another rifle.

She stood as if irresolute. They made a strange contrast, that pair—the Snow Lady and Jules the Black. Donald stirred uneasily, smitten by an impulse to interfere; for he sensed that Jules was, as usual, up to something damnable. But still he remained motionless, waiting for the situation to resolve itself more clearly. And speedily it did.

The white figure stepped back. Instantly Jules became voluble and vehement, pointing again down around the bend. A decided gesture of refusal was her reply, and she took another backward step. At that the half-breed dropped his mask. His voice rang loud and threatening:

"You go, *ma'mselle!* An' you go queeck!"

She turned to run back up the mountain. Black Jules' rifle dropped in the trail. Like a panther he sprang at her. And up at the bend Donald went into action.

Out from his covert he sprang—and hesitated. The girl was making a frenzied fight to escape. To shoot

at those struggling figures fifty yards away might mean
her death; but in the few seconds it would take him to
run down the uneven trail Jules might hurt her badly.
He did the quickest thing—yelled at them and slammed
a bullet through the timber well to one side of the path.

Even as he fired Jules tripped the girl and flung her
down. As that furious yell and the clatter of the
bullet smote his ears he whirled and stared up the
mountain. For an instant he stood motionless above
the prostrate woman. In that instant Don drew a
quick bead on his head and shot again.

Jules dropped on his face.

Donald leaped down the trail, exulting. Jules was
down! And tough though his head might be, that
bullet must have finished him. But—just as Donald
swung into top speed, up popped Jules. With one
sweep of the arm he grabbed his rifle. A dive into the
bush, and he was gone.

Donald stopped so suddenly that he skidded. A
leap, a crash of broken twigs, and he too was in the
bush. And none too soon, for as he flung himself
down a bullet ripped along the trail and the *whang* of
Jules' gun smashed the stillness. Squirming to a small
boulder, Don took another chance—stuck out his head,
flashed one glance down the path, and ducked again.
He had seen two things—a thin haze of smoke under a
pine; the woman sitting up and staring fearfully
around her.

"Get out of the trail!" shouted Don. "Move over
to this side!"

An instant of silence. Then he heard a crackle of

twigs, and knew she had moved out of the line of fire.

Whang! spoke the enemy's black-powder gun. With the report came a sudden eruption of dead leaves close beside Donald—perilously close. Jules had seen his head or marked down his voice. A cold fury seized him. He jammed two more cartridges into the receiver, giving him a full gun. Then he got cautiously to his knees, aimed through the brush at the pine where the blue haze hung, and fired as fast as he could work the lever.

Bullet after bullet tore into that tree and around it until his rifle was empty. Then he threw himself down and reloaded; rose again and belched another magazine-full of leaden death into the breed's position. And never a shot came back.

The sudden silence down there might mean two things: that Jules was killed, or that he was sitting tight and holding his fire. Common sense suddenly whispered to Don that he was not a walking arsenal, and he must be near the end of his string of cartridges. He dived a hand into his pockets and found only two bullets left.

It must be slow, sure work now. Wondering what game Jules was playing, he slipped his two remaining cartridges into the weapon. Then he waited, listening.

Up the bullet-swept trail came the voice of the Snow Lady:

" He's gone! "

" Gone where? " he asked blankly.

" I—I don't know. He crawled away."

Springing up, he rushed the enemy's position. As he sprinted down the open space he glimpsed the woman rising among the bushes, where she had been lying flat while the duel raged; but he paid no more attention to her than to a birch stump. Straight for the pine he dashed, and found that she had spoken truth. The big trunk was gashed and grooved by bullets, but the space behind it was empty. Swiftly he scanned the forest, and saw no living thing. Then he stooped and inspected the ground behind the tree. Two empty shells lay where they had been flung by the ejector; that was all. Not a drop of blood stained the forest floor. Jules had escaped unharmed.

He saw it all now. The French-Indian's fall in the trail had been but a ruse, craftily conceived and instantly executed. His two shots had been meant to kill; but he had no stomach for a fair-and-square gun-duel, and when the first hurricane of lead ceased he had fled into the trackless woods.

For the moment Donald utterly forgot the woman. He had started out to clean up Jules, and he had two cartridges left. Grim-faced, he stepped out into the trail again and started for the conical boulder where the path to his enemy's cabin began.

Behind him rang a startled cry.

" Please don't leave me here alone! "

Swift feet rushed to overtake him.

" Confound it! " he muttered, slowing his stride.

" Donald! Please wait! "

He wheeled.

" Ruth! " he said hoarsely. " You! "

"Yes, Donald, it is I. And—I'm terribly tired, and —I'm afraid." Pale, trembling, she glanced at the forest where Jules had disappeared. "Oh, take me out of this horrible place!"

"Brace up! There's no danger now. How did you get here?"

"I came up in a carriage from Warner this morning."

"All right. I'll take you back to the carriage."

"But—but it's gone! Hours ago!"

"Great guns!" he groaned. "You came up here alone, with a blizzard coming on, and sent your driver back?"

"It was foolish," she admitted. "But I'd never been up this side of the mountain before, and I had no idea it was so wild and lonely. I thought all I had to do was to walk up the path until I found your house. But I've walked and walked, and I'm tired to death— and I didn't even have breakfast this morning, either!" she added crossly. Then she smiled, a mirthless smile, and added: "So here I am. And now what are you going to do with me?"

Silent, he stood frowning down at the rifle in his fist. Into the silence came a tiny sound, faint and vague as the murmur of a far-off sea. Something impinged against his hand, his neck, his ears. Looking sharply up, he felt it on his face: the bite of snow, hard and fine as grains of sand. The murmur became more audible. He could hear the crackle of those icy particles as they hit the dead leaves.

"Go ahead," he said, nodding up the trail.

She turned away. He followed, walking crab-wise
—for Jules might not be so far away after all. If he
had been lying low and waiting for his enemy to pass
down the trail and give him another chance at the girl,
he would surely shoot when he saw his prey escaping.
But no shot rang from the timber. The breed had
fought and run away—to fight again another day.

The patter of the snow grew louder and merged into
a steady dry drumming. Thicker and thicker it fell,
until it seemed that a grayish-white haze was settling
over the woods. It bit into Don's neck until he turned
up his collar and pulled down his shapeless hat. A
wind began to sweep through the forest, and abruptly
the bleak air grew warmer. This did not fool the man
who had spent his boyhood in New Hampshire; he
knew that now the fine snow would mushroom out into
fat flakes which would speedily bury the whole countryside under a drifted blanket. And before they had
gone far his forecast proved true.

The wind increased by leaps and bounds to a furious
squall. The air filled with a veritable deluge of sticky
snow, whirling about them so thickly that it caught in
their nostrils like feathers, making them gasp for the
breath which the buffets of the wind almost smote
from their lungs. Trees and bushes blurred and faded
away into a whirling smother. They slipped and slid
on the path. At intervals they halted and turned their
backs to the wind while they caught their breath; then
forged slowly on.

Though she had seemed a Snow Lady before the
storm broke, it soon was evident that the city girl was

no daughter of the North.   She flinched under the on-
rush of the blast, and soon she stopped dead, declaring
she could go no farther.   He wasted no time in argument.   Grasping one white-gloved hand, he drew her
onward, slipping and stumbling as her high-heeled
shoes met the sloping stones of the trail.

Head down, he bored into the blizzard like a lean
destroyer bucking a frothy sea.   The blurred fringe of
timber beside the path reeled past and disappeared in
the smother.   They were out in the open once more —
the small open space where the Dales had found him.
It was barely a stone's throw in diameter, but, for all
they could see of the farther side, they might as well
have been out on the Arctic wastes.   Keeping within
arm's length of the right-hand border of brush, he
plodded onward until he found a familiar tree-trunk,
now plastered white, and plowed through the bushes to
the terrace.

In under the big trees, which caught and held much
of the snow, the air was considerably clearer.   They
stopped to breathe, and for a moment he looked down
at the wife who had driven him to the wilderness and
finally had followed him there.   Her figure drooped,
and her face was drawn into unpleasant lines of fatigue and petulance.   He glanced quickly away, then
turned and led the way onward at a more moderate
gait.

Into the stumpy clearing before his log-walled house
the snow was pouring in a flood.   Slipping on covered
roots, they lurched across the opening to the pines
among which the cabin nestled.   A moment more, and
the door was shut behind them.

CHAPTER XXVI

THE NEW YORK IDEA

" So this abominable hut is your home? "

Scornfully she looked about the dim interior of the cabin, rendered doubly dark now by the cloud of snow whirling past the one window. His mouth tightened; for no man likes to have his handiwork disdained, be it ever so crude. Yet he made no reply, but hastily re-kindled the fire and set about warming up the cold remnants of his breakfast. While the coffee was coming to a boil he turned to her.

" You're wet," he suggested.

" I suppose so," she answered, but made no move from the chair into which she had dropped. So perforce he became lady's maid, taking off the little white hat, lifting the white furs from her shoulders, turning the white coat back around the chair. Then he picked her up bodily, chair and all, and set her nearer the fire-place. After that he returned to the cooking.

As the genial warmth of the fire enveloped her she relaxed, and the pallor of weariness gave way to a pink glow in her cheeks. Speculatively she looked down at his lean, strong profile outlined by the flames. As he rose to place food on the table she caught his arm.

" Donald," she said, " I know what you think of me, but it isn't so! I haven't ——"

"Don't talk!" he cut in. "Eat!" And he swung
the table before her, poured her coffee, and then withdrew to his bunk, where he sat swabbing the wet snow
from his rifle.

She needed no second invitation. Plain fare though
it was, she ate eagerly, hesitating only at the strong
black coffee. After glancing about the table she reminded him: "You forgot to give me any cream."

"Sorry," he returned dryly, "but the milkman didn't
call this morning."

Searching his expressionless face, she laughed.

"How very careless of him! But haven't you a
cow, or—or anything?"

"Not even a goat."

"Then I suppose I have no choice," she sighed, and
sipped at the steaming liquid until the cup was nearly
empty. The hot stimulant banished her fatigue, as the
hearty food restored her strength. When she had finished she arose and inspected her coat and furs, gazed
ruefully at her wet hat, adjusted them over the backs
of the two chairs, and remarked:

"I should have brought an umbrella."

A blast of wind that shook the cabin followed her
words, and he smiled grimly. An umbrella would have
lasted less than a minute in that gale. But he went on
with his work, wordless, waiting for her to say what
she had come to say. Her next utterance, however,
was a question.

"Who was that terrible man I—we—you fought
with?"

"My nearest neighbor."

"You do not seem to be very popular with your neighbors. He looked very ugly when I asked him about you."

He glanced up, startled.

"You did that?"

"Why, yes. I had given up hope of finding you, and I thought he might know."

"What did you ask him?"

"I described you and asked him if he knew where such a man lived. I didn't tell him your name, because your friend Mr. Miller had told me you had changed it and you didn't care to be known."

"Hm! Did Harry advise you to come here?"

"No, oh no. He didn't know I was coming. He told me you were alive and where you were, and said I might write to you in care of somebody named—Daly, I think it was; but I decided to come because letters are so unsatisfactory, and I thought you might not answer anyway. And Mr. Miller was so irritating—he wouldn't tell me anything except just that, and he was very cold and formal and left almost at once. I don't like him! He's horrid!"

He smiled again, a tight-lipped smile, recalling that she had formerly considered big, genial Harry a welcome guest, and surmising that her present dislike for him was due to pique. "Go on," he said.

She glanced out of the window at the smothering storm.

"Well, maybe I'd better begin at the beginning. I'm afraid I can't catch a train back to New York to-day, so there's plenty of time.

"I came to Warner yesterday, and made arrangements to come up here very early to-day; so the driver came for me before it was really daylight, and my breakfast wasn't ready, and the people where I was staying were so slow that I left without eating. All the way to the mountain the driver kept watching the sky and worrying for fear it would snow, so that when we reached the end of the road I paid him and told him to go back. He seemed a bit doubtful, but after looking at the sky again he turned and went.

"I walked and walked, and after a while I came to an old house, but it was empty; and after I looked around I saw that nobody had been living there, so I kept on up the path for miles and miles—at least it seemed so. Finally I came into a little opening, and the path seemed to end. I called, but nobody answered. Then I hunted around and found the path again—a little path that was terribly rocky and full of holes; and I went on up, and the first thing I knew I was out on the bare summit, and it was cold and gray and awful. I was glad to get down among the trees again.

"When I came into the little opening again I called repeatedly, but I couldn't hear any answer. So I thought the old house must be the one after all, and I went away back down there and looked all around everywhere. I don't see why you had to go and build your cabin away off here, where there isn't any path or anything and nobody can find it!"

"That's just why I did build it here. Go on."

"Well, I was all tired out, but I decided to come

back once more before I gave it up. I walked up the path, and all of a sudden I felt as if something were following me. I looked around, but I couldn't see or hear anything, and so I kept on, though I was beginning to think about wolves and panthers and things. But the feeling kept getting stronger, and—well, I just couldn't keep on going; I wanted to get off the mountain. So I turned back. Then all of a sudden that—that man stepped out in front of me.

" He startled me terribly at first, but after I saw he was just a man, and not a wild animal, I felt relieved. I thought he was just a native out hunting, and though I didn't like his looks I spoke to him and asked him about you. He looked terribly ugly for a minute; but then he said yes, he knew you well, and he would take me to your cabin down the trail. Somehow, though, I felt that he was lying, and when I looked at him closely I was sure of it, and I began to be afraid of him. So I started to turn back, but he jumped at me ——"

" I know. I came into the game then."

" Yes. It was dreadful—the way you two shot at each other. Did you really intend to hit him ? "

" Hit him ? " He laughed shortly. " I was gunning for him before I saw you." Opening the rifle, he began cleaning the receiver. " I was out to kill him —if necessary."

She studied him as if almost afraid of him. Then she said: " Please put that gun away. It makes me nervous."

After a moment more of swabbing the weapon he

complied, leaning it against the fireplace where the heat would dry it thoroughly. Filling his pipe, he leaned back, clasped one knee in his hands, and suggested: "Well?"

Sinking again into her chair by the table, she rested her chin on her hands and looked steadily at him. With the soft glow of the firelight playing on her face, her dark eyes shining into his, and her little mouth drawn into a reproachful pout, she made a winsome picture—and she knew it. But he stared calmly back at her through the smoke, unmoved.

"What have you to say, Donald?"

"I? Nothing," he replied through his pipe-stem.

"You have no explanation for acting as you did?"

He shook his head. "Unnecessary," he declared.

"I do not agree with you. You should have given me an opportunity to tell you some things which you did not know, before going out to murder Elliott Duncan."

"Murder? That's hardly the word. And if there were things I didn't know you had ample opportunity to tell me of them before the crash came. Why didn't you?"

"Because——" She hesitated, then went on: "Because I did not think it was necessary. I never dreamed that any such terrible thing would ever happen. And the fact that it did happen was altogether *your* fault!"

His eyes narrowed, but he made no reply. For a moment the crackle of the fire was the only sound.

Then, seeing that he refused to be put on the defensive, she added:

"If I had thought you would ever act in such an insane manner I should have told you long ago that Elliott and I were old friends. But I had not seen him for a long time—indeed, I had nearly forgotten him— and I did not consider it at all essential that you should know of him."

He kept silence, puffing at his pipe and watching her level-eyed. Nettled by his apparent unconcern, she said spitefully: "Yes, no doubt you think I should have told you of my every deed and word and thought. That would be quite in keeping with your hide-bound New England ideas!"

The fling at the land of his birth jarred on him.

"My New England ideas may be hide-bound, but they're square!" he retorted. "They're cleaner than the New York idea which every woman in your 'society set' seems to have—that a husband is merely a beast of burden and creature of convenience!"

"Verily, now we are aroused!" she laughed. "Just as contemptuous of society as ever, aren't you? You are a wild man at heart, and I fear you'll never be anything else. Did you know that that was why I married you?"

"I've sometimes wondered why you did," he admitted.

"I never wondered about it until recently, Donald. I never really stopped to think about it. I just wanted you—and I took you. But lately, since this thing happened, I have gone back into the past and—and analyzed things, as you would say. And I realize that it was because you were so big and strong, and I'd heard so much of your athletic achievements, and you seemed so different and romantic when I first met you up here among the mountains in your camping clothes—those were the reasons why I ran away and married you so hastily that night on the lake. Do you remember that night, Donnie?"

He nodded, but his face did not change.

"Foolish children!" she sighed. "I felt that you were quite a hero, and all that sort of thing. And I thought you would be a good sport and we should have a gay life together. But then you had to spoil it all by tying yourself down to business, and refusing to be bored with 'society stuff,' and clinging to the antiquated ideas of the Puritan Fathers. I have been very much disappointed in you."

"Then the disappointment is mutual. That's better than having it all on one side. But you're not quite fair. We entertained and went out quite frequently—though I'll admit that I was bored stiff by the insincerity and artificiality of your highfalutin crowd. And of course I had to attend to business——"

"No, you didn't!" she cut in. "You need not have bothered with business. You were not poor, and I had plenty of money ——"

"Money, money, money!" he groaned disgustedly. "The New York idea again! If all you wanted was a poodle-dog to lead around on a leash you should have bought one—or married one of the Percy-boys in your own 'set.' A two-handed man wants to accomplish something in life, whether he has money or not. You can't turn him into a lounge lizard. Might as well try to convert a Canada lynx into a useless house-cat."

Again she laughed lightly.

"Your metaphors are somewhat mixed, Donnie. Poodles, lizards, and cats, all in one breath! I never wanted you to be a menagerie, you know. I wanted ——"

"Never mind. You got a bigoted barbarian. Let it go at that. Recriminations are useless. If there are to be explanations, they'll have to come from you."

"I don't know whether I'll make any explanation or not!"

"All right. I haven't asked for one."

Rising, he stepped to the door, opened it, and stood contemplating the driving snow. The first fury of the wind had passed, but the myriad flakes still were tumbling thickly down, loading the trees with a rich white mantle and covering the ragged stumps in the clearing with jaunty caps. The crude outdoor fireplace where he had cooked many a smoky meal was losing its angularity and becoming a rounded mound. The rough forest floor, with its chips and other small camp-litter, was buried beneath a smooth white carpet whereon the forest elves later might come forth and dance under the moon. It was a new world, a clean world, and when the sun came out again it would be a far brighter world.

"Shut that door!" she cried sharply. "It's cold! You're just doing that to be mean!"

His fist tightened on the edge of the door, but he quietly closed the opening.

" And you might have enough consideration for me not to smoke that filthy pipe," she added. Regretfully he knocked out the pipe and slipped it into a pocket. Then, hands hooked over his belt, he stood waiting for the explanation which she had half refused to give, but which, both knew, must come.

The fire crackled on through long minutes while they looked into each other's eyes. Presently her own gaze fell.

" I suppose," she said slowly, " that you think I—I am a very wicked girl."

He made no answer.

" I have been a little foolish, perhaps—but not *wickedly* foolish. Things were not so bad as you must have thought them. There was no real harm. What made you think there was? "

" I stood in the hall. I saw. I heard. I know what Duncan is. That's enough."

" But it isn't enough! Elliott is a little wild, and he—he scared me that night. But he isn't really bad ——"

" Oh, no. Only a little worse than a murderer."

" Why do you say that? "

" Have you heard of Virginia Davies? "

Her lip curled scornfully.

" Oh, that little fool! Yes, I've heard about her. But there wasn't any proof that her death was due to Elliott, was there? And any man with power and position is always pursued by foolish girls. And any girl who can't look out for herself must stand the consequences of her own rashness."

He stared at her in amazement. Despite what he knew, something of his old exalted opinion of her had revived in him. And now—was this the Ruth he had held so dear, this woman who uttered worldly-wise cynicism worthy of Duncan himself?

" And you, I assume, can look out for yourself? "

With a little toss of her head she replied: " Indeed I can. I was taking care of myself that night when you sneaked down and eavesdropped—and sneaked away again! What were these terrible things you saw and heard? "

Briefly, bitterly, he told her.

" I—see," she said thoughtfully. " You heard the very worst of it, and knew nothing of what had gone before. I—see. You must hear the rest of it before you can really understand. If you will sit down, instead of standing there like a stone post, I will tell you all there is to know."

He nodded, and returned to his bunk.

CHAPTER XXVII

THE SHOW-DOWN

"I was just a schoolgirl when I first met Elliott," she began in a low tone of recollection. "We three—Aunt Jessica and Cousin Rob and I—had been touring the Adirondacks and had come down to our place on one of the islands in Lake George to stay through August. We found that another island near ours, which had been used only by tenting parties the year before, now had a fine new house on it, with a boat-landing and a beautiful motor-boat. So Rob, being curious as usual, paddled over there one morning to meet the new neighbors. He brought Elliott back to luncheon.

"We soon learned that Elliott's father—a silent, secretive man who was devoting his life to making money in Wall Street—had bought the island, built the house, installed a housekeeper, and sent Elliott up there to spend the summer. Elliott was only a big boy at heart then, though he was a grown man in size, and he had been bored to death. After he met us, though, he cheered up. We all liked him. Aunt Jessica rather pitied him because he had no relatives except his father, whom he seldom saw. Rob liked him because he was always jolly, and I found him a splendid dancer

—and always a gentleman. We went to dances at the hotels, of course, and had many other merry parties together. Aunt Jessica chaperoned all these affairs.

" September came, and I had to go back to boarding-school. Elliott, too, was going back to begin his sophomore year at college. The night before we left, he proposed.

" It was a beautiful moonlight night, and I was asleep, when I woke up and heard someone softly calling. Outside my window was Elliott. He dared me to come for a midnight motor-boat ride, and it was too good a lark to miss. I threw on a few things and slipped out without waking anyone, and we went away down the lake.

" Out there on the water he stopped the boat and made the first proposal I ever had. He knew a minister near by, he said, and we could wake him up and be married and go back to the island as ' Mr. and Mrs. Elliott Duncan.' I laughed at him, for I liked him only as a good friend, and besides I wasn't even out of school yet. He seemed much disappointed, and he was very insistent—but he took me back safely to my island. Yes, he did kiss me a few times, like the big boy he was; but there was no great harm in that.

" After we both went back to school he wrote very ardent letters for a while; but I didn't answer, and finally he stopped writing. The next thing I heard about him was from Rob. When we were at home during the Christmas vacation Rob met a friend who went to the same college Elliott attended, and learned that Elliott and two other fellows had been suspended because of some wild parties—I think there were some chorus-girls mixed up in the affair, or something of the sort. And Elliott never went back to college. He could have returned, and the other two fellows did go back; but he never did. Instead, he followed his father's example and began to 'play Wall Street.'

"I heard about him occasionally through Rob, but did not meet him again for a long time. Rob said he was doing well in Wall Street, and that for so young a man he was becoming quite a 'silent power' in politics. Then, after my début, he bobbed up again at a social affair. We were both quite grown up now, but he had not forgotten me. In fact, he fell in love with me all over again, and it seemed that I couldn't go to any affair after that without meeting him. He called often, too, and about every time he called he proposed. Finally I grew tired of it. We had a rather bad quarrel, and I told him never to speak to me again.

"He went away angry, and I saw no more of him. I heard, though, that he was 'hitting the high spots along Broadway,' as Rob put it. If he wanted to be wild, that was nothing to me. I just forgot him.

"Then I met you, Donnie, and we were married."

A silence, pregnant with memory, fell between them. Presently, with a little sigh, she continued.

"As you have said, recriminations are useless. But after a while I found married life awfully slow. And the more you became immersed in business the slower it became. I tried very hard to make you take a proper interest in social matters—you will admit that!" He nodded, with a grim smile. "But you wouldn't. So

I had to carry on by myself, or be no better off than a
nun."

"You exaggerate."

"Well, perhaps it wasn't quite as bad as that—but I
couldn't let myself lose all my friends!"

"No, you'd never do that," he replied dryly. "Go
on."

"Well, I—I met Elliott again. It was this spring
and I was uptown shopping with little Mrs. Vander-
huysen—you know her."

He did, and his mouth tightened again. He knew
Mrs. Vanderhuysen as a scheming, calculating woman
of the "climber" type, who would do almost anything
to further her own petty ambitions. He knew her
husband, too, as a not over-scrupulous trader in se-
curities. He heartily despised them both, and his contempt showed in his face.

"Yes, I know you dislike her," said Ruth, "as you
seem to dislike *all* my friends! But anyway, we were
shopping, and when we came out of the store we found
that her chauffeur had disappeared—probably after a
drink. And while we were waiting, who should ap-
pear but Elliott, alone in his car. He saw the situation
at once, and offered to take us to dinner and 'show
us a good time.' And so, after leaving instructions
with the doorman to send the Vanderhuysen driver
home when he reappeared, we went with Elliott to one
of the cabarets.

"We had a dandy time. Elliott is a masterly enter-
tainer, and we danced and joked and had a little wine,
and before I knew it it was nearly eight o'clock. Then

I telephoned to the house, but the maid said you
weren't there—you had called up at five o'clock to say
you would be delayed by your old business.   Then
Elliott took us home.

"I was going to tell you about it, but you came
home late, tired and glum, and I thought I'd wait until
you felt more cheerful.   Then I decided not to say
anything, because I thought you might be jealous.
And the next time I saw Mrs. V. she advised me to
'keep mum,' as there was no harm in it, and 'what the
men don't know doesn't hurt them—or you either.'
That seemed sensible, and so I said nothing of it.

"Then I saw Elliott several times at little afternoon
teas at Mrs. Van's home, and there were a couple of
bathing parties at the beach, and—that was about all.
Everything was perfectly all right.   They were just
little parties, nothing more."

Remembering what Harry had told him on that
night when he fled New York, Donald reminded:
"You're forgetting those *thés dansants* uptown in the
afternoon."

Startled, she swiftly asked: "Who told you?"

"Never mind.   I see it's true."

She flushed, and her dark eyes flamed.

"Yes, it's true.   What of it?   There was no harm
in them—just two or three little dances now and then
with an old friend.   I suppose it was your telltale
friend Miller who told you.   I remember seeing him
once up there."

"I also heard mention of an inscrutable Jap, and of
visits to Duncan's apartment."

"You need not use the plural. I made only one visit there, and the Vans were along. It was after you and Miller came up here camping. We four went up and had a little lark in his rooms—a dinner and music and dancing—a jolly good time. The Jap —we noticed him because he was so perfectly trained. He appeared silently just when wanted, moved like an automaton, and vanished just as quietly. There wasn't anything scandalous. You might know that, with the Vans there chaperoning."

"Humph! Some chaperones, that couple! Vander-huysen plays Duncan's hunches in the Street, and he'd do anything to keep in right with him. They simply used you to feather their own nest."

"I don't believe it!"

"Very well. Kindly explain that highly decorous scene I saw before I murdered Duncan, as you put it."

"Well, that—that really was the worst thing that happened. It was the first time in my life that I was ever afraid of any man, and I did what I did because I was afraid.

"We went motoring that evening, down along the shore, in Elliott's car. We dined and danced a while, and along about eleven o'clock we came back. Elliott was—well, he was rather sentimental, and he made love to me again, for the first time since I married you. He wanted me to leave you, and promised me everything wonderful, and so on. He admitted that he'd been rather wild, but he said that was my fault—he hadn't been that way until I 'treated him badly,' and after that he didn't care what he did. But I laughed at him, and told him I couldn't get a divorce even if I wanted to, because you were no ladies' man and never would give me grounds. He said that might be 'fixed,' and I told him rather sharply that I didn't want it fixed. Then I told him not to be silly, or I wouldn't see him any more. And he drove on toward home without saying anything further.

"He took me right to the house, and then he asked if he might come in for a little music before he went on to Manhattan. I had never let him come to the house before, because I didn't want any inquisitive neighbors talking. But now I knew the Mackenzies and the Chapmans were all away, except old Mrs. Mackenzie, and it was so late she would be in bed— and she is deaf besides, so she wouldn't hear the music and be curious; and I had let the servants go out to some sort of 'racket' they were interested in. So I thought, 'Well, what's the harm?' And I let him come in.

"I took care to draw the shades, and I used the soft pedal. I played one thing after another, just as they came to me, and I may have played something that seemed to mock him—I don't know. But when I stopped and started out into the hall to see what Rajah was up to—he was making some sort of noise out there—Elliott seized me.

"'Ruth!' he said. 'You little tempter, I'm going to take you and make you love me! Ever since I've known you I've wanted you, and you can't play with me and laugh at me forever!' And he—he crushed

me so tight I couldn't move, and kissed me so fiercely
I lost my breath.

"Then I was afraid. I was alone in the house, or
thought I was; and I remembered that no neighbors
were at home who could hear me, and—I didn't know
what to do. He was reckless and determined, and I
could see he wouldn't listen to reason and any resistance would only make him more eager. All in a flash
I saw this, and I did the only thing I could do—I
played a game to get him out of the house. And everything you saw and heard, Donald, was only a pretense!

"I told him he needn't be so savage; that I hadn't
thought he cared for me so much, but had believed
him to be only flirting. And I said the servants were
likely to come in at any minute, and that the neighbors
might be watching to see how long he stayed, and we
mustn't have any scandal. I promised to meet him the
next day, and told him he must behave himself until
then—that if he did *not* behave I would never forgive
him, and he never would see me again. And—well, I
played my part, and I convinced him, and he went
away."

"And you haven't seen him since."

Her eyes wavered. Presently she admitted: "I have
seen him once or twice, but only for a few minutes.
And Mrs. Van was with me, and I haven't allowed
him to call. I've had hardly anything to say to him."

There was a long pause. Finally he asked: "What
else did you wish to say?"

"Why—why, that's about all there is to say. Now

that you understand everything, of course you will come back to New York. Only I must tell you, Donald, that if we are to live together you must be more sensible."

He stared silently at her. Absently he fumbled in his pocket, drew out his empty pipe, and clinched it between his teeth. Her manner was not at all that of a suppliant for forgiveness. Rather, it was an air of calm confidence.

" What does that mean? " he rumbled.

" It means, Donald, that I am going to get a little pleasure out of life. You must give up those old-fogy ideas of yours and allow me some freedom. If you don't want to mingle with my friends I presume you can leave them alone—though I hope you will at least be civil to them. It is going to be a bit awkward to explain your disappearance and your long absence, but it can be done. Your attack on Elliott is a matter known only to you two, I think; and I am quite sure that neither of you will say anything of it. But you *must* ——"

" That will do! *Must* nothing! "

She lifted her chin, but said no more. Wordless, he stood staring at her for minutes. Then a short, hard chuckle broke from him.

" I see," he said. " You have come up here to dictate terms, and have made this explanation first because it was necessary. My business has gone to smash. My estate has been settled. You have it all." He paused, and she nodded slightly. " So I'm a penniless outcast. But since I happen to be still alive, instead

of conveniently dead, some arrangement is necessary.
The arrangement will be that we resume living together for the sake of appearances; that you, being in
control, support me; that in return I allow you to do
just about as you please. In other words, what was a
marriage for love will now become a marriage of convenience."

She laughed again—a little tinkling laugh, but one
with an unpleasant note in it.

" You are so brutally direct in your way of speaking," she complained. " Really, you have no finesse
at all. I wouldn't have thought of saying such things.
But since you will put it in that way—why, that is
practically the situation." Swiftly then she leaned forward and added: " Now, Donnie, don't be unreasonable ——"

But he drowned her words with a roar of laughter.
Lying back in his bunk, he howled until the cabin
rang. She sat stiffly up again, an angry flush dyeing
her face.

" I am glad you find the situation so humorous," she
said icily. At which he roared anew.

" Thanks ! " he gasped. " Pardon my mirth. Your
proposition is so impossible that it's ludicrous."

" Impossible? Why, pray ? "

Rising, he spoke in dead earnest.

" Because I'm nobody's poodle. Because Donald
King of New York City is dead—and is going to stay
dead. Because Walter Macdonald, backwoodsman, in-
tends to keep on being a barbarian.

" Now wait ! I'm talking.

"All your life, Ruth, you've been a big-city girl. You love the rush and glitter of Town: theatres and dances and limousines, fine gowns and jewels—all the things of Society. You've been a little girl with plenty of money, playing around like a butterfly—and you've never grown up. Maybe some day you will, but you haven't yet. You still think that the artificial gayety of your set is Life itself. Your horizon is bounded by the perimeter of the society circle, and you don't know there is anything beyond.

"Now I'm of a different type. I'm quiet, over-silent perhaps, and accustomed to the wide, free spaces where a man can stretch himself. I don't hate the city, or despise it. But frankly, its atmosphere chokes me. Its walls seem to hem me in and crush me. Its crowds and cops and cars hold me back and shove me aside until I'm fighting mad. All my life I've been that way. It wasn't so bad when I was in small cities, for then I could easily get out into the country where I could breathe. But New York—it's the biggest city in the Americas; it's too big to get out of—and it's too small to hold me!

"There's the basic difference between us. It's not a matter of New York and New England ideas. I'm an outdoor man; you're an indoor woman. I'm used to real life; you, to an imitation. But I've played your game. I've played it square. I've gritted my teeth and bucked the line. I've hammered away for years, and I've made my gains. And I'd be pounding away yet if I hadn't been fouled.

"Now the whistle blows for a new line-up. All

right, I'm ready! But I demand fair play. And turn
about is fair play. I've played your game—now you
can play mine!"

"You mean —— ?"

"I mean that we change goals. We play according
to the rules. I will not go back to New York. But
there are smaller cities, where we can make a fresh
start; where you can meet people who are your social
equals; where I can work my way up again in business,
without your money; and where, in various ways, life
will be more worth living than in cold-blooded New
York. Of course, you've got to play fair. I'll give
you the chance."

She sprang up.

"Donald, you are preposterous!"

"How? In asking you to play fair?"

"No! Certainly not! But if you think I am going
to drag out my life in some country village ——"

"I didn't say a country village."

"What's the difference? It might as well be!"

He straightened to his full height. Eyes fixed on
hers, he asked in quiet finality: "Then you won't play
my game?"

Head high, she answered: "Absolutely not!"

He bowed.

"Very well. That's all." And he moved to the fireplace and put on more wood.

"And you—you won't come back to New York,
Donald?"

Gravely he answered in her own words: "Absolutely
not!"

It was quietly said, but the ring of iron in his tone was unmistakable.

"But—but this situation is intolerable! We can't go on like this."

"I was thinking of that. If you wish to—remarry, it can be fixed, as Duncan said. A divorce is an ugly thing, especially in New York. But if you desire it, I can come alive again long enough to put it through for you."

"Why, what do you—would you do *that?*"

"Not what you're thinking of. But enough evidence could be manufactured to get the decree. Many a divorce is based on fake evidence."

"Thank you, kind sir!" she retorted. "If ever I feel so inclined, perhaps I will accept your thoughtful offer. But I hardly think you need put yourself to the trouble. Married life is far too slow, and I have no present intention of going to the altar again."

Suddenly she leaped up, whirled toward her coat, and struggled into it.

"What's this?" he demanded.

"I'm going! I'm going out of this beastly place!" she stormed. "I'm sorry I came near you—you're not worth it! I am going straight back to town, and you can stay here in your abominable hut and live your abominable life as you please!"

She tore open the door and sprang out into the snow.

CHAPTER XXVIII

"HOLD hard!"

He leaped after her.

She had turned the wrong way, and was running into the woods at the left. In three long strides he caught her and swung her up off the ground.

"I will not go back—I will not!" she raged, squirming and kicking. "Put me down at once, I say!" But he turned back toward the door with her.

"You—you big brute!" Tears of helpless anger sprang to her eyes. With one free hand she struck him hard in the mouth.

"You're a wildcat when you get going," he said with a tight-lipped smile. Straight into the cabin he carried her, put her down, kicked the door shut and set his back against it. Then he added: "Let me give you a good motto: Don't start anything you can't finish."

"Prize-ring talk!" she retorted scornfully, looking at the window as if half minded to leap through it.

"Maybe. By the way, that window is nailed in. You started something just now which you couldn't finish. You started into the wilderness instead of toward the trail. If I'd let you go you'd have been lost in three minutes. The storm would have finished what you started—by finishing you. Now show a little sense."

She made no answer and held her chin high, but she was impressed.

" By this time the trail is well drifted. It's getting worse every minute. There's one way you can get down it—on snowshoes. You've never used them, and your French heels are poor footgear for such work. But if you insist on going now that's the only way."

" I don't care how I go, as long as I go! I want to get out of here at once!"

He nodded, strode to a corner, and picked up his new snowshoes. As he left the door she swiftly opened it; but she did not step out into the snow.

" Ruth," he said, stopping beside her, " this is the last call. Will you play the game?"

" I think we may consider that question settled. I will *not* play any game you want to play. Is that clear?"

" Quite."

Dropping the snowshoes outside, he told her to step on them. She did so. Looping the thongs loosely but surely around her feet, he gave her directions.

" Don't lift them. Slide them over each other. Let the tail drag. Walk naturally, but take a good long stride. I'll break trail."

He watched her first tentative steps. As he expected, she stepped on her snowshoes and fell. He caught her before she could touch the snow.

" A good long stride, I said," he reminded.

Angry red spots flamed in her cheeks. But she

took a longer step, and found that now she could walk.
He turned and led the way.

Slowly he went, giving her plenty of time. His long
legs made nothing of the few inches of snow under the
trees. Emerging into the open, however, he found that
the white blanket at once grew thicker, and he knew
that farther down the trail it would be worse. As he
passed down the path he noted that the footprints they
had left behind them on their upward struggle were
totally obliterated. The wind still blew erratically—
sometimes sweeping across the trail, sometimes swoop-
ing straight down it, and ever driving the flakes in
eddying gusts. This pleased him well, for he knew
that the tracks which they now were making would
soon be blotted out and no telltale furrow would be left
for Black Jules to follow to his cabin. Jules, he felt,
would hardly neglect an opportunity to assassinate him
through the window.

There was little chance for talk, even had they desired it; for the snowfall forced them to bend their
heads and keep their lips closed. Moreover, as is usually the case with the snowshoeing novice, Ruth's
whole attention was concentrated on her feet. Finally,
there was nothing more to be said. So they passed on
down the mountain without a sound, save for an occasional gasp from Ruth as she nearly upset herself,
and the labored breathing of Donald as he toiled
through a drift—for the depth already varied from
inches to feet. Not until they reached the Half-way
House clearing did they halt or speak.

" We'll take a short cut here," he said, motioning

toward the stone wall. "Over the wall and down through that pasture. Shortest way."

"The shortest way to what?"

"Road. House where you can get a horse. There are no taxis up here, you know."

"Really?" Her tone was sarcastic. "I had expected a limousine and a liveried driver. Whose house is it?"

"The Dalys, as you call them. Dale is the right name."

Bending, he examined the thongs, found they had stretched, tightened them, and knocked off the snow which had caked into slippery balls under her heels. Then he headed for the wall, and she followed. The stones now were almost buried under a smoothly rounded drift, over which she passed easily while he wallowed hip-deep. Beyond, the mountainside dropped steeply toward the valley.

"Don't try to go straight down," he warned. "A zigzag is the only safe way. Follow me." With which he began to lay a meandering trail down the slope. Even so, she fell twice on the turns, and he had to put her on her feet again.

"Oh, I never can do it!" she expostulated. "I must go back to the path."

"No. You'll be all in when you reach the house anyway, and you'll save at least a mile this way. It's easier down below."

Nevertheless, she turned to go back. A look at the stiff climb upward, however, daunted her. After a moment of indecision she followed him.

"You're mean!" she charged. "You're doing this just to make it harder for me!"

He made no answer.

As he had said, it was easier down below—easier for her, though harder for him. There the wind had swept the snow deeply into the hollows while it kept the tops of the hillocks almost bare, and she traveled with comparative ease across the places where he floundered. The rolling slopes led ever downward, and now they could walk in a direct line for the road. And on toward that road they tramped through the blurring swirl of storm.

When they reached the highway they found it smooth and unmarred by any track of vehicles. None of the few hill-dwellers along this road was abroad in such weather, and Donald felt some doubt as to his ability to hire a horse just now. Nevertheless, he meant to try.

"I—can't—go any farther!" she cried, stopping and leaning against a tree. "Go and get your old horse and come for me here."

He shook his head.

"Getting the horse may be a slow job. You'll get cold, and probably sick. Don't quit! You'll soon be where it's warm and dry and you can get some hot tea."

The thought of hot tea proved a stimulus where common-sense would have failed. They moved forward again, and did not halt until they stood before the door of Joe Dale.

There, as Donald stooped to untie the thongs, he

glimpsed Joe's face peering out at them through a kitchen window. He smiled and nodded to the old man. An excited shout came faintly to them from inside.

"Pansy! C'm'ere quick! Here's Mac, lookin' like Santy Claus, an' he's got a woman with him!"

He expected a sudden opening of the door and Pansy's usual cheery welcome, but nothing of the kind came. He did not know that the girl had paled and was standing motionless, staring at the wall of the buttery—frozen by her father's abrupt announcement that "Mac's got a woman with him."

Standing the snowshoes beside the house and slapping the "Santy Claus" snow from his head, beard, and body, Donald threw open the door and ushered his wife inside. Without preliminaries he plunged into the middle of things.

"Joe, this is my wife. Ruth, this is Joe Dale. The wind just blew us off the mountain, Joe, and we lit here. Now we'd like some hot tea and a horse."

"Heh, heh, heh! Right to the p'int, as usual," grinned Joe. "Glad to see ye, Mis'—Mis' King. Ye look pretty nigh tuckered out, an' no wonder, ef ye come all the way down the mountin on them snowshoes. Pansy, fix some tea."

"I'm makin' it, Pop," came Pansy's voice, and she emerged with a teapot. "Sit down, Mis' King, and rest." With a little nod that included both Donald and Ruth, she passed to the stove.

"Gorry, yas," seconded her father. "What be I a-thinkin' of, keepin' ye standin' like that? Take off

yer clo'es—I mean yer hat—I mean yer coat—darn
it!" He came to a full stop, red as a beet over his
"break." A slight snicker from Donald added to his
embarrassment. Pansy came to his rescue.

"Yes, do make yourself right to home. I'll have
this tea hot in no time, and wouldn't you like somethin' warm to eat too? You must be hungry."

"Thank you, no," was the cool reply. "Donald,
kindly shake this coat." Extending to him the white
garment, now doubly white with snow, she sank into
Joe's comfortable big chair.

Donald's smile disappeared; for she had spoken as if
to a servant. Nevertheless he took the coat, flapped it
out of the door a couple of times, and hung it behind
the stove to dry. Then he turned again to Joe.

"I want a horse, Joe. We are going to Warner.
Will Rob Clarke let a horse and sleigh to me?"

"Nope. He don't know ye. But he'll let *me* take
a hoss any time. I'll go git it." He reached for hat
and coat.

"But ——"

"But nawthin'! 'Tain't no trouble at all. My
roomytiz is most well, an' I ain't got a mite in my laigs
now. 'Sides, it'll do me good to git out an' walk
around. Mebbe it'll clear out my ol' fool head."

He got into his coat with hasty emphasis. Donald
grinned and said no more, for he saw the old man was
burning with chagrin at having unwittingly invited a
lady guest to undress, and that he was eager to escape.
The door slammed and Joe was gone without another
word—though Don surmised that he was making sev-

eral biting remarks to and concerning himself as he plodded away down the road.

Silence followed his exit. Donald sat down and rested his tired legs. Ruth lay back in the big chair with eyes closed. Pansy stood awaiting the simmer of the teapot, meanwhile stealing glances at the wonderfully gowned woman who was Donald's wife. The stillness grew somewhat irksome, but no one spoke until the tea was made and Pansy had brought cream, jam, cake, and other dainties from their shelves over the cellar stairway.

"Now, Mis' King, if you'll just sit up to the table," she suggested. "The tea is awful hot, an' you might drop it an' scald you if you tried to hold it in your hand. My, ain't this a hard storm! I s'pose you ain't used to this kind of weather."

"No, thank heaven!" replied the city girl, rising rather stiffly and limping a trifle as she stepped to the table. Pansy flushed a little; for, though the words carried no offense, the way in which they were uttered was a disparagement to the North Country and all things in it. Nor was Pansy's slight displeasure lessened by the visitor's next remark.

"This tea is very good, my dear."

Again it was not the words, but the air of condescension with which they were spoken, that rankled. The country girl's eyes clouded a bit, but she gave no other sign. Silently she poured more tea for the guest. Then she withdrew to her father's chair, where she sat looking straight out of the window while Ruth ate. For Ruth did eat. Nibbling at a bit of cake, she found

it so good that she took a larger piece; and when she
arose from the table there was little left of the delica-
cies which had rested there. As she pushed back her
chair the muffled thud of hoofs sounded in the yard.

"Oh, Mac!" came Joe's hail. Donald strode to the
door.

"Here's yer hoss. Rob was jest gittin' his pung out
o' the barn-cellar, so we hitched right into it. I can't
come in—the hoss wunt stand in this snow. I'll hold
him till ye're ready. An' say, git a lantern out o' the
shed-room, will ye?"

Don went and found the lantern, though he could see
no use for it. As he came back into the kitchen he
heard Pansy speak in puzzled protest.

"What's this for?"

Ruth had donned coat and furs, and now she stood
by the table. On the table lay a dollar bill.

"Why, for the excellent luncheon, my dear," she
answered in a surprised tone.

Storm shot into the blue eyes. But Pansy's voice,
as she replied, was calm.

"Thankye," she said, with quaint dignity. "But I'd
rather you'd take it away. Mebbe you don't understand. Don's our neighbor, an' neighbors don't pay
for little things like that—not up here, anyway. An'
besides, anything we can do for Don or—or any of his
folks. we're always glad to do."

For a moment the two looked straight into each
other's eyes. Then Ruth picked up the money.

"I beg your pardon. I didn't quite understand."

"All right, Mis' King." Pansy's dimpling smile

dawned. " An' we're awful glad you came in to see us."

" Mac! Be ye comin'?" demanded Joe.

" Yep."

He strode out. But Joe halted him.

" Light yer lantern, boy, light yer lantern."

" What for?"

" I'll show ye. Light it."

So he returned and lit it.

" Now," continued Joe, when Donald and Ruth were seated in the pung, " jes' put this lantern under the robes by yer feet. It's kind of smelly, mebbe, but it'll keep ye a hull lot warmer. Ye've got a long slow drive, an' the weather's turnin' colder." He hesitated, then went on: " Be ye—how will ye git the hoss back here?"

" Drive him back."

" Uh-huh." The old man now had the answer to a question which he had not liked to ask outright— whether Donald was about to return to the city. " I had to give Rob a fairy-story that I was drivin' down to meet some comp'ny on the train, an' I s'pose he'll be over here all spraddled out to-morrer to see my comp'ny. So ef ye wanter hang round here a day ye kin be the comp'ny—he don't know ye from the man in the moon. G'bye, Mis' King. Keep that lantern clus to yer feet."

The horse, restive under the sweep of the snow, abruptly ended the conversation. He threw his shoulders into the harness, and the sleigh was whisked out of the yard before Ruth could even say farewell. By the time Donald had the animal in hand the Dale home was out of earshot.

For some time they drove in silence, broken only by the occasional scrape of the runners over some spot swept bare by the wind. Then Ruth laughed in a way that somehow made Donald flush.

" There's a reason for everything, isn't there, Donald? "

He looked at her, but made no reply.

" I was mistaken when I said you were unpopular with your neighbors. There is at least one neighbor who seems to like you very well."

Still he said nothing.

" What are these farmer-folk to you? " she persisted.

" My best friends. They saved my life."

" Saved your life? How? "

" When I hit Warner I was all in—sick with fever. Had a fight with the thug who stole my clothes. Got knocked out. Came on toward the mountain and caved in. Fell in the road. Joe found me half dead and carried me home. Then he and Pansy brought me back to life. That's all."

" That's all? I think it isn't all. Isn't there a charming little romance hidden away in—in the woodpile, so to speak? Brown-haired young hero fleeing from his past—little native girl—sick-beds and white bandages on the fevered brow—really, it should be in the movies! The dashing hero becomes a hermit— most charmingly poetic, isn't it? Let me see if I can't evolve a lyric:

"There's a hermit on the mountain
And a Pansy in the Dale,
And the call of the metropolis
Is now of no avail,
For it's very, very pleasant
To philander with a peasant——"

The horse was yanked back on his haunches. The sleigh stopped. Her mockery ended abruptly. Looking into the blazing eyes of the man beside her, she paled.

"Look here!" he spat through clenched teeth—and paused. When he spoke again it was in a tone of wrath repressed.

"It's nearly five miles to town. Do you want to get out and walk?"

"N-n-no. I was just joking——"

"Don't joke any more."

She heeded the warning. She had gone too far, and she knew it. Throughout the rest of the slow drive no word was spoken.

Dull daylight was deepening into dusk as the snow-laden pung and its snow-covered passengers came into the village. Down the main street they drove to the hotel. There Donald stepped out and extended a hand to help her from the sleigh. She deliberately disregarded it and got out on the other side.

"Good-bye," she said, as impersonally as if he were some street urchin.

"Good-bye, Ruth," he answered gravely. "And good luck!"

Without another word or look she entered the house,

A yellow flood of lamplight darted out as the door opened. Then it was clipped short as the portal slammed shut. She was gone.

For minutes the man stood there in the snow, looking thoughtfully at the door. Then the horse twitched impatiently at the reins. With a slow, deep sigh he clambered back into the pung and gave the animal his head. At once the horse turned homeward. And as the wintry night closed down around him Donald set his face once more into the road he had chosen—the quiet upward road of the hill country, with its sun and storm, its sighing pines and homely hearths and kindly hearts; where the glitter and rush and turmoil of the city were not, and where a man could be a man.

CHAPTER XXIX

THE WORK OF A GUNMAN

"Mac, ye're a darn fine boy an' I like ye a lot, but thar's one good reason why I allus hate to have ye come an' see us."

Donald, who had just split a tough hardwood knot and was reaching for another, stopped his hand and glanced in astonishment at Joe. Never before had the farmer intimated that he was not a wholly welcome guest. Now Dale raised his one mittened hand and rubbed his nose, thereby masking the little grin twitching under his frosty beard; but the bright morning sunlight revealed the twinkle in his eyes. Wherefore Don relaxed from his surprised tension as he demanded: "Why?"

"Becuz I miss ye so darn much when ye go away. Heh, heh, heh!"

Don smiled, picked up the knot he was after, and balanced it on the chopping-block. Joe's gaze roved down the white road as he continued:

"Ef ye was only lazier, I could of strung out this job another week, or mebbe more. When ye come back alone from Warner that night, lookin' low-sperrited an' gloomersome, an' asked me ef I could put ye to work at suthin', I went an' had the rest o' the cordwood drawed in—wouldn't of brung it in till the

300

fust o' the year, otherways. Now ye've worked so
stiddy an' hard that—wal, ye jest worked yerself out
o' work. An' jest becuz thar ain't nawthin' more to
do, ye seem to think ye've got to go back up on the
mountin."

Don said nothing, but smote the tough chunk a
mighty blow.

" I wisht ye'd lemme pay ye for what ye've done,
anyways," added Joe. " Jest the same as I'd expect to
pay any other feller that sawed an' split for me."

A curt shake of the head was Donald's only answer.
He had all the reward he wanted—the hearty fellow-
ship of this old man and the sunny smile of his
daughter. It was for this that he had lingered nearly
a fortnight, and he had toiled fast and steadily only
because that was his two-handed way of doing things.
As Joe said, he had returned from Warner on that
stormy night with spirits at low ebb, due to brooding
through the lonely miles on the Might-Have-Been;
and, in sudden loathing of his useless hermit life, he
had asked Joe to put him to work at something.
Though he asked no questions, Dale comprehended
quite well the state of his foster-son's mind and
shrewdly surmised its cause. Wherefore he had
moved in his reserve supply of cordwood from the
forest, and day by day the pair had toiled away at it
in a sympathetic comradeship that was good for both.
To Donald the purposeful swing of saw and axe had
been a physical joy; and Joe had found his usual
pleasure in the presence of this silent, stalwart fellow
of the strong hand and the clean heart.

Thanksgiving Day had come and gone, and with it
a dinner such as only a New England cook like Pansy
can prepare on the old Puritan day of gratitude for
bounteous crops. And the day had brought more than
the feast—a closer understanding and sympathy among
these three. In the mellow atmosphere of the Dales'
hospitality, Donald at last had opened up his heart
and told them succinctly of the visit of Ruth, her
ultimatum and his counter-proposal, and of their final
cleavage. Of the initial cause of the break between
them he said nothing. But they were not dense; they
knew he had shot a man, and they had guessed very
close to the truth, though keeping their conclusions to
themselves. So now, knowing the main points of the
last chapter, they had a sufficiently accurate outline of
the whole matter; and their bond of sympathy was
strengthened all the more.

They had passed no judgment. They had studiously
refrained from any remark which might be so con-
strued. Only, after smoking thoughtfully for a time,
Joe had said:

"Every feller gits his own hand in the game o' life,
an' he's got to play it accordin' to his lights. Lots o'
times it ain't the kind of a hand he wants, an' sometimes it's awful poor. But I calc'late that ef a feller
does the best he kin with the cards he gits, an' plays
the game squar, he gin'rally comes out awright in the
end. I figger, too, that mostly no man has got a right
to tell another feller what he'd oughter do. Ye've got
yer own hand to play, lad, an' I don't aim to advise
ye. All the same, I wanter say this: Any feller that

ain't got the backbone to live his life accordin' to his best idees, but lets hisself be treated like a hoss or a dawg—that man ain't wuth a tinker's dam! That's all I got to say."

Somehow this quaint philosophy from the sturdy old farmer had heartened the younger man. And Pansy, though she said nothing, had nodded slowly as if her father spoke her own thought. Moreover, in various little intangible ways she had shown her faith that, as Joe said, he would "play the game squar." And to any man troubled in mind the unwavering faith of close friends is a mighty support and comfort.

And now the woodpile work was finished. The twisted knot into which Donald was thumping his axe was the last stick of all. So, knowing that no other work remained except the trifling winter chores which would not even keep Joe busy, he was not minded to hang around in idleness. After the midday meal he would return to his cabin.

With a final splintering bump on the block the sullen knot fell apart. Donald chucked the pieces up on the peak of the pile, spread his arms wide, and breathed deep of the nippy air.

"Ended—one job," said he.

Joe's thoughtful gaze came back from down the road.

"Awright. Le's git in an' wash up. Dinner'll be ready pretty quick." As they turned toward the door he added: "I was jest thinkin' about Rob. Gorry, he'll miss ye suthin' awful!"

Both laughed. The inquisitiveness of Rob Clarke

had become a standing joke between these two. As
Joe had predicted, Clarke had come over, the day after
Ruth's departure, to see the Dales' " company " and
to learn all he could as to the newcomer's past, present,
and future. He had gone home baffled and irritated
by the stranger's refusal to talk. Since then, on one
pretext or another, he had made several other visits
with no better luck. To-day, driving to town, he had
halted his horse for a good half-hour to watch Donald
and Joe working at the woodpile, only to leave at last
with his curiosity still unsatisfied. Now Joe added:

"I cal'late I'll hafter make up some fairy-story
about ye when ye're gone, jest to satisfy Rob. Otherways he'll be pesterin' me about ye for the nex' six
months. Most time he got back now. I bet he's been
figgerin' all the way down an' back how he could find
out all about ye. Cur'ous critter, Rob is."

Kicking the snow from their feet, they entered the
house to find the table partly set and the cook busy at
the stove.

"Wal, Pansy gal, we're losin' our boarder," Joe announced.

The girl whirled, wide-eyed.

"Are you goin', Don?"

He nodded.

"I have to return and look after my estate," he
jested. "Somebody might steal my priceless stew-
pot if I stay away much longer."

She smiled, rather soberly, and turned back to the
stove.

"I wish you wouldn't hurry," she said, "but of

course you know best." And she said no more. She had been rather silent of late, Don had noticed, and somewhat given to quiet thought. It did not occur to him that this slight change in her demeanor had taken place since his wife had come and gone. Neither had he observed that, though she smiled as of old, the smile was not quite the same—the ready smile rising from a care-free heart.

The men washed, sat down, and ate. There was little talk until the meal was done. Then Joe, preparing for a smoke, glanced out of the window and grumbled: "Aw shucks! More snow!"

The clear blue of the morning sky was gone. A gray shade had slid across it, and the grayness was thickening.

"Better stay till mornin' anyway, boy," the old man urged. "Give the ol' Snow Man a chance to bust hisself to-night, an' then start bright an' early to-morrer ef ye want to."

But Don shook his head.

"Guess I'll ramble on after my dinner settles," he said.

The farmer puffed thoughtfully.

"Wal, looky here, Mac," he ventured. "I wanter say suthin' to ye for yer own good. Mebbe I'd oughter keep my mouth shet, but before ye go I'm jest a-goin' to talk plain to ye, like I would to my own boy.

"Seems to me that up thar on yer mountin ye ain't gittin' nowhar. Ye ain't got no objeck in life. An' a man without no objeck in front o' him don't never

amount to nawthin'. What's wuss, he gits to hatin'
hisself an' everybody else. An' ye hadn't oughter put
in the hull winter settin' round up yonder by yerself,
boy. Come spring, ye'll be sour as vinegar. I know
ye ain't shif'less, an' bimeby ye'll git some objeck an'
start doin' suthin' wuth while. But ontil ye make up
yer mind what ye wanter do, take an ol' man's advice
an' git out more among men. It ain't good for a feller
to live alone so much. Ye'd oughter have suthin' to
do an' be round with other folks. I wisht ye'd stay
here with us, but I see yer mind is sot an' it's no use
to argy with ye. But ef ye want to work, thar's
lumber gangs out in the woods now an' ye could easy
git a job. That'd be a hull lot better for ye than holin'
up by yerself like a sick b'ar."

"You're right," Donald agreed. "I'll hunt a job
soon."

Impulsively Pansy stretched a hand across the table
to him.

"I'm awful glad to hear you say that, Don," she
told him. "I—we—we've been worried about you
more than once, all alone up there. You could get
hurt or sick and die without anybody to help you.
And you'd ought to have somethin' to do besides think,
think, think all the time. Please get a job somewhere!
But—but don't forget all about us when you're workin'
somewhere else."

"There's little danger of that," he replied gravely.
Their hands met, clasped, parted. A long pause followed.

Joe knocked out his pipe and arose.

"Wal ——" he began—and stopped short, one ear cocked toward the door. "Rob's comin' back. Hear his bell?"

Donald listened. Down the road came the regular tinkle of one small bell, which he recognized as the one which hung from the collar of Clarke's horse. A memory rose within him: memory of a midsummer night when he had heard the approaching squeak of Clarke's unoiled axle, bringing newspapers which he awaited almost with dread. That night he had gone out into the dark and the rain, heavy-hearted, driven by the warning of the tall clock which even now tick-tocked solemnly at his back. And now, with a graying sky above him, the memory of that night in his mind, and the jingle of the oncoming pung in his ears, there stole over him a nameless fear, a clammy feeling that this man was a harbinger of evil tidings. The bold, black-eyed face of Clarke loomed sinister in his thoughts, and he felt that his passing would leave relief in his wake.

But Clarke did not pass.

"Whoa!" came a bellow that shook the windows, followed at once by a yell to Joe. Dale stepped to the door.

"Got a letter here for Walter Macdonald, Joe," rang Clarke's voice in loud importance. "Walter Macdonald, Esquire, care of Joseph Dale. Guess that's yer talkative friend, ain't it? Letter's from Noo Yawk, too, Joe, an' it's got a big black aidge round the envelup. Mus' be somebody dead!"

Pansy and Donald paled and stared at each other.

" Awright, Rob, I'll take it," said Joe.

" Wal, whar's Mister Macdonald? Let him come an' git it—it's hisn, not yourn. Is this feller from Noo Yawk?" Obviously Clarke had determined to hold the letter until he could watch Donald's reception of it, and to learn all he could.

" Rob, I'll take that letter," repeated Joe, and there was a touch of steel in his tone.

" Will ye? Wal, I dunno about that! I'll give it to Walter Macdonald, who it's meant for. If he ain't here now he kin come to my house for it."

Donald growled and started for the door. But before he reached it Joe had taken Clarke's windy importance out of him.

" Rob, be keerful!" he warned. " Ye say the letter's addressed in care o' me. I'm responsible for it, an' ye'd better hand it over to me. Keepin' other folkses' mail is agin the law. Ef ye should lose it, now, ye might git a ride to Concord!"

The thinly veiled threat of " State's prison " was enough.

"Aw now, Joe, I was jest jollyìn'. Here's yer letter. Take it quick. Whoa! Giddap!" The jingle recommenced. Joe reëntered the room, his face serious.

" Mac, I'm afeared I got bad noos for ye." He handed Donald the letter. In a swift glance the younger man saw that the envelope was heavily bordered with black. The writing was that of Harry Miller.

Stepping to a window, he slowly opened the sinister missive and read.

DEAR DON:

By the time you have opened this the mourning envelope will have given you warning. I am sorry, old man, but I have to hand you another stiff jolt. It's going to hurt. But it can't be helped, and you'll just have to grit your teeth and bear it. I know you're man enough to take the blow without whimpering.

Don, you may remember that when I was up there I predicted that some day Duncan would be found dead with a gunman's bullets in him. That was only a guess, based on what I knew of some of Duncan's enemies. But many a random shot strikes home. This was one of those chance shots.

Duncan is dead. He was shot late last night while motoring *toward Brooklyn*. He had been at some lively party or other uptown, and it was well past midnight when the shooting came off. He was driving down Fifth Avenue, and had slowed up near Fourteenth Street because of a cross-town trolley getting in his way, when a taxi which had been following along behind him swung up alongside. A man in the taxi leaned out and turned loose with an automatic. Then the taxi jumped ahead at full speed and made a clean getaway.

Duncan's car slewed to one side and smashed through a big plate-glass window in a store before it was stopped. When the cops got to the place he was dead, with three holes in him.

Now if Duncan had been alone, this news would hardly trouble you much. But I am sorry to say, Don, that he was not alone. There was another with him, and that other also was killed.

Yes, old man, it is what you fear. The other victim of that unknown gunman was your wife. One bullet missed Duncan and killed her instantly. This will be a shock to you, I know, but remember this—it all took place so suddenly that she never even knew what had

happened.   She passed on almost without realizing
it.

There isn't anything more to say, except that a man-
hunt is on for the murderer, whose gun has been found
—he chucked it at a sewer-opening at the next corner,
but missed it, and the weapon was found in the gutter.
Of course he was some gangster hired by somebody
higher up, and whether he is caught or not is prob-
lematical.

Now buck up, old man!   You know my sympathy is
with you, and I will do everything I can ——

Donald read no farther. The letter fluttered from
his nerveless fingers to the floor. Dazed, he turned
slowly and moved toward the stove. From a hook behind it he mechanically took down his hat and coat,
and in a fumbling way he put them on. Then he
stalked toward the door.

Pansy caught his arm. But, with eyes set straight
before him, he moved on, almost unconscious of her
grasp.

"Don ——" she called, her voice athrob with sympathy, "Don—dear—what is it?"

He jerked his head toward the fallen letter.

"Read it," he mumbled. Then he opened the door
and passed out.

Minutes later, their eyes full of pity, the old man
and the girl hurried after him. But he was not in the
yard. He was not in the barn. To their calls no answer came back. Then Dale pointed silently to a nail
where Donald's snowshoes had hung. They were
gone.

In the trampled snow before the barn-door were

webbed imprints. Around the corner ran a fresh
snowshoe trail. They followed it, and saw that it led
straight toward the forest. And up on the white hill-
side, almost at the edge of the woods, moved a man
who strode slowly on, head bowed, as if he knew not
where he went. Gently around that sombre figure
floated the first soft flakes of a new snowfall, touching
him with the cool, clean caress of the Northland. He
reached the trees, faded into their protecting shadows,
and disappeared.

"Thar, thar, little gal, don't cry," Joe said huskily.
"Everything's a-comin' out awright bimeby."

CHAPTER XXX

GHOSTS AND MEN

MEMORY dogs us all. Flee whither man may, to silent solitude or to strident city, to mountain fastness or to ocean waste, to homely hamlet or to dreamy tropic isle, ever the past trails at his heels. It sleeps, perhaps, but it does not die. One may escape its pursuit for a space in the city, where the rush and roar overwhelm it and where music, lights and laughter lull it into somnolence. But even here it springs awake at unexpected moments, roused by the wail of a violin, the fragrant breath of a flower, the fleeting glimpse of a face whirled past in the maelstrom of humanity; and then for a time life becomes a mockery tinged deep with wretchedness. Still, in the hurly-burly of the metropolis these twinges of old wounds are but transitory, for ere long they are numbed by the impact of the fresh complexities starting up from every side. But in the wilderness—ah! the wilderness! It is the worst possible place for him who would forget. There the heavy stillness presses in upon him ever, weighted with brooding thought; and though the hands and body labor incessantly and the mind busy itself with problems of existence, the bulldog grip of Memory remains clinched in the heart. And when pregnant Memory whelps Remorse, the twain become hell-hounds which

312

fix their fangs in man's vitals and gnaw, gnaw, gnaw till they drive him mad.

Remorse troubled Donald not at all. But Memory's tooth was sharp, and amid the white silence of the winter woods it bit deep. Though he toiled doggedly through the days at a woodpile of his own, or snowshoed a way through the forest on still-hunts for fresh meat, this muscular activity could not banish the past from his mind. Ever there rode upon him the weight of the Days That Had Been, coupled with the bitter burden of revolt against Fate, who had made playthings of three lives and then clipped two of them short with one stroke of her shears. And when the short winter day was done and the darkness and the cold drove him into his lonely cabin, he found no surcease there.

Then, in the red heart of his fire, pictures would form and grow—ghosts of other fires which had burned in a former life, before he became a dead man to the great world outside these bleak hills; fires in whose glow he had sat with the One Girl in his arms, her warm breath beating on his lips, her eyes shining up into his, her arm entwined about his neck. And a face would look out at him, its rosebud mouth drooping and its dark eyes heavy with reproach; and despite himself a great knot would swell in his throat, and rapid winking would not clear away the blur that formed between him and the flame.

Sometimes, amid the flickering flame-fingers, this haunting face would melt away, and in its place would come another—that of a living pansy, violet-orbed,

with aura of golden hair: of her who had rescued him
from sickness of body and mind, and whose naïve
companionship had gone far toward restoring his shattered faith in humanity.   While this transitory vision
looked out from the coals the rankle of past and present hurt seemed somehow to leave him, and for a little
time his mind was at peace.   Yet this face was not
that of the merry, laughing girl whom he had first met
—it had become that of a woman; and in the depths of
the great flower-eyes he found a touch of pensiveness,
a wistful question which he could neither read nor answer.   And when the fire sank low and he rolled up in
his blankets and shut his eyes, these wraiths of the
dead and the living still hung before his mind, hovering
over him and looking in upon his soul.

Remorse, as I have said, never had taken the hermit's trail; nor did it hound him now.   He had played
a square game.   He had played it to his limit—to the
point where he could go no farther without sacrifice
of his manhood on the tinseled altar of Town; and the
thing that troubled him was not the relentless demon
born of a man's past misdeeds, but the unquiet spirit
of Regret, which vexes all men when they look backward at matters wrought by uncontrollable force of
circumstance.   Though his conscience was clear, yet
his recollections and their inevitable sting kept him
restless—so much so that he lost weight and appetite,
and his lean face grew drawn and haggard.

Then, one night as he strode his cabin floor like a
caged panther, the wise counsel of Joe Dale came
back to him:

"Take an ol' man's advice an' git out more among men. It ain't good for a feller to live alone so much. Ye'd oughter have suthin' to do an' be round with other folks."

Almost it seemed that the old man had spoken in his ear. He stopped short, looking about him. Then he answered: "You're right, old-timer. I'll hunt a job in the morning."

Picking up his axe, he inspected its edge. Then he sat down by the fire and, with file and stone, sharpened it to keen efficiency. After a moment's thought he gave his rifle a thorough oiling, lifted a loose board from the bottom of his bunk (which he had purposely built with a false flooring), and laid the weapon in a narrow hiding-place. Replacing the board, he unrolled his blankets and curled up in them. And that night, for the first time since he had left the Dale home, he slept soundly.

Up with dawn, he breakfasted heartily, shut the door hard behind him, and swung away through the woods to his left. Soon the timber thinned, and from the edge of his terrace he looked out to the north. Far below and miles away, a tiny plume of smoke rose out of a shapeless mass of trees stretching black across the white carpet of winter. There, he surmised, was a logging-camp. Fixing its direction firmly in mind, he let himself over the edge and began worming his way down the swift-dropping mountainside.

The sun was high in the forenoon sky when he snowshoed into a clearing and stopped before a shanty. In answer to his hail a short, sandy-haired, lantern-jawed man whose shrewd face bespoke Scotch-Irish ancestry stepped to the door.

" You the boss? " clipped Donald.

" Yep."

" Want a man? "

The other chewed slowly on a cud of tobacco. His sharp eyes went over the newcomer's stalwart figure, came back to his face, and bored into it like gimlets. After a time they dropped to the keen-edged axe. Squirting a brown stream expertly from a corner of his mouth, he answered:

" Mebbe."

Donald said nothing, but waited. The other ran his eyes over him again. A wintry smile stretched his mouth. He looked to left and right, spat again, and asked:

" Kin ye fight? "

Narrow-eyed, Donald tried to read his thought. He knew something of lumber-camps and their ways, but he expected any question as to his fighting ability to be brought up after he was hired, not before. However, he nodded.

" Guess ye kin handle yerself," agreed the boss. " C'm'ere a minute."

Donald stepped closer. The other sank his voice.

" I got enough men. I got one man too many. An' yit I need another man. Mebbe ye're the feller I need. I'm goin' to find out."

With which cryptic utterance he paused and chewed reflectively. Presently he continued.

" It's like this: One o' my best men is Red Hawkins.

But Red thinks he kin fight. He's got all the rest o' the men thinkin' so too. But he ain't satisfied to let it go at that—he licks somebody most every day, even when nobody wants no trouble. One o' my men got a whalin' this mornin', an' he won't be much good for a couple days. By that time somebody else'll be laid up—an' that's how it goes. Red's too good a worker for me to fire, but yit he sort o' holds back the work with his fool fightin'. D'ye git what I mean?"

Don nodded.

"Awright. Now Red ain't what ye'd call mean— that is, he wouldn't kick a feller's face off arter he was down, or nawthin' like that. He's jest a sort of a big kid—his body's growed up, but I guess his mind stopped growin' when he was about sixteen. What he needs is the same dose ye hafter give a kid oncet in a while when he gits too biggety for his britches—a good wallopin' to knock the nonsense out of him. One good solid whalin' would be the best thing ever happened to him. But nobody round here kin give it to him, an' so he's got the idee he kin lick the hull world. Now I figger mebbe ye kin turn the trick. If ye wanter muckle onto Red, an' if ye give him the medicine he needs, ye'll be doin' a good turn for me, for the rest o' the gang, an' for Red himself. Whaddye say?"

"I never start anything."

The other looked disappointed. Then his face brightened.

"Oh, I git ye! Ye never start nawthin'—ye finish what the other feller starts. Wal, ye won't hafter start nawthin' with Red. He's a genuwine self-starter—he

don't need no crankin'. If he don't start sump'n with
ye before the day's out it'll be becuz he ain't feelin'
good. An'—wal, this is jest between you an' me, o'
course—if ye give him a good trimmin' I'll slip ye a
little bonus, quiet-like, in yer fust pay. Now thar's
yer proposition. Take it or leave it."

" I'll look it over. Never mind the bonus. When
do I start work?"

" Haw, haw! Figger on stayin' a while, do ye?
Good! I'll put ye to work arter dinner—mebbe. I'm
Scotty McMahon. What's your name?"

" Macdonald."

" Oho! Ye're a Scotty too, hey? Wal, now ye've
got to lick Red, d'ye hear? If ye don't I'll—I'll kick
ye out o' camp myself!"

Donald grinned down at the bantam boss, whom he
could have thrashed with one hand.

"All right, Mac, I'll give you leave," he promised.
Stooping, he untied his snowshoes.

He soon found that Scotty had spoken truly when
he said he need not start the fight. At noon the
choppers and sawyers and teamsters came in to eat,
and among them was a big fellow with flaming red
hair, a bold eye, and a boisterous belligerence of manner. His arrogance and the over-readiness of the
other men to laugh at his rough talk proclaimed him
at once as Hawkins, camp bully. And even before the
swift, clattering meal was over Hawkins had begun
to assert himself for the benefit of the newcomer.

With a purposely clumsy elbow he upset the coffee
of the man next him and then berated the victim for

leaving the cup there. The man said nothing. Then the giant bawled facetious questions concerning the health of another man farther down the table; and Donald, looking that way, saw that the " sick " man bore a battered face, moved his arms as if they hurt him, and ate in sullen silence. Obviously he was the fellow who had been " whaled " that morning. Having amused himself by thus showing off, the bully then became more personal toward Donald.

He mimicked the stranger's way of eating, which was not the sort of pick-and-shovel work displayed by the loggers. He made loud requests for pink tea, bemoaned the fact that he had neglected to put on a " swaller-tailed " coat, and in other ways poked irritating ridicule at the silent man whose " goat " he intended to get. But Donald ate calmly on, apparently deaf, and awaited an overt act.

It came soon enough. When he completed his deliberate meal and stepped out of the eating-shack most of the men had preceded him. Before the door stood. Hawkins, chaffing a couple of grinning teamsters. As if he had not seen the tall stranger come out, he stepped casually sidewise into Donald's path. They collided.

" Pick up yer big feet! " bellowed Hawkins, wheeling with a glare. "An' look whar ye're goin'! Dig the dirt out o' yer eyes, or I'll clean 'em for ye! "

Donald made no reply. He stood ready, waiting, looking the bully straight in the eye.

"An' don't gimme no sassy looks neither! I'm Red Hawkins, I am! If ye ain't got no manners I'll larn ye some! "

The idea of Hawkins teaching him etiquette struck Donald as humorous. He grinned sardonically.

"Funny, ain't it! I'm a funny feller, ye bet! An' the funniest thing I do is knockin' grins offen fresh fellers' faces!"

With which he swung at Donald's mouth.

The blow never landed. Don parried it with a forearm and threw it aside. Then he slapped Hawkins' face twice.

A grunt ran among the other men. Some bolder spirit snickered. The face of the astonished bully turned redder than his hair. With a muttered oath he sprang in, both fists swinging.

Again Donald fended a blow and slapped him—a back-handed slap across the mouth. But the red man's other fist caught him beside the head, a savage jolt that made his ears ring. Nimbly he sprang back out of range, his hands closing. The power of that punch showed him that there must be no more slapping. Red Hawkins was strong, fast, two-handed, and mad clear through. Thrashing him would be no child's play.

The hermit adopted a jabbing game. He jabbed and got away, jabbed and got away, slipping in an occasional straight left or a hook, goading his antagonist into fury and getting his points. In a few minutes he had them. The man was a stand-up slugger, fighting with swift swings, scorning footwork, and poor at defense. Wherefore Donald made use of his own feet, darting in and out and aside, and shooting over a medley of stinging jolts from unexpected angles. A few bone-crunching smashes landed on him in return, but

most of the red man's swings hit nothing. Soon Hawkins was thoroughly bewildered.

" Stan' still, dang ye! " he growled, squinting angrily
through swelling eyelids. " Think this is a dancin'-
school? "

Nothing loath, Donald accepted the challenge. He
now had the man about where he wanted him, and he
could afford to discard his footwork. The woodsman
grunted with satisfaction and bored in. For minutes
the pair stood toe to toe and slugged in a fashion that
brought howls of delight from the tense circle of loggers about them. Then Donald stepped swiftly back.
As the other rushed he clipped him neatly on the chin.

The blow landed exactly where he aimed it. Blank
astonishment overspread the battered face of the bully.
His hands dropped. He teetered on his toes, his knees
sagged, and he slumped down into the snow.

" Purtiest knockout I ever see! " yelped Scotty Mc-
Mahon. "An' I've seen a good many. Jest a snappy
little stinger in the right place, an' good-night Red!
Neat, I call it! "

Wherewith he jumped to Hawkins' side and, swinging a pendulum arm up and down, counted him out.

As the fatal " ten " rang from his lips Hawkins
stirred—rolled over—got to his knees. There he
paused, staring at the grim figure of the victor.

" Want any more? " snapped Donald.

Red passed a hand over his face and blinked.

" I'll be ready for ye in a minute," he grunted.
" What happened to me? Did I git a stroke or
sump'n? "

McMahon cackled. The loggers howled.

"Ye got a stroke awright, Red," said one. " The fight's all over. Ye're licked."

The announcement galvanized Hawkins. He scrambled up.

" Licked? Me licked? I ain't got started yit!" he roared. " Come on, ye ——"

But McMahon stopped him.

" That'll do, Red! Ye're licked. Licked in as squar a scrap as ever I see. An' lemme tell ye sump'n—this feller's got yer number, an' from now on he kin lick ye three times a day, before or arter meals, if he feels like it. I been watchin', an' I know! Now ack like a man an' swaller yer medicine."

His words carried weight. Hawkins blinked uncertainly at him and at Donald. Don spoke.

" If you want any more come and get it. If you're satisfied, I am."

The other shuffled his feet, then grinned.

" I'm satisfied," he admitted.

Donald promptly extended his hand.

" No hard feelings? " he asked.

" Not a dang feelin'," responded the late bully, giving him a mighty grip.

"All right. Let's get to work."

And to work they got.

CHAPTER XXXI

MEN AND GHOSTS

IN the days that followed, the men found Donald something of a puzzle. At first they walked wide of him, thinking he would assume the rôle of bully in succession to Hawkins; but he did nothing of the sort. Observing this, some of the loggers went to the other extreme and became offensively familiar. They quickly dropped this attitude, however; for, without speaking, he would give such men a slow, steady stare that warned them not to presume too far. He worked hard, kept his mouth shut, and was neither tyrant nor hail-fellow-well-met. So the others did not quite know what to make of him. It was Scotty, shrewdly observant, who gave them their cue.

"This feller Macdonald's one o' them quiet men that say nawthin' an' saw wood," he said one day when Donald was out of earshot. "He ain't exackly our kind, but yit he ain't stuck-up neither. He's got sump'n on his mind, an' he's sort o' studyin' all the time. His hands work on one thing an' his head on another, an' I bet he don't see ye half o' the time, no more'n if ye was a pack o' ghosts. All ye got to do is treat him squar an' not try no monkey business. He's a good feller, an' if ye jest leave him go his own gait we'll all git along fine. Tell the rest o' the boys I said that."

Scotty's analysis was correct.   The mind of the new
man often was far from his work, and at such times
the workmen around him were little more than phantoms.   Their narrow lives and simple problems held
no interest for him, and he made no effort to enter into
them.   Yet he did not hold himself aloof.   When the
day was done he smoked his pipe with the rest, answering laconically when spoken to, and deriving a passing
amusement from their rough badinage.   As Joe Dale
had foreseen, the companionship of whole-hearted men
and the healthy activity of physical toil were good for
him.

Oddly enough, the one man among them whom he
really liked was his recent antagonist, Red Hawkins.
Possibly this was because Red, having at last met a
man who could master him, studied him with deep personal interest and thus became observant of his moods;
but more likely it was because of the fellow-feeling
that often exists between two square fighting-men, and
because Red was, as Scotty had said, " jest a big kid "
—a grown-up boy who had had some of the conceit
knocked out of him and who bore no malice.   For,
after the first sting of defeat passed off, Hawkins
regained his rough joviality, minus most of his former
arrogance.   He had learned that he could not " lick the
hull world," which is a valuable lesson to either an
individual or a nation; but he was perfectly able and
willing to thrash any of the loggers who gave him
offense, as one misguided sawyer quickly learned when
he thought to twit him on his change of status.

Donald watched this thrashing with an appreciative

smile; and afterward he gave Hawkins a few quiet tips on the finer points of boxing. This, coupled with the fact that Donald had never " crowed over " him, completely won the heart of the big red-haired man. From that time on he was never far away from Donald after working hours, and when he judged that the silent " Mac " was down-hearted he sought to cheer him up by starting a little fun. Often he succeeded, too; for he could start a frolic as readily as a fight, and the boisterous laughter attendant upon a good-natured rough-house was so infectious that it frequently exorcised the sombre thoughts from Donald's mind.

The weeks passed, and Christmas came—" lonesomest day in the hull dang year," as Red put it. All work was suspended. Several of the men, whose homes were not far away, disappeared on the night before the holiday. Somewhat to the surprise of those who were left, Hawkins also vanished in company with one of the teamsters, not to reappear until late in the evening. To questions as to where he had been he replied only by mysterious winks; and the teamster, sworn to secrecy which he feared to break with the menace of Red's fists looming in his mind, yielded no answer to quizzing. The mystery remained unsolved until the next day, when an impromptu program of sports had been run off under the loud direction of Red, self-appointed referee. Then he and the teamster disappeared again, to return presently with a cargo of snow-covered jugs.

A wild yell of joy was succeeded by a pell-mell rush as the men recognized the liquor-jars—for, though national prohibition was as yet undreamed of, the State of New Hampshire even then was disgustingly " dry." Red beat off the small mob and regulated the pouring of the drinks, taking care to get his own full share. The delight of the men became vociferous when they found that the jugs contained not mere hard cider, but home-made New England rum.

" Whar'd ye git it? " they chorused.

" None o' yer business! " Red told them bluntly. " I got friends, an' that's all ye need to know. Bimeby I'll pass the hat to pay the bill—an' any son-of-a-gun that don't chip in, I'll take him by the heels an' shake the licker outen him. Hey thar, Big Mac, ain't ye drinkin'? "

Donald, standing back, shook his head.

" Don't touch it unless I'm sick," he explained.

" Ye don't? Gorry mighty, I never took ye for a parson! Say, be a good feller an' git sick quick, will ye? This is dang good stuff! "

Don smiled, but again shook his head. Red, however, was not to be denied.

" Then, by jing, ye'll hafter save some till ye do git sick. Hey thar, Jake, go git a bottle somewhar! An' git a move on! "

Jake went, and returned with a bottle suspiciously resembling a flask. Red filled it, corked it, and held it out.

" Compliments o' Red Hawkins an' Sandy Claws! " he proclaimed. " Come an' git it, Mac! "

So Donald sauntered over and took it, with an exaggerated bow to Red and the gang. He had little thought of using it. But the time was not far off when he was to find excellent use for his Christmas gift.

By noon everybody except Donald had a glorious souse, and the Christmas dinner—though it varied from the ordinary fare only by the addition of hot plum-pudding—was the merriest ever eaten in that camp. Backwoods jokes, songs of robust humor, and roars of laughter kept the shack quivering throughout the meal. At its end Red draped a mackinaw around his hips, clambered tipsily into the middle of the table, and performed a ludicrous skirt-dance which reduced all hands to hiccoughing helplessness. When they recovered they clamored for more dancing, and Red told them to do it themselves. Forthwith the table was cast out into the snow, benches followed, and the room was cleared for action. But then somebody discovered that there was no music.

" I can play a mouth-organ," volunteered Donald. "Anybody got one? "

Somebody had one—a battered instrument minus several keys, squeaky and discordant. But to the loggers it was something to dance by, and that was enough. So Donald got into a corner, tongued the instrument into a waltz, and the dance was on.

It lasted all the afternoon. The hardened muscles of the woodsmen, stimulated and fortified by the rum, knew no exhaustion, and pauses came only when the musician stopped for breath and the dancers craved a smoke or a drink. The men took turns at being " wimmin," adopting high falsetto notes and affecting

a simpering coyness that was ridiculous in the extreme.
Yet on Donald, who was sober, the festivity presently
palled, and he kept playing only to make a holiday for
the others.

In the thickening tobacco-smoke the stamping men
whirled past like ghosts—noisy, hilarious ghosts, but
phantoms nevertheless. His playing became mechanical, and his thoughts winged from this uproarious
lumber-camp to a far more quiet scene—the home of
the Dales, with its solemn clock, its kindly master and
its pansy-faced mistress. Father and daughter were
thinking of him this day, he knew, and wondering why
he did not come to join them in their Christmas dinner.
He wished himself there with them, as he had done
more than once since coming into camp. And as his
mind dwelt on the Dale farm and his own forsaken
cabin, slowly there grew up in him an aversion to his
present surroundings and an irresistible longing to return to his own forest and his own friends.

His absent gaze rested on the doorway, thrown open
to cool the heated dancers. Presently he became conscious of the answering stare of Scotty McMahon,
lounging in the opening and watching him. Scotty
was well lit up, but he was not dancing; he was keeping a weather eye on the gang to see that no free-for-
all fight developed. For some time he had also been
studying Donald's face. Now Don stopped abruptly
and strode over to him.

" I'll take my time, Mac," he announced.

Scotty nodded reluctantly.

" I calc'lated ye was gittin' ready to quit," he said.

"Yer eyes showed it. Dang sorry to lose ye, too, big feller. Mebbe ye'll come back?"

"Maybe. Don't know."

"Awright—hic—come back any time. When ye goin'?"

"Pay me off Saturday."

Scotty nodded again. Further talk was cut off by bawls from the dance-hungry gang.

"Come on, Big Mac! Whoop 'er up! Blow the guts out o' yer mouth-organ! Christmas is goin' fast, and we got to work to-morrer!"

So Donald, though his mouth already was rubbed raw, started in anew and played until everyone at last was satisfied.

Saturday brought snow—a steady downfall blown hither and yon by a shifting wind. At noon Donald drew his pay, shook hands around, and left camp with the jovial farewells of the gang ringing in his ears. Up through the storm-blurred pastures and forest he tramped toward his cabin. It was a stiff climb up the mountainside, and the early winter night was drawing on as he stopped before the door which he had slammed shut weeks ago.

By the time supper was cooked and eaten darkness had come. The wind increased. It hissed through the needly pines, shrilled at the corners of the cabin, moaned drearily in the chimney. Over the hermit, fresh from the roistering companionship of the camp, settled a depression which the snap and glow of the fire could not banish. He tried to disregard the dismal sounds, to think of amusing incidents of his life as a lumberjack, but the effort failed. The melancholy wind dominated him, for it seemed freighted with malicious spirits and menacing voices—voices now stilled for all time. Now and then the door rattled as if ghostly enemies sought to shove it open and swarm in. At the black window glimmered faces that were gone from his life: the leering visage of Bull the thug, the crafty face of Sniffy the Weasel, the shark eyes of Duncan. It seemed that evil things were abroad in the night, beleaguering the lonely cabin and urging one another to rush it and destroy the man inside.

So strong did this feeling become that the hermit strode to the window and peered out. Of disembodied things he had no fear, but the thought had come to him that he had a live and deadly enemy on this mountain —Black Jules; and it was always possible that Jules would find this covert. But Jules was not there. Steady staring into the gloom showed no living thing outside. With a short laugh he turned back and went to his bunk.

Out from its hiding-place he lifted his rifle. It was still slippery with the oil he had put on it weeks before. Sitting down, he swabbed the weapon dry, then ejected the cartridges, laid them beside him, and began wiping out the receiver.

Suddenly his hand stopped. He leaned forward, tense, staring and listening.

Above the ghostly noises of the wind rose a quavering cry.

CHAPTER XXXII

THE BLOODHOUND

IT was a man's voice—a fear-ridden voice—a voice of agony and despair, imploring help.

Donald tore open the door and leaped out into the snow.

" Hello there! " he roared.

Instantly the cry came again, from the tangled timber between the cabin and the trail—a broken, gasping, inarticulate call. In the thick blackness Donald could see nothing, but he could hear something—a spent man hurling himself on through the storm. And as he came he whimpered. The sound chilled the waiting man's blood.

Jumping back into the house, he seized the gas lamp which Harry had left and swiftly lit it. Another bound, and he was again outside, shooting the searchlight ray at the place whence came that fearsome sound. Then out from the forest, floundering, staggering, stumbling, but driven on by an awful fear, reeled a figure with its head hanging and swaying in the last extremity of exhaustion. From its stiffened lips came a hoarse whisper:

" Mac! Mac! "

" Joe! " cried the hermit.

"Yuh," gasped the old man—and fell on his face.

Donald sprang to his side. Swiftly he raised him and bore him inside. His face was that of the dead.

Down beside the fireplace Donald laid him. Then, straddling the inert body, he began strenuous work of resuscitation. As he toiled, across his mind flashed the memory of the Christmas rum given him by Red Hawkins. He yanked it from his hip and poured the pungent fluid between the gray lips.

The old man's eyes opened. He rolled his head feebly away from the bottle.

"Mac!" he gasped. "Pansy!"

That name, and the naked fear in the farmer's face, struck Donald rigid for an instant.

"What—what ——" he mumbled.

The other tried to struggle up, but fell back. His old eyes glazed with horror, he jerked out:

"Gone! Kerried off! Jules!"

Don's face went dead white. He leaped for coat and gun.

As he struggled into the coat Joe reeled up from the floor, reviving under the stimulus of the liquor, and staggered toward him.

"Oh Gawd, Mac!" he whimpered. "Save my little gal—ef ye kin! Mebbe it's too late now—it took me a thousand y'ars—to git here! Ye know whar he lives —oh, help us, Mac! Help us—nobody else kin!"

"I'm going!" gritted Donald, snatching up the light. "Stay here!"

Dale slumped into a chair, muttering over and over: "Oh Gawd, Mac!"

Outside and tying on his snowshoes with frenzied fingers, Donald shot one question through the doorway.

" Joe! Are you sure it was Jules? "

The old man started up. " Couldn't of been nobody else! She fit him—kitchin's all tore up. I found tracks—snowshoes an' a sled—long narrer shoes—one of 'em had a patch in the toe. The tracks come up the mountin—oh, help us, Mac ——"

Donald heard no more. He was off and away. Through the snow, now falling thinly, his gas lamp glared ahead like a locomotive headlight. And like an engine of death running wild, he tore along the terrace and out to the open trail.

As he ran he gave thanks to the grim goddess Nemesis that the path led down-hill and the way was clear. Downward he plunged like an avalanche, his flying shoes smashing a smother of snow outward and upward. Well was it for him then that he had snowshoed much in other years; for now he sped so fast that a flounder would have meant violent collision with tree or boulder. But there was no floundering. The walls of brush fled past on either side with unbroken speed.

When he reached the fallen tree, now partly buried but still an obstruction, he growled because he lost a few seconds in climbing over. Farther down, when he sought the conical boulder and could not find it—for it had sunk well down into the drifts, and even the trees looked unfamiliar in their winter garb—the dread that he might be too late to save sunny little Pansy girl smote him to the heart. He took an iron grip on himself while he sought the stone which would point out the way, but it seemed that an endless night passed before he discovered it. Then, overmastered by impatience, he smashed his way into the brush at mad speed.

The whipping of the branches across his face brought him to his senses.

"Got to make haste slowly," he muttered. The words were hardly out of his mouth when he caught a foot and fell sprawling. His rifle flew from his hand and dived into a drift.

Several more minutes were lost while he swept the light back and forth, seeking the lost gun. When he spied its butt barely showing above the snow he pounced on it, yanked it forth, and worked the action once to assure himself that it was uninjured. Suddenly he grew rigid.

"Great God!" he croaked.

The gun was not broken. It was empty.

In sudden frenzy he pumped the lever up and down, seeking to draw from the magazine a cartridge which was not there. The vacant clatter of the ejector mocked him. He had unloaded the weapon in order to clean it. When he heard that cry from the forest he had flung it aside. Dazed by Joe's terrible tidings, he had swooped it up without a thought that it was not reloaded. His cartridges now lay useless on his bunk.

The shock staggered him. Gray-faced, he stood staring hopelessly down into the bare receiver. Then his fingers began to fumble in his pockets. Something whispered to him that he had a cartridge somewhere in his clothing. And the tiny mentor was right. In a coat pocket he found one cartridge.

It was a " dud "—one which had failed to explode on a previous hunting trip, and which he had not thrown away because his ammunition was scarce and precious. A cartridge which fails on the first trial will sometimes work the second time, he knew. Now, staring down at the defective primer with the blunt dent of the firing-pin showing plain in its copper, he savagely vowed that it *must* work. It was his only hope of saving Pansy. With a fierce but unspoken prayer he forced it into the barrel. Then he ran on toward the cabin of Jules the Black.

Guiding himself by tree and bush-clump, he forged ahead as fast as the bewildering darkness would allow. Ever the need for haste hammered upon his brain, and it was more through blind instinct than by recognition of his surroundings that he held his way true through the wilderness. On and on, with cold fear for Pansy gnawing at his heart; on and on, armed only with one cartridge which already had failed to stand the test— so he sped through the night, driven by wrath and hate, while in his ears still rang an old man's beseeching cry: " Oh Gawd, Mac! Help us! "

Suddenly he leaped away with new speed. He had cut the half-breed's trail.

Before him, hardly blurred by the falling flakes, ran the track of a sledge. Its broad runners had sunk well down into the soft snow, and the body of it had scraped smoothly along and smeared out the marks of

the snowshoes which preceded it. It had been heavily
laden, that sledge—burdened with the weight of Pansy,
whom the breed had dragged up the mountain and
through the pathless woods. No doubt he thought the
storm would wipe out that trail before morning, and
deemed himself safe from all pursuit. But the storm-
gods had failed him.

Along that unmistakable trail Donald raced on
faster, ever faster, lifting his eyes now and then to
dart glances at tree and boulder and hillock. At length,
the winding track swerved sharp around the base of a
steep, bare slope. He slowed, stopped, and shot the
light up along the declivity. It was the deceptive hill,
smoothly rounded on one side and precipitous on the
other, where the lair of Jules was hidden. His goal
was just around the turn.

He put out the light. With the clipping off of that
white ray the darkness seemed Stygian. Stealthily but
swiftly he tramped around the hill; and as he went his
eyes righted themselves and the double track of the
runners again became visible, dim ruts in the wan
snow. Then a small rectangle of yellow light showed
in the blackness under the hill. He knew it came from
an oil lamp shining beyond the little window in Jules'
door.

Throttling down a fierce impulse to hurl himself
headlong at that door, he trod silently up to it, balanced
himself with long arms outspread against the solid logs
beside it, and peered through the dirty glass. As he
saw what was going on inside a hot wave of joy surged
through him.

He had come in time.

Like the animal he was, Jules had attended first to the call of his belly. He sat on a stool before a crude table near the stove, and his tin plate was bare. Now, his normal appetite glutted, he was feeding his abnormal craving for liquor and feasting his ghoulish eyes on poor little Pansy girl, who cowered against the wall. She was white to the lips with the pallor of hopeless terror. But she was not crying, nor pleading, nor looking about her for a way of escape; she knew it to be useless. A forlorn little figure of despair, she only shrank away from him as far as she could, watching him as a trapped little bird might watch a snake crawling upward to destroy it.

And Jules, true to the Indian strain in his mongrel blood, was enjoying her helpless torture. And he was boisterous, boastful, as his type ever is when inflamed by drink. His loud voice came through the ill-fitting door.

"An' you t'eenk you fool me, you laugh at me on the trail wit' your lovair!" he jeered. "You laugh about how I speet blood—*sacre!*—an' how I t'eenk your lovair ees your brothair. An' all de tam Jules ees right beside you, ma leetle wil'cat! But he ees no fool, Jules LeNoir—*mais non!* He wait an' he watch, an' bimeby he grab you—so!"

He stretched a dirty paw at her and pinched thumb and forefinger together, grinning a devilish grin.

"Ho ho! Who laugh now, leetle liar? You are los' in de woods where your lovair can't fin' you, an' *I* am your lovair now, *moi!* Mebbe when de spreeng-

time come I tire of you, an' you can go back to de beeg
peeg you love—after Jules ees t'rough!'"

He threw back his head and laughed harshly, his
glittering eyes still dwelling on her through black-
lashed slits. She shrank still more against the wall.
Don's hands curled into fists against the logs. The
breed poured another drink from the bottle into his
thick throat.

"*Mais non!*" he bellowed, as the fiery rotgut put a
new kink into his brain. " I t'eenk I keell your lovair,
moi. Mebbe I keell you too bimeby. *Mais* first I'll
tame you, ma leetle devil, an' mak' you do w'atever I
want. *Oui,* by gar! I mak' you show me hees cabin.
I mak' you lead me to heem. I have mak' heem run
from me, but I ain't find hees place where he hide.
He's afraid, de beeg peeg, afraid o' Black Jules, an' so
he hide away. Ho ho! Now you'll lead me to heem
an' watch Jules keell heem. *Mais oui!*"

Then Pansy defied him. In her extremity and despair, she defied him. She straightened against the
wall, her chin came up, her big blue eyes flashed.
What she said Donald could not hear through the
door, but her resolute attitude told him. No matter
what happened to her, she would never lead this fiend
on the trail of the stalwart fellow who had watched
over her through the days when her father was gone.

The heart of the silent watcher swelled within him,
and his fierce eyes softened. Simultaneously two
thoughts struck him—that he must reach the rear window, and that he must untie his snowshoes. His one
poor cartridge might do its work this time, but he

dared not trust it. In any case he must get into the cabin, and the only way was through the window; for the door, he knew, must be barred. Without touching the door, which might squeak and give warning, he slipped his webbed feet backward preparatory to turning away. As he did so a roar of laughter arose inside.

"Ho ho ho! You leetle speetfire! But yes, you weell! You t'eenk I can't mak' you show me de place? Eef you don't I keell you—I keell you *slow!* I keelled wan woman so, een Quebec—*oui!*"

Donald started. In a flash he saw again the fear in that black-bearded face when Pansy had threatened him with hanging, down there in the Dale dooryard months ago. So the half-breed was a fugitive.

"De police hunt me for dat, but I fool 'em—ho ho, *oui!*"

Again the human bloodhound outside choked down an impulse to assault that door. Noiselessly he sped around to the rear of the house. Like a spectre of the storm he strode to the window. There he stooped and loosed his snowshoes.

The voice of Jules came again, loud and ugly.

"I tame you, ma Lucee! I tame you queeck! *Sacre,* I tame you now!"

Up rose Donald, his feet unfettered. Through the window he saw Jules rising slowly, his face aflame. Her back to the wall, desperation and loathing in her eyes, Pansy braced herself to fight him to the uttermost. With a hoarse growl Donald swung his rifle hard against the window.

CHAPTER XXXIII

THE DEATH-GRAPPLE

SMASH! Shattering glass crashed. Through the opening Donald shoved the barrel of his gun, its muzzle menacing the breed's head.

" Back up!" he snapped. " Stand away from her!"

Rooted to the floor, Jules stared slack-jawed at the deadly gun and deadly face framed in the broken window. The girl, all hope long since fled, stood staring incredulously at her rescuer. Then a sobbing cry of gladness broke from her, and with arms outstretched she started from the wall.

" Back, Pansy!" warned Donald. " Don't get in line with him. You Jules! Open that door!"

Slowly Jules turned as if to obey. He took one step. Then, quicker than light, his left hand licked out and knocked the glass lamp from the table. Instantly the cabin was dark.

Donald pulled trigger.

A thunderous report—a streak of flame—a sudden scream. The rescuer dropped his gun and hurled himself through the window.

Scrambling up from the floor, he jumped toward where Jules should be. Some unseen obstruction tripped him. He fell, striking violently on a rising body, and knocked it flat. A gasping snarl came from

340

under him. He had fallen on Jules, who, escaping the bullet by throwing himself sidewise, had turned toward the window and now was springing up.

The impact against the floor knocked the wind out of the half-breed. But the collision smote the breath out of Donald too. He grabbed the enemy's legs, locked his own knees around the breed's neck, and hung on.

Flame was licking upward from the floor—flame from the shattered lamp, whose oil had ignited. By its weird light he saw Pansy, half-dazed from the concussion of the rifle-shot, staring down at him like a ghost in the dark.

" Out! " he managed to gasp.

She started, sprang to the door, unbarred it and fled into the night.

Breath was coming back to him. Jules was squirming under him. He began to rise in air, as the breed got his hands beneath him and pushed himself up. Locking his feet, he squeezed that black head between his knees with all his power. At the same time he seized one of Jules' ankles with both hands and twisted it. A choking groan broke from the man underneath. But still, doggedly, he rose. Donald began to slip off his enemy's back. Still holding that relentless knee-grip, he snapped his legs sidewise. The unexpected yank threw Jules off balance. He crashed down again, upsetting the table.

Both had recovered their wind. Now, even as Jules hit the floor, Donald let go. Up on his feet he sprang. Jules seemed to rebound from the boards. He rushed, his face hideous with hate.

Two smashing blows Donald shot into that distorted visage: blows that cracked like gunshots. Jules reeled, but came on. His powerful talons swooped at his assailant's throat. They missed; for Donald burst straight through them, landing a frightful blow under the breed's heart. The clutching thumbs tore his neck and slid over his shoulders. Then they grappled.

Wrenching, racking, striking, clawing, they reeled about the flaming room in abysmal combat. Each saw nothing but his enemy. Each felt nothing but the wild blood-lust which bereft him of sense, of reason, of all but the primitive madness to kill.

But human flesh could not forever endure such battering; human framework could not stand such wrenching, nor human lungs such furious conflict. At length, from pure exhaustion, the combatants fell apart. They swayed on wobbling legs, watched each other with glazed eyes, and gasped. Though the fire was growing fiercer, the smoke bothered them little; for the open door and the broken window at either end of the place formed a sort of flue, and a wind sweeping in at the entrance carried off much of the smoke while it fanned the flames.

They got their breath again, and Donald attacked. This time Jules did not spring at him, but waited. He ducked one blow; reeled under another; tried for a deadly back-hold, and lost it. Then, in the hot grapple again, they battled with renewed fury.

It took a stunning crack on the head to knock some reason back into them. Both got it at the same time. Though they had fought the length of the cabin time after time, wrecking all they struck, the dilapidated old stove still stood untouched. Now, in one whirling, snarling clinch, they fell headlong across it. Their skulls whacked against the log wall with dizzying force. The stove, rotten with rust, overturned beneath their weight and fell apart. Its blazing fuel and red-hot coals scattered over the floor. Its blistering heat bit through their thick winter clothing like the fangs of an adder. They broke, squirmed off the hot iron, and stood apart, blinking dizzily at each other.

Dazed by the impact, yet they were sobered by it. Heretofore they had fought with the paroxysmal fury of jungle animals striving to rend each other. Now, though their deadly hatred was undiminished, they became reasoning creatures and their fighting craft reasserted itself.

Jules fumbled at his waistband. His hand jerked upward, gripping a naked blade. Instantly Donald was upon him, seizing his wrist with one hand, choking him with the other. A fearful struggle ensued. Savagely Jules strove to drive the knife into his opponent's body and to break that hold on his throat. With all his power Donald fought to keep his bulldog grip on wrist and windpipe. The breed's face grew purple; his eyes protruded; his mouth gaped. Then a terrific drive of his pinioned right arm carried the knife-point slashing up his antagonist's side.

From that cutting pain Don instinctively dodged away—and lost his throat-hold. In the same instant he tripped over something. Jules hurled him off his feet and down. As he fell, the dread knife-hand was wrenched from his grasp.

Now the fire was burning higher along one side of the cabin. The floor-boards too were blazing hotly. Struck repeatedly by the battling bodies, the over-turned table had been buffeted about and now lay with its legs in the flames. Across the upturned edge of the table-top Donald fell sidewise with a force that seemed to crush in his ribs. Before he could move Jules was on him in snarling triumph.

The knife flashed up, started down. But before the blade could pierce his struggling body it halted abruptly. It hung poised a few inches above him. The Indian half of the breed's nature had halted that death-stroke: halted it because it saw a chance for torture.

Pinned down on that rigid table-edge, the fallen man had no chance. More than half of him was off the floor, held helpless by the table and his enemy's grip. His moccasined feet slipped uselessly on the boards. His hands could clutch nothing but his foe. His head and shoulders hung above the flames, which licked greedily up at him. All Jules had to do was to hold him there—and let him burn.

A shrill cackle yammered from the Canuck's aching throat.

" Burn, peeg! " he taunted. " Roas', peeg! Bimeby I steeck you in de t'roat lak any odder peeg! "

Madly Donald heaved and kicked and squirmed. But the utmost he could achieve was a turn of his body. He got his face upward, away from the blaze;

but now he hung across the sharp edge on his back, and that sharp edge bit into his spine. Above him leered the vindictive face of Jules. Clamped around his throat was the iron hand of Jules. Into his despairing eyes burned the baleful eyes of Jules. And flashing lurid in the red light hung that naked steel.

"Burn, peeg!" mocked the half-breed again. "I keell you—slow! I t'eenk I cut you up w'ile you roas'."

He cackled afresh in demoniac mirth. Slowly, with torturing deliberation, the knife descended toward Donald's eyes. He strained back from it, fought to clutch his enemy's wrist again; but his arms were held down by the full weight of the other's body. He could not free them. Backward he bent until it seemed his vertebræ must snap. The flames bit into his neck. And still the knife crept nearer.

The table broke. The two lower legs were burned half through. Suddenly, under the combined weight of the men, they snapped off short. The top fell over, carrying the combatants with it. The other two legs struck with a grinding jar that nearly broke Don's back. The knife came down in a vicious jab; but its aim was deflected by the unexpected upset, and it merely slashed along its victim's scalp above the ear. Then the upper table-legs, unable to bear the strain, cracked and tore away from the top, which fell flat. Jules lost his grip and landed on his face amid the flames. Donald rolled out of the fire and sprang up.

His back seemed paralyzed, his head was bursting, his nerves were shaken. Yet, as Jules scrambled up, gasping and blinded, he rushed at him once more. Jules still held the knife. With both hands now Donald seized that wrist from the side. Then he whirled his back to Jules. He twisted the wrist sidewise. He heaved the arm up high. With every atom of his power he brought that rigid arm down on his shoulder.

Above the snap of the flames sounded a dull crack. Jules screeched. The knife fell. Donald threw the arm aside. He had broken it.

Then, in the thickening smoke, the half-breed saw the fiery eyes of Pauguk, Indian god of Death. Around his heart he felt the icy hand of Pauguk. In the hiss of the flames he heard the summons of Pauguk. Stark fear smote him. He fell on his craven knees and begged.

Donald looked down on a face turned ghastly. Blackened by smoke and flame, blistered by burns, reddened with blood from fist-cuts and split lips and broken nose, yet the breed's countenance seemed pallid. On it was stamped an awful terror. In the swollen black eyes which a moment ago had danced in devilish delight over a tortured victim now stared the naked fear of death. From his writhing lips fell a babble of pleas for mercy.

Sickened, Donald cut him short.

"You killed a woman in Quebec!" he charged.

"*Mais non—mais oui—oh Dieu,* you are de police!" screamed the wretch, and his face grew yet more distorted. A torrent of unintelligible patois burst from him. He dragged himself forward on his knees and one hand, imploring mercy in a way that nauseated

Donald. It seemed that the groveling creature was about to clasp his legs, and he gave back sharply.

"Get up!" he growled. "Stand up like a man, you whining cur!"

But still that miserable figure hunched itself along toward him, and he gave back again. In the bare nick of time he glanced at the breed's one good hand. It was just darting out toward the fallen knife.

Donald promptly kicked him in the body. The kick lifted him half off the floor, away from the knife. With another kick he sent the blade slithering across the floor and out of the door.

With a baffled snarl Jules sprang up. Desperately he launched himself at his conqueror, striking savagely with the broken arm as well as the good one. Donald ducked. He caught him around the hips. With a mighty heave he swung him up—up—hurled him over his head and let go.

Once more Jules screamed. It was his death-shriek. On his face he smashed to the floor. On his face. And his heavy body whirled over backward. Far backward. Mingled with the thud of his impact sounded a crackling crunch.

Donald stared down at the sprawling figure, which lay like a huddle of old clothes. He shoved it with his foot. It rolled a little, then flopped back. Stooping, he lifted it by the shoulders, turning it face upward. The head rolled sidewise, then backward, hanging far down, unnaturally limp. The neck was broken.

Thus died Black Jules.

CHAPTER XXXIV

THE LITTLE BLIND GOD

THE farther wall was now a solid sheet of flame. The heat was intolerable. The smoke was stifling. Out from that wall darted a long, curving tongue which licked around his face like the tentacle of an octopus. Gasping, choking, blinded, he reeled to the door and stumbled headlong out into the snow.

Once down, he stayed down for a time, his face upturned to the grateful coolness of the snowflakes, his hot body relaxed in the soft embrace of a drift. He might have stayed there overlong had not a compelling thought pulled him up as if a hand had seized him. Where was Pansy?

Floundering hip-deep, he pitched to his feet and turned his face to the night.

"Pansy!" he bellowed.

No answer came back.

"Pansy! Here!" he roared.

Silence, dreary silence hung heavy over the blackness, broken only by the hiss of the flames. Scanning the snow, he saw her tracks where she had struggled away in frantic fright. He started to follow. A few difficult strides, however, roused him to the fact that his snowshoes were behind the burning cabin. Turning, he lurched back along his own trail and around to the break in the wall of snow.

348

Flame and smoke now were rolling out from the broken window, making the rough cavern among the boulders a pocket of reddish light and choking fumes. Awaiting an instant when an air-current sucked the fire back into the house, he dashed at the logs, swooped on snowshoes and rifle, and dodged away just in time to avoid another blast of heat. Once again in the open, he looped the thongs around his moccasins and ran back to the door, seeking the gas lamp he had dropped there. He found it; and in the glare of the fire he found something else as well—the sledge on which Pansy had been brought helpless to her prison. Yanking at its rope, he slewed it around. Then, the lamp once more shooting its white beam ahead and the dead man's sledge trailing behind, he tramped away on the track of the fugitive.

He called as he went, and ere long he raised an answer. Huddled under a huge pine he found her, down in the black woods. Blindly she had fought her way through the drifts until she could go no farther; and it was an exhausted, half-frozen girl who awaited him beneath the shaggy arms of the forest giant.

"Are you hurt?" he asked anxiously. "You screamed when I fired."

"No, I—I wasn't hit. I guess I screamed—I was so scared. I'm awful cold an' tired an' lame—he choked me down there in the house—but I ain't really hurt. Oh, Don ——"

"There, there! All's well, little sister. Now we'll just run along home and get warm."

Up into his arms he swung her, as if she were only

a little girl who had run out to play and been lost in the snow. And safe at last in those strong arms, her overtaxed nerves snapped, and she dropped her head on his shoulder and burst into hysterical weeping.

Holding her close, he stood quiet and let her have her cry out, for he knew it would do her good. And while her arms clung about him and her breast heaved against his, comfort came to the man as well as to the maid. The ferocity of battle, the yet-rankling hatred of the dead half-breed—these faded out; and in their wake came an infinite tenderness toward this little girl who in bygone days had lifted him from a red abyss of phantoms, who had shielded him from Jules by claiming him as her brother, and who even in the hour of her extremity had refused to imperil him by telling her captor of his covert.

Nor was this all. With her in his embrace there grew in him a great calm strength, a feeling that a load had been lifted and that now he could stand straight and breathe deep. Had he tried to analyze this feeling he would have said it was relief because she was safe forevermore from the menace of Jules. Yet it was far more than that. Here in the darkness and the storm, with his enemy dead behind him and the vision of Pansy girl's unwavering loyalty shining clear before him, the last bitter dregs of grief and cynicism and rebellion were swept away. His redemption had become complete.

Presently she grew calmer, and lifted her head.

"I'm—I'm an awful cry-baby," she said. "I'll be all right now. You can—let me down."

But he did not release her at once. He stood looking down into the big eyes upturned to his. His head drooped lower and lower. Her mouth rose to meet him. Their lips touched and clung. And then for a time the cold and the snow and the darkness were not, and life itself seemed to fade into nothing; for, in that meeting of the lips, soul merged with soul.

At last he straightened. Turning, he set her gently down on the sledge.

"You're going to ride," he decreed. "You have no snowshoes. It will be rough going for a while, so hang tight. Now bundle yourself up." Stripping off his torn mackinaw, he wrapped it around her despite her muffled protests.

"I'll be warm enough," he assured her. "I'm going to be the horse." Turning the broad collar up around her head, he added: "Curl up and keep your head down, or the bushes will switch your face. Now mind, or I'll tell Pop to spank you!"

She laughed a little, as he hoped she would. But she pushed back the collar to ask: "Don, what—what about Jules?"

"Don't worry about him," he replied grimly. "I'll tell you all about it later on. Now curl up!"

She obeyed. He had two objects in thus muffling her face—to keep her warm and to prevent her from seeing any light from the burning cabin; for she had had more than enough of horror. Picking up the lamp, which he had so placed in the snow that its light would not strike him and clearly show his hurts, he gave a warning tug at the rope and then started away through the forest.

For a hundred yards or so he plowed away through untrodden snow before swinging back to his trail. When he knew the cabin must be hidden behind its hill he swerved to the left, and soon came out in the open. As he did so he began to talk, in order to keep his passenger's eyes to the front. He told how her father had come to warn him, and something of his dash down the mountain.

"Why, poor Pop!" she exclaimed. "I don't see how he ever did it! Why, he's been half crippled with his 'roomytiz,' and he didn't have any snowshoes!"

And Donald too, though he knew that a man can do the impossible under the stress of overmastering fear or wrath, marveled at the feat of the crippled old farmer in battling all that distance up the snow-buried mountain in time to save his daughter. Fervently he hoped that Dale had stayed in the cabin to await their return; for the man was so far spent that if he attempted to follow the trail left by the flying avenger he would certainly go down—and possibly out. Pushing on as fast as he could, he still sought to make talk by asking her the particulars of her abduction.

Rob Clarke, he learned, had unwittingly given Jules his chance to strike. One of his horses being sick, he had driven over to get Joe's opinion on the nature of the ailment; and Dale, always sympathetic toward horses, had promptly offered to go and examine the sick animal, despite his own indisposition. So, well bundled up, he had been driven away. And soon thereafter Jules had sprung into the kitchen where the girl was making preparations for supper when her father should return. Without preliminaries he had leaped at her, snarling a command to come with him.

"I was just movin' a kettle of hot water back on the stove," she said, "an' I threw it right at him! It nearly knocked him down, an' it must have burnt him some. An' then he was like a mad dog! I was scared most to death, but I grabbed a chair an' tried to drive him out with it; an' he grabbed the chair too, an' we fought all round the room until by an' by he got me into a corner. Then he yanked the chair away an'— an' choked me! Oh, Don, it was awful! He choked me so hard I didn't half know where I was for a while, an' the first thing I did know I was tied on the sled an' he was runnin' away toward the woods."

She had struggled hard to loosen her bonds, but to no avail. At length she had grown numb from the cold. He had freed her for a time then and compelled her to wade in the snow until she was past the danger of freezing from inaction; then tied her up again, and kept her so until the cabin was reached. By that time she was numb again.

"An' he lugged me in an' dumped me on the floor like a sack of 'taters!" she cried. "An' when I got thawed out again he made me cook his supper for him. An' while I was cookin' he sat there an' kept drinkin' —an' lookin' at me—oh, Don ——"

"Forget it, Pansy dear," he interrupted. "It's all past now."

As he spoke, one sled-runner hit a boulder masked

under the snow. The sledge tilted so swiftly that the girl was pitched off.

"There, now I'm all wet again!" she cried, pulling herself up. "Oh, look! There's a fire!"

His stratagem having failed, he stood her up on the sled, brushed the snow from her, and gazed at what lay behind them. Red upon the ink-black curtain of night glared a lurid patch of flame. He knew the fire had burst through the roof. The girl, wondering, began to voice a conjecture; but suddenly, as the sinister significance of that murky redness struck her, she broke off her sentence with a gasp.

In utter silence they stood gazing through the storm at the ominous glow. Weird, uncanny, it hung against the Stygian gloom like a flare from the infernal Pit erupting through the crust of earth to overwhelm a demon who had stalked among mortals for a time and whose tether had run out. Beneath it, they knew, toppled the timbers of an abode of dread, which ere morn would be wiped off the face of earth; and under those blazing logs lay the black devil who would prowl these woods no more, and who now was being consumed in a roaring hell which he had lit for himself. A chill which was not that of the wintry storm struck them. Pansy sank down on the sledge and sat very quiet. Wordless, Donald turned away and forged out to the open trail, which henceforth would be safe.

Up that trail they passed; Donald stalking silently onward, each stride drawing the girl nearer to his fire-lit cabin and her father's yearning arms; Pansy trembling with cold and the aftermath of terror, yet throbbing with the memory of that long kiss down in the forest. And as they went, her wide eyes studied the back of this man who could be so grim and fierce, or so gentle and tender. Only a little country girl, unversed in the ways of love and men, her sensations now were a riotous confusion of joy and dread, desire and doubt. For he had said no word of love, and he treated her always like a child. Now that he had aroused her to the wild, sweet emotions of full womanhood, would he still remain only a "big brother," or ——

Ah, my Pansy girl, fear not! Before another nightfall you shall know that you and he are not the only ones abroad to-night on this darksome trail; that another now is passing up the bleak mountainside with you; and that that other is a little blind god, who rides unseen on the sledge between you and your mate.

CHAPTER XXXV

THE HEART OF A MAID

" D'ye know, Mac, I ain't got a mite o' roomytiz to-day!" declared Joe, smoking his pipe at Donald's fireside. " I'm all lamed up an' I feel like I'd been drawed through a knot-hole, but it's my muscles that's lame, not my bones. Did ye ever hear o' the like? "

Donald, sprawling in the other chair with long legs outspread and pipe in fist, nodded.

" I've heard of such cases, but I never saw one," he answered. " The shock of finding Pansy gone and your fight to get here knocked it clean out of you. Cheer up! Maybe it will come back."

" Gorry, I hope not," grinned Dale. " With the roomytiz an' Jules both gone I feel ten year younger. Bet ye I'll beat both of ye to the house to-morrer— that is, ef ye'll leave off them snowshoes o' yourn. Say, by gorry, I got an idee! We'll slide down! The snow's froze so hard all we got to do is to set down on Jules's sled an' let 'er rip! "

" Why, Pop!" reproved Pansy. " We'd break our necks."

" Heh, heh, heh! Wal, Pansy darlin', I guess I'm gittin' foolish in my head. Besides, I'm so glad to have ye back safe it seems like I got to do suthin' childish jest to let out my feelin's."

The girl, seated on Donald's bunk and busy with

some mysterious dish she was evolving from his raided supplies, smiled her reponse. The eyes of the men rested fondly on the fair face softly illumined by the firelight. She alone of these three showed no signs of the harrowing night that had gone. Donald's battered face, burnt hair, bandaged scalp and skinned knuckles bore eloquent testimony to the deadly fight he had waged. Joe's face was haggard with the lines of the anguish he had suffered in the dark hours before the baby of his heart came back to him, and his abrupt movements at times showed that his nerves still were on edge. But Pansy, after sleeping well bundled up in Harry's former bunk, was her usual rosy, sprightly self again. And now, preparing for the evening meal of her " men folks," she made a picture of sweet simplicity that filled them with contentment.

It had been a lazy day: a day during which the men had done little but rest, eat, and renew the strength from which the past few hours had taken heavy toll. Also, it had been a day of keen cold. Soon after Donald's return the snowfall had stopped, to be followed almost at once by one of those swift drops in temperature that come so abruptly in the northern mountains. So now, as Joe said, the snow was crusted thick, and his whimsical suggestion that they slide home was quite practicable—though also quite dangerous. But Donald had decreed that they be his guests for at least one more night; and after the long weeks of recent separation they had gladly acquiesced. In their idleness they had found much to talk about, and the day had gone fast.

"Pipe's smoked out agin, Mac," suggested Joe. "Seems like I've burnt up more tobacker to-day than I gin'rally use in a week—an' I ain't got enough yit."

"Pardon me. Thought I left the tobacco on the table," apologized Don, digging up his pouch from a trousers pocket.

"Awright, boy. I can't smoke much more this y'ar anyway."

"Why not?"

"Don't ye know what day it is? Last one in December."

"Then this will be New Year's Eve," mused Don, looking abstractedly at the wall. "Hm! Down in town there will be dances and theatre-parties, and Broadway will be full of folks throwing confetti and blowing horns and ringing cowbells, and the cabarets will be jammed. And people are mailing New Year cards to all their friends—wonder if Harry will remember me."

Joe started.

"By mighty, Mac, I forgot! A couple o' letters come for ye more'n a fortni't ago, an' they was both from yer friend Harry—leastways the envellups had his name in the corner. I been kerryin' 'em round till I could see ye agin. Look in the inside pockit o' my coat."

For a moment the hermit sat as if unwilling. The thoughts of all three went back to the last letter he had received from Harry—the black-edged missive which had driven him blindly from the Dale home into the solitudes. Abruptly then he arose, drew from the inner pocket of the farmer's coat two slightly soiled letters, glanced at the dates, and tore off the end of the first. From the envelope he drew two sheets— one a brief note, the other considerably longer and typewritten on a business letter-head.

Father and daughter watched him with sympathetic concern while he read. They saw his brows lift slightly as he glanced through the note; observed the interest with which he examined the printed business matter at the top of the longer sheet; and relaxed as they saw a smile grow on his face while he scanned the close-typed lines below. Then they leaned forward again. Surprise had shot into his eyes, followed at once by joy. He read a paragraph for the second time, stared wide-eyed at Pansy and Joe, and broke into a jubilant laugh.

Vastly interested, but struggling to repress any indication of curiosity, Joe ventured:

" Guess ye got good noos this time."

" I've got a job," announced Donald.

A silent pause followed. Involuntarily Joe glanced at his girl. Then he stared at his pipe, put it in his mouth, and with expressionless face guessed: " A job in Noo Yawk, I s'pose."

" No. Not New York. I wouldn't go back there if they'd give me the whole town."

Whereat Joe, and Pansy too, brightened again.

" It's a job in Maine," continued Don. " A man's work, out in the open. My chum Harry has an uncle over there—George Miller, a lumber king. I met him after a game, years ago when I was playing football, and found him a great old scout. Now Harry has written to him about me, and the old boy comes back with a letter saying he will give me a good chance to work up in the lumber business if I want to come over and try it out. Harry was up to his ears in work when he received the answer, so he shot the letter itself along to me. His own note says that if I make good—and there's no reason why I shouldn't—George Miller will shove me ahead so fast that it will make me dizzy. It's a great chance at the sort of thing I'd like to do."

"Oh, Don, that's fine! I'm awful glad!" cried Pansy. Then she bent her head far down, concealing her face, and became very busy with her work. Once more her father glanced at her.

"Yas, that's fine," he assented soberly. "I know ye'll do mighty well, an' I—we both wish ye all the luck in the world. But we're a-goin' to miss ye, boy— miss ye a lot."

The hermit's smile, which he had been vainly trying to subdue, flashed into another joyous laugh.

"But that isn't all," he added. "There's another paragraph in George Miller's letter which I'm going to read to you. Listen:

"'I was much interested in your account of your hunting and camping trip at King's cabin on the mountain. You speak of a family named Dale near Warner. Now I have recently learned that one of my foremen is from Warner, and I wonder if he is related to that family. He will not talk about himself, but I am told that he left home some three years ago because of family trouble and is too proud and stubborn to write to his people. He is a first-class man, energetic and thrifty, and may be intending to go home again when he has saved up what he considers enough, though this is only a surmise on my part. I make it my practice to keep my hands off the private affairs of my men, and of course have not given him any unsought advice. At the same time, it may be that news of his whereabouts will be greatly appreciated by his people, and if you think it advisable you can notify them. I leave it to your judgment. This young man's name appears on the pay-roll as Thomas F. Dale.'"

Pansy leaped from the bunk.

" Oh, Pop! Tom! Our Tom!" she cried.

The old man swallowed hard.

" Thomas F. Dale," he repeated hoarsely. " It's him! The F stands for Fernald, my wife's maiden name." His eyes suddenly filled. " I—I knowed he mus' be alive," he went on brokenly. " But sometimes I been awful afeared—Pansy gal!"

His one hand reached for her and drew her into his lap. Then he broke down and sobbed in thanksgiving. Donald turned away and tiptoed to the window, where he stood smiling out at the waning day.

Presently he remembered the second letter and quietly opened it. This one had no enclosure, and was written in Harry's own sweeping hand.

DEAR DON:

Now that I have a little more time I will add something to my hasty note which went forward two days ago.

First, you are not supposed to have seen that letter from Uncle George to me. Return it to me, please,

and let me know what you intend to do about it. If
you take up the proposition (and you're seventeen
kinds of a fool if you don't) I'll have him write you
direct. Also, I'll give you another good boost while
I'm writing him.

Now listen hard. Since the death of your wife I
have made it my business to horn into your affairs and
see if I couldn't retrieve something for you. I knew
you wouldn't come back to make any claims, but there
is no sense in your staying broke when nobody but
your wife's relatives will benefit by it. Therefore I
have brought matters to a show-down with Mrs. Delancey, your wife's aunt, who has been busily acquir-
ing unto herself everything of value left from your
estate. To speak frankly, I had some difficulty with
her, as she showed a determination not to unhook her
claws without a squall. But I have brought pressure
to bear which has changed this attitude, and she now
is willing to make a settlement. Unless you give me
specific orders to draw in my horns I am going to get
that settlement, too. You know as well as I that she is
a selfish, high-and-mighty person, and I don't believe
you want to handicap yourself for her benefit. She
has more than enough now.

Details will be sent you later on. I don't know yet
how much will be coming to you, and will make no
forecast at this time. But you can rest assured that
it will be a snug little sum, and if you like Uncle
George and his business you can undoubtedly invest
your nest-egg where it will mean prosperity. That's
up to you.

So now I would suggest that you go down to the
village and blow yourself to a hair-cut and shave.
Also that you make arrangements to buy some civilized
clothing. And while I'm making suggestions I'll add
one more:

You've had a pretty rough deal all around. It's

quite possible that you are still sick and sore mentally. But there's a wonderful cure for that, and—well, Pansies are heart's-ease.

Now put that in your pipe and smoke it.

Sincerely,

HARRY.

Thoughtfully the hermit folded the letter and pocketed it. Again he looked out at the snow and the pines. Into his deep eyes came a warm, steady glow.

"Mac!" came Joe's voice, and he turned. The old man was standing now, an arm around his daughter, his face wet but full of happiness.

"Ye've give me back my gal an' my boy. Ye've done more for me than any other livin' man could do. I—I——" He put out his hand. Donald gripped it hard.

"Enough said," he answered tersely. "But I rather think you're going to lose your girl again."

"Whaddye mean?"

"I'm going to take her——" He paused. Then he went on: "—to take her up on the summit and show her the sunset."

The men stood looking steadily into each other's eyes. Joe's grip tightened. A fatherly smile widened his gray-bearded mouth.

"Awright, boy. Take her!"

His arm drew his Pansy girl closer to him. He dropped his head and kissed her on the lips. Then he released her.

"Come!" said Donald.

Without question, she obeyed. Muffled in her fa-

ther's coat, but hatless, she went with him out into
the fading light. Donald closed the door gently behind him, leaving the old man alone with his pipe and
his dreams.

Walking easily on the crusted snow, they passed
away arm in arm into the forest and up the terrace
to the narrow trail that led to the top. All this side of
the mountain lay in shadow deepening slowly into the
winter twilight; but a little cloud floating high up in
the blue, and tinged with the soft light of the sunset,
told him that evening had not quite come. He pointed
to it, and said:

"We are coming up out of the shadows into the
light, Pansy girl."

Her hand pressed his arm, but she made no answer.
Wordless, they climbed up, up, up into the higher
spaces. Along the edge of the crater bog they passed,
and slowly, carefully, they climbed the frozen slope
of the topmost knob of all that knobby summit. On
its crest they stood side by side and looked out across
the snowbound hills.

Far down, the last sun of the dying year was sinking to his rest. Banked along the horizon floated soft,
plumy clouds, waiting to receive him in a fluffy bed.
Already his rim touched their upper edges, dyeing
them molten red and splashing the lower banks with
orange and salmon. Above him arched the great vault
of the sky, a clear, liquid blue; below stretched the
winter world, its hollows filled with transparent grayish shadows, its hilltops kissed by the good-night rays
of the ending day.

" ' And the devil taketh him up into an exceeding high mountain,' " quoted Donald whimsically, " ' and sheweth him all the kingdoms of the world, and the glory of them: And saith unto him, All these things will I give thee, if thou wilt fall down and worship me.' "

She looked up at him, questioning.

" And even so, my girl, I have brought you up to the top of my mountain, to show you what I have to offer you. I don't ask you to fall down and worship me. I merely show you my kingdom, and ask you whether you want to share it with me."

Puzzled, she looked out across the long-shadowed landscape.

" I—I'm afraid I don't understand, Don."

" I'm going away into my kingdom—not these hills down below, but the forests and lakes of the great North Woods. I'm through with cities. I'm going over into Maine, the big Pine-Tree State, and make a fresh start in life. And I want you, Pansy dear, to come along with me and make my new start worth while—and to keep me going after I've started."

A wonderful light sprang into the rosy face and the big blue eyes. But suddenly it faded. She dropped her head.

" I'm awful glad—you like me so much, Don. But —I can't."

Blankly he stared down at her tumbled hair. Then, gently but firmly, he put a hand beneath her chin and lifted her face to his.

"Pansy girl! Surely you don't misunderstand. I want you to marry me."

"Oh, Don, I know that,—of course you couldn't mean anything else. But—I can't, Don—I can't!"

Steadily he looked into her eyes, and in them he saw gathering tears. Into his own eyes came slow pain. His hand fell, and he breathed deep.

"I'm sorry," he said simply. "I have only just realized—last night—how much you meant to me. I've been away lately. I might have known some other man would come into your life. But—well, it hurts."

"Oh, that ain't it! There's nobody else. It's because—Don, I ain't fit!"

"Not fit! You—not fit to be my wife? What do you mean?"

Her lips quivered and her eyes overflowed. Yet her voice was resolute as she told him.

"I don't know enough. I never had much schoolin', an' I've never been anywhere or seen anything, an' I haven't had a chance to learn the things your wife ought to know. About all I'm good for is to marry some man round here, that don't know any more than I do an' only needs somebody to cook an' keep house. You've been to college an' you've lived in New York, an' you know most everything. You're goin' away now, an' pretty soon you'll be mighty prosperous—oh, yes you will, with that Mister Miller to help you along —an' you'll be with folks that ain't lived in the woods all the time like I have. An'—an'—oh, Don, I'd rather die than have my husband be ashamed of me!"

" Why, dear girl!" he replied gently. " Is that all that's troubling your pretty head?"

" Ain't that enough?"

" No, indeed, it's not enough. You're making a mountain out of a mole-hill. All the education in the world couldn't make you any sweeter or better than you are now. In fact, sometimes it works the other way—I've known folks whose heads were so full of book-stuff that they forgot how to be human. Ashamed of you? If the time ever comes when I feel that way I hope somebody will knock me in the head."

He smiled again.

" Besides," he added, " if there's anything you want to learn why not ask me? I'll tell you all I know, and then you'll know as much as I do, won't you? Marry me first and ask questions afterward. You'll have me then where I can't get away."

She broke into a tearful little laugh. But her eyes searched his as she asked:

" An' you—you don't want to marry me just because you're lonesome an' because you're kind of sorry for me?"

" Not a bit of it," he denied earnestly. " I want you, Pansy girl, because I love you so much I just can't get along without you. Say you'll come over to Maine with me and help me to make good. Let's start the new year right."

The light came back into her face. Wide-eyed, she stood looking out across the snow. Then, her gaze on the flaming clouds floating on the rim of her world, she answered him.

" I'll go with you, Don—anywhere. An' as long as I live I'll be your good girl an' do everything I can to make you happy."

Out and around her swept the strong arm to which she clung. She nestled in its embrace. So, their eyes on the golden glory of the departing day, their souls attuned to a new and perfect love, they stood silent.

Far in the west the afterglow faded out. Up from the lowlands flowed the soft shadows of eventide. Above, serene and pure, shone forth the evening star. And on them, on their mountain, on all that vast countryside, settled perfect peace.

THE END